Beyond the Glass Doors

by JS Ririe

Jan Hill Books

Beyond the Glass Doors by JS Ririe
Publisher: Jan Hill Books
ISBN: 978-1-7333027-3-9
Copyright 2020: Jan Hill Books
Cover Image by: Antonio Guillem
Cover Design by William Gensburger

Praise for: Beyond the Glass Doors

"This is a well-written story that has a lot of twists and turns that keep you turning the pages as fast as you can read."

- LCD

"This book kept my attention from first page to last sentence. It brings out the best and worst attributes of the mortal experience while capitalizing on the resiliency of the human spirit. It's a great story with plenty of excitement."

- Matt J.

Dedication:

To all those dealing with challenges they would rather not face. I've certainly struggled with some of mine, but I would not trade the compassion, understanding and knowledge I've gained. It has made me reach inside, learn how to walk by greater faith and enjoy the relatively peaceful times. May God bless us all as we walk our individual paths, and may we be sensitive and caring enough to help shoulder someone else's burdens when given the opportunity.

~JS Ririe

Chapter 1

My head was pressed against the cool glass doors as cascading rain slipped away into obscurity. How I wished I could become part of it. I didn't want to exist now that my other half—my best half—had been called back to his heavenly home. It wasn't fair that I had been left to go on living when ever fiber of my being wanted to rend the air with mourning like women in other lands were expected to do.

Ken and I had promised to be there for each other until we were old and gray. We were supposed to share disappointment and sorrow and bask in the ecstasy our union had already brought. Now fate had landed a most pitiless blow, and I was left to pick up the fragile pieces of my broken heart and continue the course we had set when making the decision to become parents—a two-person job that wasn't meant to be done alone.

Part of that job was taking time to fortify and replenish our marriage. We had decided to do that by taking a much-needed mini vacation. Our children were not happy about being left behind, but the promise of taking them somewhere fun when we got back helped sooth their troubled souls. Unfortunately, while they were awaiting our return, we were plunged into a series of bizarre events we never saw coming.

Landi and Kenny were too young to understand their own loss, let alone the depth of my grief and despair at having lost the only man I would ever love. But expecting me to keep it together when my own world had been irrevocably shattered wasn't fair. The very thought of having to make it on my own was enough to keep me confined to my bed.

People had been texting, stopping by the house or making personal cell phone calls for days. I appreciated their condolences, expressions of support and genuine concern, but what did they know about the darkness of being left alone to navigate through a hostile and lonely existence unless they had been through it themselves? It wasn't something that could be reversed, and the pain was too intense to believe it would diminish in a hundred lifetimes.

Memories of our final hours together might bring a sense of comfort someday, but I didn't feel capable of carrying the heavy cross of acceptance right now. Maybe I never would. I wanted the life I had built with Ken to return, and no one could give me a satisfactory reason as to why bad things had to happen to good Christian people who were trying to do what was right.

I continued to watch the rain as it carelessly beat upon the flowers and shrubs in the backyard below the master bedroom balcony. My arms were wrapped tightly against my body, and my limp, brown hair looked as if it had been shaped to my head by a hard hat. The unexpected downpour had done that, but I didn't care. I would never care how I looked again.

I felt as lifeless inside as the stone statue of Benjamin Franklin in the town square. Why had my perfect world been allowed to crash so unmercifully around me? Every dream I had ever entertained had been right at my fingertips, and Ken had been the very heartbeat of my life.

He was the perfect man for me—tall and masculine with thick, blonde hair and the most incredible blue eyes that cast an undeniable spell the moment they found mine. I hadn't expected to fall in love instantly. Stuff like that only happened in the movies, but I felt like I had known him forever when he inadvertently knocked the papers from my arms as we tried to force our way into the same overcrowded elevator in the business section of downtown Boston, Massachusetts.

I tried to act cool and aloof—a futile attempt for an inexperienced farm girl who had just taken up residence in a bustling city—when he bent down to help retrieve the scattered conglomeration of what had once been carefully written resumes and samples of work I had done in the past. But inside, my eggshell feelings of self-worth were shattering. This was it, my last chance to secure a job. If this interview failed, it was a one-way ticket back to Hurricane, Utah, and the unwelcome sneers of all the hometown folk who had told me that I was being more than naïve to think I could move to a big Eastern city and find a glamorous job without having the right kind of connections.

"I'm sorry for bumping into you," I stammered, dropping to my knees beside him while a dozen pairs of hostile eyes waiting in the open elevator burned a hole in my back. "It was rude of me to think there was room for one more when this elevator was already full, but I didn't want to be late for a very important interview."

He was wearing a charcoal gray suit with a blue shirt and colorful silk tie, and his back was keeping the elevator door from closing. I brushed a strand of hair from off my forehead and tried not to melt under his thoughtful gaze.

"A beautiful woman should never feel the need to apologize for something that was clearly an accident," the man kneeling on the tile floor beside me said while two strong hands pushed rumpled papers towards me. "I was late myself, and certainly not being a gentleman by trying to beat you inside."

The hot color of embarrassment rushed to my cheeks as I glanced up at him. He was like a sun god. His eyes were clear and calming, and the broad, unassuming smile on his handsomely sculptured face made me look away it was so warm and inviting.

The man of my dreams was just inches away, and instead of melting into his arms like heroines in books and movies do, I wanted to slither through the cracks in the brown, tile floor so he could forget about ever bumping into me. We were still blocking the door to the elevator, and the moans and forced coughing coming from inside were getting louder.

"You're much too kind," I replied as the last of my scattered belongings were placed in my arms. "I wasn't watching where I was going."

He rose to his feet and then cupped his hand underneath my elbow and helped me to mine. "Not another word of censure. I'm so tall I automatically assume people will see me coming and clear the way."

"Well, bully for you," a deep, surly voice boomed from somewhere inside the elevator. "I'm all for apologies, but in case you love-birds haven't noticed, there's an elevator full of people that you've already made late for work."

I swallowed hard, glad that I no longer had the annoying habit of chewing gum. I would have swallowed it and choked. An unexpected meeting with a handsome man was supposed to make a day seem magical, not turn it into a nightmare, and it was only a little after nine in the morning.

"You take the elevator," the handsome man politely offered. "I'm sure the company I work for won't fold just because I'm a few minutes late getting back from an early morning meeting."

The commanding tone of his voice silenced the angry and outspoken adult male, but I felt my heart plummet as the man of my dreams ushered me into the elevator and the door made a grating sound as it closed with him on the other side.

No one spoke as we moved from floor to floor. I watched the back of people's heads as they exited the confining space and tried to convince myself that no one would remember what had happened once the work day began. I had never been so embarrassed and wished I could ride the elevator back to the lobby of the brick and glass building that overlooked a public square with trees, flowers, benches and kiosks where coffee, sodas and pastries could be purchased. But if I did that, I might be forfeiting my only chance for employment. So I made my exit on the seventeenth floor.

"What's wrong with you?" I asked myself as the feeling of moving upwards on suspended cables subsided. I was standing on a tightly-woven carpeted floor, and surrounded by freshly painted walls, bright light fixtures, a colorful bouquet of fresh flowers and impressive artwork. My heart immediately seemed to take another nosedive. "A dirt farmer's daughter should marry a dirt farmer's son. At least then she would retain some of her dignity."

With a heartfelt sigh, I glanced down at the stack of crumpled papers in my hands. They looked nothing like the carefully constructed portfolio I had spent hours assembling. Since there wasn't time to put them in order again if I wanted to keep my appointment, I tossed them into the nearest trash receptacle. This one was made of gold-colored metal instead of the cheap plastic version I had grown up with on the farm.

My arms now free, I straightened the front of the tailored, black suit I had purchased so I would at least look like I belonged and made sure the cuffs of my white blouse were still soil free. Then I squared my shoulders and placed one foot in front of the other. I was wearing stylish stiletto heels. They made me feel more in control, but they were far from being comfortable.

My thoughts turned to the past as the long walk down the hallway began. I had no one to blame, other than myself, for anything that happened. I had decided while still in high school that being the wife of an accomplished, professional man in some exciting city was what I wanted. There would be no riding plows in some Utah dust bowl for me, even if I had to move some proverbial mountain to prevent it.

So I had devised a seemingly foolproof plan. I dropped the names of what I considered the most exciting cities in the United States into a hat, closed my eyes, and let fate do the rest. It sounded more than a little reckless when I thought about it now, but I hadn't left everything to chance. I had enrolled in the best business school in the state—although it had taken me longer than anticipated to save up the cost of tuition—and could have landed a job with any number of firms in the Western half of the United States. But Boston was the chosen city, and I was determined to make it my home.

My poor parents thought I had lost my mind when I told them what I was going to do, but my stance was firm. I didn't want to be one of those girls who married a hometown boy and never left the state. I wanted to see what life had to offer away from the confines of a tightly-knit community where all the neighbors weighed in on every decision that was made.

"You're crazy if you think we're going to let you throw your life away like this, Maya," my father had said. "You're a good girl who has gone to church your entire life. Do you have any idea the kinds of people you're going to meet in some big city where most of the people don't even believe there is a God? Satan will pull out all the stops in trying to deceive you, and you won't have your family around to help when times get tough. What's so bad about staying here and finding some nice boy to marry who believes the same things you do?"

"There's nothing wrong with Hurricane, dad, but I want to see more than sagebrush, rattlesnakes and red cliffs," I retorted. "Besides, who said all the eligible, Christian men live in Utah? You always taught me that good people exist in every part of the world, and I need to do what feels right for me. If I make a few mistakes along the way, then so be it. I'll learn from them and start over if necessary. I need to figure out what God has in mind for me, not some busybody down the street."

"But it's so far away," my mother lamented as she dried her hands in the folds of the apron she always wore when baking. "You won't be able to come home any time you want to. And what if you don't find the right kind of man? You could end up with some heathen."

I laughed. "That's not going to happen. I know what I'm planning may sound crazy, but this is the twenty-first century, and you won't even know I'm gone. We can FaceTime every day, and I'll tell you all about my adventures. And if things don't work out, I'll come back."

That put an end to their protests, although I was certain they discussed my foolishness long after I went to bed that night. But as I packed my bags for the big move after graduating from business school, I wasn't so sure I really believed what I had told them. I knew Heavenly Father would take care of me, but what if it wasn't the spirit guiding me to Boston? What if it was only my desire to be different from everyone else?

I thought about my decision as I drove from Hurricane to Boston. It took me three days and two nights, and I was ready to drop by the time I got there. I would be sharing an apartment with a young woman I had found through a listing on the bulletin board at school. Her name was Teri Johnson, and she had been working for an advertising firm for the past three years. Like me, her dreams for finding the perfect job and the perfect man were lofty. But unlike me, she came from a well-to-do Philadelphia family who had distant relatives in Boston.

She seemed nice enough when I called her on the phone, but her words were less than encouraging when I told her where I was from. She explained that it wouldn't be easy for a farm girl from Southern Utah to find the kind of job I was looking for in Boston. While city people were kind and generous, most CEO's came from affluence and liked to surround themselves with people from similar economic backgrounds. Without referrals or inside help, I would be lucky to secure an interview.

She almost caused me to rethink my plan. I wasn't exactly the life of the party when it came to socializing, and I certainly knew nothing about living a pampered life. I could irrigate crops, herd bothersome animals and babysit neighborhood children, but I could hardly converse about trips to exotic locations, dealing with household staff or attending a prestigious school. Everyone told me I was pretty, but I wasn't particularly polished or poised. I worked hard, knew how to set goals and had graduated with honors, but those things did not automatically mean success.

"Oh, well," I thought, forcing my mind back to the present and the critical situation I was in. "This is it! The end of the line! If I don't get the job, I'll be only way back to Utah by the end of the month—penniless, defeated and forced to live with my parents until someone takes pity on me."

I looked at my reflection in the clear glass that covered one of the etchings. I looked like a little, lost puppy with eyes almost too big for my face, but I wasn't about to go down without a fight. If I was truly meant to be here, someone at the firm of Turner, Holden and Holden would recognize a diamond in the rough whose portfolio was now is in the trash.

Suite 1790 was at the end of the corridor. I took a deep breath to help steady my racing heart and dry my sweating palms before turning the doorknob to enter the reception area.

Across the threshold was an elegantly furnished room—just the kind I had always imagined in my daydreams. It was decorated in shades of brown and tan with deep pile carpet and expensive-looking, upholstered furniture. The woman at the receptionist's desk was wearing a rust-colored, linen suit and looked as if she had been placed there by an interior decorator.

She glanced up as the door closed behind me. "May I help you?" she pleasantly inquired.

"Yes," I said, summoning all the feeble courage I had left. "I'm Maya Kincaid. I have an interview with Mr. Holden. I would have been here earlier, but there was a little trouble with the elevator."

"Nothing serious, I hope," the lady returned with a smile. "Those elevators can be infuriating at times."

"I suppose they can," I replied.

The last thing I needed was to explain my part in what had happened to a stranger. Besides, I had learned through numerous failed interviews that the person sitting at the front desk had a great deal to do with who actually got the kind of job I was looking for.

"Well, you're here now," she said. "I'll let you know when Mr. Holden is ready to see you. Have you worked in a firm like this before?"

Her question was disheartening. I hadn't done anything of a professional nature since finishing my business degree, but that didn't mean I wasn't capable of running an office. I just needed someone who was willing to give me a chance.

"No," I responded before sitting down on a brown, leather sofa in front of a window to wait. My knees were beginning to tremble, and the knot in my stomach had risen to my throat. If I wasn't careful, I would worry myself into being sick.

I didn't want this to be the end of my quest, but even if it was, I wouldn't surrender what was left of my dignity. I would simply thank my interviewer for his time and walk out the door with my shoulders back and my head erect. No one would ever know what awaited me when I left.

I glanced out the window as the phone began to jingle. Seventeen floors up! It was a long way to the ground, and people really did look like tiny, sugar ants walking along the sidewalk. I couldn't help but wonder how I would be feeling when I joined them again.

"Good morning, Mr. Holden," I heard the woman say a few moments later.

I was on the edge of my seat in an instant with the blood pounding in my temples. I didn't want to seem overly anxious, but the money I had managed to save was almost gone. I had been subsisting on boxed meals like macaroni and cheese and Ramen noodles for weeks now.

"Yes, your appointment has arrived. Do you want me to show her back?" The headset was back in its holder before she addressed me. "Mr. Holden is ready to see you now."

"Thank you," I said, rising to my feet.

She looked at me with real compassion and a certain amount of discomfort as she escorted me across the room. "I should have introduced myself, but this is first time I've worked at the front desk. My name is Fiona Turner. My husband is a senior partner and persuaded me to fill in until a new receptionist is found. The last one got married rather unexpectedly. You're not engaged, are you?"

Her abrupt question caught me off guard. "Not even close, but I thought this job was for a personal assistant."

"You can all it what you like, Miss Kincaid. We do financial advising for both individuals and corporations, and the person in the reception area must be smart, discreet and have the knowledge and skills necessary to fill in whenever the need arises. People trust us with their financial success, and every member of the team must be committed to excellence, honesty and personal accountability."

"Well stated," I replied, feeling like I had been politely reprimanded for not doing enough research on the company I hoped to be working for.

But as we passed through a set of carved, oak doors, I realized this was exactly the kind of job I was looking for—one with prestige, a certain amount of glamour and enough variety to keep me from getting bored. But what if they didn't want a country girl who was willing to give her all to fit in? Or even worse, what if they were willing to give me a chance, and I wasn't ready for the responsibility.

"You'll like Mr. Holden," Fiona Turner remarked as we passed by a large, formal conference room and several closed doors with name placards stating positions of prominence in the firm. "Ken is our newest shareholder and quite available for some lucky girl. This was supposed to be a family business for both senior partners, but H. Holden was the only one who had a son. My husband and I have three daughters. We love them dearly, but not one of them is interested in financial advising."

"I'm sorry," I said, finding that I quite liked the amiable woman who was trying to be both informative and accommodating. "Maybe a son-in-law will join the firm one day."

"Possibly! I still have one daughter who isn't married. I was hoping she and Ken would get together, but they seem to prefer being friends."

She wrapped lightly on another oak door and then pushed it open. A blonde man in a dark gray suit sat behind the desk.

"Miss. Kincaid," the eligible and irresistible gentleman I had literally run into earlier said as he looked up at me. His eyes were dancing with amusement, but when his fingers closed over mine I knew he would never reveal our unfortunate encounter at the elevator. "I'm delighted to meet you."

My second apology began the moment the door closed behind my escort. "I'm so sorry about what happened on the ground floor. You must think I'm one of the rudest persons on the planet."

"Not at all," he replied, releasing my hand and motioning for me to sit down in one of the two chairs that faced his desk.

I felt an unexpected moment of exile from something more than wonderful. His eyes were the clearest blue I had ever seen, and the strength of his hand matched that of any of the boys I had known growing up who milked cows by hand and stacked heavy bales of hay and straw. I was so mesmerized by his presence that I almost missed what he was saying.

"You were a little pre-occupied, Miss Kincade, but that goes with the territory. Interviews are always unnerving."

"That doesn't excuse my behavior. I was deliberately trying to force my way underneath your arm so I wouldn't be late."

"Is that so," he said as he began drumming the tips of his long fingers on the desktop while he continued to study me.

Looking away was impossible since I didn't want to appear ineffectual or weak, but my portfolio was gone. I had used what it contained as a springboard to move the conversation forward during an interview. Without it, I wasn't sure I could express exactly what my qualifications were. It wasn't like I had some huge list of people who could be contacted about my capabilities since I had never worked in the professional sector before. I was still in the process of finding someone who would give me a chance.

But as the silence—only broken by the sound of light tapping—continued, I knew my somewhat bold and unrealistic expectations might rapidly be coming to an end. I had taken my coursework seriously and knew how to handle most people, but I needed the opportunity to put what I had learned into action. I just wished he would either criticize my actions or laugh. Anything would be better than sitting in his presence when I had no idea what he was thinking.

After what seemed like forever, he spoke again. "You make it sound like this interview is important to you. Do you mind telling me why? You're quite unlike anyone I've met with thus far, and I am curious as to why you no longer have the samples of work I helped you retrieve from the floor."

I resisted the urge to bite my bottom lip as I usually did when I was given something perplexing to consider. Different could mean anything, but if I wasn't completely honest, I had the strong feeling he would know it. So I took a deep breath and clasp my hands firmly together in my lap before giving my answer.

"Coming to Boston was a calculated risk, sir. I'm from a small farming community in southern Utah where everyone in town feels like family, but I felt the need to see what could do on my own away from the safety of everything familiar. So I learned everything I could about how businesses operate. I just received my degree and have never had a job of real significance before, but I'm a hard worker and learn fast. As for my carefully constructed portfolio, I threw it in the trash because it would take more time than I had to reorganize. And quite truthfully, it only showed what I had done as a student who wanted to excel."

"I like an honest woman, Miss Kincaid," he responded. "Most of the ones I meet like to embellish. That doesn't do either of us any good. Why don't you tell me what kind of work you have done."

"Nothing terribly exciting, sir. Before I was old enough to get a real job, I babysat neighborhood children and helped my father irrigate ground and take care of crops and animals. I know how to drive a tractor, plow a field, lay out irrigation pipe, change sprinkler heads and deliver baby calves and sheep. I can even preserve fruit and vegetables and bake bread from scratch. I know those aren't the employability skills you're looking for, but they taught me responsibility, exactness and the determination to finish what I started. When I was sixteen, I began working at the local Dairy Queen. I stayed there until after I graduated from high school."

"Did you work while going to college?"

I allowed myself to give him a timid smile. "I had to, sir. My parents are wonderful, kind and loving people, but farming isn't the most lucrative profession. I worked in the shoe depart at Macys and tutored underclassmen."

"It sounds like you've been busy, but what about hobbies or other interests? This work is demanding, and people need a way to relax and release tension at the end of the day. There are many ways for doing that, but some are more counterproductive than helpful."

HIs innuendo was clear, but I had never so much as set foot in a bar. "My social life is non-existent at the moment since I've only been in the city for a few weeks, but I don't drink, smoke or take drugs. I try to live what I believe, and when I have free time, I like to watch movies or go running. I also enjoy reading, painting with pastels and watercolors and trying new recipes. I live a simple life and don't need to be on the go all the time to be happy."

"But you wouldn't be opposed to planning or attending the right kind of parties. We host those occasionally as a way to express our thanks to our clients. Without them, there wouldn't be a firm. Everything we do is geared towards making them feel that their livelihoods are safe with us. Sometimes there is a fine line between being unwavering when it comes to what is best for their financial future and showing sensitivity to their feelings. That skill is not easy to learn."

"Understood," I replied as my brow began to furrow. "I know we didn't get off to a very good start, but I'm usually a very organized and amiable person."

"There's little doubt in my mind that you could handle the demands, but you have yet to tell me why you want to work for us. There are dozens of firms like ours scattered throughout this city."

Telling him that I needed this job because I had run out of money and would have to go home without it wouldn't win me any favorable points. Nor would telling him that he was the most gorgeous man I had ever seen and appeared to possess all the qualities I had ever wanted in a man. And if I tried to act like I knew what I was talking about, he would see through my lame attempt in an instant.

"I don't exactly know how to answer that," I replied. "You're already aware of my history. While it's true that I like helping people and understand the benefit of making the right financial decisions, I have no practical experience to draw from. I can only say that I felt something inviting when I walked through the door into your front office. I'm looking for a place where I can use what I have learned to become a valued member of the right firm, and this feels like the perfect place for that."

"That's hardly the answer I expected, Miss Kincaid. However, it is nice to know that the atmosphere we're trying to create can be felt. This is a rewarding line of work, but it's also a very demanding one. Whoever greets our clients and assists with other important tasks, even while learning the ropes, must be a soul of integrity and dependability. I can teach most anyone how to make the right calculations and which investments to avoid, but personal character comes from within. Fortunes can be made or lost on a single phone call. That is an incredible responsibility and a very daunting challenge at times."

"I understand," I replied. "And I didn't mean to sound altruistic or patronizing. I know what it means to work hard, and I also know what it means to lose everything. As a family, we lost our crops more than once because the elements wouldn't cooperate. We had to take out loans and sacrifice in order to pay them back. My father has never believed in government bailouts or getting something for nothing. He believes in hard work, prayer and faith."

"You're a Christian!" he exclaimed.

"Is that a problem?" I asked.

He put his head back and laughed. "Hardly! Most of the people I meet don't seem to believe in anything other than their own ability to succeed or fail, and some of them can be more than ruthless when it comes to making money. You have an honest, refreshing outlook on life with a deep sense of loyalty and a willingness to work hard for the right reasons. That's as hard to find in Boston as perpetual sunshine. My dad keeps telling me I should have found someone to share my life with before I left college because the women I meet in the corporate world can be even more aggressive than their counterparts."

"Why didn't you?" I asked, finding it hard to believe that a man as handsome as he was didn't have dozens of suitable girls waiting in line for a marriage proposal.

"I don't know," he replied, settling back in his chair and fixing me with a look that made the blood rush to my head. "Maybe I was waiting for you to grow up and come looking for me."

From that moment on, my life took a dramatic and unexpected turn. My roommate, Teri, gave me a very puzzled look when I came waltzing into the apartment later that afternoon with a bottle of sparkling, white grape juice in one hand and two long-stemmed glasses in the other. She had been having a few rough days and was trying to decide if she should quit her job. She was at the bottom of the ladder leading towards success, and people above her at the advertising firm were always trying to pillage her clients and take credit for the work she had done. Like me, she was a Christian who wanted to live a good life, but the handwriting was on the wall. Either she compromised her values and began acting like everyone else, or she started looking for something else to do.

"Your day must have gone better than expected," she said as I handed her one of the glasses.

I kicked off my shoes, dropped my purse to the floor and popped the lid off the bottle. "It was the most incredible day of my life. Not only did I get the job, but I think I'm in love."

"Really," she responded as I poured some of the lightly-tinted liquid into her glass. "I thought they were looking for someone with experience."

I let some of the warm beverage slide down my throat before answering. Teri wasn't trying to be rude or disagreeable. She was simply frustrated and a little scared. I knew how many hours she spent after work sequestered in her room on the computer coming up with new mottos and designs. She was artistically gifted and very bright, but she wanted to fit in and be liked.

"I guess they figured I was worth taking a chance on," I replied. "If I'm in over my head, I'm sure I'll discover it soon enough."

She set her glass on the counter without finishing what was inside. "Don't let me rain on your parade. I'm just in a rotten mood. Howard made another play for one of my clients, and I'm afraid I'll lose him. Tell me everything, and I'll try to respond appropriately. I know how much you hate the idea of going home empty-handed, and I really am trying to think about someone other than myself."

My frown was quick, and I hoped she didn't notice. "I'm not saying this is a panacea to all my troubles, but I feel good just getting a job."

"What about your new employer? I hope he isn't the one you think has stollen your heart. Men are seldom who they claim to be, and I haven't met one yet who didn't want to see just how far he could push without causing fallout in his personal life."

"Is there something you want to tell me?" I asked.

The sadness behind her infrequent smiles let me know that she was drifting from where she wanted to be. But I didn't feel as if I knew her well enough to pry, and any accolades when it came to the man who had set my heart to racing were best left unuttered. Rules were in place for a reason, and once a certain line had been crossed there was no going back.

"No," she responded much too quickly. "Maybe I'm just jealous because you've found a man worth considering. I've been here for nearly a year, and the only ones I've met are at work since I refuse to get involved with online dating or going to bars."

"You're probably right when it comes to activities like that," I told her. "The horror stories I've heard outweigh the successes ten to one. And I'm not really in love. It's just nice to know there are still men around who can make me feel safe and worthwhile. I was beginning to feel as if I was destined to remain jobless and alone."

She reached out and touched my arm reassuringly. "That's not going to happen to either of us. We've just been overrun with moments of doubt and uncertainty recently. I'm really happy for you and hope this job is everything you've been looking for. When do you start?"

"Monday. That only gives me the weekend to get prepared."

"If there's anything I can do to help, all you have to do is ask."

"Thanks," I responded. "How was your day? I know you've been stressed out the past few weeks."

"Only because I had to do things my own way. I could have become an instant executive in one of my father's firms, but I needed to see how the rest of the world lived. I just didn't expect starting at the bottom to be so hard. Having others question my decisions, or my abilities, drives me crazy. And I simply detest people who step on others to further their own agendas. I hope you know what you're doing. What seems like such a great beginning can backfire. I'm living proof of that, but I'll stick it out for awhile longer because I'm in no hurry to go back to my family either. They'll just insist that I marry Cyrus Klosterman."

"Cyrus Klosterman," I repeated. "You haven't mentioned him before."

"That's because I never really considered him as husband material until recently. We grew up together, and he always seemed a little boring. I mean he did everything right—got good grades in school, played varsity basketball and became an anesthesiologist who now owns an incredible house and is a member of the most elite country club in town."

"Doesn't sound so bad to me."

"He's a good guy, but I always thought that falling in love meant fireworks and steamy, passionate kisses like we see in almost every movie. I wanted the bad-boy, the anti-hero, the illusive heartthrob who was always just out of reach."

"I guess falling in love with a guy like that might have its perks, but I've never seen a followup movie about what happens once the good girl marries the bad boy. It seems to me that having similar values would be a real plus."

"So you think I should give Cyrus a chance?"

"That's something only you can decide, but the fact that you're thinking about him tells me that you aren't completely disinterested. Some of the best marriages I know of began when two friends decided that something more might not be such a bad idea."

"I guess I never thought about it that way before. I just figured he would always be there if I didn't find someone else."

"Your version of a back-up plan?" I asked.

She laughed and picked up the glass of sparkling grape juice I had poured for her. "It sounds rather Machiavellian when you put it that way. But yes, that's exactly what he's been."

"Would it hurt if he became involved with someone else?"

"You don't think he's done that, do you?" she asked. "He always said he would wait until I came to my senses and realized he was the only man for me."

"It sounds like he really cares. But if he's a good man—who is who he claims to be—someone else will eventually notice and make a move."

"Maybe I ought to go home more often, but I wanted to prove my worth as a member of the professional community before deciding about marriage and family. Was that so wrong of me?"

"You're asking the girl who put her future in fate's hands for advice?" I countered. "I wish I had a backup plan, but if this job falls through I have nothing waiting for me back home, except the knowing glances of everyone who was kind enough to keep their opinions to themselves when I told them what I planned to do. If you feel like you might have a future with someone, I think you owe it to yourself to give the relationship a chance."

"What about all the passion, excitement, and tingling a girl is supposed to feel when the right man comes along? I don't want to miss out on that."

I thought back to meeting Ken Holden that morning. I had certainly felt all of those things when his eyes found mine, but I was a romantic who still believed in white knights and fairytale endings. The problem with that approach to living was distinguishing between what was real and what was simply a very carefully crafted illusion.

"It's my belief that intense emotions seldom last. Real life is hard, and marriage takes work. I can't speak from experience, but I know I would rather be married to my best friend than chasing some fictional dream. He would understand and appreciate who I am—my weaknesses as well as my strengths—and would never push me to become anyone else."

"And you don't think knowing so much about someone else would lead to an utterly boring life?"

"Hardly! I want someone I can count on. We're not going to stay young forever, and there will always be younger, more beautiful, and more aggressive girls who want what we have. If a relationship is build on superficial values, it will never survive."

"I suppose that makes sense. I've always been the pampered, little rich girl who was told she could have anything she wanted."

"We aren't so different, even if our socio-economic backgrounds are world's apart," I responded as my eyes took in the room we were sitting in. Teri had furnished it with money coming from a trust fund that would last her for the rest of her life. My only contribution was the trunk my grandmother had given me. It was filled with homemade linens she had embroidered, knitted or crocheted for my future home. "I was a dirt farmer's daughter, but my parents told me the same thing about having my heart's desires. The only variation was having to work hard and sacrifice to get them. Most parents want their children to be happy, productive adults."

"Did they have a guy all picked out for you to marry? My parents love Cyrus. My dad calls him a thoroughbred of a guy who has a remarkable linage, and my mother looks for opportunities to invite him to family gatherings where everyone can praise his many accomplishments. Maybe that's why I've tried to distance myself from him. I want to make my own decisions."

"And undo pressure can easily be construed as discriminatory manipulation."

"So you do understand."

"Only in a minor way. Hurricane is a very small town. And my parents really didn't expect me to marry the boy who grew up on the adjoining farm, but I can't say that I ever gave anyone a chance. I thought my real life couldn't begin until I left everything familiar behind."

"And how has that been working for you?"

Her question made me laugh. "At least I finally have something positive to share with them."

"Do you really think they'll rejoice when you tell them you've found a job?"

"Probably not! They've never made it a secret that they would rather I come home, but they will support my decision."

"My parents would be over the moon with joy if I told them I was going to marry Cyrus. We could share Sunday brunch at the club, and both sets of grandparents could spoil our children. I would never have to worry about anything."

"But if it's not the life you want . . . . "

"I'm beginning to think I've let my fantasy life override reason because I wanted to live life on my own terms." She suddenly slapped her palms down on the countertop with such force that her empty glass almost seemed to dance. "Thanks for the pep talk, Maya. It's good to know I'm not the only one with irrational expectations. But right now, I have laundry to do."

I didn't try to keep her talking. Some things in life were just too personal, like my meeting Ken. My heart had definitely come alive when I first saw him, but what I liked most was his frank and honest openness. He was a man people could rely on, and I couldn't stop replaying the moment when he told me that maybe he had been waiting for me.

Sleep that night was intermittent at best, and I spent Saturday trying to decide which of the five career suits I had purchased for my dream job would be best to wear on my first day. I had taken a course on how to dress for success on a limited budget, and it was all about classic cuts that could be mixed or matched, basic colors and accessorizing. I had done my best in securing what I felt was necessary, but anyone with a trained eye would know exactly what I was trying to do. I kept telling myself that clothes didn't define a person's worth, but they most assuredly gave a boost when it came to appearing poised and self-assured.

Fiona Turner rose to greet me when I walked into the office shortly before eight on Monday morning.

"I am so glad Ken had the sense to hire you," she said, coming around the reception desk and giving me a friendly hug. "You have no idea how long we've been waiting for someone like you to walk through that door. Not that we haven't had a lot of lovely, qualified people interview for the job, but you are exactly the right fit. There are so many individuals who become offended by everything—even a simple Merry Christmas, Happy Easter or hope you enjoy the 4th of July. But here I am running on when I should be showing you around the office before the partners come in for the day."

I liked both H. Holden and Winston Turner immediately. They were more than just competent and professional. They genuinely cared about people and made me feel like I belonged. I listened intently as they described the company's mission statement and what they expected in an employee. I could find no fault with any of their goals or expectations. I only hoped I would not disappoint anyone. This was my first experience in the corporate world, and I was definitely out of my comfort zone. I had learned that well enough over the weekend by spending what little free time I had researching financial advising practices and how easily they could either make or break someone's life.

After our short meeting ended, Ken remained in the conference room with me while the others went back to work. I felt my jaw begin to tremble when he looked at me and smiled.

"So how does it feel to be part of the family?" he asked as I steadied my body against the edge of the long, wooden table and forced myself to breathe more deeply so I wouldn't become light-headed. "I mean, part of our business family, at least for now."

Without conscious thought, the lines between my eyes deepened, and I bit down on my bottom lip. Every flutter of emotion I had felt on Friday was returning. I would have to figure out how to remain aloof when my heart was turning summersaults if I didn't want to mess anything up.

"You frown," he responded, touching my arm as the expression on his face became serious. "I know I'm one of your bosses, but I'm not into playing games or trying to manipulate people. We only get one shot at life, and I want to make sure mine counts for all the right reasons. I haven't married by choice because none of the girls I've met had that special something I couldn't even identify until I met you. Maybe it's simply because you know how to do some extraordinary things like drive a tractor and bake bread from scratch, but I got the feeling that you weren't trying to play it coy or impress me. You were simply telling me like it was. I don't think any other woman has ever been that honest with me."

"Is that why I got the job?" I asked. "I know I'm not the most qualified applicant you had."

"Like I told you on Friday, anyone can learn the mechanics. It's that innate sense of propriety, honesty and genuine caring I was looking for. I hope my boldness hasn't offended you or caused undo concern. I would never overstep any boundaries of propriety, but I knew if I let you walk out of that door I would regret it for the rest of my life."

This was not a conversation I had anticipated having on my first day of employment, but for some reason I wasn't disturbed or even worried about it. I had known from the moment we met that Ken Holden wasn't like other men. He was unassuming and straightforward, and when he said something I needed to listen because he wouldn't repeat himself.

"Nothing you've said has been upsetting, just a little surprising," I said. "Men aren't usually so open, unless they have an ulterior motive."

"My motives are pure. I can assure you of that. But I felt an instant attraction when we bumped into each other, and when you walked into my office I knew I was being given a second chance for something I couldn't even define. Please correct me if my assumptions were wrong. It won't affect your job. Meeting you was like a breath of fresh air, and we really do need you here."

I smiled up at him as goose flesh covered my arms, regardless of the fact that the temperature in the conference room was perfect like everything else within these offices. I had to give this golden opportunity a chance. God had answered my prayers exactly the way I had hoped he would.

"I did feel something, but I'm realistic enough to understand that situations change, and I need this job," I said as my jaw began to quiver. "I won't do anything to jeopardize it. I know what I need to be happy, and it isn't some office romance that ends badly."

"That's exactly what I thought you would say and precisely why I decided to lay my cards on the table so soon. I don't believe in karma or even old-fashioned good luck. I think everything happens for a reason. I just didn't want to risk having some other guy make his move before I had a chance to make mine."

"You have nothing to fear in that respect," I responded. "I haven't been on a single date since I got here."

"That's only because the guys in this city have blinders on, but you have things to do and so do I. If there's anything you need, my door is always open."

He left me alone to digest what had just happened, but it would take more time than I had to do that. Normal people didn't throw the names of cities into a hat and then draw one out to determine their destiny. But then I had never been like other girls, and maybe that wasn't so bad.

If Fiona noticed my lack of concentration while explaining my duties, she let it pass. "You are a very quick learner," she assured me as I was getting ready to leave for the day. "It's taken me what seems like forever to feel as if I have something to contribute to this firm, and Winston and I have been married for over forty years. But you look and act like you've always been here."

"That's only because you're such a great teacher."

"Hardly," she responded. "But I do believe things have a way of coming together when they're right."

When I got home, I called my parents. I didn't want to jinx my perfect job by speaking about it too soon. But after spending a day learning the rudiments, I was ready to share my excitement. However, I would keep what I said about my employers to a minimum, especially the the man with the amazing, blue eyes and an openness that seemed to have set my entire world on fire. I had only spoken to him one additional time, and it was all about business. Maybe he was waiting for me to make the next move. Well, I would bake a batch of chocolate chip cookies and leave them in the conference room the next day to show my gratitude at having been hired.

"Good for you," my mother said, but I could sense the underlying disappointment. As much as she wanted me to be happy, she still wished I could find it a little closer to home. "So things really are working out just like you planned."

"It's an amazing opportunity, mom. I know my decision to come here was a little unorthodox, but I never doubted that it was the right thing to do."

"Then you have my blessing, Maya. Not every girl can manipulate her dreams into coming true."

"That's not exactly how it happened, but this is a very promising beginning."

It was hard to say much after that. And once the screen on my cell phone went dark, I looked up at the white ceiling in my bedroom that had sparkling flecks mixed into the paint. Others might not agree with what I had done, but after today, I knew it was more than coincidence that I had been led to the office of Turner, Holden and Holden.

Fiona told me, in confidence, that Ken had been looking for the right girl for a very long time. He would be thirty-four in January and wanted to settle down. I was nearly twenty-two and wanted the same thing, but there was a twelve-year difference in our ages. When he really got to know me, he might decide that what he thought of as being desirable qualities were really just a matter of inexperience and naiveté.

I saw very little of him, or the other partners, during my first week. They spent their time in meetings, while I spent mine with Fiona learning filing and billing systems, where to find necessary information, and as much about each client as was prudent. Even minor details, overheard by accident, were privileged and not to be repeated. It was a lot to absorb, but my commitment to the firm only deepened as each day began and ended. I liked what I was learning and felt confident that I could handle things on my own once my mentor was no longer around to offer help and encouragement.

Ken and I tried to take things slow. We didn't want to make any mistakes, but the more time we spent together, the more we realized that we never wanted to be apart. We got each other and were soon spending time together away from the office. We would laugh and talk until the early morning hours, but only if we were in a place where the temptation wasn't too great. We knew the world equated dating with having sex, but we wanted that part of our relationship to remain unexplored until our wedding night. That way it would be a truly sacred union to be celebrated with nothing but joy because past encumbrances, of any kind, would never become an issue.

Three months later, he wanted to speak to my father. I knew what was on his mind, so I took him home to meet my family. He had never been to southern Utah and found it hard to believe that people would voluntarily live in a desert where the temperature only went from hot to hotter. But after a few days, he began to love the red-baked soil and low-growing shrubs almost as much as I did. It was an awesome beginning to the rest of my story.

Chapter 2

"Maya."

The familiar voice brought me brutally back to the present—to the cold, the rain and the emptiness of a heart that wished it could stop beating.

"What did you say, mom?" I asked, turning away from the rain-streaked glass door that lead onto a private balcony and wiping the tears from my eyes. It was getting dark, and the house must be nearly empty by now. I had escaped the confines of the rooms below because I could no longer handle words of condolence or encouragement. They were taking away my right to feel unrelenting and absolute pain.

"I merely wanted to know if you were okay," she responded as the door moved inward and her head came into view. "You've been locked away in your room for hours. Everyone has gone, the left over food has been put away and the children are ready for bed. They need you to listen to their prayers and tuck them in for the night."

I choked back a sob as she crossed the room and enfolded me in her arms. My greatest desire was to push her away. I had listened to more than enough words of unfounded optimism the past few days, but I didn't want to appear overly callous or rude.

"Come on, Maya," she said, trying to lift my chin with one finger as she had done so many times when I was a child. "I know this isn't what you want, but you're not alone. Your father and I will stay for as long as you need us, and Harold and all of your friends are only a phone call away."

My icy glare, when she was only trying to help, was both unnecessary and unkind. She had been nothing but supportive since I'd placed the call that let everyone in my family know my life was over. But if I lost control now, I might not be able to contain the outcome. All the rage, fear and despondency was just below the surface, and letting any of it escape might lead to a total breakdown.

"I know that, mom," I said as my chest rose with pain. "And I do appreciate everyone's support. Ken would have been pleased to know how many people really care. He was the most humble, gentle and real person I have ever known."

"He was also a strong, wise and compassionate man who chose you to be his wife because he knew he could count on you to make it through any obstacle placed in your path. He's depending on you to raise the family you created together the way he would have done had he been allowed to stay."

I sniffed back more tears. I didn't want to think about the future without the man I loved. The present was difficult enough.

"Please don't push, mom. I'm barely holding it together."

"I'm not discounting the depth of your grief. I know it's real, but it's been six weeks since the accident."

"It seems like only yesterday."

She moved away from me and sat down on the edge of the bed Ken and I had shared. "Everything I say lately is wrong, but I'm only trying to help."

"Nobody can help," I responded. "Ken's gone, and I don't want to go on without him. It's as simple as that."

"Nothing about this is simple, Maya. But despite what happened, you're still part of a wonderful family. Maybe the time will come when you can draw comfort from the fact that you actually found the man God had in mind for you. Not everyone gets a blessing like that."

"Stop with the platitudes!" I almost shouted. "They mean nothing right now."

"Not even the knowledge that this separation is only temporary? You will be reunited with Ken someday."

"What am I supposed to do in the meantime? Ken was everything I ever wanted or needed, and I don't know how to make it through life without him."

"You'll do it by moving forward one minute at a time if necessary, and by never forgetting how much he loves you and the children. He's building a heavenly home for his family, and you have to do your part if you want to share it with him."

"But I should have been the one to die, not him. You said it yourself that Ken was the strong one. He knew how to make me feel safe. Every time I had a problem that was too big to handle on my own, he was there to walk me though it."

"He was an amazing man, but he had his own doubts and fears. He just didn't let them stop him from moving forward. He lived each day to the fullest because he valued everything he had been given, even the unexpected and complex. He's completed his earthly mission. Now it's time for you to work through the remainder of yours."

"What if I'm not up to it? I just want to be with him."

"Maya Kincade Holden," she said, placing her hands beside her on the bed. "That's the most selfish thing I've ever heard. I know you're hurting, but you have two beautiful children who are counting on you to help them make sense of an impossible situation. You've got to let them know that they still have one parent who will be there for them. They're too young to understand why any of this happened."

"Too young," I almost shouted through tears I could no longer control. "I'm almost thirty-five years old, and I don't even understand why it had to happen. How am I supposed to convince them that losing their father was in anyone's best interest? Ken's death has destroyed everything. No one in this family will ever be happy again."

"That's not a given, Maya. While you'll never forget Ken and what you shared, you will find a way to go on. You have to believe that God knows our innermost desires and dreams, and he will never give us more than we can endure."

My laugh was acidic. "Maybe I am having a crisis of faith, but you and dad have been together for nearly fifty years. Where's the justice when one couple has half a century together and another one only gets a few years? And I certainly don't see some magic window opening now that the door to my happiness has closed. All I see is a lifetime of loneliness and desolation. Those old clichés only sound good until something really awful happens."

My mother shook her head, and I detected a look of more than just concern in her eyes. "Listen, Maya. I haven't been where you are, but I know when I hear pain and grief talking. You have more compassion and strength in your little finger than most people have in their entire hand. And the amount of courage you possess is astounding. You went up against the advice of an entire town to search for your dreams and found them. Ken cherished you in this life, and he'll be waiting for you in the next. But if you really think about it, you're not the only one who has been asked to make an unwanted sacrifice. You still get to cradle your children and grandchildren and guide them through life's greatest challenges. You'll watch them survive their first heartbreak, attend their first prom, graduate from college, buy their first home and be there when their first child is born. Ken won't be able to do any of those things. Don't you think he feels a sense of loss too?"

"I suppose," I relented.

"Then do what you must to make it through a very difficult process, but never discount the blessings you still have."

"You make it sound easy, but this isn't something I can forgot about in a month, a year or even a dozen years."

"Oh, Maya," she said, pulling me down beside her. This time, I didn't resist. "I know it won't be easy, but each day will bring added perspective. Use that to help you take another step into the unknown, and never forget that God really is on your side. He could stop all your pain and sorrow, but that might cause you to miss out on something really important."

"I won't ever forget Ken," I declared with firm conviction. "He's the only man I will ever truly love."

She didn't make some useless comeback like saying I was too young to be alone for the rest of my life. She knew I would explode if she did. I had told her often enough that I would only fall in love once.

"Just baby steps, Maya," she replied instead. "That's all you can take right now, but your children need you, and whether or not you want to accept it, you need them."

"There isn't anything left I can say. They just watched their father's body get lowered into the ground. I'm not sure they will ever get over seeing that."

"Maybe not, but your presence will be enough for now. You can make it on your own, can't you?"

"Sure," I said, putting on a false façade of bravado. "My leg is almost as good as new. The doctor said the cast can come off in another two weeks."

But before leaving the room where both of my children had been conceived, I hugged the woman who had given me life and years of wise advice. She was just trying to help, but this was a journey I had to make on my own, and all the kind and sympathetic words in the world would not take away the misery that was consuming my soul.

Instead of using my crutches like I had been doing all day, I limped down the upstairs hallway towards Kenny's room. My leg hurt almost as much as my heart, but slow progress gave me time to contemplate how I was going to face my son. He looked so much like his father with thick, blonde hair, clear blue eyes and a lanky frame now that most of his baby fat was gone. He was barely six-years old and would begin first grade in the fall, but he was the only man in the house now. I would have to be careful not to overburden him with tasks or emotions beyond his years.

When I got to his bedroom door, I paused for a moment and listened to the soft moans that were coming from inside his room.

"Kenny, it's mom," I called out. "Can I come in?"

It seemed like forever until his soft response came, and I pushed the door inward. His room was layered in shadows as the light from the hallway drifted past me. My heart crumbled when I saw him laying on his bed, his cheeks streaked with tears and a torn, toy pony gripped tightly in his arms.

How was I going to take care of my children, and the demands of daily living, when I wasn't even capable of taking care of myself? Surely God could have found someone more capable to test in such a harsh and formidable way. But my own questions, needs and concerns would have to wait until I knew my children were okay, at least for tonight.

"It's going to be all right," I encouraged, propelling myself across the room to the bed with wild horses painted on its wooden frame.

Kenny had been mesmerized by their beauty and grace when he saw one running through a canyon near my childhood home the year before. He now had dozens of plastic replicas placed strategically on the shelves in his room. He and his father had played with them every night before prayers were said and the lights turned off.

When I got close enough, I sat down beside him and pulled him into my arms. "Would you like me to read you a story?"

"No," he promptly retorted as his lips continued to quiver. "Daddy's the one who always did that before bed. He said he loved me for always, but he doesn't because he left."

Warm moisture slid down my own cheeks as I pulled him even closer and stroked his tousled mane. "Daddy still loves us, Kenny, and he didn't want to leave. But Heavenly Father needed him. He'll always be in our hearts."

"I don't want him in my heart!" my son lamented, giving me a look of defiance that felt as if it had come directly from some frozen tundra. "I want him here to play with Roscoe and me. He said we'd be buddies forever."

My son pulled away from me and buried his face in his pillow, his small body shaking with each tortured sob. Watching his misery, I found myself wanting to join him. I needed Ken too. He was my protector, my friend, my confidant and my lover. But my mother was right. I couldn't fall apart, at least not completely, and not in front of my children.

"Kenny, will you come with me?" I asked, lightly touching his shoulder. "I think we should check on Landi. She might be needing us a great deal right now."

The small figure began to stir, and two small arms found their way around my neck. I rose carefully to my feet and shifted my beloved burden to the right side where it would not weigh so heavily on my injured limb. Each step was painful and slow. I was tempted to put him down and have him walk, but I found that I needed the comfort his arms brought as much as he needed my strength.

"Landi," I said, rapping lightly on her door just in case she was sleeping. No one had slept much at our house recently. "It's mom and Kenny. Can we come in?"

I waited until she pulled it open for us. "I thought you'd forgotten all about me!" she said as I stepped inside a darkened room where posters of teen idols covered one complete wall. I could tangibly feel the weight of her sorrow.

"I could never forget you," I said as I followed her the short distance to a canopy bed. Kenny was still in my arms, and he didn't release the hold he had on me as I sat down beside her. "Your presence in my life has brought nothing but joy."

Getting her into my free arm wasn't easy with Kenny's legs dangling between us. But somehow we managed, and I was surprised to learn that my independent, talented and stubborn eleven-year-old still needed to snuggle.

I struggled to find the words that would make our loss seem less tragic, but only time would dull some of the pain. "I'm sorry I didn't come sooner. I was being selfish and unfair. But I didn't know how to explain something I don't understand myself. I kept thinking I would find the right words, but I'm not sure they exist. Maybe life is just some giant puzzle where we have to decide where all the moving pieces fit. But right now, there are only three pieces I'm concerned about."

"What are they?" Landi asked.

"You, Kenny and me! Everything else can wait until another day. We're going to make it, you know. Daddy didn't raise a bunch of quitters."

Quitters! I reflected as the word slipped out without forethought. That's exactly what I wanted to be—one gigantic quitter who didn't care what anyone else thought. Even the idea of trying to make it on my own sounded ludicrous. Ken was everything to me, and going on without him was impossible.

It wasn't long until the two small forms in my arms were silent. Trying not to wake them, I lay them side-by-side on Landi's bed and pulled a patchwork quilt my mother had made over their still forms. They were my life now and, regardless of how much I wished it could be otherwise, fate had landed our family a significant blow. Instead of being a wife and mother with nothing more serious to think about than caring for the needs of the people I loved, I was now a widow with two children to raise and a business to help keep alive. Bitterness entered by heart with such force that I knew it would consume me if I didn't do something about it.

I looked down at my sleeping children—enchanting Landi whose very nature expressed love. She would keep me on my toes. She already liked boys too much, and they were not indifferent to her. I needed to help her remain focused on the things that really mattered. But while we shared a great mother-daughter relationship, she was the apple of her daddy's eye. That was a bond even my greatest strides forward could never touch.

And little Kenny—the miracle we thought would never be ours to keep—who came two and a half months early and spent the first nine weeks of life in the hospital. How fearful I had been bringing him home after watching all the doctors and nurses had done to keep him alive. Who would help when he got into trouble now? He needed his father's wisdom as he began navigating his own world.

There would be no more children for me in this life, but I had to believe that when I joined Ken on the other side of mortality's veil that we would spend eternity creating more children to love.

It was after midnight when I placed a moist kiss on both their cheeks and returned to my room. I undressed in the darkness and prayed for the strength to endure being alone. Then I pulled back the warm comforter that covered the king-size bed. There had only been a handful of nights in my entire married life when Ken had not been sleeping beside me. I lay in my accustomed place, clutching the covers to my chin and trying to fight back the awful emptiness that seemed to be consuming my soul.

How could I face life without the man of my dreams? I reached across the bed and placed my hand on his pillow. Without even trying, I recalled each feature of his handsome face and tried tracing them with fingers of memory. I smiled as my fingertips reached the cleft in his chin and moved upwards across soft, inviting lips, prominent cheekbones and laughing eyes to the scar on his forehead that he'd gotten while playing high school football. Then I listened intently until I could hear the rich tones of his voice as we made our nightly accountings to each other of all that was important in our world.

What would happen when I could no longer recall each texture, expression or feeling regarding our life together so clearly? I wanted to get lost in his embrace one more time, tell him how perfect he was for me, and how each moment we spent together was even more beautiful and flawless than the last. I needed the firm assurance that our time together wasn't over for always, but all I had left was hope.

"Oh, Ken," I cried out in my heart because doing so vocally might awaken someone in the house who was trying to sleep. "Why did you have to leave me alone in that room to go off with all the others? It wasn't your responsibility."

I didn't want to relive our last few days together after enduring his funeral. But there was something comforting—albeit incredibly painful—about recalling just what an incredible and Christlike man he truly was. Those attributes of compassion, understanding and genuine love for others was part of what had drawn me to him in the first place. He was always the first one in the office, or the neighborhood, to offer assistance when anyone needed help, and he seemed to have a sixth sense when it came to discerning who might be calling out for a friend. And it certainly wasn't in his nature to remain safe, warm and happy when others were in trouble.

The words coming from the pulpit that morning about what an extraordinary man he was might bring added comfort someday, but right now, they only made me question why such a good man had been summoned home when so many truly horrid people were allowed to stay. I bit down on my bottom lip as I curled into the fetal position wishing I had even half the strength and wisdom he did.

Nothing about what had happened was fair, but I couldn't go back and change any of it.

I must have fallen into a troubled sleep because at some point during the moonless and drizzly night my mind took an unprepared for journey. Ken's father had insisted we leave the children with him and go on a weekend retreat to our favorite mountain resort. I wasn't sure my skiing lessons would allow me to remain even a respectable distance behind as my husband raced down the slopes, but I had to try.

Ken was an all-around athlete, and skiing was his favorite sport. I was hopeless! My knees still buckled and my poles and skis never seemed to be heading in the same direction. I told him a hundred times that I would never be a snow bunny. People from Hurricane, Utah, weren't meant to get cold. But he would only laugh, hold me even closer and tell me that it didn't matter if I spent more time on my back than upright, as long as I didn't get hurt. The fun was just being together.

I couldn't deny that he made chores like cleaning the gutters along the outside edges of the roof seem like a game. He was never cross or belittling, even when my natural clumsiness undid hours of work or caused another repair. Besides, we hadn't been away together for months, and Ken was beginning to show signs of stress from the monumental workload he carried while both senior partners at Turner, Holden and Holden moved more cautiously towards retirement.

It was a heavenly winter morning in mid-January—clear skies, no wind and plenty of fresh, powdery snow—when we loaded our suitcases into the car, kissed our children good-bye and left the busy city streets behind. The tires on our reliable family SUV were new, and I had no doubts when it came to my husband's ability to keep us safe. We talked and laughed and made each other exorbitant promises as we wound our way up the mountain road leading to Heaven's Glen.

The remainder of our day would be spent on the slopes. I really didn't mind the exercise, the sunburn on my exposed face or the throbbing muscles I would feel once my boots were removed. My time of pure bliss would come after we had eaten a robust meal of homemade chili or freshly grilled steak and retired to our room. That's when we would sit in front of our private fire and soak in our own jetted tub.

I thought about the possibilities the evening would bring as we rode the lift to the top of the mountain and made our way back to the lodge three times after checking into our room. I had packed a bottle of fake champagne, along with my sexiest nightie, in the bottom of my suitcase so he wouldn't see them outright if he wanted to help me unpack. Doing unexpected and special things for each other was just how we lived, and it was never a burden to find thoughtful ways of expressing our love. But sometimes a complete break from routine was needed, especially when children were involved.

We loved Landi and Kenny wholly and completely. But as I watched Ken stoke the fire, his muscular biceps glistening in the soft, flickering light, I knew I needed this mini-vacation as much as he did. There was just something about being in a romantic setting, away from home and family, that made me feel like an innocent bride again. One who had yet to experience the total abandon and bliss of making love for the first time. I ran my fingers across my lips as I waited for him to return to my side. I was ready to show my husband that our years together had only increased my desire to be with him.

Not surprisingly, we stayed awake until the early hours of the morning as our acts of recommitment to each other, and the life we had chosen, took us to heights we had not experienced before. I wished our magical time could last forever. But as I lay on a soft, fluffy rug in front of the dying embers of a once-roaring fire and took a sip of warm, fake champagne from a mug, I thanked God again for leading me to Ken. He fulfilled my every desire.

"I love you, Maya. You know that, don't you?" he said, removing the mug from my hand and giving me the strangest look.

"Always," I responded, turning so my body was facing his. "I love you too."

"I know, but it seems like we never say it often enough. You are my life, my sunshine, my hope for everything precious and dear.

You've given me more than words can ever express. You've given me immortality."

"How?" I asked, unsure of what he was getting at.

"By giving me the most priceless gifts in the world—our two beautiful children. I wish we could have a dozen more. Watching them grow means I'll never really grow old and disappear. A part of me—of us—will always be alive in them, and in the countless others each of their unions bring. When I look in their faces, it's as if I'm looking into reflecting mirrors where there is no end. The immensity of what we've been able to create keeps me awake sometimes. I know this life isn't the end. It's just the beginning of a never-ending eternity of possibilities."

"What brought that up?" I asked as I placed my hand in his.

"I don't know. Maybe I'm just in a pensive mood. It seems like I've been so involved with work lately that I haven't had time to be the husband and father I promised I would be when I asked you to join me on this incredible journey."

"You've always given us everything you could. I know it's been hard shouldering so much added responsibility, but it won't last forever. Your dad and Winston will decide on their replacements eventually. Would it help if I spent a little more time helping out at the office? I'm sure I could find someone to watch Kenny for a few hours each day."

Instead of answering, he lifted my hand to his lips and began kissing each fingertip.

"I love it when you do that, Ken, but you haven't answered my question. Is there something you're not telling me? You know I don't like being left in the dark about anything. It's not the way we do things."

His movements stopped a little too abruptly. "Maybe I'm just resisting the inevitable too hard. But sometimes I hate change, even if it is necessary. There's no way I'll be able to fill the gap when both of my mentors are gone. The've always had my back, and I'm not ready to be the one in charge."

"I can't see either of those men walking away for good. Your dad would go crazy with nothing to do besides driving to the country club to eat, play tennis or golf, and Fiona will make Winston's life miserable with all her demands. I've seen the list of chores she's compiled for him."

"It's not just that. I'm as close to fifty as I am to forty—way past my prime. That never bothered me until I realized that I entered middle age about the time we got married since it's doubtful I'll live to be a hundred. Don't you sometimes wish you'd married a man a little closer to your age since woman are supposed to live longer anyway?"

"Never," I said, placing my free hand on his cheeks. "Twelve years is nothing. I used to be afraid of growing old myself—afraid that I might lose your love when I was covered with wrinkles and mantled in white."

"I'll get there long before you do, Maya."

"You're deliberately missing my point! Young love is so powerful and all-consuming that it's hard to imagine anything being more desirable. But I've learned over the years that those rockets firing are just the beginning of an extraordinary voyage of discovery. When that special someone becomes a living part of your heart and soul then you know you've found love. And Ken, that's how I feel about you. I can't imagine living a moment without you."

"Well, Mrs. Holden," he said, kissing my eager lips. "I hope you'll always feel like that because you're never going to get rid of this somewhat older man. I love what we have, and it's only going to get better. Now what do you say about climbing into bed for a few hours? I could use a little sleep before heading to the slopes again."

I didn't want to leave the warmth of the blanket, but the fire was almost out and one of us would have to step outside if we wanted more wood.

"I could be persuaded," I replied. "Just don't make me get up too early. I like being lazy, especially when I can do it with you."

His spontaneous laughter lit up the room as he pulled me to my feet. "You do know how to say just the right thing, but the night isn't over yet. I still have a few surprises up my proverbial sleeve. Can you believe we've been married for twelve years? It seems like only yesterday that we made our vows to love, cherish and be there for each other. Do you think we'll feel the same way in another fifty years?"

"I think we'll be even more in love. Do you really believe in forever?"

"I do, but I wouldn't want to be part of it without you."

Snuggling into his open arms was easy as the bed covers drifted over our heads. His breath was soon caressing my face, and we were swept into loving each other again. Our marriage was good. It was strong. And there was enough love building inside both of us to last a lifetime and beyond.

When he awakened me with a gentle kiss, I saw the morning rays of a bright, winter sun peaking underneath the heavy window curtains. I stretched luxuriously like a playful kitten, opened my heavy eyes and smiled. "What time is it? I've been having the most wonderful dreams."

"About me, I hope?"

"Who else, but nothing compares to how you make me feel when I'm awake and in your arms."

"You little wench," he teased, trying to pull the blanket away so I wouldn't notice how deeply my expression of love and contentment had touched him. I tried to fight back, but it was all just a delicious game I really didn't want to end. "You would say anything to keep from heading to the top of my favorite mountain again, but we came here to have all kinds of fun."

I felt the corners of my lips turn upwards as we wrestled with a pillow. He could read me like an open book and didn't seem to mind that a few of my pages were a little smudged. That's what made being with him so easy and natural.

"Would not," I playfully retorted as more of the room room came into focus. "But can't we be lazy for just a while longer? My body isn't ready to get cold again. What time is it anyway?"

He took his cell phone from off the nightstand and waited for the face to light up. "It appears we've dozed more than just the embers away. It's eleven-thirty."

"In the morning?" I asked, trying to push myself upright. I hadn't slept that late for ages.

"Afraid so, but there's still time for a few runs. We could grab some lunch before leaving the lodge. How long will it take for you to get ready?"

"All I have to do is pull on some clothes, if you don't mind spending the rest of the day with some who hasn't showered."

He pulled me to my feet and quite literally danced me across the room. "I wouldn't normally say this, but I feel like a kid today and perfect hygiene is the last thing on my mind. Why don't we save that for later. I would even be willing to throw in a full body massage when we get back."

I didn't need further encouragement and was dressed before he was. We took what we wanted from the buffet table that had been set up in the lodge's dining room, and ate all we could comfortably consume while sitting in front of a floor to ceiling window. Guests were everywhere, both inside and out, and bright splotches of color were moving so rapidly in front of my eyes that I felt like I was looking through the handheld kaleidoscope I'd had as a child. It gave me a dizzying feeling as if the entire earth had momentarily shifted.

"Don't you ever get tired of being around so many people?" I asked my handsome husband as I waited for the sensation to lift. "You never have any time alone."

"People interest me. I like trying to figure out where they're from, what they do for a living, and if they're planning for their futures. Even when the economy seems strong, it's unpredictable, and we need to be prepared for anything."

"We're prepared, aren't we?" I asked.

He reached across the smooth surface where empty plates were sitting. "We're as prepared as we can possibly be, without having unlimited resources. Why the sudden interest in our financial affairs? You helped set up our entire portfolio and know exactly where we stand."

I looked down at the strong hands that were holding mine. "Maybe I'm just feeling incredibly blessed and a little scared. Not many people get to live their dreams."

"We've worked hard to get where we are, and we deserve a break from the rat-race once in a while. Have I told you lately how grateful I am that you're always so willing to try new things—even when you know you aren't going to like them."

"Skiing is fun," I replied. "I'm just not very good at it. Even Landi and Kenny show more grace on the slopes than I do."

"That's because they've never learned to be afraid. You've seen what happens when people are careless or take unnecessary risks."

"I'm not afraid, Ken Holden, and I certainly don't take the kind of chances I used to," I said, giving him a rare look of defiance. "I know where my weaknesses lay, but I'm feeling fairly positive today. How about making a little wager."

"That's not necessary, Maya. My only concern is that you don't get hurt."

"I have no intention of doing that! The den needs a new rug, and I've found the perfect one. Its a little pricey, but what would you say about buying it for me if I can make the longest run down that mountain without falling?"

"That's a fool's bet, Maya. Even I've lost my footing on that one."

"Then you have nothing to lose."

"Except my wife! I have no intention of taking you back to our children damaged."

"But you could make a counter wager. What would you most like if I lose without breaking any bones?"

The return look he gave me let me know that he was reconsidering. "Just where do you plan on getting enough money to buy a mountain cabin complete with a trout-stocked stream."

"I won't need any money because I intend to win."

He caught me in his arms as I rose to my feet and gave me a heavenly kiss. It was magical being loved by a man like him.

"You had this planned all along, didn't you?" he accused. "You wanted to catch your old hubbie when his defenses were down."

"Did it work?" I asked.

"Probably, but what if it backfires? I'm not going to back down on my mountain cabin either. You might find yourself working some incredibly long hours for the rest of your life to pay for it."

"That wouldn't be so bad, as long as I was working for you," I responded as we made our way to the hooks by the front doors where all sorts of winter gear had been stashed. "Now grab your parka because this lady is on a roll."

He carried my skis to the lift and, despite the chill in the air, I felt all warm and toasty inside. I almost believed I could pull off my bet, but it wouldn't really matter if I didn't. Ken would only chide and tease me if I lost, and the whole thing would be forgotten before we got home—even the cabin and stream.

I was the luckiest woman in the world, I told myself for the millionth time as we slipped into our skis before climbing onto the lift and making sure the gate that would keep us from falling to our deaths was closed securely in front of us. There was no stinging wind today that burned tender cheeks and made traversing the slopes almost impossible at times. Just the bright, winter sun that was now at its apex and the laughter of people not so far away from us.

All I could see in every direction was snow covered peaks as we moved beyond the tree line. The lodge and parking lot had become nothing more than colorful dots against a very white and bright landscape. I loved being with my husband like this. I reached for his gloved hand as the distance between us and the earth increased. Maybe I should reconsider my bravery and ask to be let off at one of the lower runs, but when I looked up into his smiling face, I knew he would make sure I was safe. I had never felt anything other than love, protection and fulfillment when I was with him. He was everything in the world to me.

Sometimes I felt slightly guilty when I thought about how perfectly my decision to move to Boston on a whim had turned out. Not only had I found the perfect man, but I had two precious children and had been able to stay home to raise them. As I leaned into Ken's shoulder before it was our turn to get off the chair lift, I knew I was ready to have another child. Landi and Kenny had been talking about it for months, but I hadn't been in the right frame of mind to even think about more diapers and late night feedings until now.

But something about the moment we were sharing, in the vast beauty of the world God had created, made me see how self-centered it would be not to give another one of his children an earthly home. I would bring it up when we returned to the lodge that night and see how Ken felt. We had been through so much trying to have Kenny, and the doctor had cautioned us that a premature delivery could happen again, but our son was thriving. So why not give it another try?

As an only child, Ken had always been open to having a big family, but he was leaving the timing to me. Maybe we would have twins. That wouldn't be such a heavy burden because there would be plenty of help. My heart was even lighter than before when the lift came to a stop. I used my poles to push me into an open spot so I wouldn't be in anyone's way.

"Are your bindings tight enough?" Ken asked, and then bent down to check them for himself.

"Of course," I replied. "You made sure of that before we left the lodge."

He rose to his feet with a bright smile and placed his hands on my arms. "Am I being over-protective again?"

"A little, but I love it," I said, wriggling my nose as I stretched upwards and placed a kiss on his cheek. If anyone was watching, I didn't care. I was totally and completely in love with my husband. There would never be anyone else for me. "Now let's go! I want to make this run at least a half a dozen times before dark. I'm so glad we came."

"So it wasn't such a bad idea, even if we had to leave the kids at home?" he asked.

"This vacation is just what we needed after being cooped up in the house since long before Christmas. The pharmacist is rapidly becoming one of my best friends. It seems like I've visited with him almost weekly since this cold and flu season began. We can bring the kids next time. Right now, I feel like a bride all over again."

"Every day is a new beginning to the life we're living, Maya, and I feel like the luckiest guy in the world to be sharing it all with you."

"Cut it out, Ken" I said, slugging him playfully on the arm. "You're going to make me cry."

"Why? Because we have everything?"

"Yes! And sometimes I wonder when our balloon is going to burst."

"It's not going to burst. We'll sail along together through whatever God has in mind for us until the end of time."

"Promise," I said. "I couldn't bare it if something happened to our world."

"Nothing's going to happen, but if it should, you would make it just fine."

"I wouldn't want to make it without you," I said as a shivering kind of foreboding seemed to wash over me. This was much too nice a day to think about anything unpleasant.

But instead of walking away or changing the subject, Ken simply looked at me with such tenderness that I thought I might melt into a pool of crystal, clear water.

"Still, you could if you had to," he said. "Landi and Kenny would need your strength more than ever if I wasn't around to take care of you."

"But you're going to be around just as long as I am," I responded. "That's the way we've always planned it."

"And I intend to stick with our plan, but just supposing something unexpected happened. I want you to make me a promise."

"What kind of a promise?" I asked.

"That you would go on with your life—find a new husband to love and care for you and the kids. I have to know that you wouldn't sit home and mourn for me. Your happiness is all I've ever wanted."

"Then don't talk like that," I said as my agitation rose to a dangerous level. I was a generally a very calm person, but I had my limits, and talking about us not being together was one of them. "When we were married it was forever, and that's the way I intend to keep it. Don't you know by now that you are my life, my world, my everything? You're all I've ever wanted or needed."

"I know," he said, placing his hands on my shoulders so I couldn't turn away. "Do you think I like the idea of another man in my wife's life? But we have to be realistic. Chances are that one of us will be taken before the other, and I don't want you to spend your life alone. You have too much love and vitality inside. It wouldn't be right to throw that away for a memory."

"I won't listen to this crazy talk," I hotly retorted, trying to break free of his grasp. "You're being morbid."

"Not without reason. We can't always control what happens, and I have to know that you wouldn't give up if something happened to me."

"But you're going to be around until we're both old and gray and so crippled with arthritis that we can't even walk without leaning on each other."

It wasn't often I got mad enough to lash out, but something about the raw intensity behind his words was giving me the creeps, and I felt the irrevocable need to get away. I had never faced the death of someone close to me, and even the idea of it happening terrified me.

"Maybe you're right," he relented, releasing my arms and dropping his hands to his sides. "This was supposed to be a vacation, unmarred by work or dismal thoughts that came out of nowhere. I'm sorry for putting a blight on our day. It just seemed important, that's all."

I sighed with relief and looked down at my poles. They had kept me from taking hundred of spills in the past. "You don't have to apologize. I know it was hard losing your mother, but that's not going to happen to us. We need each other, and our children need both of us. Now let's aim for all of our dreams and forget this nonsense. People are going to think we're fighting."

I pulled on my goggles, and with a mighty thrust of my poles was soon racing down the snow packed trail. I felt gloriously alive and free, and more deeply in love with the man I had married than ever before.

"This is delicious," I called to the wind as it played with my streaming hair.

And then I inhaled deeply the sweet, brisk mountain air. If there was anything I loved, other than being with my family, it was being at one with nature where I could see God's hand with vivid clarity. It echoed through the leafless branches of snow-covered trees and caused cool, white mists to swirl upwards as skiers moved almost effortlessly past me. The sky above was a brilliant blue, and I couldn't help but wonder how many other worlds, like ours, existed in such a vast universe.

I was progressing at lightening speed, twisting and turning my knees so I wouldn't run into anyone else. Ken was somewhere behind me, but I didn't look around to see how close he was. He would catch up with me, and most likely leave me behind any moment now. My job was to remain upright if I was going to claim my prize. This wasn't the most difficult run on the mountain, but it was one I had never taken before. Ken had cautioned me about getting off the path. There were sharp drops into ravines, icy spots that could propel me into trees and other skiers who might not be able to avoid a collision if I moved back and forth too rapidly.

It was the perfect outdoor adventure until a sudden movement beneath my feet nearly sent me sprawling.

"Steady, old girl," I muttered to myself since there was no one else around to hear. "You haven't quite got your snow legs yet. And if you intend to see that rug on the floor of the den you'd better be careful. It's still a long way to the bottom."

That was certainly true, and I had a habit of not breathing deeply, or often, enough when I was concentrating too hard. No wonder it felt as if the earth had moved. Oxygen was less prevalent at such a high altitude, and I needed to remember every lesson Ken had taught me about survival in the mountains, not just the ones that would help me capture my prize. But by the time I reached the half way mark, my knees were ready to crumble. Maybe skiing for such a wanted reward had been a bad idea. The idea of sitting down in the middle of the trail was definitely appealing, but I couldn't quit yet. It wouldn't be long until the lodge came into view.

And then I heard a sound—not unlike someone calling my name. But I was moving too fast for it to be anything other than the rushing wind playing tricks with my head. So I dismissed it and kept moving. But it was impossible not to feel a little shaken when some of the skiers around me began digging their poles into the snow to get an extra thrust forward.

"Maya!"

There it was again, but this time the sound was muffled beneath a raw, smothering noise I had only heard on the television or movie screen. I peered cautiously over my shoulder and saw Ken coming towards me. But he wasn't smiling, and behind him was a rolling mountain of white. The look of sheer panic on his handsome face let me know that this was no game.

"It's an avalanche, Maya! Get to the bottom and don't stop for anything."

I didn't take the time to judge anything for myself. There was another thundering roar, and then a surge of freezing ice flakes was sweeping over both us as the mountain seemed to move spasmodically beneath our feet.

Fear hung like heavy weights from every appendage of my body. "I can't do it," I screamed without even looking at him.

"Yes, you can!" he hollered back through an awful reality I didn't want to accept. "Now stick in those poles and travel."

One of his hands was suddenly on my back, and I felt every muscle in his body tense as he hefted me forward. This couldn't be happening! But from the reeling movement underneath my feet I knew I wasn't dreaming.

"Oh, Ken" I silently prayed as my skies continued to propel me downward. "I love you so much. Please be okay. We have so many dreams left to live."

Swirling, loose snow was making it impossible for me to see anything. I only knew that I was going down the mountainside faster than I had ever thought possible. Through a swirling curtain of white I saw brilliant flashes of color. People were stumbling and sliding spasmodically to safety. This was a fight for survival, and an angry Mother Nature seemed determined to win.

I clung desperately to my poles. They were my only life-line to safety, but one mighty thrust of snow and ice and they were gone. Before I had time to scream, I fell to my knees as an agonizing pain gripped my legs. So this was death—the darkness, the pain and the cold before the brightness. I tried to recall all that I knew about passing to the other side of the veil. There was supposed to be a tunnel and then a glorious light.

But what came after that? Someone I loved was supposed to greet me. But who would it be—a grandparent or my older sister, Mattie, who drowned in an irrigation canal before I was born? I had never known her in this life, but I loved her because I had been told how good and beautiful she was. I wouldn't mind getting to know her. In ways it would be quite wonderful, but I didn't want to leave my family behind, and I certainly didn't want to see my husband with anyone else.

"What you said was true, Ken," my mind suddenly cried out. "One of us is going to die before the other but please don't forget about me."

And then my face felt warmer, but I couldn't bring myself to open my eyes. I didn't want to leave mortality. Like Emily, the young woman in Thornton Wilder's play *Our Town* who knew she was dying, there was too much on earth that I loved. Her last soliloquy recounted all the things she would miss when she was gone like fresh bread baking and newly ironed clothes. Recalling anything else was impossible, but her sentiment was certainly hitting home I couldn't imagine not watching my children grow up, spending my nights in Ken's arms, or going about daily living with all the people I loved. Time was supposed be on my side. I was still a young woman and should never have taken anything for granted.

If this was death, I didn't want any part of it. And then from somewhere in the distance it seemed as if another voice was floating towards me.

"Breath for her, man! She'll never make it if you don't."

Through a foggy sort of awareness, I felt lips press against my own and my chest begin to rise and fall. My body wanted to move, but something was pinning me down—something heavy, cold and unrelenting. Death was supposed to be a release from suffering, but I had never felt such incredible agony. And then the cold returned, and I realized where I was. The snow from the mountain had overtaken me, but I was not alone. Shrill and commanding voices were trying to get me to respond.

I needed to take some action that would let the people helping me know that I was still alive. So I forced my eyes open and then felt a low, choking sound die away in my throat when I saw Ken looking down at me. It seemed as if a lifetime of desires, hopes and dreams passed between us during that one, brief moment. As startling as it was, I suddenly knew that death was not the enemy I had always supposed it to be. It was simply a gateway into the next part of living, and I had been given a glimpse of what it might be like to greet a loved one after a short, or long, separation.

"Don't try to talk," he whispered against my cheek. "Everything's going to be all right. We just have to free you from all the snow."

It was only then I realized that every part of my body was encased, with the exception of my head and shoulders. I couldn't tell if I was laying down or curled into a ball. I only knew that it was becoming more difficult to breath.

"Keep her calm while we do the digging," someone I couldn't see said. "The weight of the snow is constricting her lungs."

My fear-filled eyes focused on the man who meant everything to me. "Guess you were right talking about the future, but I certainly didn't expect this. If I don't make it, you need to remember the advice you gave me and use it for yourself."

"Stop with the nonsense," he replied, brushing at my hair with his gloveless hands. He would get frostbite without them. It was bitterly cold outside. "I was wrong tempting fate that way. You'll soon be back in the lodge all toasty warm and comfortable. Our love is too strong to be destroyed by an angry mountain."

"I hope you're right," I responded as my brain seemed to start reeling again. "But if I don't make it, you need to know that I will love you forever and always."

My head fell backwards, but I knew Ken was cradling it in his arms. His words of comfort and love were still floating towards me, but I was too tired to respond. Every so often I felt him force more air into my lungs, but the sound of my rescuers clawing at the snow that imprisoned me seemed to be receding. But instead of floating away into a pleasant sort of oblivion, I knew the exact moment when all the snow had been pushed away and Ken tried to lift me because my scream shattered the silent, mountain air.

"What is it?" he asked as my body collapsed against his.

"My legs! I can't seem to move them."

"They're probably broken," someone said. "You'd better get her back to your room and try to make her comfortable. If she isn't in shock now, she soon will be, and there's no way of knowing how long it will take to get enough doctors here to take care of all the injuries. You're lucky she was close to the bottom or we might never have found her. That swale took most of the snow."

"I couldn't have freed her without you," Ken replied.

"It could have been any one of us under that snow," a woman said. "But I'm afraid there are other people on that mountain who weren't quite as lucky. I've never seen an avalanche come on that quickly. There was no time to get anyone to safety."

Ken didn't say anything in return, but it was impossible not to recall the two small jolts I had felt earlier in the day. Maybe if I had mentioned them we wouldn't be sitting in what was left of an avalanche now.

Every muscle in his body tensed as he lifted me into his arms and rose to his feet. I wanted to tell him I could make it on my own but knew I wouldn't even be able to crawl. His show of both bravery and love made me suppress cries of agony as he climbed inclines and slipped into crevices in the loose, binding snow. The men and women who had assisted in my rescue were helping others, and I knew he wished he could go with them. But without complaint, he carried me as if I were a child in need of the most tender care. I marveled at his display of physical endurance, and I would not make his job harder by being a coward. He needed to know that his wife was strong enough to face whatever else might come her way.

Chapter 3

It was almost dusk when we reached the lodge. The clamor in the lobby was both deafening and disheartening as help was administered to people who had been hurt and lists were compiled of those who were missing. I tried not to listen as calls went out for volunteers who would be willing to join rescue parties. I wouldn't be any good—even if I hadn't been hurt—but Ken would be the first one to join if it my condition wasn't holding him back.

One of the porters helped him get me up the stairs to our room. Once I was laying on the bed, he told Ken that he would send medical help as soon as it arrived. Reports coming from town said the road leading down the mountain was blocked, and it might be morning before emergency vehicles were able to make it through. He would send extra towels and bedding to our room, along with a pleasant dinner, but there wasn't a doctor on staff and all they had in the way of painkillers was what could be found in the gift shop.

I tried not to let my fear or my pain consume me as Ken removed my torn parka and damp turtleneck sweater and then eased my stretch pants down my legs. Before covering me with all the blankets he could find, he checked my body for open wounds or any sign of internal injuries. Then he hunted through my overnight bag for the extra-strength Tylenol I always carried with me.

"Sorry I don't have something stronger," he said as he got a bottle of water and opened it. "This isn't the way I planned on spending the evening. Are you in a great deal of pain?"

"No more than when I was giving birth to our children," I said, fighting back the nausea that increased proportionately to the throbbing in my legs. "How would you feel about having more?"

"What brought that up?" he asked, tilting my head so water wouldn't saturate the nightgown he'd slipped over my head. "You know I'd like at least half a dozen, but this is hardly the time to talk about making an addition to our family."

"Why not?" I asked. "I need a diversion to keep me from asking you to go down to the bar and bring back a bottle of the strongest alcohol they have. I've heard it numbs pain."

"I can do that, if it's what you really want."

He started to move away, but I reached for his arm. "It's the pain talking, not me, Ken. Now is hardly the time to take my first drink. There's no telling how I might react. I can handle this until the doctor gets here, but I wasn't kidding about needing a distraction."

"And talking about having another child will do that? You know what the doctor said."

"He said having another preemie was a possibility, not an absolute. And now that we know the risk, and what caused it, we'll be better prepared. Even if I have to stay in bed for a couple of months it would be worth it. I love being a wife and mother. Nothing brings me greater joy."

He sat down beside me again but didn't try to get underneath the covers. His parka was laying across the back of a chair to dry, but he was still wearing his water-repellant snow pants. Once his adrenaline quit pumping so hard, he would be as cold as I was. I almost said something about it, but the look of devotion in his eyes let me know he wasn't thinking about his physical comfort. Nor was he opposed to my surprise request.

"If things were different, I would let you know just how much I want to fulfill your every desire—starting immediately—Maya Kincade Holden. We've been given another incredible gift. I thought I had lost you forever when you disappeared under all that snow."

"How did you even know where to look for me?" I asked.

Talking about what had happened wouldn't make anyone's problems disappear, but it would give us something to do while we waited. And I had a feeling it was going to be one of the longest and roughest nights of my life. It was all I could do to keep from screaming the pain was so intense.

"Divine intervention!" he replied while I was still lost in my own miserable thoughts. "I was right behind you when the first wave came, but the snow took you at least 100 yards down that mountain. It was swirling so hard I couldn't see my hand in front of my face. I lost my poles and one of my skis immediately. I bent down to release the other one so it wouldn't get in the way. When I stood up, I caught a glimpse of the bright, red headband that was covering your ears. I focused on that while I stumbled, and then rolled, to where it was."

"And it was still on my head?"

He shook his head solemnly as he reached for my hand. "It was several feet away, but something led me to where you were, and I started digging. I had your head cleared by the time someone stopped to help. You have no idea how hard I prayed that I would find you alive. The thought of losing you, or one of our children, is the only thing that's ever kept me awake at night. By all rights, we should have been buried together."

His body started to quiver, and I felt the tears come as I clung to his hand. "We should never take anything for granted again, Ken."

"I don't intend to, but I feel like the worst husband in the world because I can't even get the help you need."

"You saved my life while risking your own. There's no greater way of showing love than that. And despite a little stress and inconvenience, we're safe and warm now. How many others are still lost and might never be found?"

"People won't stop looking for survivors, but we need more wood if we want to stay warm. The power lines are down, and the backup generators will only last for a few hours now that the lodge is filled to capacity. The people who came for the day, with no intention of staying overnight, have no way to leave, and the staff will have to find some place for them to sleep."

"Should we offer our room?" I asked. "The sofa is comfortable, and there's plenty of space on the floor."

He stood up and tucked the blankets more tightly around me, making sure not to touch my legs.

"I'll tell someone at the front desk that we have extra room when I get more wood. What we have will last most of the night, but I don't want to be hunting around for more in the dark. Will you be okay if I leave for a few minutes? I don't want to bother anyone in room service. They'll be busy helping others."

"I'm not going anywhere," I said, putting on a mask of false bravado.

Ken would never leave me alone unless it was necessary, and I could never be one of those helpless females who needed constant attention. But as I turned my head to watch him put on his parka I had the sudden realization that something was very wrong. While the rest of my body felt as if it had been tossed about in a cement mixer, my legs were no longer throbbing. In fact, I could barely feel them at all.

Ken kissed me before leaving the room. "I love you, Maya. I promise we will make it through this, and we will have more children."

"Shush," I whispered as the tears in my eyes threatened to slide down my cheeks. "We don't need to make any more promises. We just need to be there for each other. Everything else will work out as it's meant to."

But while I waited for him to return I knew that life, as I had always known it, might be over for good. A spinal cord injury was the most logical reason I could no longer feel anything below my waist. If I couldn't walk, I wouldn't be able to have another child. I might not even be able to take care of Landi and Kenny. I closed my eyes and prayed harder than I ever had before. Now was not the time to give in to self-pity. I would trust in God's wisdom and mercy as I had never trusted before.

Somewhere during my pleadings for more divine intervention and the ability to accept what had already been set in place, I must have fallen asleep. I don't remember dreaming, but when I opened my eyes again it was completely dark outside and a fire was burning brightly in the hearth. Ken was standing in front of the window that faced the mountain. His arms were folded across his chest and his head lowered. I almost called out so he would know I was finally awake but realized in time that he, too, was seeking comfort in prayer.

I watched him for some moments, caught up in the love I felt for the strong, dependable and righteous man who had been my husband for twelve, joyous years. We would make it through this latest challenge, and our marriage would be even stronger because of the sacrifices we might yet have to make. But as my thoughts continued to turn inward, an abrupt rapping on the door brought both of us back to a very uncertain present.

Ken opened it to admit a short, thin-haired man in a snow-covered parka. It was impossible to tell his age, but he was holding a black bag in one hand.

"My name is Dr. Miller," he said. "They told me at the front desk you could use some help."

Ken breathed an audible sigh of relief as he stepped back so the doctor could approach the bed. "Thank you for coming, Dr. Miller."

"It's my pleasure," he replied, giving me a look that was impossible to read." I understand that your wife was buried in the avalanche. It's a miracle you were able to find her so quickly. Can you tell me anything that might be helpful before I begin my examination? I've found that patients, and the ones who love them, are often able to provide valuable clues that can lead to a quicker diagnosis. Was she conscious when you got to her?"

"No," Ken said without hesitation. "We had to bring her back, but she's been lucid since she regained consciousness. She wasn't able to walk, so I carried her back to the lodge. Then I checked for open wounds and the possibility of internal injuries as best I could."

"Do you have medical training?" the doctor asked him while I lay still hoping the next few moments would not confirm my worst fears.

"Just what it takes to be part of a rescue team. There wasn't anything that could be used to mobilize her neck. And with the chance of more tremors, I did the only thing I could—move her to a safer place."

"I'm not here to condemn your actions, Mr. Holden. You did what was necessary to keep both of you alive. Now it's my turn to see what else needs to be done to get your wife back on her feet. I'll do what I can for her here, but we need to get her to the hospital as soon as possible."

"How long will that take?" Ken asked.

"We have one chopper in the air and more on the way. They will transport the most critical patients first, but it will be a few hours until ambulances arrive. I've lived in this area all my life and have been called in to help after several similar incidents, but this is the most far-reaching avalanche yet. Is there anything more you can tell me about your wife's condition?"

I should have expressed my own concerns but overreacting, or becoming hysterical, wouldn't help anyone. So I lay where I was and tried not to cry as the doctor gave me an initial examination. He checked my eyes, my throat and my heart. He asked simple, but direct, questions as he looked at the bruises that had now formed on my arms and torso. But when he got to my legs and checked for broken bones and reflexes, his look became a little more solemn.

"What's wrong with her legs?" Ken asked. "She was feeling plenty of pain when we got her out of the snow."

"I wish I could give you a definitive answer. There's obviously more than one broken bone, but the lack of sensation is cause for concern. It may be something as simple as the mind's reaction to acute trauma since there were no painkillers available, but we won't know anything until we're able to do more comprehensive tests. The good news is that there's still a sufficient supply of blood to her feet, but we can't risk any sudden movements. I'll give her something to help her sleep. Her body needs to fully relax so it can begin healing. You're not afraid of needles, are you, Mrs. Kincade?"

"No, doctor, but I need to know just how critical my situation is. Will the feeling in my legs return? I haven't felt anything for several hours."

"That's what I'm hoping will happen, but we need to take things one step at a time. We'll get you back to town on the first available chopper, and I'll notify my colleagues so an operating room will be ready. The best thing you can do right now is rest."

He filled a syringe from a small bottle he withdrew from his bag, and then I bit my bottom lip as the needle stung my arm.

"Just how bad is it out there?" I asked.

"Bad enough, but you shouldn't be worrying about that now. Everyone capable of helping is doing everything he or she can. You're a mighty lucky young woman, Mrs. Holden. There aren't many avalanche victims who live to tell about it. Now try to sleep. I have to attend to other injuries, but I will see you at the hospital later."

He closed his bag and then motioned for Ken to follow him into the hallway. I felt a jolt of uncertainty when they were gone. I believed in miracles. They happened all the time, but I wasn't fond of waiting—especially this time. There were outside forces at work, and sometimes truly innocent people were simply in the wrong place at the wrong time.

And what was it the doctor had to say that he didn't want me to hear? I chewed down on my lip again as I stared at the closed door. The knot in my throat was threatening to choke me. I may never walk again, but Ken and I could face anything as long as we were together. I just wanted to be home in my own bed with my children playing contentedly on the floor beside me.

I listened to the sputtering flames in the hearth while I waited. My mind seemed to be losing focus, but I couldn't go to sleep before Ken returned. He might not want to tell me what had been said, but he would never intentionally lie. Our marriage was built on more than love. We had promised to always tell each other the truth—even if we didn't want to.

I was feeling a little fuzzy when he reappeared. He tried to convince me that the doctor had just given him additional information about what was happening on the mountain. At least fifty people were still missing, but rescue operations had been suspended until morning. I would be the next one leaving on a chopper. We just had to wait for it to get back from town.

"Are you sure that's all?" I asked as my words seemed to slur. "Shouldn't we be talking about that very large elephant in the room that we both seem so intent on dismissing?"

"Nonsense," he replied, crossing the distance between us and running his hand down the side of my cheek. "This is just another test, like so many others we've had to endure. Even the doctor can't tell us what the prognosis will be. We'll know more in a few hours. But for now, you need to let the drugs do their job so I can catch a little shuteye too. I'm not as young as I used to be, and this day has pretty much taken all my excess reserves."

"Thank you for always being there for me. I will never quit saying that I'm the luckiest girl in the world."

"I hope you still feel that way when you aren't quite so groggy."

He kissed my forehead, and I knew I would never get enough of his touch. "You won't leave if I go to sleep, will you?"

"Wouldn't dream of it," he responded. "I intend to stay right by your side until you're safe and sound in the hospital and fully on the road to recovery."

If I hadn't been so disoriented from the medication, I might have protested his seemingly comforting words. But knowing him as I did, he was already making preliminary plans to help in the rescue operations.

When I woke from my drug-induced sleep, my left leg was in a plaster cast that came up to my hip. It hung suspended from a pulley in the ceiling of a stark, white hospital room. I couldn't see my right leg. It was hidden underneath the covers. Ken sat in a chair near the window with his eyes closed. I looked tenderly at his tense, drawn face. How tired he must be! As if sensing that I was finally awake, he stirred, stretched and looked over at me.

"Glad you're finally awake," he said with a forced smile. "That was some shot Dr. Miller gave you. You didn't even stir in the helicopter when the medics brought us here."

"That must be why everything is still a little out of focus," I said, trying to lick my dry lips. My mouth felt as if it had been stuffed with dry cotton balls my tongue couldn't dislodge. "How long have I been asleep? It's not even morning yet."

"A whole day and night have come and gone since we left the resort. Are you telling me that you don't remember any of it."

"Not a moment," I replied.

"I suppose that's a blessing. It took the doctors over five hours to get your left leg back together again. The right one only had a hairline fracture. How are you feeling? Any pain?"

I knew what he was really asking, but my entire body was numb, and I could barely keep my eyes open.

"Just tell me what the doctor said, Ken. I'm too tired for guessing games, and I can't even feel my fingers right now. I only need to know if I've ever going to get out of this bed."

Instead of answering my question directly, he crossed the room to my side and brushed the hair away from my eyes. "The surgeon found no evidence of permanent paralysis. The feeling in your right leg has already come back, and I watched your left big toe twitch just an hour ago."

"You've been with me the entire time?"

"Where else would I be," he chided.

My hand instinctively reached out to touch him. Now that the worst was over, I needed to feel more connected to him in a physical way.

"Hey, not so fast," he said, stopping it in mid-air. "The doctors have you all wired up."

The burst of pain as the IV needle shot forward in my vein caused me to cry out as Ken lowered my arm to my side. "I guess I won't be going on any more skiing trips at Heaven's Glen this year."

He looked at me with a mixture of sorrow and compassion. "No one will be skiing at Heaven's Glen for a very long time. It was the worst avalanche they've ever had."

"Casualties?" I asked, even though I already knew the answer.

"Five, so far, and at least twenty people still unaccounted for. The search and rescue teams have been out all day, and they're asking for more volunteers. They won't stop until everyone is found."

"And you want to go with them, don't you?"

"I have to, Maya. I know that mountain like the back of my hand. I've skied there all my life. Don't you see how lucky we've been? We're alive! But there are others out there who may not be so lucky if we don't act quickly . . ." His voice trailed off, and I felt myself wanting to slip back into oblivion so I wouldn't have to face what was coming.

"I'm not going to beg you to stay with me, Ken," I finally said, almost wishing I could be a little more shrew-like and demanding. "But I'm scared. What if something happens to you?"

He bend down and kissed me again. "Nothing is going to happen to either of us. We beat that old mountain once, and we can do it again. Besides, I've already told the kids I'll have you home by the end of next week—cast and all. It might be a slow recovery, but you'll be ready to chase them again by the time school is out."

"Gosh," I said, allowing my head to sink back into the pillow. "I haven't even thought about how this will impact our children. Landi is a huge help around the house, but I can't ask her to take on more responsibility. And Kenny is just a little boy who still wants me to give him piggyback rides. What kind of a mother am I going to be if I can't even stand on my own for the next few months?"

"You'll be the same wonderful, caring mother you've always been. And the kids will adjust. Just think of this as another way of teaching them how to serve others. After all, kindness is supposed to begin at home."

It was a struggle not to let my eyes roll the way Landi's so often did. "But not this way, Ken. My leg is hanging from the ceiling, and there's no way this contraption will fit in our bedroom."

"So we sleep in the front room for awhile! All I care about is having my family back together again. The details will take care of themselves. By the way, dad sends his love."

"I bet this is the last time he suggests we go away for a vacation."

"He did mention something to that effect, but he's mostly glad we're okay. News reports have been flooding the airwaves for the past twenty-six hours."

"So the kids know what happened."

"Only the basics. I figured we could share details once we decided how much they needed to hear. There's no reason to give them nightmares. I think the two of us will have that covered for awhile. I know I'll never forget how close I came to losing you. It comes back in graphic detail every time I close my eyes."

"I guess I'm lucky in that regard. I could feel myself slipping away, but I didn't get to see some great shaft of light. I think your heroic measures were responsible for that."

"I was fighting for my life because without you, I wouldn't have one."

"That's precisely why I think it's foolish to even think about taking more risks. We've already tempted fate enough, and I couldn't live without you either. What else did your father say?"

"He said he'd get in touch with your parents and take care of the kids until we get home."

"What about work? He never misses a day unless he was sick."

"Don't worry about that. He's got everything covered. Maybe we're all being told it's time to slow down. I know I feel bad for spending so much time at the office lately."

"Your dad needs you during this time of transition. We all understand that. Have you eaten anything lately? I know you haven't had any sleep."

"I've taken a few catnaps, and I've eaten enough food to keep me going. My concern right now is for you and all the people who are still missing. I got a little taste of what their families are going through yesterday, and . . . "

I stopped listening because I knew what was happening in his heart. He wasn't a man who could walk away when someone was in trouble, but he needed to understand that his place was with me. I couldn't even move into another position without assistance.

He walked towards the frost-tinted window as tears tickled the end of my nose. His back was straight and his shoulders firm. He wouldn't mention returning to the resort to help in the rescue efforts unless I brought it up. But was it right of me to keep him from doing what so many other people couldn't? Buried resentment was a very ugly thing.

"I know exactly what you're thinking," I said as my heart began to crumble. "I won't be the one to stop you from going, but you need to understand that Mother Nature knows how to be angry. What if she isn't through with her outbursts yet?"

He was back by my side in an instant. "Your ability to understand what drives me is just one of the reasons I love you so completely. You won't be sorry. I promise."

"I'm already sorry, but I know you can't do anything here. Just make sure you come back to me. We've already been through enough on this vacation."

"I'll be back. There haven't been any sizable tremors the past seven hours. And while it's unlikely that anyone else will be found alive, the families of the victims need closure. If I can help give even one person that, I would feel so much better about touting the miracle we've experienced. Reporters have been roaming the halls since the first victim was brought in looking for a human interest story. I've managed to keep them away from our door, but now that you're awake it will be next to impossible."

"I don't want anyone talking about us," I responded as tears slid from the corners of my eyes. "It's nobody's business."

"That's not going to stop them. The only way to put an end their interference is to give them a bigger story to write about. I know you're scared, and you have every right to be. But I also know this isn't the end for us. We'll leave this hospital together. And when we get home, I'm going to treat you like the cherished queen of my heart that you are. I even told dad I'm taking a couple of weeks off so I can nurse you back to health personally."

"You don't have to do that," I said as my eyes continued to swim in tears. He was trying to give me hope, but we weren't out of the woods yet, and his father needed him. "I'm sure the kids and I can manage."

"That's a given. My family is the strongest one ever, but I want to take care of you for a change. Isn't that what a husband is supposed to do?"

"You were helping your father and Winston while providing for us."

"But at what cost? Landi and Kenny are growing up so fast. I want to be the kind of father they will never forget because I've spent quality time with them doing the things they love. When I think of all the nights I worked late, leaving you and the children to eat diner alone, I could just kick myself."

"You spent every weekend doing things with your family."

"Most of that was work."

"Maybe, but it was still fun," I responded, reaching for his hand a little more carefully than I had done before. The warm sensation when his fingers closed around mine made me realize just how irrational I had been in wanting him to stay with me. God wouldn't bring us together after such a tragedy just to tear us apart. "The kids and I understand, but I have to admit that having you around a little more would be wonderful. I've really missed our time together as a family, and what came after the children were in bed."

"So have I," he admitted. "That's why this trip was so important. We needed time to reevaluate our priorities. I know it's nice having all the little extras, but I'm not sure they're worth the cost. When you brought up having another baby, it made me realize how one-sided my life has become. All I do is think about work and how the company will survive with me at the helm. I'm not ready to be the big boss."

"Then tell your dad that! I get the feeling he's only talking about retirement because Winston makes it sound so desirable."

He bend down and kissed my lips. "I should be letting you rest, not talking about all my troubles."

"Never apologize for being the kind of husband you promised to be—one who included me in everything he possible could. I've certainly placed enough of my burdens on your shoulders over the years. And I could do a little simplification of my own. Someone else can chair the local charity drive and volunteer to chaperone at school for awhile. As for our children, they would find far more pleasure doing things with their father than being involved in all the dancing lessons or little league teams society claims are so important to their development."

"Some kind of second honeymoon this turned out to be," Ken laughed. "Instead of the romantic retreat I envisioned, I almost got the love of my life killed."

"But I'm not dead," I said. "I may be out of commission for awhile, but in an odd sort of way, maybe there was a practical reason behind it. We've certainly been given the opportunity to do some unintended soul-searching. I doubt I'll be taking life for granted again any time soon."

"Me either," he responded. "I just wish you weren't the one suffering because I suggested we go skiing instead of to some tropical island. I promise to make it up to you once you're standing upright on your own again."

I might have laughed, but it took too much effort. "I won't forget you said that. My passport is in the safe just waiting to be used again, but I know all the money in the world can't buy what I want most."

"And what's that," he asked.

"Just being with you and the kids. I don't care about having a bigger house, taking elaborate vacations or even putting in the swimming pool we've been talking about. I just want to spend the rest of my life taking care of you during the day and sleeping in your arms at night. That's really all I'll ever need to be happy."

"So you wouldn't mind scaling back a little if we had to?"

"I wouldn't mind living in a grass shack, as long as our family can be together and well."

"It may come to that some day," Ken replied. "We've looked at dozens of qualified applicants for partnership, but none of them have exactly what we're looking for. If we don't find at least one person soon, we may be forced to relinquish some of our clients. That's the first step towards closing the doors for good. No one wants to be affiliated with a firm who can't take care of all its clients."

"You'll find the right person, and you'll make an incredible boss when the time comes. But don't discount your dad just yet. Like I said earlier, he isn't ready to walk away."

Ken took my face in his hands and looked deep into my eyes. "I could stay here forever, but it will be light soon, and I need to make it back to the lodge before the first teams are sent out."

"I know. I just wish everyone else had been as lucky as we were."

"That's why I have to do what I can to help. I'm not going into this blind. I've been on a dozen rescue missions before and know the dangers. Believe me when I say there's nothing in life more important than being with you and our children. I won't do anything to mess that up, but this is something I have to do. Just try to get some rest while I'm gone."

"Apparently, that's all I've been doing the past day and a half, but I'll give it the old college try. You do know it's going to be an incredibly long day since I'll be spending it along."

"Don't give me that. You'll be sleeping most of the time, or at least you should be. Search and Rescue are working their teams in twelve-hour shifts. That should put me back in your room before dark. I love you, Maya Holden, every little part of you."

"And I love you," I replied as he moved towards the chair where his parka was dry and ready. He was still wearing his ski pants and boots. "What are you going to use for skis and poles?"

"I'll rent some at the lodge, and please try not to worry. I intend to give you every sponge-bath from now on."

"Stop it!" I said. "You're going to make me cry, and both my ribs and my legs are killing me."

"I'll let the nurse know before I go, and thank you for believing in me. This is something I have to do. I couldn't live with myself if I didn't."

"I get it! Just hurry back. I'm missing you already."

He gave me another kiss and was gone. I listened until I could no longer hear his footsteps in the hallway. Then I buried my face in my hands and let the tears flow.

It was approaching dusk that afternoon when Dr. Miller finally came into the room to check on me. Nurses had been interrupting my supposed rest all day—changing bags of fluid, checking monitors and writing notes on their electronic pads—but I was ready to ask questions and voice concerns. All the feeling in my legs had returned, and there was a throbbing in my head that hadn't been there before.

"How are you this evening, Mrs. Holden?" he asked, looking carefully over my chart but avoiding eye contact."

"I'm fine, but I'm getting tired of not being able to move. How long is my leg going to be suspended? I feel like all the blood in my body has rushed to my head."

He suddenly looked up and smiled. "That's the best news I've heard all day. It means you're no longer in shock, and the surgery accomplished what we hoped it would."

"I'm not doubting your skill as a surgeon. At least I'm assuming you were the one who worked on me. I'm just frustrated because I can't move anything more than my arms without sending spasms of pain everywhere."

"You can thank Dr. Maynard that you'll be able to use both of your legs once the cast comes off, but it will be a week or two before the pulley comes down. You did some serious damage, and your leg must remain motionless until the healing has begun. I'm sure my colleague will be more than willing to answer any questions when he has some free time. He's been in the operating room almost nonstop since this tragedy began."

"Has there been more news from the lodge?" I asked, my mind suddenly shifting in a different direction. My needs would be taken care of, but Ken was risking his life to help others. And while few skiers could rival his skill on the slopes, no one could stop another avalanche. "My husband went back to look for other survivors this morning."

He pushed his glasses a little further up the bridge of his nose before answering. "That was a courageous thing for him do. SAR teams have been in the field since the first rumble on that mountain, and patients with diverse kinds of injuries have been arriving almost steadily since you got here. That's why we haven't spoken sooner. I wish I had more time to spend with you now, but I only stopped by to see how you were doing. I'll try to check in with you later, but it's a little busy around here. Meanwhile, I'll have a nurse give you another sedative so you can sleep."

"I'm tired of sleeping, and I don't want another sedative. I want to be awake when my husband gets here."

"That might not happen as soon as you expect."

"Why not?" I demanded as I felt my blood-pressure rise. "Are you trying to keep something from me?"

"Not at all, Mrs. Holden. It's just that I've dealt with situations like this before. More often than not, volunteers will stay at the site for additional shifts if the help is needed. I know waiting isn't easy, but there's nothing you can do to hurry it along. Now, I'm going to get that nurse."

"I can make it with some extra strength Tylenol, Dr. Miller. But I would like to use a phone if possible. I haven't spoken to my children yet."

"A nurse can make sure a phone is available, but I'm afraid I'll have to insist on a sedative. The morphine in your IV will take care of the pain, but you still need sleep. Worrying about what is happening elsewhere won't do anyone any good."

I wanted to argue with him, but I couldn't move by myself, and nobody on staff would help me without orders from him. So I was left with no choice, other than doing what he asked.

Once a phone was close enough to use, I keyed in my father-in-law's cell phone number, but he didn't answer. The same thing happened when I called the landline at home. That set my mind off in a dozen directions because home was where I expected my family to be. Ken's father found it easier to take care of Landi and Kenny when they were around their own things and sleeping in their own beds. Perhaps he had taken them out to eat or to a movie to help pass the time. They could be a real handful when they were overly stressed, hungry or tired. But instead of allowing myself to get upset, I left them a message I hoped was filled with enough encouragement to put everyone's minds at ease. Then I took the pills the nurse brought in a small, white, paper cup and tried to settle in for a long, restless night.

I slept the troubled sleep of someone who was trying to fight the effects of medication so she could face an uncertain future. While it sounded as if my recovery would eventually be complete, there could be months of inactivity and therapy before I was ready to resume even a semblance of normal living. And that meant more stressors for every member of my family. And try as I might, I couldn't think of anything that would move the situation we were in along any faster.

My dreams were jumbled, and they were all filled with flashes of my husband—our last night together at the lodge where we explored the depths of our love, the invigorating mountain air before the avalanche and the feel of blinding cold just prior to the darkness.

I fought for the light to return, but my subconscious only took me in another direction. It was almost a relief when I woke up, but when I looked around for Ken—the only one capable of understanding my greatest desires and fears—he wasn't there. In fact, there was nothing in the room except equipment, furniture and shadows. I rang for the on-duty nurse, but she only gave me another sedative and told me he was likely spending the night at the lodge. Traffic to and from the resort had been suspended, except for emergency vehicles.

That took care of a few more hours, but by the time the cleaning lady came in on her rounds the next morning, I was ready to explode.

"Excuse me," I said much too curtly. "Has there been any news from the lodge?"

She looked at me with large, dark eyes as she moved her mop back and forth over the already clean-looking hospital floor. From her demeanor, I suspected that she hadn't been in the country for long.

"I have just arrived for the day," she said in broken English that only confirmed my suspicion. "The news will not begin until six."

"Even with a disaster like this!" I heard myself say. While an avalanche would not remain a topic on national stations for long, local media should be eating it up.

"I can turn on the television, but we are not a big city. Do you have someone on that mountain?"

"Yes, my husband," I said, wishing I could push myself upright without asking for help. "He went out with search and rescue twenty-four hours ago. I should have heard from him by now."

"It is a big mountain, and there are so few willing to help. I am sure you will hear from him soon."

"Maybe, but he could have used one of our cellphones to call," I thought as she bowed her head and continued to work. "If he didn't have his with him, mine was still in our room. Surely housekeeping would have left our belongings alone knowing what we've been through and what my . . ."

But I didn't have time to continue with that line of thought, or even wonder why my father-in-law had not returned my call, because a disturbance had erupted in the hallway outside my door.

My heart lurched to my throat as shouting voices and pounding feet broke the eerie stillness of the hospital. I tried pulling myself upright so I could get a better view since the cleaning lady had left the door partially ajar when leaving. But the suspended weight of my injured leg made that impossible, so I did the only thing I could. I tipped over the pitcher of water on the stand by my bed. Half of it went on my hospital gown and half on the floor. Then I pushed the call button connected to the nurse's station long and hard.

Water was running underneath my bed by the time the door moved inward and a pretty, young nurse appeared. "How can I help you?" she asked.

My voice was a little strained when I made my reply because I wasn't used to fabricating or telling lies. "I've had a little accident. Could I get me a dry gown and pillow?"

"Certainly," she replied, forcing a smile. "I'll see that someone is here as soon as it can be arranged. I would it myself, but all available nurses have been ordered to the emergency room."

"What happened?" I asked as the hair bristled on the back of my neck, and I felt my arms go limp.

"Something to do with rescue operations at the resort. A group of volunteers got stranded. They're bringing them in now."

"Were there casualties?" I managed to ask.

"I don't know, but it must be pretty bad to disrupt the entire hospital. Listen, I have to go. Just try to stay calm until someone can get to you."

"Volunteers stranded! Possible dead!" Those thoughts like blinding flashes of light were causing my brain to reel. I couldn't wait for help. I needed answers now. With a great deal of twisting and and indescribable amount of pain, I managed to maneuver the stand with the portable phone close to my bed. The nurse who had been helping me the night before had forgotten to put it away.

I punched in my father-in-law's number and then offered a silent prayer as I waited. It was 5:15 a.m.

A sleepy voice answered.

"Dad," I said, trying to fight back rising panic.

"What's wrong, Maya?" he asked.

"Some volunteers got stranded."

"Ken? He told me what he planned to do."

"I don't know. That's why I called. Everyone here is too busy to tell me anything."

"I'll get Fiona to watch the kids and be on my way as soon as I can. Just hang tight. We don't need to borrow any more trouble."

Not long after I hung up the phone, two orderlies entered to room with dry bedding and another hospital gown. It was humiliating being shifted from one side to another in a sheet by men who were younger than I was, but I simply closed my eyes against the embarrassing event and tried to keep my heart from racing. The tumult had moved to another section of the hospital, and I was too afraid to ask any questions for fear of what I might learn.

Once they had gone, I lay still as a hard, marble statue and watched the sun come up. Someone put a tray holding my breakfast on the stand next to my bed but didn't remove the cover. My stomach was too upset for even a sip of water. I wasn't a superstitious person by nature, and premonitions were not my thing, but something didn't feel right. Ken had never kept me waiting, and he certainly wouldn't take on a second shift without letting me know.

The time for morning rounds had come and gone—with only a nurse available to check on me—before H. Holden was holding my trembling hands. He must have driven like a mad man to make the trip in under three hours.

"Any news?" he asked as I watched tears fill his eyes. He was a man of deep emotion like his son, and family meant everything to him. He still talked about his wife as if she had just gone to the grocery store, and she had been dead for over thirty years. That's how I had known Ken would be a faithful and loving husband. He had learned what it meant to be a man from his father.

"Not a word! It's been like a ghost town in this part of the hospital since it happened."

"That's to be expected," he encouraged. "If people have been hurt, the doctors will see to their injuries before attending to anything else. And someone would have told you if Ken was among them."

"How can you be so sure?" I asked.

"Because I can't lose anyone else. Give me a few minutes to see what I can learn, and then you and I are going to have a nice, long chat. Ken told me what happened, but I need to hear it from you."

I was ready to tell my side of the miraculous story, but not before I knew my husband was safe. Misfortune had already knocked at our door, and while I didn't want anyone else to suffer as a result of the avalanche, I needed Ken by my side. There was a long and difficult recovery waiting for me.

But when my father-in-law returned to my room, I knew that life, as I had known it, was over.

"Not Ken!" I begged.

"He's not dead, Maya, but the prognosis isn't good."

I took a few deep breaths of air, and the darkness I wished would engulf me began to lift. "Just tell me what you know and don't leave anything out."

He gave me a compassionate smile. "Sometime yesterday afternoon the snow Ken and his party were climbing on shifted."

I gasped and then shoved my fist into my mouth so he would continue.

"Ken, along with everyone else in his group, fell over 100 feet into a ravine. There were internal injuries—stomach, spleen, intestines and liver. The fall tore up just about everything in the ones who survived. The doctors have him in surgery, but they won't give us any false hope. Ken may not make it off the operating table. And even if he does, he may never regain consciousness."

"Ken's a fighter. He's not going to give up."

"And neither are we, but we have to be prepared. His life is in God's hands now, and all we can do is pray."

Ken remained in a coma for six weeks and then he was gone. His heart simply quit beating. I was by his side, in my own hospital bed, until the end speaking words of love and comfort that I knew he heard at some level of consciousness. I longed to hold him in my arms and plant kisses on his pale, lifeless lips but, in my own state of recovery, I could do nothing more than hold his hand.

My parents came to take care of Landi and Kenny so Ken's father could return to work and keep the company afloat. They brought the kids to visit, but seeing me unable to move on my own, and Ken hooked up to beeping machines with tubes running in and out of his body was so traumatizing I told them not to come again.

Chapter 4

H. Holden was the one who picked up our things at the lodge and drove our car back to the city once the roads had been cleared for more than emergency vehicles. He also made arrangements for Ken's body to be taken to a local mortuary and then made a bed for me in the back of our SUV so I wouldn't have to make the three-hour trip home by ambulance.

I'd had weeks to come to terms with the inevitable, but when Ken took his last breath I felt something inside of me die. Gone was the man I had lived for and loved. Never again in this life would I see his smiling face or hear his deep, melodious voice as we made nightly accountings to each other about all that was happening in our world. My dreams were still filled with horror, and my waking hours were not much better. I tried to keep from blaming God but knew I would never understand why Ken's life had not been spared. He had everything to live for, and our desire to have another child would always be just another bittersweet memory.

Landi and Kenny were trilled to have me home again. Not that they hadn't enjoyed their time with my mother and Ken's father. They had been pampered and given massive amounts of love and distractions, but they were no closer to accepting the loss of their father than I was. My role in life was now that of a young widow with two children to raise.

The first few weeks, after my mother returned home to Utah, were filled with adjustments I didn't want to make. I cried whenever something new had to be done and could barely admit even a close friend into our home. I fought through hours of physical therapy once my cast came off and ordered what few groceries were needed online so they could be delivered to our front door. I found the inner reserves to be pleasant and positive during the hours my children were awake, but once they were in bed, I huddled beneath the covers and tried not to scream out in agonizing, emotional pain.

Financially, we had nothing to worry about. Ken had taken out a very healthy insurance policy to protect us in case it was needed, and we held 33.3 percent of the stock in *Turner, Holden and Holden*. If I was careful with our investments, and if someone reliable could be found to take over my husband's accounts, I would not have to join the workforce until our children were old enough to live on their own. But I wasn't sure my mental health could withstand prolonged exposure to the home he would never walk through again.

My father-in-law was advising me about the stock market. He and Ken had similar philosophies, and I knew H. Holden would make no decisions that could adversely affect the lives of his only grandchildren. He had set up trust funds for both Landi and Kenny so they could attend any university they desired when the time came. He was my rock, but I couldn't confide in him about everything. He had his own loss to deal with, but at least Winston Turner had decided to postpone his retirement. I tried to look on it as one of God's tender mercies. It was certainly that, but he was a practical man who didn't want to see what he had helped build fall apart.

So it wasn't financial concerns that caused me to feel so much unrest. It was the emptiness inside, and no matter how full I tried to pack each day with incidentals necessary for living, it was never enough. That longing for my perfect friend and confidant only grew more intense. A million times a day I would start to speak to Ken and then realize he wasn't there. And sometimes, late at night, when tears were soaking my pillow and all thoughts of sleep had fled, I could feel his presence in the room, and his voice would come to me, giving me the courage to face another day without him.

The first year was excruciating, and I marked off each special occasion as a sort of milestone when it came and went because there was nothing else I could do. My job was simple—keep my children from falling apart. So I planned activities that I hoped would give all of us a few moments of relief. But most of them were dismal failures, especially birthdays and Christmas. Even simple plans backfired. If we went to the park or the zoo, we pictured Ken's exuberance as he made the outing more fun. If we went to church, we pictured him sitting in the pew with us and interacting with his numerous friends. If we went to the mall, every man's blonde head became his and every sound of male laughter made us cringe.

But home was the worst. Every room held memories of the man we loved—his favorite chair, his books, his desk, his tools, his laughter and his smiles. Mealtime was almost unbearable because we were all so painfully aware that the chair at the head of the table would never be filled again—at least not in this life.

After eighteen grueling months, I decided that something had to change. It was early June and school had been out for nearly two weeks. I was determined to find something fun for my children to do over summer vacation. The tears were by no means gone, but I could see that the pain in my children's eyes was not as intense as it had once been.

It was hard to believe that time could heal such an all-consuming wound, but Landi and Kenny needed to know that their lives still held a great deal of promise. Continuing to live in a world of maybes and whys and might-have-beens was no longer productive. There were no mortal answers to the questions I continued to ask. And fate would intervene again, even if I wasn't ready for it. That day came much sooner than anticipated.

I was in my garden—my hair tied back with a rose-colored ribbon and my hands gloved—determined to dig out every weed that was trying to strangle tender seedlings as they poked their heads through the fertile, brown soil. It was a glorious day, despite the heaviness that still lingered all around me. The sun was bright and warm and the sky blue and calming. I was feeling more at peace now that I had allowed myself to accept the fact that Ken's death was not meant as a punishment for anything either of us had done.

He had been helping others, and he was not the only one who had lost his life on the mountain that day. I had contacted one of the other widows whose husband had been with Ken when the earth shook again, but our friendship had never taken off. She was suing everyone she could think of for her loss. I preferred to believe I had something powerful to learn from mine, and no amount of money or public exposure would help me sleep any better at night. God must have needed Ken, or he would still be with us.

Just as I was about to spare the life of a tiny bachelor button, Landi threw open the screen door and hollered in that youthful voice that could still send chills up and down my spine. "It's for you, mom, and it's long distance."

I rose to my feet, brushed the dirt from the knees of my Levis and straightened my aching back. I had been bent over in the garden for the better part of the morning. It was my place to forget, and I always left my cell phone indoors.

"Who is it?" I asked as I headed towards the back door of the house. The roses were starting to bloom, and I inhaled of their fragrance as I passed by them. I had a dozen colors, but the yellow bush was still my favorite. It was the first, and Ken had planted it the day I told him he was going to be a father.

"Some lady! She called on the landline so I figured it was okay to answer. No one uses that except family and people we know. I don't know why we still have one. None of my friends do," Landi said as she moved across the flagstone patio towards me. "She didn't give her name, and she sounded kind of scary so I didn't ask."

"Are you sure it wasn't Grandma Kincade? She may have been coming down with one of her summer colds, and they always make her sound a little cranky," I replied.

"It isn't grandma. She always talks to me when she calls, and this woman didn't seem to know who I was," Landi continued as I stepped into the cool, clean kitchen behind her. "We're still going to the farm this summer to see them, aren't we? You said we would discuss it after we got through with our chores today."

I smiled at my precocious daughter. She was eleven going on fifteen and wanted to be treated like an adult.

"That's the plan, and the day is still young."

Landi handed me the phone but didn't leave my side. She was like a pit-bull when she wanted something. I just hoped the person on the other end of the line wasn't some telemarketer. I hated having my morning routine disturbed by infuriating nonsense like that.

"This is Maya," I said, trying to smile at my daughter.

"Oh my darling," an unfamiliar voice literally gushed. "I hope I didn't get you from something important, but I simply had to talk to you."

"I was just weeding in the garden."

"Well, isn't that just like you," the voice continued as I searched my mind for whom it might be. "Poor dear! It's been nearly two years since I've spoken to anyone in the family. I've been on nearly every island throughout the South Pacific. It's been glorious, and since people always say that no news is good news, I simply decided not to bother with any of it. I figured I would find out everything I needed to know when I got back. But mercy me, Maya, I had no idea that wonderful Ken of yours had been killed."

The light was starting to dawn, but that didn't stop the new surge of grief or the quick bristling of hair on my arms. Landi noticed my discomfort but didn't say anything more. She simply sat down on a stool next to the kitchen counter with the smooth, granite top.

"Why, it's the most horrible thing I've ever heard. And so young! I feel just awful that I wasn't around when you needed me. But I'm back now, and I intend to do everything I can to help you get over this frightful tragedy."

Nobody in the world could become so caught up in her own affairs that she knew absolutely nothing about what was going on in her family, except for Great Aunt Lillian Farrow, Grandfather Kincade's youngest sister. She had moved to Los Angeles before graduating high school to escape what she considered a fate worse than death. Hurricane, Utah during the 1950's had nothing to offer an enterprising young woman who had no desire to get married. A real beauty, by most anyone's standards, she'd disappeared with an insurance salesman who offered her a life she had only dreamed of having.

I had thought about her occasionally because her life sounded strangely like my own. But with marriage all of the similarities ended. While my union with Ken had been ideal, her marriage to August Farrow had been short-lived and bittersweet. Eighteen months after their wedding he was convicted of embezzling company funds and sentenced to fifteen years in the state penitentiary.

She immediately sued for divorce and got it, but instead of going back home, she opted to stay in L.A. There were rumors about her life after that, but no one in the family took a trip to the coast to find out if any of them were true. She was a teenage girl, without an education, who had been hoodwinked by a shyster. But somewhere along the way, she started her own advertising firm, and by the time August got out of prison she was a well-respected business woman with an investment portfolio anyone would be proud of.

He tried to get back into her good graces by claiming he was a reformed man, but she closed every door in his face. According to her, men no longer had a place in her personal life. They were simply a means to an end—and that end was being completely independent of them.

"Listen, darling," she continued as musings stopped. "I've had the most marvelous idea. Why don't you come to Los Angeles and spend the summer with me? I need a rest from traveling, and I would dearly love the company. We could have a wonderful time— one social engagement after another. I can assure you that boredom would not be a complaint, and it would keep your mind off matters that can't be changed."

"I don't need to be entertained," I replied. "There's enough for me to do right here in Boston. Besides, I'm not sure Los Angeles is the right place for my children, and I've already planned to spend the entire summer with them."

"Doing what?" she demanded. "Acting like some mother hen and hovering too much? That seldom works out in a positive way. I don't mean to sound crass or unsympathetic, but you need time away from that house and all your sad memories so you can figure out who you are now that your world has been turned upside down. And those children need the freedom to come to terms with their own grief. That's not going to happen if they have you to tun to every time they feel a pinch of sorrow. Take it from someone who knows, you can't live in the past if you want to have a future."

Her words cut like a knife because I had thought the same thing on occasion, but she didn't know anything about me, and she certainly didn't know my children.

Who did she think she was anyway, trying to give me advice when I hadn't seen her since I was a child even younger than Kenny? Besides that, what did she know about love, commitment and family? She had thrown all of that away for wealth, power and the illusion of grandeur. She had never remarried or had any children. Other people might respect and even idolize her, but she lacked sensitivity and the ability to relate.

"You make it sound like I've locked my children away in a prison, Aunt Lil," I said. "But we're surviving, and we're even managing to have a little bit of fun."

"Now, I've offended you," she replied in most sullen tone. "I would say I'm sorry, but I'm not! I'm a realist, and I have always expressed exactly what's on my mind. It's not an endearing habit, but it is a necessary one, especially for a woman who must learn how to stand on her own. Ken may have left you with financial security, but we're not living in a world where that's a woman's only concern. I'm surprised the piranhas have kept away from you this long. But mark my word, they're going to come out in circling masses once your mourning period is over. What will you do when that happens? Most men refuse to take no for an answer, especially when an attratkicve widow is involved who has something they want."

"Ken was the love of my life. I will never be interested in anyone else."

"Now that's just foolishness," she responded. "You're a young woman in the prime of her life, and men will sit up and take notice. You can bury your head in the sand as much as you like, but denial isn't practical. Even if you want to remain single, you need to know how to fight off the gentleman callers. Some of them can be very persuasive."

"Why are you saying this to me? We haven't spoken to each other for thirty years."

"That was my mistake. I should have stayed in touch, but no one in the family has ever taken what I've said seriously. I may be the black sheep, but I will not apologize for how I've lived my life. I have done things and been places most people only dream about, and I have learned how to turn disaster into an asset. I just want to share that knowledge with you. Have you even been away from your children one night since you got out of the hospital?"

"I haven't felt it was necessary."

"What about going to see your folks?"

"We were planning to do that this summer."

"Good to hear, but it won't be enough to give you the break you really need."

"It will be enough. All I have left is my children."

"You believe that because it's what you've been told. There's an entire world out there for you to explore, and I'm not just talking about places you haven't seen yet. The journey inward can be as revealing and exciting as any place you can visit in the physical world."

"I don't mean to be unkind, Aunt Lil, but you have no idea what you're talking about. My children have been troupers the past year and a half and deserve my undivided attention. Not only did they lose their father to some freak accident that never should have happened, but I couldn't do much more than dress myself and feed them for nearly six months. They've already lost a good portion of their childhood, and I intend to make sure they don't lose any more."

"I can see that your temperament hasn't improved all that much since you were a child. When you made up your mind to do something no one could get you back down. In that sense, we are very much alike. Why else would you run off to Boston simply because it was the name of the city you drew out of a hat. It's not so unlike what I did as a young woman who didn't want to spend my life in the desert either. And whether you believe it or not, children are resilient. But they will take their clues on how quickly it's okay to heal from you."

"You make it sound like I've been holding them back."

"Never intentionally, but there is a natural tendency to hover too much when a tragedy occurs. I know you better than you think I do, even if we haven't had any contact for years. You'll devote every ounce of strength you possess to your family, and doing good works for others who may or may not appreciate it, just trying to fill the hole in your life because Ken is no longer here. That may seem like enough for awhile, but mark my words carefully. Your children's scars are already starting to heal, but yours never will as long as you stay locked away in that house trying to build a life out of memories. It isn't healthy and will come to no good."

"That's not fair," I retorted, my fragile self-control on the verge of collapse. I should have hung up on her, but I didn't quite dare. She would only call back, and part of what she was saying held a morsel of truth. "I love my children, and despite what you may think, they need me. You've never had to worry about anyone but yourself."

"I suppose I deserve that," she replied, and I could almost see the line of her jaw harden. Perhaps it had not been her desire to live life without having a family. "I married a man I thought I couldn't live without, but all he ended up giving me was a lot of debt and the desire to prove to everyone that I could survive on my own. But I've seen more families than I can count ruined because someone could not face the harsh and grim realities of life. Everyone lies, and few people get what they really want. Your children do need you, but they need you to be whole and willing to embrace life and all that it has to offer again."

Her insinuation made me bristle. I wasn't some robot that could move on command. I was an adult who had seen my own share of sorrow. And I certainly wasn't interested in having another man in my life. Not now! Not ever! As far as I was concerned, Ken and I were still married and always would be.

"I'm not interested in having a different life or meeting someone else," I told her.

"Well, you should be. The Ken your parent's described lived every day to the fullest and would never want you to be alone. He was honest, sensitive, hard-working, dependable, kind, faithful and loving. In retrospect, maybe he really was the perfect man, and you did have it all."

"I had twelve of the happiest years any woman could ever hope for. We lived every moment for each other and our children. There was nothing we didn't share."

"It sounds like perfection, but it's all in the past," she responded, and I knew her moment of empathetic understanding had ended. The old straight-shooting Lillian Farrow was back and feistier than ever. "But what about your future? You simply cannot lock yourself away for the rest of your life and hope your children won't be affected. Do you want them to feel like they owe their lives to you simply because of what you've lost?"

"Of course not, but it's going to be a long time before they're ready to be out in the world on their own."

"I'm not proposing you throw them to the wolves. I'm merely suggesting that they need the next few years to learn how to trust again. Your mother told me how they feel like they've been betrayed because the father, who said he would always be there to love and protect them, was gone. What if something happened to you? They might not be able to survive another loss like that."

"They'd manage," I replied. "They have a wonderful support system."

"Filled with old people and casual acquaintances who have their own lives to live. You do have my sympathy. I know what it's like to suffer tremendous setbacks and loss, but it's time for you to be practical. No one can live in a self-imposed vacuum forever."

"I'm under no delusions, Aunt Lil. I know I'm being overprotective, but I don't think taking my children to Los Angeles where they will be exposed to a totally foreign way of living is the right way to proceed."

"Your response comes as no surprise. Despite living in a big city, away from family for most of your adult life, you still have those hometown values your parents were determined to instill. They never let you stay with me because they felt I would be a bad influence on an impressionable, young mind. I will admit that I haven't been to church since I was a kid, and I do like to attend parties where the best champagne is served. But I am not an alcoholic, a drug addict, or a sexual deviant, and I no longer smoke cigarettes or bet on anything bigger than a simple game of chess. I can honestly say that I am an upright member of the community, and I can help you adjust to a life you didn't choose."

My head was spinning, but nothing she'd said would force me into changing my mind. California was no place for anyone in my family. We would learn to adjust in much less troublesome environment.

"I appreciate your thoughtfulness, Aunt Lil, but the timing isn't right. Maybe in a few years when the children are older."

"Time isn't going to shield them from life. You already know that, Maya. And if you really don't want to bring your children here, leave them with your folks for a few weeks and come out by yourself. You could go home any time you wanted, or you could fly the children out to join us. My desire is not to corrupt anyone. I simply want to help you through this."

"You make it sound so easy, but I have other responsibilities besides the children. And I haven't even talked to my folks about an extended visit. They usually have plans of their own for at least part of the summer."

"I've already discussed my idea with both of them."

"And they agreed to it?"

"Let's just say that they want what will be best for all of you. I know leaving the security of the life you've been living won't be easy, but you've taken a calculated risk before. All I'm asking is that you give me the chance to prove that I can still be a useful member of this family. I won't force you to do anything against your will. I just want to spend some time with you. So pack your bags. I'll have plane tickets on the way to your address this afternoon."

"I haven't said we were coming," I replied as a feeling I couldn't quite put into words seemed to wash over me.

"But you will come—once you've decided that I'm right."

I put the receiver back on the wall, unable to digest all that had transpired during the past few minutes. My great Aunt Lillian was a force to be reckoned with, but I wasn't sure I had the energy, or the desire, to do as she'd asked.

"Who was that?" Landi demanded as she planted her chin on the palms of her hands and looked up at me. She had been perched on a stool during the entire conversation. "I couldn't tell if you even liked her."

"That was your great, great Aunt Lillian Farrow," I responded, smiling at my nearly teenage daughter. "And it's not that I don't like her. I don't even know her. She hasn't been part of my life since I was younger than you are. But it does appear that she and I have been cut from the same bolt of stubborn Kincade cloth."

Her nose wrinkled like it always did when she was perplexed.

"Never mind," I said, giving her a hug. "Suffice it to say that she's a long lost relative that has resurfaced at a most inconvenient time."

"But I don't understand," Landi lamented. "You said something about California. I've been dreaming about going there."

"Dream or not, that's a trip we won't be taking this year, but I have been making other plans."

"They won't be as good as going to a real beach and maybe even Disneyland and Sea World. Most all of my friends have already been there. They've even been on cruises. We haven't been anywhere fun since you got out of the hospital."

Her assessment of the situation made me cringe. I wasn't trying to be difficult, but I couldn't deny that I was scared. I wanted my children close by me so I could keep them safe. But the determined look on Landi's face let me know that she wasn't about to back down, and I was in no mood for another disagreeable conversation. If I could just get her to understand . . .

"Come sit by me," I said. "I think there are a few things we need to discuss."

"You're just going to tell me we can't go."

"Maybe, but don't you want to know why?"

With a total lack of enthusiasm, she followed me across the room to the overstuffed sofa we always sat on as a family to talk or watch movies. Her arms were folded defiantly in front of her chest. This wasn't going to be an easy sell.

"My great aunt has never been interested in anyone, other than herself, until now. She didn't come to my wedding or even acknowledge you or Kenny's births. I'm not saying she isn't a good woman, but I know nothing about her, and I'm not sure what motivated her sudden interest in us. I wouldn't feel comfortable in her home since I've never been there, and I certainly don't want my children in an unfamiliar environment."

"But it could be so much fun!"

"That may be true, but wouldn't you rather spend time with your grandparents? You always have fun on the farm, and your cousins are excited to see you."

"I suppose," she reluctantly admitted. "Could we stay for more than a few days? Grandpa said he'd take us to the Grand Canyon and let us look for Indian relics in the foothills. I want to have something fun to share when I go back to school. All I did last summer was cry."

I felt her pain almost as deeply as my own. We had talked about Ken's death on numerous occasions, but I had always tried to soften the blow. Maybe she was ready for something more than platitudes about her father being in a better place and needing us to be strong. Even the concept of him missing us as much as we missed him no longer brought the comfort it once had.

"Have I been making things harder for you, Landi?" I asked, drawing her into my arms.

"Maybe a little," she replied. "I know you and daddy were planning to take us to Disneyland when Kenny was old enough to have fun. But he's gone now, and he's not coming back. I don't want to spend the rest of my life sitting home and feeling bad because I'm not like my friends any more."

"Is that how you really feel?"

"All the time, and I'm tired of doing chores and pretending. I just want to be happy again."

"But you understand that California might not be the place for any of us right now."

"I really don't care where we go. I only know I don't want to sit around here all summer like we did last year. Kenny feels the same way I do."

"You've talked to him about it?"

"Not in so many words, but he cries even more than I do. He likes doing things with Grandpa H., but it isn't the same as being with daddy."

I looked into my daughter's bright, green eyes and suddenly recognized just how wise she had become in under twelve years. I had been trying to give my children what I thought was a normal childhood in a very atypical time. But they were growing beyond their grief and needed more than I was capable of giving them on my own. Landi could even talk about her father without crying.

"I promise we will do something fun together this summer. I just have to make the arrangements first. Now why don't you gather up my garden tools and put them in the shed while I fix lunch. After that, I'll take you and Kenny to the pool on Vista Drive. I have some serious thinking to do."

Landi put her arms around my neck before rising to her feet. "I'm sorry I made you sad, mom. I know how much you miss daddy, but it's going to be all right. Remember, we still have each other— the only three pieces of the puzzle we'll ever need."

It had been over a year since I'd made that comment about the puzzle, and I was surprised that she even remembered it.

"How did you get to be so smart?" I asked.

"I guess it's because I'll be in junior high next year."

My heavy sigh was felt clear down to the tips of my toes "It's hard to believe my little girl is almost a teenager. That means I must be getting old."

"You're not old, mom," she said as her brow knit into two short lines. "You're the prettiest mother I know."

"Flatterer," I responded.

"I mean it, mom! You are pretty. I just worry that some man is going to notice and want to take daddy's place."

"That's not going to happen, Landi," I said with a fervent shake of my head. "When your father and I were married we promised to love each other until the end of time. No one is ever going to take his place."

"But you miss him so much."

"I'll never stop missing him. But when my heart chose his, I knew there would never be anyone else for me. I know waiting for our family to be complete again isn't going to be easy, but what your father and I have transcends most everything else in my life. We will have eternity together, and I don't want anything messing that up."

"You really think we'll get to be together for always?"

"With all my heart, Landi. This life is just a test to see what we're made of, and I can assure you that we come from devoted pioneer stock who would not give in or give up."

"I know," she said. "Our ancestors built homes out of sticks and clay blocks in a red desert where only rattlesnakes, Black Widow spiders and scorpions could thrive. Grandma's told me that story at least a hundred times."

"You believe her, don't you?"

"I guess, but sometimes I get scared. So many of the kids at school have new mothers or fathers, and they hate it. I want things to stay the way they are right now—just you, me and Kenny."

I kissed her shinning hair, knowing that she had just given me a glimpse into what was really bothering her. "I promise that the three of us will be together until we're reunited with your father."

"Good!" she responded. "That's the only way I want it. Now, we can start talking about our summer vacation. I want to go to Utah. It's where I have the most fun, and grandma and grandpa have the coolest stuff."

"Did somebody say we're going to the farm?"

The back door slammed shut with a jarring bang, and my precious son came racing into the kitchen, a smile on his face and the rest of his body caked in mud. I had left the sprinkler running on the far end of the garden, and his footprints were clearly visible on my once-clean hardwood floor.

"Not again, Kenny," I said, unable to keep from smiling at both my beautiful children. They were amazingly resilient, and thank goodness they were made that way. Otherwise, they might not survive in a world plagued with so much turmoil, violence, unrest, setbacks and heartaches. "You haven't been digging in the garden again."

"But mom," he retorted, wrinkling his nose the way Ken had always done. "Dad said boys were meant to get dirty."

I took both of my children into my arms, although I couldn't see them through the tears. There was so much I had yet to learn about raising a family. And it really didn't matter that I had already planted most of our garden twice. I just wanted my children to feel loved and safe.

"You two are pretty terrific," I said, as the tears trickled off the end of my nose. Ken might not be with us any longer, but he had left me with two incredible gifts.

"So are we going?" Kenny asked, struggling to free himself from my embrace. He was all male and getting to an age where tender moments were best left for bedtime. "Grandpa said I could drive the tractor next time we came."

"That's something we'll have to discuss when we get there, but I haven't made up my mind about anything yet. A trip of more than a few days takes a lot of planning on both ends."

He gave me his most irresistible look. "But we can still go, can't we?"

"We'll talk about that after you take a bath. Lunch will be on the table in thirty minutes, so make it fast."

I called my parents after evening prayers were said. But instead of the usual salutations and questions about how each of us was doing, my mother surprised me by saying that she and my father had been waiting to hear from me.

"Is something wrong?" I asked to speed up the conversation so we could get to the place where we needed to be.

"Nothing serious! Dad and I are both doing well. We had the whole family over for dinner tonight. Jason got a summer job with a construction firm in St. George. It's hard to believe I have a grandson old enough to work a full-time job. I wish you and the children could have been here. It would be wonderful having the whole family together for special occasions."

She wasn't intentionally trying to make me feel guilty, but I hadn't been home since the summer before Ken's accident. The thought of making that journey without him was intolerable. Our last visit to Utah with the children had been superb. We'd gone to

Lake Powell and rented a houseboat for a week. There would never be another real family vacation for me—just feeble attempts at trying to feel somewhat normal again.

"Are the kids excited to be out of school?" mom asked when I didn't respond.

"They are," I said, biting down on my bottom lip to keep the tears of loneliness and frustration at bay. "But I'm afraid Landi is already bored. I don't remember feeling that way about summer vacation when I was her age. Bill and I would hurry through our chores as fast as possible so we could explore the canyons around the house. I know you hated our adventurous spirits, but dad taught us what to look for so we'd be safe."

"What else was he supposed to do?" she countered. "You and your brother were drawn to those hills from the time you could unlatch the back door. I count my blessings ever day that you both made it to adulthood. But life isn't as simple as it once was, and most kids today are growing up in the city where they have too much free time and not nearly enough productive things to do."

"I try to keep Landi and Kenny busy."

"You're a great mom, Maya, but maybe they need a change of scenery."

"Like the cactuses and red-baked soil of southern Utah?"

"That thought has crossed my mind several times recently. It tends to have a healing effect on most everyone."

"Not when it comes to something like what I've been going through, mom. Besides, my garden will go to weeds if I'm not there to take care of it every couple of weeks."

"Are you sure that's not just an excuse? Your reluctance to strike out on your own is understandable. You feel safe where you are because it's familiar, and you can control much of what goes on. It won't be that way if you get on a plane. You'll have to learn how to trust people again."

"I trust people," I said.

"Then book flights for you and the kids. It isn't that hard to do. I know the world can seem like a frightening place, and people aren't always who they claim to be. But your children need to know that you're not afraid, or they'll grow up to be that way too."

"Do I really give off that kind of vibe?" I asked.

"Not intentionally! I know you derive comfort being in the home Ken built for you and the children. I would feel the same way if something happened to your father, but you need to include the rest of your family in your life. We can't replace what you've lost, but we can give you love and support, and we'd like to do some of that in person."

"I guess we could come for a few days."

"If that's all you feel you can give us right now, then we'll take it. I'll get your old room ready for you and Landi and fix up Bill's room for Kenny. By the way, did you get a rather strange phone call this afternoon?"

"From Aunt Lil?" I asked. "It was quite a surprise since she hasn't wanted to be included as a member of this family since I was a child. She certainly knows how to stir things up."

"That's exactly the reaction I had when she called here to get your phone number earlier today. Your father's aunt is like some mini-tornado no one sees coming, but the effects can certainly be felt once she's made contact. I hope she didn't upset you too much."

"Let's just say that she gave me some unsolicited advice and an offer that makes a certain amount of sense."

"Please don't let Lillian Farrow draw you into one of her schemes, Maya. She talks big and has plenty of money to indulge any fantasy, but she won't stick around when times get tough. Whatever she wants is simply a whim that will be forgotten if you don't give in to it. She's not a woman who should be trusted when it comes to anything personal."

"Is that why you wouldn't let me stay with her when I was growing up? I overheard phone calls and even saw a letter she wrote once."

"Your father and I didn't want you exposed to the kind of life she was living. She was ruthless when it came to business dealings, and her private life was a mess. Once she and August were divorced, and she found out she could be successful in her own right, she began using people to get what she wanted. Some of the stories we heard were truly frightening."

"She lived in a different time and age. Women had to be tough to survive."

"But she didn't have to turn her back on everyone who loved her? I can't tell you the number of times your grandfather tried to convince her to come home, even for a short visit, but she was always too busy to be bothered with family."

"Maybe she's changed. She wants me to bring the kids and visit her this summer. She said she was getting plane tickets for us today."

My mother's intake of breath was audible, even over the phone. "She mentioned the same thing to me, but I hope you're not seriously considering it. Los Angeles is no place for impressionable children who have lived what the world considers rather sheltered lives."

"I'm not naive about everything, mom," I protested. "In her own way, I really think she wants to help."

"Lillian Farrow thinks a new dress and a party can cure anything, along with the best wine and champagne money can buy. I'm not saying that she was ever involved in anything illegal, but she's done her share of skirting the parameters of the law over the years. According to your grandfather, Lillian wanted to do everything, see everything, and be both rich and famous. She has everything the world can offer—millions of dollars in the bank, a fabulous home with servants at her beckoned call, and a chauffeur-driven limousine, but she's missed out on the most important part of living—building something that will go on forever. She never had a family, and she's outlived most of her friends. In many ways, I feel sorry for her."

"When you put it that way, she's more to be pitied than anything else," I said. "I already told the kids there was no way we were going to L.A."

"So coming here is simply a compromise to keep them from being upset? I thought they enjoyed spending time with us."

"They do, and so do I. But you have to understand that my entire life changed when Ken died. I always thought we would spend the rest of our lives together, and all we got was twelve years.

Moving forward with anything makes me feel like I'm being unfaithful to him."

"That's not how he sees it, I'm sure. He made preparations for your future because he wanted you to go on living, regardless of what happened to him. You are a very special young woman, and I'm not just saying that because you're my daughter. You have the strength, courage and determination to do anything you set your mind to. Just don't get swept away by an offer that amounts to nothing more than a temporary fix."

I thought about what my mother had said a lot over the next few hours, but I was not some simple-minded teenager who had never been away from home. While my risks would never rival those of Lillian Farrow, I couldn't dismiss the idea that we had several inherited characteristics in common. And when a voucher for first-class plane tickets arrived by express mail the next day, I made up my mind that the time for being afraid was over. I might not like what life had thrown my way, but I couldn't bow down to debilitating grief any longer. Ready or not, I had to take the next step into the unknown. That was the only way I would learn why God thought I was strong enough to make it on my own.

So I decided on the dates—little more than a week away—that might be best for us to travel and called the airline to make the necessary arrangements. It was the hardest thing I had ever done, but once the initial terror subsided, I found a young man in the neighborhood to take care of the yard and garden. Then I helped Landi and Kenny pick out what they were going to take before packing my own bag.

I had no idea what I would say to my father-in-law. He always took care of anything left undone when we took a family vacation, checked on the house and even drove us to the airport when necessary. But this trip seemed different somehow, and not only because it was my first solo adventure. I was moving away from my past in hopes of salvaging a better future for my children.

He surprised me by saying he thought the trip would be beneficial, but I knew he felt otherwise when he knocked on the front door the morning of our departure, dressed for another day at the office. He was as apposed to change as I was, and we were all the family he had left.

To keep from giving in to my own emotional fragility, I took one last walk through my home memorizing details as if I would never see them again. It had always been our family's haven—the place we returned to each night to refuel our souls with the security and peace needed to face another day in a very fallen world.

We had good neighbors and wonderful friends who were always ready to help when needed, and I knew my way around most of the city. The outside world represented a very real treat to my fragile independence. I had never traveled alone since driving across the country to Boston nearly fifteen years earlier, and when I added to my inexperience as a traveler two active children, I felt totally overwhelmed.

"I wish you were coming with us, dad," I said after placing the last of our suitcases on the floor in the entry hall. Landi and Kenny were saying goodbye to their best friends.

"So do I," he responded. "I'll never forget the time I went to the farm with you and Ken before the wedding so I could meet your family—more than a hundred of them if I remembered the details of that barbecue correctly. Your father had me so busy hunting and fishing I didn't have time to get homesick for work. That was the first time I'd been anywhere since my wife died. It was just easier to focus on my career than deal with my loss."

"You could come with us now. There's plenty of room at the house, and my folks would love it. It wouldn't be that hard to get another plane ticket."

He placed his arm fondly around my shoulders. "Maybe not, but it would have to be a different flight on a different day, and that's a lot of driving back and forth on both ends. Hurricane isn't exactly a thriving metropolis. I used to think that I would never get old and tired, but I have. Sometimes I wonder if losing Ken wasn't harder on me than it was on you and the kids. I know that's an unfair assumption, but he was all I had left when his mother was gone. Millicent and I wanted lots of children, but try as we might, God only sent us one. If it wasn't for you and my grandchildren, I might already have given up."

"Not you," I responded with a sad smile. "You're the strongest man I've ever known, and you've been an absolute rock for me and the children. If anything, we've relied on you too heavily the past few months—coming to you with every little problem that surfaced. That wasn't fair."

"Nothing about the past few months has been fair, Maya, but God doesn't ask for our permission before giving us some unexpected trial. He knows there's something useful for us to learn if we look hard enough."

"So you haven't lost your faith."

"Hardly! But I'm still human, and I would bring back everyone I've loved and lost if I could. If that makes me less of a man in your eyes, then I'll just have to get used to it."

I kissed his cheek. The wrinkles had become far more pronounced since Ken's death. "I couldn't love you more, dad. I've had plenty of soul-searching hours myself, but I've come to the conclusion that there is a reason some of us are still here and why we are a family."

"But I'm nearly seventy, Maya. That's old in the eyes of the world. Don't I have a right to feel tired?"

"Of course you do, but you can't give up. The children and I need you too much."

"Maybe that's why I feel so blue. Ever since you told me about your plan to go home, I haven't been able to shake the feeling that you'll never be back here to stay."

"Nothing could be further from the truth," I replied as a sick foreboding seemed to wash over me too. "This is our home. It's where we will always want to be."

"I know that's how you feel now, but you're young and beautiful. Somewhere out there is a man who is going to fall in love with you "

"No, dad," I said, placing my hands firmly on his lower arms. "I don't want some man falling in love with me. Ken is the one who has my heart. That's never going to change."

"You say that now because you're still grieving, but in time, life will take on new meaning and another love will come along. It might not be the same as what you had with my son, but it can still be very powerful and consuming. Your children need a man's influence too."

"Landi already told me that she never wants another father, and I'm sure Kenny feels the same way. Besides, they have you."

"That's true, but I'm not young enough to be a father-figure, and I would never aspire for that role anyway. I like being a grandfather too much. Now, let's get off this subject before you decide to cancel your tip and stay here to baby sit me."

"I would do it in a heartbeat. All you have to do is ask."

"While that's a comforting thought, you and the children need this vacation. I've got more than enough to keep me busy while you're gone, and that brings me to the reason I came a few minutes early. Winston and I have been discussing the future of the company. We're both well-past retirement age, and with Ken gone, trying to sell the company seems more logical than simply closing the doors. We've been looking around, and there are a few interested parties. The name *Turner, Holden and Holden* still carries some weight in this city. We need to capitalize on that while there's still time."

"Oh, dad!" I exclaimed, having to steady myself on the back of the sofa to keep from collapsing. "Isn't there some way we can keep it going? The business was as much a dream of Ken's as it was yours. I know he wanted Kenny to join him when he was old enough, provided that's what he wanted to do."

"His intentions in that regard were clear. That's why I'm discussing this with you now. Winston has decided to call it quits at the end of the year, and I don't have the heart to run it with junior partners, regardless of how invested or talented they are. It isn't a family-run business just because it says so on the door."

"Would it help if I came back?" I volunteered. "You could teach me what I needed to know, and I could go back to school so I would have the right credentials. I need something challenging to fill up part of the hours during the day anyway."

"You'd be a quick learner and a loyal colleague, Maya, but you're a mother and need to be home with your children."

"Most of the women in the world work today, especially after losing a spouse. Ken had our finances worked out so I could be a full-time wife and mother, but half of that role is already gone."

"Do you really think you could handle it? Your children need to be your first priority. If we sold out, you would get a sizable amount of money."

"I already have what I need, and there's only so much cooking and cleaning with three people in the house. Besides, both of the kids are in school during the day, and getting a degree online is a popular alternative for furthering one's education. I know it wouldn't be easy, but it is doable."

"Only if financial advising is what you really want to do with your life. There are hundreds of other careers you could choose from if you feel the need to take on added responsibilities. I don't want you to to feel pressured into doing something just because I need to make a decision."

"This isn't the first time I've considered taking a more active role. Ken and I often talked about me coming back to the firm when the kids were older. If I had a degree, I could do more than just sit at the front desk and run errands."

"Your job was always more important than that. But if I knew you'd be there, I might be convinced to stay on for a few more years. I always figured retirement was a time for enjoying life, but it's hard to do that alone."

"I know what you mean, dad," I responded as tears filled the corners of my eyes. Losing Ken had been a devastating blow for both of us.

But instead of acknowledging his own pain, he squeezed my hands affectionately. "I shouldn't have brought this up today. You need to enjoy this vacation. We can talk when you get back."

"We will talk more then, but I'm glad you brought it up now. I need to feel connected to something more than this house and my children. But it will take a couple of years until I'm ready for an office of my own. If Winston leaves, how will you manage until then?"

"I've been thinking about that. We've already brought in Todd Foster. He's a competent associate, but he's certainly not ready to be made a partner. We need someone with more experience who could lead out until you're ready to sit at the helm."

"Not so fast, dad! I haven't even started school yet."

"We have to think long-term if this is going to work. No transition will be entirely smooth, but we have to plan for the unexpected. Ken's death taught me that. I always believed he would be there to run the family business long after I was gone. Knowing that you're willing to stand beside me, despite all we've lost, gives me hope. If we work together, we can keep this company alive for Landi and Kenny. I'm not ready to think beyond that yet."

"But how would we do it? Just having a degree doesn't mean I'll be successful. It takes years to build a portfolio of clients and earn their trust."

"You could start by coming into work for a few hours a week when you get back. I could introduce you to some of our clients, have you sit in on a few meetings and let them know what your plans are. By the time you've finished school, you'd already have a firm foothold."

"What about Todd? Won't he feel like you're showing preferential treatment to a family member if I advance more rapidly than he does?"

"I'm not saying there won't be a few bumps along the way, but he already knows you own a third interest in the company. What's to stop you from taking on more responsibility? It's certainly within your rights, and quite frankly, to be expected. Do you remember Jeff Talbot?"

"Ken's cousin?" I asked. "I thought he owned a competing firm."

"He does, but it's hard for small, recently-formed and independent businesses to make it when there are so many large companies with deep pockets, plenty of exposure and no aversion to pushing ethical boundaries when the payoff if big enough. Winston has already approached him about a merger, and he's willing to talk."

"It sounds like change is in the air, regardless of what I decide to do."

"Time remains still for no man, but I like the sounds of what we've discussed. Why not take some time while you're away and really give it some thought. You don't have to make a decision today."

"I'll do that, but you have to promise me something in return."

"And what's that?' he asked.

"That you'll cheer up. Life doesn't have to be over for either of us, and I know for a fact that there are dozens of women out there who would love to spend time with a man as handsome and thoughtful as you. What about Mrs. James? She's been a widow for nearly five years."

"Now you're being patronizing. Rachel James is a young, vibrant woman."

"She's sixty-one and a great-grandmother who has lived down the block from you for years. I know she's interested because of all the treats she brings, other than the ones for traditional holidays. Why don't you invite her out to dinner while I'm in Utah. It might do both of you a lot of good."

"So you think this old goat needs to be seen with a beautiful woman, do you?"

"It couldn't hurt! And it would make me feel less guilty about leaving if I knew you wouldn't be spending all of your time alone."

He assured me that he would think about it, and we left for the airport a few minutes later.

My intention had been to fly directly into Salt Lake City so there would be no layovers or hurried treks through unfamiliar terminals to catch a connecting flight. But I had waited until too late in the season. Most of the flights were full and finding three seats together was a real challenge. That meant flying into Dallas and waiting inside the terminal for nearly four hours. Landi and Kenny wanted to go exploring, but I felt it would be too easy to get lost in the tumult of a busy, international airport where each airline had its own base of operations.

Had Ken been with us, this minor inconvenience would have been a glorious adventure, but here we sat in a small concourse restaurant drawing pictures on our napkins and counting the number of airplanes that landed and took off on the tarmac outside the window.

I hated being a single parent. Decisions, like the one that had surfaced that morning, swamped me almost daily. And I still spent the majority of my nights sobbing into my pillow and asking God why this burden had not been given to someone else. Most of the time, I felt incapable of giving my children the proper attention and discipline without being overprotective or too indulgent. I needed Ken! I needed the strength and encouragement he had always given me. Without him, I was walking through a long, dark tunnel that seemed to have no end.

"Is that our plane?" Landi asked, shaking my arm and pulling me back into the present moment where I could no longer pretend that my entire world wasn't changing.

"I don't know," I said. "I wasn't listening."

She gave me an exasperated look. I wasn't helping anyone with my negativity and unfounded fears. "Is 215 our flight? They've announced it three times."

"Then I guess we'd better be going," I replied, reaching for my carryon item and then telling my children to do the same with theirs.

Landi was so pretty—tall for her age and imposing like her father. She would grow into a beautiful, kind and sensitive woman with the right attention and care, and boys would soon be knocking down our door for a chance to spend time with her. But like most everything else, I couldn't think about the challenges of raising a teenager alone. I wasn't even sure I would survive this vacation. People would try to be kind, but there was no way they could ever understand the extent of my loss or my grief.

My parents met us at the airport. It was good to see them again, but it brought back memories of the last time we had been together. I tried to fake excitement so my children would feel like they could express their own emotions at being with family again. It helped with a difficult reunion. But I knew the bandaid that was holding my fragile world together would be forcefully ripped off once we were on familiar soil, and my parents knew I wouldn't be able to bolt without someone's help.

Still, despite trepidation and a certain amount of fear, home was home. I allowed myself to be pampered for several days before I saw how futile it was to think I could escape reality by pretending it wasn't there. I had talked to Ken's father only once. That was to tell him we had arrived safely and wished he could be with us.

Mother and I were walking along the edge of the big feeder canal one afternoon when suddenly I stopped, bent down and plucked a blade of snake grass from its hiding place near an open marsh.

"Do you remember the first time I brought Ken home, mom?" I asked.

"Of course," she replied, pausing beside me and looking up into the blue, cloudless sky. "He had never been to the country before and couldn't believe how backward Utah farmers were. We didn't even have a computer in our home to keep track of farming expenses. You sent us one that Christmas, and it took dad nearly six months to garner the courage to take it out of the box."

"That was a happy time, wasn't it? Despite a rather dubious beginning, it only took that one visit for Ken to fall in love with the land. He told me on several occasions that someday we would retire and build a little cottage right over on that knoll." I nodded in the direction of the small rise in the land where willow trees rustled slightly in the breeze and a few wild flowers nodded their tiny heads in the sparse, dry grass. "All we had to do was to convince dad to sell us that piece of ground. It seemed like such a simple, realistic dream."

"All of your dreams don't have to end, Maya. You and the children could still move home. Dad would help you build that house."

Tears dimmed my vision and then rolled slowly down my cheeks. "I know he would, and sometimes I'm tempted to do it, but I can't leave Harold alone. We're all the family he has left."

She smiled reassuringly, and then took my hand as we walked along the narrow cow trail underneath the spreading branches of juniper and poplar trees. Neither of us said anything until we were standing in the middle of a floating bridge that spanned the big feeder canal at its widest point. I began popping the snake grass at its joints and tossing the pieces into the water that rushed along below us.

"Why couldn't life have been different, mom?" I asked as familiar pangs of pain and loneliness washed over me for the zillionth time. "All we ever wanted was to be together as a family. I can understand something tragic happening if we'd asked for the world, but we didn't. All we wanted was our own little corner of it."

Mom looked compassionately in my direction, and I knew she would willingly take away my pain if she could. "I don't have the answers you're looking for, Maya. All I know is that God must have needed Ken for some special purpose, like teaching countless others who both lived and died without knowing they had a Savior who was willing to make the ultimate sacrifice for their sins. He was an amazing man with many gifts and talents, but I know that doesn't seem like a very good reason when you need him so much."

"Thank you for not saying that we won't be given more than we can handle. That phrase has lost all meaning for me."

"Don't allow bitterness to consume you, Maya. I know you loved Ken with all your heart."

"He was the very center of my universe. How am I supposed to go on when there's nothing left to build on?"

"Nothing!" she exclaimed as her countenance changed from understanding to disbelief. "How dare you stand there and say you have nothing? You had twelve of the happiest years any woman could ask for, and you have two of the most precious children in the world. You have a beautiful home, good health, plenty of food and clothing and people all around who care. You and Ken will to be together again, but you have to live worthy of having that blessing. I would say you have a lot more than most of the people in the world, even if you have lost something important."

There it was. The rebuke I had been waiting for and deserved.

"I'm sorry, mom," I said, resting my elbows on the wooden rail and staring into the swirling, blue water. "I don't mean to question God's will all the time, but I'm scared. The kids are growing up so fast, and I feel totally incapable of filling all their needs. There are still days when I don't want to get out of bed."

"And yet you do it because that's the person you are inside. Disappointment and heartache are the downside to living a rich and full life, but you can't let those feelings consume all your energy. You have to figure out who you are as a person now that so much in your life has changed. And I'm not talking about Maya the daughter, the mother, the sister, the aunt, or even the widow, but Maya the woman."

"I'm the same person I've always been. I just have different problems than most women my age."

"You've been trying to keep things going as if nothing has changed. That isn't healthy, and I'm afraid you're heading towards an emotional breakdown that will not have a pleasant ending. Bringing this up is a last resort, but I think you need to get away by yourself to figure things out."

"I can't leave my children alone," I protested. "I'm all they have left."

"No, you're not, Maya! Your children have plenty of people who will love and support them, regardless of what the future brings."

I opened mouth to argue with her, but she silenced me with one of her mother-knows-best looks.

"I'm not saying that your children don't need you, but they need you as more than an empty shell."

"That's a little harsh, don't you think?"

"Maybe, but they've got to see you smile and laugh again."

"I do that all the time," I replied. But inside I knew I hadn't been spontaneously happy since Ken's death, and it was affecting both Landi and Kenny. They had become more like little adults than children. "What do you suggest?"

"Go see Aunt Lil."

I looked at her with nothing short of amazement. She couldn't possibly be serious? Aunt Lil was the most self-indulgent person I had ever heard of, and she'd never had room in her life for members of the family—until now.

"Heaven help me, but for once I agree with her," my mother continued. " You have to get away from your everyday problems for a while, or you'll never be able to guide your children when they have serious difficulties of their own. Of all the people I know, she's the perfect person to help you do it."

"I thought coming here would be enough."

"Apparently, it isn't. Maybe you need a complete break from your past so you can start building a slightly different future."

"Isn't that being disloyal? I don't want to stop thinking about Ken. I'm afraid if I do all the memories will fade and then I really won't have anything left."

"You and Ken will have eternity together, but part of that eternity is living through today and tomorrow and making the best of each opportunity for growth as it comes your way. Ken is growing and changing where he's at, and he would expect no less from you. That means experiencing new friendships, new places and new ideas. No one expects you to forget what you had, but that part of your life is over, and you have to adjust."

I allowed more tears to fall before commenting. I didn't like new beginnings, unless they ended up the way they had with Ken. But my mother was right about one thing. I couldn't continue the way I was. That breakdown she mentioned was coming. I could feel it with every part of my soul. "You really think that's the right move, mom?"

"I do, and I'm not the only one. Landi told me how sad you've been and how nothing she and Kenny do seems to cheer you up. Your children are worried. They don't want to lose anyone else."

"That's not going to happen!"

"You can't guarantee that. No one can. All anyone can do is take precautionary measures and hope for the best."

"So my acting has been less than stellar. I thought I had been hiding my feelings quite well."

"Children see more than we think they do, and they seldom know how to express what they're feeling. That makes them vulnerable to so many things."

"But why couldn't she just talk to me? We've always been able to share things."

"She's growing up and learning how to reach out to others for support. That's not a bad thing."

"Then why does it seem like it is?"

"Because you're not seeing some parts of life as clearly as you might. That's another reason I think you should go. Kenny has already talked your father into letting him raise one of our wiener pigs for the county fair, and Landi and I have a few plans of our own."

"It sounds as if you have everything worked out for the rest of the summer with no room left over for me."

She put her arm reassuringly around my shoulders. "There's always room for you, sweetie. And despite how you may feel right now, your children will always need you. But they can survive for a few days, or even a few weeks, on their own. Take the word of someone who has lived well over half a century and who loves you dearly. You won't regret going, if for no other reason than just having some time to gain a little more perspective."

I wanted to believe her, but I had my doubts. Aunt Lil didn't seem like a person who would have a calming influence on anyone, and I doubted she would allow me to just lie on the beach and think. She would want to make sure every moment counted.

Chapter 5

Lillian Farrow was an eccentric from the tip of her platinum blonde hair to her 1956 Rolls Royce and chauffeur. And that was just for starters. She lived in what I considered a celebrity-type mansion and had friends in all the right places. I knew my life would never be the same from the moment I spotted her chatting leisurely to airline personnel when I walked off my plane and into the Los Angeles International Airport late one Friday afternoon near the end of July.

"Maya, darling," she gushed, rushing across the floor, her three-inch heels clicking unmercifully on the polished tile floor. She was slender and petite, dressed in a fire-engine red suit jacket and short skirt with a silver fox stole dangling carelessly over one shoulder. She appeared to be a boundless bundle of energy, and no one could possibly guess her age without looking at the telltale neck and hands which also appeared to be surprisingly young. She was seventy-three but looked closer to fifty. It was impossible not to wonder how much time and money she spent trying to look so vibrant. "My goodness. It's hard to believe you're all grown up."

"What did you expect, Aunt Lil?" I replied, trying to stifle my amusement as she brushed both of my cheeks with her painted lips and then stood back to appraise my appearance while her hands still clutched my arms. It made me wish I was wearing something other than jeans and the light top I had purchased at a local department store. I felt like a country bumpkin standing next to her. "It's been nearly thirty years since we last saw each other."

"Please don't remind me of that," she countered, glancing quickly around in every direction. "People don't like to admit they're getting older, but just look at you—all grown up and absolutely ravishing. It makes an older woman almost jealous."

"Whatever for," I said, unmistakably aware of my mysterious great-aunt's need to be noticed. My mental image of her had been anything but accurate. She was no closer to being arthritic or a victim of mental decline than I was. "You're just what I imagined you would be."

"I hope that's a good thing, my dear," she said as her face lit up with another warm smile. "I've told everyone here that my favorite niece was coming to town for a long and relaxing visit. I wouldn't want them to think we're strangers, even if we are."

Her not-so-subtle statement let me know that this visit would be anything but restful. She had plans for me, and I needed to play along for a day or two before deciding if it had been a mistake to come. So I put my arms around her slender shoulders and gave her a hug. "It's good to see you again, Aunt Lil. Thank you for inviting me."

"No thanking me yet, young lady. We're family, and while I'm a little late with my help, I'm ready to give it now. So you'd better get used to being indulged because that's exactly what I intend to do."

My return smile was unexpected. Maybe a little pampering from this rather strange, but very intriguing, dynamo was just what I needed. I was certainly finding it difficult to think about digging weeds or scrubbing a bathroom while standing next to her.

"Now, darling," she said, taking my arm and propelling me towards a tall, robust man who was standing near one of the exits. "I think it's time to go. Otto can pick up your luggage if you tell him what to look for. He's an expert when it comes to finding things. We can grab a drink while we wait. He'll let us know when the car is outside the terminal."

The man she indicated with a slight incline of her head was wearing a black chauffeur's uniform and had his fingers wrapped around the brim of an official-looking cap. His feet were planted slightly apart on the floor, and his eyes were methodically scanning the terminal. For a fleeting moment, I got the impression that his duties included more than just driving my aunt where she wanted to go. He was big and powerful and looked like he could stop a small army single handedly. But I couldn't worry about the extent of his duties right now. I had a more pressing problem.

"A soda would be fine, Aunt Lil, but I don't drink anything stronger."

"Of course you don't," she responded as I hurried along beside her. "I was just testing the water to see how deeply engrained some of the family values were. I hope you don't mind if I indulge. A little wine in the afternoon keeps the entire circulatory system healthy, or so I've been told."

"Please don't feel you have to change anything just because I'm here."

"That thought never crossed my mind. I no longer let the fact that I'm the family reprobate bother me, and life is too short to give up certain pleasures. You'll realize that when you get to be my age. Now, I would like you to meet Otto. He's been with me for over twenty-five years. This is my niece, Maya Holden."

"Ms. Holden," the formidable-looking man said as he briefly lowered his head. "I hope you enjoy your stay."

"I'm sure I will," I replied before searching through my handbag for the baggage claim ticket. The scrutiny with which his bold, gray eyes were looking at me made me feel more than exposed. "My suitcase is black like most of the others, but I tied a purple and white, stripped ribbon to the handle so it would be easier to recognize."

"That's what I always do," Aunt Lil said. "Only my signature color is red. In case you haven't already noticed, I like to make my appearance known. It keeps things simple when dealing with others, and let's them know that I have nothing to hide."

I handed the ticket to Otto instead of saying anything more. I was in a very different world where people played by rules I might never understand.

"No reason to look so anxious," Aunt Lil said as he hurried away. "Otto is perfectly harmless, but he does take care of many of life's pesky little details. I think you'll like the rest of my staff. There's Hildie in the kitchen—she and I have become particularly close—and Sofia who does the cleaning. Pedro takes care of the grounds and Marty gives in-home massages on a twice-weekly basis. Randolph, my butler, was there when I bought the house. He might seem a little stiff at first, but he's old-school and loyal to a fault. I wouldn't be able to survive without him, but I quit relying on him for certain things years ago. His mind isn't as clear as it once was. Other than that, I go to the salon once a week and have an indoor gym if I feel the need to do more than swim. Time spent in my pool is much easier on the joints, and I feel it a shame not to utilize what is cared for so meticulously. Is there anything you might like to know?"

My head was swimming but formulating a question seemed impossible, so I simply followed her to one of the airport's many lounges. All the tables and booths were filled, but she didn't see to mind sitting at the bar.

"A club soda for my niece and a glass of your best house wine for me," she told the waiter who had a damp rag in his hand. After her order was taken, she glanced over at me. "You're deep in thought, Maya. I do hope you're not worried about your children. I am more than sure your parents can keep them safe and occupied."

"I'm not worried about them," I replied, hoping she would never guess what was really on in my mind. I was beginning to regret my decision about coming already. I had never sat in a lounge before.

"Well, that's good because everyone deserves a vacation. There's so much in this world to enjoy, and I sincerely believe it's a sin to waste one precious moment of the time we've been given."

"I can't imagine you wasting time on anything, Aunt Lil. You're the most successful woman I know, and you've been absolutely everywhere."

"I've seen a great deal of the world and have known many interesting people searching for fame and fortune. But I haven't created a legacy that will matter to anyone when I'm gone."

A single tear slipped from the corner of her eye. She wiped it away with the tip of her ring finger where a wedding band could have been. I merely bit my bottom lip and stared at the soda the barkeeper was putting on the counter in front of me.

"Now look what you've done!" she tartly stated as he turned to get her drink. "I'm too old for tears, and this is supposed to be a celebration, not a wake. Now tell me, does your Landi like large, stuffed animals?"

"Certainly," I responded. "What young girl doesn't?"

"That's good," she said, taking a sip of red wine. "And what about young Kenny? I don't suppose he cares much for baseball."

"He lives for little league."

"That's what I hoped because your children will be receiving a large package tonight with a message from you inside. I thought a large giraffe and a baseball mitt and glove might help ease the pain of losing you to the city for a few weeks. I hope I haven't overstepped my bounds since I've never met them."

"Not at all. They'll be delighted, but you should have told them the gifts were from you. They would have appreciated them twice as much."

"I doubt that! Besides, I have a few surprises reserved for when you bring them to stay with us."

"You sound like you think they're coming," I said, taking a sip of my soda and wondering how she could possibly believe I would bring two young and innocent children to stay with a woman I found totally disconcerting.

"I know they're going to come," she said, interrupting my thoughts. "Maybe not while you're here this time, but I would be willing to make a small wager that they will see California soil before the snow flies in your part of the country. It's almost always pleasant weather here."

I had never been to Los Angeles and found it impossible to tear my eyes from the limousine window as we passed through the industrial section of the city, down busy freeways where the cars traveled bumper to bumper and into a fairytale land where only the very rich or famous could live. Aunt Lil's home was located high in the Hollywood Hills—a spacious Spanish Villa surrounded by stone walls and an elaborately executed alarm system. Two Dobermans were leashed near the front door. They looked even more formidable than Otto.

"Well, this is it," Aunt Lil matter-of-factly stated with a sweep of a bejeweled hand as we pulled to a stop in a circular driveway. Palm trees, green grass, ornamental shrubs and flowers in every variety and hue imaginable surrounded us. "I hope you won't find it too uncomfortable."

"That would be impossible," I replied, unable to stop my eyes from trying to take in everything at once. "I feel like Cinderella being taken to live at the palace."

"This isn't exactly a palace. But I fell in love with the house the moment I saw it and decided to do whatever was necessary to live here. It took a few years of scrimping and saving, along with some rather risky investments, but my dream finally came true."

The gates closed behind us, and I felt a moment of unease—not unlike being imprisoned in what appeared to be paradise. "And you don't mind living with all the security?"

"When one is successful the way I am, precautions must be taken. The only way I get any privacy is to lock myself away behind impenetrable walls and security dogs. I suppose that must seem rather silly and pretentious for a girl who grew up with the wide open spaces as her back yard, just as you did."

I tried not to frown as visions of my own simplistic life of normalcy floated in front of my eyes. Nothing earth shattering or monumental had even happened to me—except for losing Ken—and that was a once in a lifetime experience.

When I didn't respond, Aunt Lil took the conversation in a less incriminating direction. "How would you like to do something a little bold and daring tonight?"

"Like what?" I asked.

"Nothing illegal. I've given up involvement in activities that push the confines of the law. I just thought you might enjoy viewing, first-hand, the kind of life I've lived for the past fifty years. Madame

Estelle Dubois—who claims her late husband descended from French royalty—has invited us to join her aboard her yacht for an intimate dinner party. She's limited the guest list to a hundred of her closest friends."

"That's an intimate gathering," I replied as I watched Otto get out of the car and move towards my aunt's door. I had only been to dinners that large when someone was trying to collect donations for a charitable organization. "It must be an awfully big yacht."

"Listen, my dear niece," Aunt Lil said, giving me a look of impatience. "This is Los Angeles. It is like no other place on the face of the earth, and that includes New York City and Las Vegas. You'll soon discover that nothing here is done on a small scale, especially when the wealthy are involved."

I watched as Otto took her hand and helped lift her to her feet. I was tempted to open my own door so he wouldn't have to bother but decided that my lack of sophisticated and genial behavior was apparent enough. Once I was standing beside her again, I made my apology.

"I'm sorry for being flippant, but I'm not accustomed to going to parties of any kind. Ken and I lived a very uncomplicated life. Our weekends were devoted to each other and our children. I get tongue-tied when there are more than ten people in the room and would hate to embarrass you."

We were making our way up an inlaid, tile walkway towards two magnificently carved wooden doors before she spoke again.

"That's not an excuse I'm willing to accept. You don't have to be the life of the party, but you're never going to move forward if you won't give something new a try. I promise to steer you away from the most aggressive men who only have have conquest on their mind, but I'm afraid there's nothing I can do about the women. Even the ones who are barely legal will be jealous of your captivating innocence and down-home beauty."

This compliment was different than the one she had extended at the airport, and I didn't know quite how to take it because I recognized that it came from her heart—all-be-it a little grudgingly. Lillian Farrow was still an incredibly beautiful woman who could command the attention of most any man.

"I smell roses," I said, looking around to see where the heavenly aroma was coming from. They would always be my favorite flower.

Aunt Lil took a deep breath and smiled. "My gardener claims we have nearly every variety that does well in this climate. Naturally, I don't believe him, but I am satisfied with what he has chosen. I'll take you on a tour of the grounds in the morning. They're at their most beautiful when the dew is still on the ground."

A man in the black uniform opened the front door to the villa before we had time to knock. Aunt Lil addressed him as Randolph, and I knew immediately why she had given me a more complete description of him than she had of her other employees. His face was as lined as a piece of driftwood, but despite visible signs of frailty, he stood erect and composed. The stories he had stored away after a lifetime of serving others would be worth hearing.

"Please see that Otto takes my niece's suitcase to the east guest room. It should be prepared by now," Aunt Lil told him.

"Yes, Ms Farrow," he replied. "Is there anything else?"

When she told him that would be all, he merely bowed and disappeared.

I stood in awe gazing at my surroundings. Ken and I had not been poor, but we had chosen to live an uncluttered and simple life. Everything about Lillian Farrow's residence was bigger than life, and she undoubtedly knew it. The dark, hardwood floor seemed to go on forever and shimmered in the light of a single multi-tiered chandelier that hung suspended from a two-story ceiling. The windows facing the front of the house were draped in heavy red velvet as were the sofas and chairs in the entry. A two-sided fireplace stood in the middle of the hall with Spanish shields placed at cross angles above it. Beyond that was a sunken room and floor to ceiling windows that overlooked the back gardens and what appeared to be a very steep cliff. There was a marble staircase to the right and several doors to the left.

"It's a little ostentatious," Aunt Lil admitted. "But I think you'll find the rest of the rooms in the villa more relaxing. I keep the main part of the house this way because it exudes a certain kind of strength that discourages some of my colleagues from thinking they can take advantage of me. Women have it a little easier today than when I was starting out, but men still run most of the corporations."

"You don't need to explain anything to me, Aunt Lil. I think your home is beautiful, and you're right when it comes to certain people wanting to take advantage of single women. I've been learning a little about that myself recently. I admire what you've been able to accomplish."

She gave me a brief tour of the lower level before escorting me to the room I would be using. It was decorated in pleasant yellows and greens with a balcony overlooking one of the side gardens. I stood next to the iron railing for some minutes looking down on white, pebble pathways, an arboretum, and lush green foliage that hid the security fence. The only sound I could hear was a few birds warbling.

Sofia brought me a tray filled with fresh fruits, cheese and dry, fancy crackers. I nibbled at them while I unpacked, knowing that too much food on a nervous stomach was a recipe for disaster. Then I put my personal grooming items in the white, tile bathroom that had both a shower and a jetted tub. But when I opened the closet door to hang up my jacket and the only dress I had brought—a lightweight frock that could be worn sightseeing—I saw two evening gowns. Both were fashionable and stylishly cut—one blue and the other one white. On the floor were matching sandals for each of them.

I took a step backwards in astonishment before checking the size. Aunt Lil was a master at manipulation who seemed determined to get me back to the land of living, but the draw to feel like a princess for just one night was too much to resist. So I showered and curled my hair, and when I returned to the bedroom to try on each dress before deciding which one I would wear, I saw a small box sitting in the middle of the bed. There was a note resting on top of it.

"I hope you mind that I took the liberty of selecting what I felt would look best on you for tonight," Aunt Lil had written in a bold, clear, cursive hand. *"I knew there wouldn't be time for shopping, so I asked your mother to send me the information I needed. The dresses are yours to keep, but the pearls are simply on loan. They are the only perfect thing August ever gave me."*

At precisely seven o'clock, I joined my aunt in the foyer of her magnificent home. I was wearing the blue, satin gown with short, capped sleeves, a gathered front and a slit that came up past my knees. The strand of genuine pearls was around my neck and matching earrings could be seen when I lifted my hair. The high, stiletto heels she had selected were surprisingly comfortable.

"You look absolutely ravishing, Maya," Aunt Lil said. She was dressed in black with stunning diamonds at her neck, wrist and ears.

"If I do, it's only because of you. I had almost forgotten how good it feels to dress up."

"It is one of life's pleasures I simply could not do without," she replied. "That's why I felt it was necessary to do a little arm-twisting to convince you to come with me. Whenever I'm most out of sorts, I always have my hair done, put on a pretty dress and find some party to attend. I let the idle chatter wash over me until I start to see that my own life isn't so bad. And if I'm very lucky, I will find someone truly interesting to talk to. I hope it will be like that for you tonight."

"And I'm hoping I won't trip or spill something. I would hate to ruin this amazing dress."

"The dress can be easily replaced," she said as we stepping into the warm night air. Otto was already holding the limousine door open for her. He must have done it a million times in the past. "I just want you to relax and try to have a good time. I know some of the people will seem a little over-the-top, but their goal is simply to impress everyone with all their success. Despite my many, obvious flaws, I've never felt the need to push myself, or my accomplishments, on others. I know I have genuine worth that goes far beyond what happens in the boardroom or the bedroom."

"So you really haven't forgotten your country roots."

"Not completely, but If you tell anyone, I will deny it. I'm a firm believer in the Golden Rule and have no doubt that I will have to account to my maker one day. But I've lived in a society where a woman has to bear her claws and fight for what she wants. Unlike some members of our family, my dreams have always always bigger than life. That's one of the reasons I left home and never locked back. I got tired of seeing the displeasure, and downright abhorrence, in some people's eyes when I verbally expressed what I wanted. But I've never forgotten who I am inside. I only bring that up now because you need to know that most of the people you'll be meeting tonight play hard ball. If they want something, they'll try to take it. Sometimes you have to be forceful, and even a little deceitful, not to get hurt."

"I'm not sure I have the capacity for doing that, and I don't plan on getting close enough to anyone to get hurt. I only came along tonight because you made it rather hard for me to refuse."

Lillian Farrow threw back her head and laughed. "Not only are you refreshingly honest, but you're totally naïve when it comes to what this world is all about. It's not going to be easy to keep you from meeting the wrong people. Most everyone in tinsel town is looking for innocence—innocence to corrupt."

"Then why take me to a place like that?" I asked as Otto navigated unfamiliar streets.

"I have my reasons, and they don't include harming you in any way. Maybe I only want to show you that your life is pretty spectacular just the way it is, even after all you have lost."

We drove for some time in silence because I couldn't think of anything else to say. Aunt Lil closed her eyes but made sure the back of her head didn't come in contact with the seat. I stared out the window wondering just what mess I may have gotten myself into without even trying. I was a suburban housewife with two children to raise, not some starlet looking for her big break.

It wasn't long until Otto pulled to a stop in a marina where hundreds of luxurious sailing vessels were docked. He would wait in the parking lot until we were ready to leave. The deck of Madame DuBois' yacht was filled with people who acted and looked like they had nothing better to do than have a good time. Waiters, in black jackets and white shirts, worked their way through the crowds with bottles of chilled champagne and odd-looking delicacies on oblong, silver trays. The women were wearing elegant evening gowns, most of them low cut and revealing. Diamonds, rubies, sapphires and emeralds sparkled everywhere. The men looked affluent, articulate and somewhat dangerous, especially for a woman who had not yet become accustomed to being on her own.

The hairs on my arms began to rise and a sense of trepidation settled in the pit of my stomach as I climbed a slight incline the join them. Aunt Lil was a few steps ahead. Tonight would be pure enjoyment for her, but I doubted that the warm night, soft music and light breeze coming from the ocean could calm my racing heart. I was no longer willing to make such a bold and daring move. I just wanted to be back in Ken's arms.

"Lil, darling," a woman came floating towards us in a silver, chiffon gown. Once they shared a quick embrace, her brightly painted lips brushed both of my aunt's cheeks. Then she turned to look at me. "Don't tell me this is your niece from Utah? I thought I would be meeting some quaint creature in a homespun frock. Do see that she meets all the right men. They'll find her a delightful change from all of the silly creatures who usually accompany so many of our friends."

Aunt Lil appeared to be amused by her statement, but I caught her eyes drift to the young man standing by Madame Dubois' side. He was very handsome in a European way with dark eyes, very tanned skin and an aloofness that made me wonder what he might be thinking. He looked young enough to be her son, or grandson, but even in my naivety I knew he wasn't.

"You can rest assured that no one unacceptable will come near her, Stella. But I must admit that I was rather surprised by your unexpected invitation. I thought you planned on staying here for a few months."

Stella Dubois pushed a bejeweled hand through the crook of the young man's arm and smiled demurely up at him. "All my plans changed the moment I met Karl. He's such a fascinating boy and has promised to show me sights I have never seen. We're leaving day after tomorrow for places unknown before returning to Paris for the holiday season, and I wanted to bid a fond farewell to all of my friends here before leaving. Help yourself to some hors d'oeuvres. Dinner will be served in an hour. We need to make the rounds before then."

She left, taking the young man with her. But before they disappeared into the moving crowd, Karl looked over his shoulder and gave me a suggestive smile.

"Don't worry about him," Aunt Lil said. "The piranha's are always lurking about at events like this. They may undress you with their eyes, but they would never make an overt move in front of the women they are with. Personal scruples may not be an issue, but they admire them in others and know what would happen if they made their companions mad."

We edged our way to the center of the spacious deck, stopping every few seconds so Aunt Lil could greet others and introduce me. I had to refuse glasses of champagne three times, but my aunt was ready for her second drink by the time we reached a large table with more than a dozen silver trays, filled to an artistic capacity with things I would never eat.

"Do you think it would be rude to ask for something non-alcoholic, Aunt Lil?" I questioned while looking for the most identifiable morsel.

"I'm sure soft drinks can be found somewhere. Some of people here are actually trying to remain clean and sober. Why don't you try a few of these dainty tidbits while I ask around."

She dropped something round, smooth and faintly orange into her mouth. My nose automatically wrinkled, just as my children's did when I put something unfamiliar on the dinner table.

"What was that?" I asked.

"It might be best if you don't know the ingredients. Stella like to serve the exotic, but I can tell you that most everything has a bit if seafood in it, in case you have allergies."

"None that I know of, but I've never eaten much that comes from the ocean."

"Then perhaps you should go easy on the canapés. I'm sure something a little more traditional will be served at dinner."

I took her advice and waited, empty-handed, until a waiter brought me a glass of club soda. It wasn't my favorite beverage—a little too bitter and bland—but it made me feel less conspicuous.

Aunt Lil seemed to know everyone who came our way by name, and one introduction casually followed another. I soon found myself forgetting just how uncomfortable I was as strangers told us about their latest escapades. Helen Van Orten had just returned from a trip to the Far East to look for silk. Her Indian guide had been bitten by a Cobra, and according to her tale, it had been simply agonizing watching him die. The Charles Rutterfords had been burglarized, and the police were no closer to finding who had stolen their valuables than the day it happened. And Pete and Mazzie Chamberlain had made a killing in the stock market and were planning another trip to Africa.

I was glad no one asked what had transpired in my life during the past few months. Weeding my vegetable garden, cleaning the house or driving my children to school could scarcely compare to the interests of these socially-minded people. But my mundane and somewhat boring life was perfectly okay with me. It had given me everything I had ever wanted until Ken died.

Not wanting to cry, I forced myself to look across the room to where a cluster of women were loudly laughing and holding their champagne glasses in the air.

"What's going on over there, Aunt Lil?" I asked as soon as there was a lull in her most recent conversation.

"It's probably Peter Richards and his flock of female admirers. They cling to him like flies to honey whenever he's out and about. You've hear of him, haven't you? He's the heartthrob of daytime television."

"I'm not into soap operas," I said, glancing in the direction of the dark-haired man who seemed to tower above almost everyone else on the deck.

"Well maybe you should be. Despite the public persona needed to keep his career booming, Peter is one of the most down-to-earth, single men I've ever met. Would you like to meet him?"

"No!" I replied, feeling a flush of color rush to my cheeks. "I'm a little old to be starstruck."

"That's too bad because he really is a good man, and you do have something in common."

"What could that possibly be?" I asked.

"Don't let his appearance fool you, Maya. He was raised on a farm somewhere in the Midwest and hasn't been completely ruined by success yet."

"Then I'm happy for him, but I didn't come here to meet anyone. I just needed a few days to decide what I'm going to do with the rest of my life. I've been thinking about furthering my degree so can join Ken's firm as a full partner. His father is delighted at the prospect of having me there."

"I'm sure he is, but do you really want to be stuck in some stuffy office all day? I've been there and done that, and it's not the life for a woman like you."

"What do you mean by that? I'm perfectly capable of having a career and taking care of my children at the same time. Women do it all the time."

"Perhaps, but there's more to living that keeping busy. What about that big hole in your heart? It needs to be filled wth something besides work and taking care of others."

I was just about to say something less than tactful when a jarring gong sounded, and people began moving towards the yacht's lower level.

"Where will everyone sit?" I asked, grateful our conversation had been interrupted.

"There's plenty of room in the ballroom below. Personally, I think having a yacht three times as big as anything else in the marina is ridiculous. It takes a crew of a dozen men just to keep it running. But her late husband left her with billions, and she bought this with the interest from his investments the first year he was gone. How would you like being that wealthy?"

I shook my head before responding. "I like being able to pay my bills and put something away for my children's future, but too much money might cause me to look at others differently. That's not who I am inside."

"Smart girl," she replied, taking my arm and leading me towards the stairs. "It can be lonely at the top of the food chain. Stella always has people around, but she will never be sure if they like her for who she is or simply because of the amusements she can offer."

"I'm perfectly content with my family and a few close friends."

She smiled up at me. "See, this evening hasn't been a total waste. You're already counting your blessings."

We were seated at the head table just to the left of a top fashion designer and directly across from a Hollywood producer and his very young companion. During the main course, he expounded on the impact and enormous cost of his latest film. Since I rarely attended the movies, I had no idea what he was talking about, but everyone else seemed to, including Aunt Lil. Her knowledge, and the ease with which she interacted with others, made it unnecessary for me to say much.

That left me free to watch the other guests—something I immensely enjoyed. I soon noticed that the young starlet was making eyes at a very virile-looking man who was seated at one end of the table with a rather intense-looking woman who may, or may not, have been his wife. When the producer saw what she was doing, he gave her a look that reduced her to tears, and she lowered her head and actually began eating.

Her disgrace gave the fashion designer the opening he needed to discuss his upcoming show and the designs he hoped would rock the industry. Once again, I was left with nothing to say. But thanks to Aunt Lil's impeccable taste, when he began making cryptic remarks about some of the women's chosen attire, I was left alone. Otherwise, I might have been the next one reduced to feelings of shame.

After that, I was able to disengage myself from what was going on around me and focus my attention on the woman who sat at the head of the table. Madame Dubois had the regality of a queen who knew how to rule her subjects. After chocolate éclairs had been served and wine glasses refilled—except for mine that had remained turned upside down during the entire meal—she rose almost wearily to her feet. And heavily resting her hand on the arm of the young man who had not left her side all evening, she began to speak.

"My dear friends, I am so pleased you were able to join us this evening on such short notice. My mind has been in turmoil of late trying to come to a very difficult decision. I have had such a lovely time in your country, but I do not wish to wear out my welcome. That is why I intend to return to my home once our travels have ended. I miss my chateau, my old friends and my vineyards. It is unlikely I will ever return."

There were a few gasps and then the room turned silent again.

"Please do not feel any distress over my departure. I have been here longer than first intended. Your warmth and acceptance have been over whelming during my several visits, but I feel an urgency to return to my past and try to rekindle some very pleasant memories. Now, I am rather tired, and if Karl will help me below, I will bid you all a fond *Au Revoir*. Feel free to stay and mingle. The yacht will not leave the marina until noon tomorrow."

She floated out of the dining room on the arm of her young escort. I longed to ask Aunt Lil what was happening. Perhaps Madame Dubois was terminally ill and didn't want her friends to grieve, or maybe she had pressing business in France. But my aunt seemed undisturbed by what had happened. She had already risen from the table and was engaged in an intimate conversation with the renowned Dr. Frederick Winthrop. He was an anthropologist who had written numerous books and articles on the psyche of people who chose to live their lives in the public eye. I had found him a little stuffy and condescending when we were introduced, but that was likely because I had never read anything he had written.

I wandered aimlessly around the banquet hall for what seemed like forever waiting for Aunt Lil, but it appeared that she had all but forgotten me. I knew she was having a wonderful time and wished I could say the same thing. But while the partygoers had been both interesting and agreeable, instigating a conversation with someone I would never see again seemed a little needy.

I was looking out a porthole window at the shimmering water and thinking about Ken when a deep voice addressed me, and I felt a hand on my shoulder. The pressure so startled me that I immediately whipped around. It was one of those fight or flight instances I had mostly read about. Aunt Lil was no where to be seen, but the handsome, daytime heartthrob, Peter Richards, stood less than six inches away from me. His hands were hanging unceremoniously to his sides, and he looked as if I had just slapped him across the face.

"Please excuse my boldness for addressing you without a proper introduction, but you looked like you could use a friend," he said as I felt his dark eyes boring into mine. "These affairs tend to lose their appeal once the big reveal has been announced. Have you known the extraordinary Madame DuBois for long?"

"I just met her tonight and only came at someone else's insistence," I firmly replied, not wanting him to notice my discomfort. I hadn't felt a man's touch—other than in a friendly handshake—since Ken's death, and the warmth of his fingers through the thin fabric of my dress had been horribly unsettling. "I'm waiting for my aunt. She'll be ready to leave soon."

"So Lillian Farrow is your aunt. I couldn't help but wonder what the connection might be when I saw you walk in with her. She usually attends gatherings like this alone so she can skip out right after dessert. She must have had a special reason for staying."

"What are you implying?" I asked as my eyes narrowed without conscious thought.

"Not a thing," he responded. "I'm simply trying to start a conversation with an attractive woman who's spent the entire evening alone when nearly every man in this room has been watching her."

"Including you?" I asked as the blood seemed to rush to my head again. This was beginning to feel like an ambush, and I hoped Aunt Lil wasn't responsible. She would get an earful when we got back to her house if she was.

His smile was slow and methodical. "I tried to keep my date from noticing my interest, but yes, I found myself watching you whenever I got the chance. You aren't from around here, and that's a refreshing change from all the women I usually meet. You're also very good at pretending that you could care less about meeting me."

"That wasn't pretense since I had no idea who you were until my aunt told me. I seldom watch television, especially during the day."

"And you never look at the tabloids while standing in line at the supermarket? I find that hard to believe since they can be entertaining, if not exactly factual."

My only desire was to get away from him, but the look of genuine interest in his eyes stopped me from causing an unwarranted scene.

"I usually have other things on my mind while shopping, Mr. Richards. And please don't be offended by my lack of interest. My aunt told me that you were a great guy, but I've never been any good at small talk and really don't belong here."

"I can see that now," he replied. "It hasn't been that long since I was the new guy in town and had to learn that all that glitters isn't gold. But I've managed to survive."

"Then you've done better than most, but I won't be around long enough to worry about either fame or fortune. I only came for a very short visit—not more than a day or two."

"That's too bad. I wouldn't mind showing you around Hollywood."

Before I could think of an acceptable comeback, a beautiful blonde girl was tugging on his arm and giving me a venomous look that told me quite clearly that Peter Richards had already been tagged private property.

"We have to go right now," she told him.

"Is that so?" he responded, sliding his arm effortless around her slim waist. "I thought you wanted to talk to everyone before we left."

"I've talked to everyone who matters, but I don't appreciate looking around to see that my man has deserted me to talk to some older woman neither of us has ever seen before. Why even bother?"

Her words stung, and my cheeks began to quiver. I was in my mid-thirties, not someone over-the-hill, but it was doubtful either of my companions noticed. They were much too absorbed with each other.

"Pull back the claws, Lana," he told her. "You have nothing to worry about. We've only been talking for a moment, and I don't even know her name."

"Then it won't be that difficult to disengage. I have a callback first thing in the morning and don't want to be late."

Something about me had set her off, but I had no idea what it was. She was young, scary-thin and beautiful with perfectly applied makeup and wearing a sparking, emerald gown. She couldn't be a day over twenty-one, but it was apparent from her attitude and mannerism that she was trying to make a name for herself before someone even younger came along.

"I didn't forget, but there's no need to be rude," Peter Richards was saying when I forced my mind back to the conversation that had gone from uncomfortable to completely disagreeable in less then three minutes. "The young woman I've been speaking with is Lillian

Farrow's niece. While she may not belong to our closely-knit group of acquaintances who enjoy playing these ridiculous games, she still deserves a kind word. Unlike you and me, she has yet to become tarnished by what this city has to offer."

"Then I apologize for my behavior," Lana said. "I was unaware that Lillian had any family. She's always seemed like a loner to me—a very rich and powerful one who is held in high esteem by all her associates. Is this the first time you've been in L.A.?"

Her abrupt change let me know that she had crossed the wrong people before and had no intention of doing it again, even if she had to eat a little humble crow. There was no reason for me to do anything other than set her mind at ease because she had nothing to fear from me.

"It is, but I won't be staying long. I have responsibilities elsewhere."

"Then enjoy what time you have here, but Peter and I really must be going. He has to be on the set before I even crawl out of bed."

There wasn't time to say anything more. I watched while she whisked him away. My life might not be the greatest right now, but at least I was past the point of chasing impossible dreams.

"Well," Aunt Lil said a short time later. "I see that you met Peter Richards without my help. Did you have a nice visit?"

"It was more like a brief exchange of words with little meaning behind them."

"I'm sure that's all it took to make Lana Laraine's blood boil. She's been after him since the day she arrived in town. That was two years ago, but as far as I know, she hasn't been able to extract a commitment from him. Marriage seems to be a career-breaker for most everyone around here."

"Are you speaking from personal experience or making a general observation?" I asked. "It's clear that she cares about him."

"Let's just say that I've had my share of flings over the years but decided it was more advantageous to keep my assets protected than enter into another doomed marriage. I never needed the headaches or the tears. There are plenty of those in the corporate world. You'll find that out for yourself if you commit to joining your late husband's firm. Men enjoy having pretty women around to spar with, but they seldom take them seriously when it comes to finances. As for Lana, while she has the looks to make it big and isn't without talent, she devotes most of her energies to obtaining what might not be hers to have. Maybe that's why Peter is such a novelty to her. He is likely the only man she's ever met that can't be wrapped around her dainty, little finger. But you can be certain that if he ever pledged his undying love she would be bored before the ink was dry on the marriage certificate."

"You must know her rather well."

"I'm an old fixture around here, and people talk to me as if I already knew everything. Lana's not a bad person, she's just been pampered by an over-indulgent father and a mother who is more interested in going to the gym or visiting some exotic spa than raising a daughter."

"Maybe Peter will help her become the person she could be," I said, surprised that I could so easily defend a woman who had been deliberately rude to me. "People can change if the motivation is strong enough."

"Spoken like a true optimist," Aunt Lil said, linking my arm with hers and leading me towards the stairs. There were no more than half a dozen people left in the ballroom, and most of those were cleaning up.

Over the next few days, Aunt Lil kept me so busy I didn't have time to think. I was okay with that because the limo was comfortable and her stories entertaining. We drove through narrow canyons, up steep hills to houses where famous people lived and took a day trip to Catalina Island where we could view the ocean through a glass-bottomed boat. We sat in the audience of a fast-paced game show, walked leisurely down Hollywood Boulevard and past TCL Chinese Theater and even spent an afternoon absorbing the ambiance on the Santa Monica Pier. Each night we dined at a different restaurant or attended another well-attended, but stuffy, party. By the end of the week, I was ready to collapse, but all she could talk about was what we had left to see and how we should save Disneyland, Universal Studios, Sea World and all the other children's attractions until Landi and Kenny could be with us.

"Aunt Lil," I sighed as we came through the front door of her villa at two o'clock in the morning. We had been to the opening of Percival's Art Gallery. "How can you do this every night and still get up in the morning? I'm exhausted!"

She kicked off her shoes before reclining on the red velvet sofa in front of the massive fireplace. I had only made it as far as the nearest chair, and the stairs to my room looked like some gilded mountain I had yet to climb.

"This is nothing," she replied with a mischievous smile. "You should be here during
the holiday season. There are social engagements back-to-back most every day of the
week. It does wonders for a girl's ego to be in such demand."

"I'm sure it does, but you look more radiant with each passing day while I'm just
becoming all blurry-eyed and rummy. That hardly seems fair."

"Nothing about life is fair, Maya, but if you have good friends and interesting things to do, you can learn to be happy. That's what I've had to do. I don't talk much about August Ferrell because he was a backstabbing womanizer, but he was my first love, and I've never completely gotten over him. Heaven's knows I've tried, but I chose to be cautious with my heart rather than dive into another relationship just because I couldn't see myself without a man. I'm sure your parents, or even your grandfather, have explained all my foibles in a very uncharitable way. What they don't understand is why I never went back to Hurricane after my marriage ended."

"All I've ever been told is that you were too busy with your business interests to come back to a town you only wanted to escape."

"They weren't wrong in that. I hated growing up in a backwater town with one pair of shoes to my name. I vowed from the time I saw my first movie at the drive-in theater that I would find my way to the big city where I could experience what life was really all about. August Ferrell arrived soon after that in his big, black car selling insurance. I was fourteen. He was handsome, mysterious and knew how to captivate an audience. All the girls had their eyes on him, and all the fathers purchased a policy they couldn't afford to keep him away."

I settled back in my chair so I could internalize all she was willing to say.

"I knew he was dangerous with his highly-polished shoes, clean, white shirt and broad-rimmed, felt hat. But when his eyes found mine, I didn't care about logic or self-restraint. I could only see the ocean, the house in the hills and the good life he had waiting for him when he returned from this trip. So when he told me loved me and wanted me to be part of his life, I couldn't refuse. I packed my suitcase and left town with him a week after we met."

"That was fast."

"I thought it was romantic, but I was still a girl with small-town values. When we got to Las Vegas, he suggested we get married. You could do that without anyone's permission back then, and he'd found someone willing to forge a birth certificate saying I was nineteen instead of what became termed jail-bait later on. Since I believed I was in love and had left everything familiar behind, I agreed. We were married in a small chapel on the strip and spent our first night making love in some large casino where he won big at the Blackjack table. Even discovering that he lived in rundown tenement housing instead of at the beach didn't phase me. He always had money in his pocket and treated me like a queen."

"When did you find out he wasn't who he claimed to be?"

"A couple of years later. He claimed I was his good-luck charm. I waited tables and kept the home fires burning while he traveled around selling insurance. We moved to a better neighborhood and even talked about having a child. And then one day two men came to my door saying they were from the government, and my husband was being investigated for insurance fraud. It seemed he had been pocketing some of the money from the policies he sold. I was left alone and practically penniless, but the people at the diner where I worked believed in me. I was given a room above the shop where I could live without paying rent, and my boss taught me what he could about surviving in the business world. I wasn't interested in running a diner, but I had an aptitude for designing ads that got results. When people in the neighborhood saw what I could do, they started paying me to do work for them, and the rest you could say is history."

"You took an awful situation and turned it into a success story. You should have been proud to go home and tell others what you had accomplished."

"Maybe I was too much of coward to face my past. I knew the mindset of small-town people who had never been more than twenty miles away from the house where they were born. I left home with an older man when I was still a child, and he ended up in prison. That's how people would remember me if I told anyone my story, and I didn't want anyone speculating on how I had risen to the top of a very competitive business."

"I can understand that."

"Then you can also understand that I forgave my husband for destroying my innocence, but I could never invite him back into my life. He died a few years later, and I've never loved anyone else."

"What about Senator Hughes? He's a very handsome man and has been at nearly every function we've attended the past few days. I couldn't help but notice that you were more relaxed around him than anyone else I met."

"I was wondering when you'd get around to asking about Tom," she said, the light in her blue eyes dancing. "I haven't said anything about him for fear it might jinx what we have."

"And what's that?" I asked, hoping she was still in a reflective mood.

"Just a very dear friendship, and one I wouldn't want to live without. Tom and I have known each other for over thirty years. His wife, Grace, was my closest friend and the loveliest woman I've ever known. We co-shared dozens of philanthropic events. She had a heart attack three years ago. Tom and I stood vigil at her bedside for weeks before she died. The last thing she did was take both our hands in hers and beg us to take care of each other after she was gone. You see, they hadn't had a family either."

"Do you love him?"

"A part of me has always loved Tom, but not in the way you're thinking. He was more like my brother until as few months ago."

"And now?"

"And now, I love him dearly. I guess that's what happens when you put someone else's feelings above your own. My life with August was less than I had hoped it would be. I was young and impressionable and believed nothing bad could ever happen to me. I suppose if I had stayed in Hurricane my life would have been much different, but I took a risk for what I thought was love. We might have been truly happy together if he hadn't stolen from his company. But he was even a bigger dreamer than me, and he was used to taking shortcuts. In many ways, I owe all of my financial success to him, but I came out of that marriage a bitter woman. I trusted no man until Tom came along."

"And he was married to your best friend."

"That's probably the only reason our friendship worked. He was devoted to Grace and never looked at another woman all the years they were married. That gave me a chance to be myself around him without worrying about whether or not he would try to take advantage of me. He knew how to accept a woman's weaknesses, fears and tears, and he never complained about anything that wasn't associated with politics."

"He sounds like a wonderful person. I hope I'll get to know him better while I'm here."

"That would be nice, but I'm afraid he won't be around much longer."

"Why not?" I asked.

"Because he told me tonight that he's dying and has decided to go to Switzerland in the morning."

Her words brought back chilling memories I had been trying to put behind me. "Cancer?"

"All though his body apparently, and there's nothing any of the doctors he's seen can do. He waited too long to seek treatment for what he thought was an ulcer."

"I'm so sorry, Aunt Lil," I responded, quickly crossing the room to her side. The lighthearted woman of a few moments ago was gone, and I knew she had been trying to remain strong for me. "But I don't understand why he would chose to go away at a time like this. He needs people around who care."

She patted my hand affectionately. "He thinks he's doing me a favor by leaving, and I can't blame him for how he feels. I made a horrible mistake last year. He asked me to marry him, but I said I needed time to think because it was a huge commitment after all the years I'd spent alone. I wasn't sure I was capable of living with anyone again."

"Surely he understood that."

"He said he would give me all the time I needed, but I got scared. So I booked a trip and told him we'd talk when I got back."

"That doesn't sound unreasonable. There was a lot to be considered."

"Please don't make excuses for me, Maya. I only planned on being gone a few weeks, but every time I thought about giving up my freedom I made excuses to stay away longer. By the time I got back, his condition had been diagnosed, and he'd changed his mind."

"Then make him change it again."

She gave me a look of unadulterated remorse. "He won't give me that chance. The only time we ever see each other is in a group setting where we can't talk privately. My heart feels like it's already stopped beating I love him so much."

"Then go with him, if you can't get him to stay. There's nothing more important than loving someone else. I would give everything I possess to hold Ken in my arms just one more time."

"But what if he rejects me again? That would be more painful than being told he no longer loved me."

"He's not going to tell you that, Aunt Lil. Can't you see that the only reason he's leaving is to save you the pain of watching him die?"

"How can you be so sure?" she asked.

I allowed my own tears to surface before responding. "Because I sat with Ken all those weeks when he was dying, and even though he was never able to respond to anything I said, I know he felt my presence. People really don't want to be alone when death comes, regardless of the circumstances, but they do want to stop some of the pain felt by the ones they're leaving behind."

"Spoken like a true Kincade, but what about you? Are you going to spend the rest of your life mourning a past that can't be retrieved, or will you be brave enough to give love another try?"

"We're hardly in the same boat, Aunt Lil."

"Aren't we, Maya?" she replied, twisting around so she could get a good look at my face. "We might not be the same age or have the same interests, but we've both experienced a once-in-a-lifetime kind of love. While the men we chose were very different, they held the key to our hearts. I let my relationship with August cloud every part of my existence. Because of him, I had to be strong, unemotional and immovable just to survive, or at least I thought I did. That belief served me well in the business community, but it wrecked havoc with my personal life. I thought needing someone else was a sign of weakness, so I pretended I was above that until it became a reality no one even tried to challenge. I don't want that to happen to you."

"It won't! I have my children."

"If they were supplying everything you need, there would be no reason to rejoin the workforce when Ken made adequate provisions for your future needs."

"Nothing has been decided. I was just thinking ahead. But this isn't about me right now. We were talking about your relationship with Senator Hastings and how you don't want it to end like this."

She clasp her hands tightly together in the folds of the gown she was wearing. "So we were, but if I'm willing to go all the way to Switzerland to prove my love for Tom—and risk his total rejection— then there has to be someone right here in Los Angeles that could help you reconsider spending the rest of your life alone. I'm not saying that you have to fall in love, but it's a big city with plenty of eligible bachelors."

"What makes you think I would be susceptible to anyone's charms?"

"Call it woman's intuition! You know how to love. It would be a shame to waste that gift. Now, I have some serious thinking to do. How about calling it a night? We can talk more tomorrow."

"What about Senator Hastings? I thought he was leaving in the morning."

"It's morning already, and he's probably on his way to the airport as we speak. He's even more determine to live life on his own terms than I am, and he's always been an early riser."

"But you've got to try!"

"Whatever I do must be carefully planned. He's a proud man, and my indecision hurt him. Whatever gesture I make must be one he cannot find fault with.

"Is there anything I can do to help?"

"Nothing, unless you can turn back the proverbial hands-of-time. I caused someone I love great pain and saying I'm sorry won't cut it. He has to believe that more than guilt is driving my desire to be with him."

"It's just so sad," I said, sliding to the edge of the sofa. "Loving someone shouldn't be so hard."

"I count any feeling a blessing. I've lived so much of my life without them. How would you feel about going deep-sea fishing tomorrow? I know someone who would be more than willing to take us."

"Maybe another day," I responded, fully aware of what she was trying to do. "I've had a wonderful time, but I should start thinking about going home."

Aunt Lil did something very unlike herself then. She leaned over and kissed my cheek. "You're a good person, Maya Holden. You haven't complained or criticized even once, and I know I've taken you to places you'd rather not be. My friends aren't exactly the go-to-church-on-Sunday type."

"Your friends are nice, and I'm glad I got to meet so many of them."

"So am I. My only regret is that you weren't able to come sooner. It took a long time to get where I am, and I did a number of things I wish I hadn't. But I've still tried to live by the Christian principles I was taught as a child."

"That's all any of us can do, Aunt Lil. I know I would never presume to judge anyone else."

"Your tolerance is much appreciated. Most of the family thinks I went over to the dark side when I left town with August."

"Maybe you should think about coming back with me. I could run interference if things got dicy."

She laughed and rose to her feet. "Now I know we could both use some sleep. What you just said actually makes sense. I've loved having you here the past few days. It makes me wish I had a child of my own to help guide and protect. The only legacy I will leave behind is a whole lot of money for people to fight over."

We went to bed shortly after that, but Aunt Lila had given me a great deal to think about. How effectively was I using my time on earth, and what legacy would I be leaving for Landi and Kenny? I didn't want them remembering me as a mother who had forgotten how to have fun.

Chapter 6

The sun was streaming into my bedroom through the cracks around the window blinds when I next opened my eyes. I tried to blink the weariness away and focus on the face of the alarm clock that was sitting on the night stand next to my bed. I moaned and sank back into the folds of the soft, feather pillow when I saw that it approaching noon. Aunt Lil would think I had deserted her since I was usually a very early riser.

With that thought in mind, I practically jumped from the bed, took a quick shower to help awaken both my mind and body and slipped into a pair of blue jeans and a light shirt. Then I hurried down the staircase to find Aunt Lil and apologize for sleeping so late. She was laying in a recliner on the sundeck behind the house with a glass of lemonade in her hand. The air was sweet and warm.

"Good morning, Aunt Lil," I said, standing stiff and still in the sunlight. "Or perhaps I should be saying good afternoon. I never meant to sleep so late."

"The time of day doesn't matter, Maya. You were tired."

"I guess I was, but you look as if you've hardly slept."

She was wearing dark glasses, but I could tell that she had been crying. Her cheeks were puffy and her lips drawn. She patted the seat of the chair next to hers.

"I got all the sleep I need for now. Come sit by me while I pour you some lemonade. There's something we need to discuss, and I'm not sure how to begin."

I did as instructed, but it was hard to keep the anxiety at bay. I had never seen my aunt quite so intense and cheerless. I knew instinctively that I wasn't going to like what she had to say.

"Try not to look quite so fierce," she said as I took a sip of lemonade. "I know you are no fonder of surprises than I am, so I'll get right to the point. I've decided to go to Switzerland to talk to Tom. I got the address of the house he's renting from his housekeeper. She was reluctant to give it to me at first, but I can be very persuasive when I want to be. There's a flight leaving at four this afternoon, and I intend to be on it. That means I'll be on my way to the airport within the hour. My suitcases are already packed."

"That's wonderful. You need to be with Tom," I said, wondering what was going to happen to me. It would take more than an hour to arrange a flight back to Utah and let my parents know I was coming. I didn't want to be stranded anywhere, but I couldn't stay in her home once she was gone.

"I agree, but it wasn't an easy decision for an old woman to make. I'm not sure what my reception will be. Tom didn't go back to his house after the party last night. Obviously, he'd been planning this for quite some time and saying goodbye to his friends was the last thing on his to-do list before boarding the plane that would take him away from me permanently. My only regret, other than some very misguided decisions in the past, is bailing on you. My intention was to have you with me for as long as you felt you could stay."

"Don't worry about me," I said as the emotion behind her words began to take hold. The Aunt Lil I had met less then a week ago would not allow sentiment to overshadow of any kind of self-inflicted duty. "I've had a wonderful time, but I really should be getting back to my children."

That was certainly true enough, but I was still confused and uncertain about who Maya Holden, the woman, was. If I returned to Hurricane today, I would go with the same fears I had harbored since the moment Ken died. How could I let Landi and Kenny move forward with lives of their own when they were all I had in mine?

Aunt Lil looked at me as if she knew what I was thinking. "I want you to stay here as long as you want to, Maya. I shouldn't be gone for more than a few days. My intention is to bring Tom back with me. He needs his friends to help him through this, and I need to make sure his doctors have done everything they can."

She removed her sunglasses and wiped away the tears that were floating in her eyes. I felt my own brimming, so I did likewise. No one should die alone. Death was as much a part of plan of Life and Salvation as birth, and it should be celebrated accordingly.

"I think you show a lot of wisdom and courage, Aunt Lil."

"I hope you can still say that after I've told you what else I've been planning this morning." She pulled herself to her feet and walked to the edge of the veranda. "I've been meddling in your life again, and this time, even I think I may have too far."

A hard knot of anxiety dropped to the bottom of my stomach. "I'm sure it's not that bad. You've been nothing but kindness itself since I arrived."

She stared down at the sharp rocks and brush just below the well-manicured lawn and gardens while I rose to my feet and joined her. She waited to say something more until my hands were resting on her shoulders, but she didn't turn to face me.

"You're like the daughter I never had, Maya, and I love you to the moon and back. We've walked in similar paths of self-discovery, adventure and loss. That's why I think I know you better than you know yourself right now, and why I've taken matters into my own hands. You need someone to help you find real purpose in living again, and some job with your father-in-law isn't going to cut it."

The lump in my stomach seemed to explode. "You haven't signed me up as a mail-order bride, or something even worse, have you?"

Her laugh was hollow. "It's nothing as risky as that. I know you'll find love again when the time and circumstances are right. What I've done is made arrangements for you to be a housekeep for a week."

It took a moment for her words to register, and when they did I started to laugh.

"I'm serious, Maya," she said.

"But I'm not a housekeeper, Aunt Lil."

"Sure you are. What do you think you've been doing the past thirteen years? You're the most qualified person I know."

"I'm qualified to take care of my own home, not someone else's."

"I can't see how that matters. One house is pretty much the same as another."

"That may be, but the people living in it certainly aren't. I'm a farm girl, Aunt Lil. What do I know about the lifestyles of the rich and famous?"

"You don't have to know anything. This is a special case."

"You're really serious," I said.

"I've never been more serious. You aren't ready to go home, and this is a trip I need to take. I was contemplating what I could suggest that might keep you here when the perfect opportunity presented itself. You took a chance when you moved back east and found the love of your life. Why not try it again? The results might not be the same, but seven days isn't such a long time, and you'll have plenty of time to the think. The owner is rarely at home, the neighborhood is safe, and it's not too far from the beach. That's one place we haven't spent much time, and it's perfect for serous contemplation."

I gripped the railing on the deck as acute nausea rose to my throat. Aunt Lil had been wonderful to me, but everyone knew she was just a little crazy. What if she had finally gone off the deep end and was plotting to take me with her?

"Please hear me out before making an irrevocable decision. I know this sounds like a bizarre request, but Hildie was in complete turmoil when she brought my breakfast tray this morning."

"And why is that?" I asked, trying to keep my voice level.

"Because my sudden departure has made it impossible for her to keep a promise she'd already made. One of her friends got an emergency phone call from her daughter not long after we left for the party last night. There was an automobile accident and her only grandchild—a little boy about Kenny's age—was hospitalized. He's in critical condition, and Mrs. Newbold wants to be with him."

"That's awful! I'll pray for his speedy recovery, but I still don't see what it has to do with me."

"Hildie said she'd cover for her while she was gone. Normally, that wouldn't be a problem. I allow my employees a great deal of latitude when it comes to helping others since I never know when I might need a return favor. But I'm relying on Hildie to see that everything runs smoothly during my absence. She has a great rapport with everyone in my household and knows how to keep them in line."

"I'm glad you have someone you can rely on, Aunt Lil, but why can't she just call an agency like anyone else in the same situation?"

"Because it's my fault she can't go, and no one likes strangers taking care of their home. Besides, like I said before, this is a special case."

"You can't play God, Aunt Lil."

"I'm not trying to, but I do believe he will only help those who are willing to help themselves."

"And just where is it that you think God wants me to go?" I asked.

"To Peter Richards!"

My mouth dropped open at such an audacious assumption. "The daytime heartthrob I met at the party the first night I got here? He'd see through my charade the moment he saw my face and most likely have me thrown in jail for impersonating a qualified housekeeper. I'm sure this would be far from the first time a woman tried something similar to get close to him. It's a recipe for complete disaster, and I'm surprised you'd even suggest it considering your standing in this community. While it's been a lovely visit, my only alternative is to go back home where I belong."

I turned to leave. Her logic defied reason, but her hand caught my wrist.

"No one is going to jail. Peter Richards is one of the most genuine, likable men I've ever known, and he needs our help. I can't believe you won't even consider the possibility of stepping outside the safety net you've built for yourself. Things like this don't happen by chance. Something greater than what we can comprehend is at work here."

"And you're absolutely certain you didn't play a more prominent hand in it?"

"While I can take credit for some pretty amazing things happening in the boardroom, this is outside my area of expertise. I'm not exactly known for my matchmaking skills."

"That's good because I still love Ken and always will. There isn't room in my heart for another man."

"Then your heart is a lot smaller than I thought it was. You disappoint me, Maya. I thought you were a person who valued living, but you buried yourself with your husband. Go ahead! Leave! Crawl back to Utah or Boston and your glorious dreams of the past. Forget that we were meant to make every day of this life count. I know I haven't been much of a Christian in the true sense of the word, but I've never turned my back on someone in need."

Pent-up tears suddenly gushed out, and I didn't even try to stop them. "I've never turned my back on anyone, Aunt Lil. But what you're suggesting is ludicrous. I'm not a housekeeper and Peter Richards is no fool."

"That may be true, but I have a feeling both of you could use another friend."

"I've got friends and so does he."

"His are far from being the kind he needs, especially when it comes to the women he lets into his life. He needs to see that a woman can be genuinely sensitive, caring and understanding without wanting anything in return."

"I'm sure he already knows that."

"Perhaps! But he's not as happy as he should be after all the success he's attained. He's wallowing in some quagmire and needs help getting on track again. I was thinking you might be able to help each other."

"We're not pawns, Aunt Lil. We're people, and he already has a girlfriend who's not going to let anyone interfere."

"Lana has a ferocious bark, but she's not what he needs."

I looked at the white, fluffy clouds above my head before responding. One of them looked like the Labradoodle my neighbors had back home. "How can you be so sure?"

"Because she'll drop him the moment someone who can be more of an asset to her career comes alone. I've seen it happen a thousand times over the years. And if you're really not interested in him, she'll figure it out and leave you alone. A few angry words never hurt anyone, and you'd be helping both HIldie and me."

"I'm not sure that makes me feel any better about your proposal."

"Then maybe this will. If Peter is truly in love with Lana, your presence in his home for a few days won't cause so much as a hiccup in anyone's life. He needs someone who can keep things tidy and run a few errands. That leaves him free to work and socialize as he's always done. He really won't care who is cooking his meals or cleaning his bathrooms as long as nothing in his orderly life is upset. I know you're capable of doing that. And if the situation progresses to a point where you have a genuine conversation, then what's the problem with that? Two wonderful young people getting to know each other better shouldn't be construed as a problem. Your different perspectives might give each of you something new to think about."

"I'm not exactly a kid, Aunt Lil. I'll be thirty-five next year."

"And Peter's almost thirty. What difference does age make in either life or love? You can still be friends."

Aunt Lil had me right where she wanted, caught somewhere between feelings of guilt over not being more generous with my time and anxiety over what my future might bright without the love of my life in it.

I wasn't some starlet whom men passionately pursued. I was a mature woman who had married a marvelous man, given him two beautiful children, and then been brought to my knees in despair when he died. My heart was still cankered by what I had lost, but perhaps there were some words of wisdom I could share.

"All right, I'll do it, Aunt Lil, but only because you're asking it as a favor. If I get any bad vibes, I'm out of there."

"I would expect no less," she replied. "I'll inform Otto that he may be receiving a call from you while I'm gone, but I have a feeling an escape won't be necessary. And now, I'm off for an adventure of my own. I hope we both have exciting tales to share when we see each other again."

Shortly after three that afternoon, my suitcase and overnight bag were put into the trunk of Aunt Lil's limo, and I was on my way.

I still couldn't believe I had allowed her to talk me into doing something so foreign to my basic nature. I had always weighed my decisions carefully before making any move. Even going to Boston fourteen years earlier had been the culmination of a long-planned dream. That dream was now gone, at least for the remainder of this lifetime.

"Oh, Ken," my mind thought as I bit my lip and looked out at the passing, scenic landscape to keep from crying. "Why did you have to die? We had our lives so meticulously planned. And here I am, your level-headed, no nonsense wife off on a fool's errand. Well, it won't be for long. I'll take care of Peter Richard's house, but the moment my stint as an indentured servant ends, I'm taking our children home where we all belong. And then I'm going to help your father with the business. Landi and Kenny will have everything we planned for them, and they will have a mother who lives life joyously and smiles from her heart. I won't fail you again."

My resolves made, I settled back in the seat of the car and closed my eyes. The situation was unbelievably preposterous and going along with it was sheer folly. But if I could pull it off—with some memento that would prove my sojourn was not the figment of an overactive imagination—my adventure might keep Landi entertained for weeks. Besides, how difficult could it be to take care of a bachelor's house for a few days? If what I'd heard about movie and televisions stars was true, Peter Richards would seldom be around, and I would have plenty of time for thinking, soul-searching and relaxation.

Otto stopped the limousine in front of a modern, sandstone house that stood at the end of another gated driveway. Hildie had provided the access code. It was large and open-looking with plenty of windows to let in the warm, California sun. Oak and maple trees grew in groves throughout the front yard, and a wooden bench had been built around one of them. Not even the sound of a plane flying overhead disrupted the peaceful setting.

"Mrs. Farrow left this for you," Otto said as he opened the car door and placed a silver key in the palm of my hand. "It opens the back door to the house. Your instructions are waiting on the kitchen counter. If you need anything, just call. Mrs. Farrow said I was to be at your disposal day or night."

"Thank you, Otto," I said, squeezing his hand as an impulsive child might have done as I stood upright. "This is a new experience for me, and I'm not sure what I've gotten myself into. While I am hoping for the best, that doesn't stop me from being scared."

"There is no need for concern. Mrs. Farrow has only your best interests in mind."

"You're very close to my aunt, aren't you?"

I thought I detected a look of sadness in his eyes before he spoke again, but it quickly passed. "I have been her driver for a long time, and she has been very good to me."

He led me around the corner of the house, through another gate and up some steps to a covered patio. I couldn't help but notice how clean and spotless everything looked as I opened the back door with the designated key. Otto didn't need directions as to where my suitcase and overnight bag belonged. There was a small bedroom located off to one side of the kitchen where pots of every size hung suspended from hooks over a center island.

"Will there be anything else, Mrs. Holden?" he asked, after placing them on the tan carpet and straightening his back.

"Nothing I can think of," I replied while looking around for signs of another person having occupied the bedroom. But finding none, I could only assume that Peter Richard's housekeeper, Mrs. Newbold, did not live on the premises.

"As you wish," he said tipping his cap and turning to leave.

But I wasn't ready to be left alone. I was miles away from my aunt's house and feeling quite vulnerable now that she was no longer in the city. If I allowed him to walk away, I would truly be on my own in what could so easily turn into a hostile situation. In order to delay his departure, I decided to ask the question that had been on my mind for hours.

"Do you think my aunt will be able to convince Senator Hughes into returning with her? I know she's taking an intentional risk."

"That's not for me to say, but if anyone can persuade a person to do something, Mrs. Farrow can," he replied.

I smiled, despite my desire to pick up my suitcases and run. "You're absolutely right, Otto. I've just had a sampling of her persuasion, and I hope it won't be my complete downfall."

He touched the rim of his hat before pulling open the back door to leave. "Never give up on yourself or your aunt. Things have a way of working out the way they were meant to. Sometimes they just need a gentle push in the right direction."

That was my cue to sit down on a stool and read the instructions Mrs. Newbold had left. Monday through Friday, Mr. Richards left for the studio at four in the morning. He ate his daily meals there but expected his dinner to be on the table at eight each evening, unless he had another engagement. The menus had been planned, the shopping done, and the recipes for his favorite meals left in the top drawer next to the stove.

The laundry service came on Tuesday, and I was to have his shirts, slacks and suits bagged and ready to be sent out by ten. Everything else could be washed at home. Garbage pickup was scheduled for Monday, and the gardener came on Saturday. Other than that, my only responsibility was keeping the house in order until she returned. There was a more personal addition that thanked me for coming on such short notice.

I thought it sounded simple enough until I turned the page and read the postscript. *"By the way, he's having a small dinner party tonight—just a few of his closest friends. The food has already been prepared. There's a lasagna in the freezer that needs to come out by four so it will be ready for baking and a tossed salad and dessert in the refrigerator. The table has already been set in the dining room. All you have to do is serve the food and clean up afterwards. Mr. Richards is very easy to work for. All he expects is an orderly home without conflict or confusion."*

"Great!" I muttered, placing my hands behind my neck and stretching as if I had been bent over a difficult task for hours. Here I was standing alone in a stranger's kitchen and wishing I was anywhere else. Regardless of what my aunt had said, Peter Richards was expecting a bonafide, substitute housekeeper who knew how to take care of his needs. And it would be anything but an orderly and tranquil arrangement if he remembered meeting me before. Lillian

Farrow's niece would not be masquerading as an employee in his home, unless she had something underhanded in mind.

That thought caused a whole slew of undesirable possibilities to surface, but there wasn't much I could do until he got home. Then I would explain what had happened and hope he found it amusing. Aunt Lil could be upset if she wanted, but I wasn't a person who could live a lie—even a small one that could easily be rectified.

My decision made, I felt somewhat better. But I still needed to know my way around the main part of the house in case he wanted me to stay through dinner. None of this was his fault, and I could survive putting food on the table if I had to. I had done it plenty of times in the past.

In the dining room was a massive, hardwood table with matching chairs and breakfront. It had been tastefully set with china, silver, crystal, and freshly cut flowers. I ran my hand over the smooth, polished wood of the chair nearest me. Mrs. Newbold appeared to be an immaculate and talented housekeeper.

The inlaid, hardwood floor extended through open French doors into the living area where leather upholstery and an oriental rug had been placed in front of a white, stone fireplace. There were sculptures and paintings everywhere. It was apparent that Peter Richards liked the finer things of life and could afford to have them.

From there, I took a hallway that veered to the left of the house where three bedrooms, a guest bathroom and a small laundry room stood. I didn't need to open any doors since none of them were closed—even the one leading into the master bedroom. It was uncluttered, dignified and masculine with a large walk-in closet and a private bath. The furnishing were in the same rich, earth tones as the rest of the house.

But when I turned another corner and saw his den, I walked in without thinking. There were at least a dozen shelves of books, and a few trophies and ribbons displayed in a built-in glass case on one of the walls. There were countless reminders of past ballgames, science projects, fishing trips, motorcycles, personal performances and activities that made the headlines. There were also pictures of smiling people that looked so much like him that they could only be members of his family.

It reminded me of Ken's den, and I sat down at his desk and put my head in my hands. No matter how much I might disappoint Aunt Lil, I couldn't do what I had promised. The only man I had ever taken care of was Ken, and I had no desire to serve another man in that special and all-consuming way.

I finished my wanderings in the garage. I should have made myself go back to the kitchen to wait, but I was restless and no longer thinking as clearly as I should. Unfortunately, I was soon to discover that I wasn't immune from making a bad situation even worse.

There wasn't anything unusual inside the main part of the garage, just an old, blue pickup truck and room for another vehicle. But when I saw another door leading to the back of the building and all of my instincts told me to leave it alone, I didn't heed the warning. One turn of the handle and I was standing in Peter's private workroom. It was filled with carvings made from seasoned driftwood. There were animals, birds and all kinds of abstract figures. But most of all, there were faces filled with every emotion known to man—love, hate, envy, greed, pride, jealousy, fear, compassion, joy, sorrow, and timidity. The feelings elicited nearly took my breath away.

I cradled a figure of a fisherman in my hand and wondered what had happened in Peter's life that had turned him into such a sensitive and skilled artist. It was almost like seeing inside of his soul, and I had entered that most intimate sphere without his permission.

Tears filled my eyes as I walked away. I had never invaded anyone's privacy before, and it left me with a very clear picture of the person I would become if I stayed where I was any longer than necessary.

"Bread!" The word hit me with all the force of an exploding landmine before I made it across the patio and back to the house. I hadn't baked a single loaf since leaving Boston, but the sudden thought of butter dripping over hot, crisp crust made my mouth water. I knew the recipe by heart. Perhaps if I did something useful it would help calm my troubled heart and keep me from getting into any further mischief. And if I began immediately, there would be five, fresh loaves waiting on the counter by the time Peter Richard's came home for his dinner party.

So I forced well-deserved feelings of anguish to the back of my mind and set to work. An idle mind was indeed the devil's workshop, and I never wanted to go there again.

An indescribably wonderful aroma was coming from the oven when I decided it was time to put the lasagna in the microwave to start the unthawing process so it would be ready for the oven once the bread came out. I opened the freezing compartment of the refrigerator to remove a large, bronze casserole dish.

"How delicious," I thought. "If it tastes even half as good as it looks, I'll write and ask Mrs. Newbold for the recipe. Once I'm safely back home in Boston, that is."

The casserole dish was much larger and heavier than anticipated, but that wouldn't have been a problem if I'd swept and moped after setting the bread to rise and washing the dishes. My left foot raced past the rest of my body when it came came in contact with something on the floor, and I landed with a screaming crash while the casserole dish sailed across the kitchen floor and shattered into a million, tiny pieces.

I just sat where I landed, my hand clasped over my mouth, too stunned to cry out in either embarrassment or pain. Dinner was gone, and Peter Richards would be home in less than thirty minutes.

"This is all your fault, Aunt Lil," I lamented as I looked around the once orderly room and then pulled myself to my feet with the aid of the kitchen cupboard. There was food and glass everywhere. It covered the floor, the cupboards, the appliances and the walls.

I wanted to open the back door and disappear, but I had no one to blame but myself for this mishap. It was divine retribution for snooping. So I worked as rapidly as I could to clean up the mess. Since the largest pieces of the broken casserole were most accessible, I started with them. Then I took the dustpan and slid it underneath intact slabs of noodles, meat, tomatoes and cheese.

It was a revolting undertaking and one that could have been avoided, but that wasn't an option now, so I found a bucket and filled it with hot, soapy water. I would take care of the floor before starting an everything else. I was bending down to put a dishrag into the water when a decidedly masculine voice startled me.

"Mrs. Newbold, are you in the kitchen? Something smells delicious. If I didn't know better, I would think you were baking bread."

The door leading into the dining room swung inward before I had time to call out my presence or move. My knee hit the top rim of the bucket as the door slammed into my side. It flipped over, and floating bubbles of food and fragments of broken glass were swirling everywhere when Peter Richards tried to step into his own kitchen.

"What the devil happened in here?" he demanded as dirty water moved around his shoes. "And you're not Mrs. Newbold. She would never allow anything like this to happen."

I tried to straighten myself to my full height and tilt my chin in the air in hopes of swallowing back some of the humiliation I felt inside. "I'm her replacement. She was called away unexpectedly. I was just preparing your dinner when a slight accident occurred."

"Slight," he responded. "It looks like you've destroyed my kitchen. You are aware that my guests will be arriving momentarily?"

"Yes, sir," I said, as the last shred of dignity left me. "I'll get this cleaned up and have something on the table as fast as I can."

"Who are you anyway?" he demanded. "Mrs. Newbold didn't say anything about leaving."

"It's a long story, Mr. Richards, and I'll tell you all about it later. Right now, I need to work fast or water will get underneath everything."

He looked around the room again, and as he did so, his frown was replaced with an almost amused grin. "It looks like it already has. Do you need some help?"

"Probably, but I can handle it," I admitted. "This isn't the first time I've seen a flooded kitchen."

He didn't say anything more. He simply sloshed through the water and took a mop from the closet. "Don't tell me you make it a habit of doing this. It must be rather hard to keep a job as a housekeeper."

"This is the first job I've had in a number of years," I replied as I began wiping down walls, cupboards and appliances with a damp dishcloth, as if cleaning up near-disasters was some thing I did everyday.

"Well, don't let it get to you," he said while working on the floor. "I've had plenty of first-day jitters myself. Fortunately, we all seem to live through them. By the way, I didn't catch your name."

"It's Maya Holden, and I really do want to explain . . . " I responded, grateful that introducing myself by name hadn't come up the first time we met. It was quite obvious he didn't recognize me when I was not dressed up in finery, but he likely met dozens of women each day. And there was nothing really remarkable about me, except for my seeming ability to get into trouble.

"Don't worry about it right now, Maya Holden. I'm sure Mrs. Newbold would not have recommended you if you weren't qualified. Accidents can happen to anyone."

"You're being very understanding."

"Why shouldn't I be? I've had a good day and can afford to be generous."

I watched the muscles on his arms and back ripple as he pulled out the refrigerator and moped behind it. Aunt Lil was right about one thing. Peter Richards was a gentleman.

A few minutes later, the floor was finished, and Peter was carrying the pail to the alley to dump.

"Listen, Maya," he said, when he returned. "Why don't you take the rest of the night off? You've had a rough, first day, and I can always take my guests out to dinner."

"I wish you wouldn't," I replied, wanting to remain indifferent to him. But that was rather hard to do since he'd so readily made allowances for such obvious blunders. "I would like to make it up to you for the inconvenience I've caused. I'll replace the casserole dish tomorrow."

"None of that is necessary. You've been through enough."

"I bounce back fast," I lied. "And I'm sure I can come up with something else for the main course. Mrs. Newbold had everything ready, and I haven't destroyed the salad or the dessert."

He was thoughtful for a moment. But I knew if he sent me away, I would never come back. I would take my still-packed luggage, and he would never get so much as a lame excuse for my undignified behavior and reprehensible charade.

"I suppose we could always eat lots of bread with the salad," he finally said.

That snapped me back to the mirky present in a hurry, and I hurried to the oven and pulled open the door. Five loaves of perfectly browned bread were ready to be pulled out and placed on a rack to cool. Peter was looking over my shoulder.

"I haven't smelled anything that wonderful since I left home. Nobody bakes bread anymore, not even Mrs. Newbold. She gets hers from the neighborhood bakery. You must be from some other planet."

"Not quite," I said. "Would you mind handing me some hot pads?"

"Coming right up," he replied. "Do you want me to get the wire racks out too?"

"Sure, if you know where they are."

"Why shouldn't I?" he asked as a drawer opened and closed. "I do my own cooking on Mrs. Newbold's days off. Maybe I can treat you to one of my home cooked meals before she gets back."

"That would be nice," I said as I turned the bread onto the racks and rubbed butter on each top. "Thank you for helping me and for being so understanding. I really didn't mean to destroy anything."

"No permanent harm done. This little adventure has livened up an otherwise ordinary day. Why don't you join us for dinner?"

I smiled and shook my head. "I don't think so."

"Why not?" he asked. "Nobody has to know you're the housekeeper."

"Because I have a job to do that doesn't include eating with your guests," I said, giving him a nudge towards the dining room door. "Why don't you do whatever need to be done while I figure out something to serve."

By ten minutes to eight, I had a thick summer stew simmering on the stove. I still had the condiments and water to put on the table, but that could wait until I had changed into something more fitting than soiled, damp jeans. I was on my way to Mrs. Newbold's room to change when I heard the front doorbell ring. I paused for a moment, wondering if it was one of my duties to answer it.

But then I heard the door open, and Peter was greeting someone named Bridgette. "You're right on time, but where is that handsome devil you're always dragging around?"

"He's coming in a second car. I told Barry I wasn't about to wait while he chased Randolf down the beach. That dog is incorrigible, but according to my husband, he's just a playful baby who likes to run."

I lost track of the conversation as I changed into the only light, summer dress I had brought with me from Boston, ran a brush through my hair, and headed back to the kitchen to stir the stew. I had just taken the lid from the pot when the back door to the house burst open.

"Tally ho, Mrs. Newbold. Where's my Peter? I've been waiting all day for one of his delectable kisses."

The moment of truth had arrived. Peter might not recognize my face after our brief encounter, but Lana certainly would. I saw the color rush to her cheeks and her eyes narrow when she saw me standing in front of the stove. I was still trying to figure a way out of a very disagreeable situation when she asked me another question.

"Where's Peter's regular housekeeper? He didn't tell me she was leaving."

"Mrs. Newbold will only be gone a few days," I responded with as much decorum as I could muster. One false move on my part could destroy what was left of a very uncomfortable evening. "I'm only here to help out while she's gone."

"Over my dead body." Lana seethed. "Does Peter know you're here?"

"That I do!" I heard the man I was supposed to be helping say as he entered the kitchen through the dining room doorway, and placed his arm fondly around her shoulders. "I can't believe this is the same room I entered just a few minutes ago, and you clean up quite well too, Ms. Holden."

Despite the fact that I knew he was only trying to help me feel less awkward, his unexpected compliment made my heart race It had been over a year and a half since anyone had taken more than a casual interest in my appearance—including me.

"Thank you, Mr. Richards," I said, afraid to face the couple that was standing on the far side of the kitchen table. It was much safer just to keep stirring the vegetables in the pot.

"Just what's going on here?" Lana demanded. "And where is Mrs. Newbold?"

"Can't tell you that, my love," Peter said. "Ms. Holden was here when I got home from work. And to tell you the truth, we were so busy with other things that I forgot to ask why Mrs. Newbold was even gone."

"And just what was keeping you so busy?" Lana asked as the animosity in her voice seemed to increase.

"It's not important, Lana, just a little mishap that could have happened to anyone. Besides, we should be thanking her for helping out. If she wasn't here, you would be the one serving dinner tonight. Now, why don't we join Bridgette in the living room? I'm sure Ms. Holden has everything under control in here."

"I suppose I can do that, but I know I've met that woman somewhere before." Impulsively she broke from Peter's grasp and moved across the room to where I was still wishing I could simply disappear. "Are you the Windell's regular housekeeper?"

"No," I replied. "I've never worked for anyone around here."

"But, if you're not a housekeeper for one of our friends . . . "

"Let it go, Lana," Peter interrupted, taking her arm and escorting her towards the dining room door. "Her past employment is none of our business, as long as she does what's required here. By the way, you look ravishing."

"I should! I spent the entire day shopping for the perfect dress so you wouldn't forget what I looked like. You said you would call today, but you didn't."

"My time isn't always my own on the set. You should know that by now. But I must say that you outdid yourself tonight. It would be hard for any man to keep his eyes off you. Now, let's keep Bridgette company before she wears a hole in my rug. Randolph escaped again, and Barry is out looking for him."

"That animal," Lana scoffed. "If he was mine, I would have him put to sleep. The city is no place for a St. Bernard. He should be living in the Arctic. By the way, are Mitchell and Suzi coming? I heard there was some kind of a row at their place recently."

The front door opened and closed three more times before Lana poked her head back in the kitchen to announce that dinner could now be served.

I sliced bread and put in on the table at the same time I served the salads, but I felt like crying inside. I wasn't a domestic, and I hated being ordered around. Ken had never demanded that I do anything the entire time we were married. We each knew what our roles in the marriage were, but we were partners in everything. That meant picking up the slack, regardless of which one of us needed additional help. He had washed dishes and done the laundry far more times than I'd ever mowed the lawn or taken the cars to the shop for repairs.

"What's this?" Lana's nostrils flared with distain after I had cleared away the salad plates and put a bowl of stew on the table in front of her. Since she was acting as hostess, I had made the assumption that she should be the first one to get the main course.

"Summer stew," I responded with a wane smile. "I hope you enjoy it."

Lana opened her mouth to protest, but Peter interrupted. "I know you had your heart set on lasagna, but there was a little setback in the kitchen before anyone got here, and Ms. Holden was gracious enough to fix us another meal."

"We could have gone to Jaspers," she pouted. "You promised us one of Mrs. Newbold's famous meals. This looks like something from the farm."

I winced. It was a farm recipe—one I had learned from my grandmother—but it was also wholesome and filling. People should appreciate the simple things in life more. They would be healthier and likely much happier too.

"Let it go, Lana," Peter said. And regardless of the fact that I wasn't looking at him, I could tell from the tone of his voice that he wasn't smiling as he looked from one guest to another. "Ms. Holden has been kind enough to prepare this entrée, and it's the one we're going to eat. I hope that meets with everyone's approval."

The room was deathly still until Barry McDaniels spoke. "I ate stew all the time as a child, and with fresh, homemade bread I'm game. You others can do as you like, but I'm eating here."

"I suppose if we must, we must," Lana conceded with an exaggerated shrug of her pretty shoulders. "But I do have my heart set on Chocolate Moose for dessert. That wasn't destroyed as well, was it?"

"No, the dessert's fine," I said, struggling to control my rising temper. There was no reason for Lana to be so openly hostile? I had done nothing to provoke her, other than being alive. But when I went back to the kitchen to begin cleaning up, I could hear the dinner conversation above the music playing on the radio.

"What's gotten into you tonight, Lana?" Peter asked. "Ms. Holden is only trying to do her job."

"Maybe so, but there's something fishy about her. I haven't been able to put my finger on it yet, but until I do, I'm going on record as saying that she shouldn't be here."

"And why not?" Barry asked. "I think she's nice, in a warm, homebody way."

"Just so she doesn't get too homey around here," Lana snapped back. "I could swear I've seen her some place before, and she doesn't look like much like a housekeeper to me. Peter needs to get to the bottom of this before everything of value in his home comes up missing. Mrs. Newbold has never been gone without advance warning before."

"While there may be some truth to what you're saying, I think it may simply be a case of that old, green-eyed monster rearing its ugly head. You've never been accepting of any woman, under the age of fifty, who has gotten anywhere near Peter," Barry retorted with a short laugh.

"So what?" was her quick response. "I care about what happens in this house. I've spent plenty of time here and have no intention of sharing Peter with anyone, especially a domestic."

"You're overreacting, Lana," Peter said. "I haven't gotten any bad vibes, and there hasn't been time to find out why Mrs. Newbold left in such a hurry. I promise to find out what's going on but not before we finish eating. You're just upset because she isn't the person you're used to seeing in my kitchen. But that isn't being fair to either of us. You have to know how I feel about you after all the months we've spent together."

"Well, I don't!" she exclaimed. "You've never made a verbal commitment to me."

"I didn't think one was necessary. I was under the impression that we trusted each other."

"Come on, you two," Bridgette cut into the conversation. "You sound like Barry and me before we tied the knot. I was jealous of every woman who even looked in his direction, and she didn't even have to be as attractive as Ms. Holden. She just had to be alive."

Barry clapped his hands. "Well, spoken, my dear. But I thought we were here for a party. Where's the hard stuff, Peter? I think we're all going to need more than a glass of wine before this evening is over."

"I'll join you," Lana said, and I heard the sideboard open.

That was my cue to return to the small bedroom at the back of the house until someone called for me to clear the table again so dessert could be served. I had overheard enough for one evening, and if what I'd been told about people who drank in excess was true, the conversation was only going to get more heated and disagreeable as the night progressed. Alcohol lowered inhibitions and made people careless. That was only one of the reasons I had never indulged.

"Is this what my life has been reduced to, Ken," I whispered as the stark reality of allowing someone else to determine even a portion of how I spent my time washed over me.

My head was in my hands as I sat on the edge of the single bed in the dark. I was too frustrated with myself to bother with turning on a light or closing the door. My loneliness and fear would subside when I left this city behind because I had a family who loved and supported me, but it was getting through the present that had me down.

"I hope you're getting a good laugh over this one wherever you are, Ken," my thoughts continued. "You always told me I was hopelessly naïve and needed a keeper when the outside world got too close. I can't believe I allowed Aunt Lil to talk me into doing this. It's the worst decision I've ever made."

"Now I remember where I've seen you before," an accusing voice said. "You were at Madame Dubois' farewell party. You're related to Lillian Farrow."

My head shot upright. Lana had slipped silently to the edge of my door with a martini glass in one hand and a salt shaker in the other. Apparently, she'd eaten all of the stew she could stomach.

It would have been so easy to go on the defensive, but two wrongs would never make a right. It was one childhood lesson I had never forgotten. "Your memory is correct, Lana. I'm her great niece."

"I knew it! I never forget a face. But if you're related to advertising royalty, then what are you doing here?"

"A favor for a friend," I responded.

"Don't give me that. I saw the way you looked at my boyfriend. You want him for yourself so you devised some diabolical plan to get into his home. Well, I'm putting an end to it right now. He may think you have no ulterior motives, but you and I both know that isn't true. Every woman in this city has her eyes set on Peter."

"That's not true," I responded, forcing myself to my feet. I was a good three inches taller, but the way she carried herself made me feel insignificant. She might not be able to inflict bodily harm without a weapon, even if she chose to try, but I knew what her cutting words could do. "I already have the only man I'll ever want."

"That's good! Then you won't have to make any more aggressive moves towards mine. I'm glad to see that your bags haven't been unpacked. That will make it easier for you to call a cab. I'll make sure Peter knows about your departure."

"What about serving dessert and cleaning up after the party?"

"I'll make arrangements with a temp agency first thing in the morning. It's really lucky for you I discovered your deceit before Peter did. He hates a fraud and will call the police if you don't leave before I tell him what I know."

I had to bite my bottom lip to keep from expressing myself in anything but unladylike words. Lana was positively exasperating. She had everything a man could possibly want—youth, beauty, the regal prominence of a princess and the ability to satisfy primal urges —but what she lacked was evident. There was nothing soft or submissive about her, and those qualities were necessary for maintaining an enduring, fulfilling and peaceful relationship.

The problem was that she had already made up her mind about me, and I couldn't refute anything she'd said with a clear conscience. I was a fraud, but not for the reason she thought. I had no interest in Peter Richards. I had simply been remiss in thinking I could do someone a ill-advised favor without getting caught.

"There's no need for that," I said. "I have every intention of leaving tonight, but I will not run away as if I've done something wrong. I came here because my aunt asked me to do something her housekeeper, Hildie, was unable to at the last minute. If it's upsetting, you have my sincere apology, but I will tell your boyfriend about what you call my deception after his dinner party ends. I see no reason to distress anyone else. Now, if there's something I can do for you, it would be my pleasure to assist. Otherwise, I would suggest you back to the table and enjoy the rest of your meal. There's nothing to be gained by being adversarial. My only intention was to help."

She gave me a look that could freeze boiling water. "Everything about you seems suspicious to me, but since Peter isn't fond of scenes, I'll keep your secret for the moment, but if you don't come clean the moment everyone else has gone, I won't hesitate telling him exactly who you are. Now, this salt shaker is nearly empty. You really must be more careful with your responsibilities if you want a decent recommendation."

I took the salt shaker from her. It wasn't needed for anything now that the main course had been eaten. Then I cleared the table again and took the dessert Mrs. Newbold had prepared to the table. It was impossible not to wonder at the depth of her patience if she had to face Lana often. But then maybe she posed no threat to the moody blonde who was so determined that no one would have the opportunity to steal her man.

While everyone was in another part of the house talking, drinking and playing pool, I cleared the table, put the leftover food away and took care of the dishes. I was ready to talk to Peter

Richards and explain what I could, but asking him to leave his guests so I could clear my conscience and disappear didn't seem like the best way to handle a rather absurd situation.

After what had happened in the kitchen earlier, I knew he was a reasonable man and would find no reason to call anyone about my removal from his property. In fact, he would likely find the entire incident humorous, as long as Lana wasn't there to express her beliefs and concerns and try to turn him against me.

Still, that thought didn't stop me from berating myself over becoming part of a plot that was doomed to failure from the moment of inception. But instead of pacing the kitchen floor in hopes of making the time go by faster, I retired to the housekeeper's room to wait until he had time to talk. The night was warm, but I was still trembling when I sat down on the edge of the bed again. The laughter coming from the room where everyone else was enjoying a pleasant evening penetrated the walls and slipped underneath the doors making me feel more lonely and vulnerable then ever. Since it was only a little after ten, I knew I might have to wait an hour or two before I could set things straight, so I kicked off my shoes and pulled back the top cover.

The light was on in the kitchen, and despite the fact that the housekeeper's room was dark, I would hear anyone who approached the door. I had left it partially open so no one would get any more wrong ideas, but punishing myself for making a poor decision would not stop any of the backlash. In a few hours, I would be on my way home, and I needed some rest. So I lay down on the top sheet, pulled the light quilt up to my chin and closed my eyes.

Regardless of how miserable I felt inside, I was not a person who could hold a grudge or plot revenge against anyone. Lana was only aggressive towards me because she was in love with Peter Richards and afraid of losing him. Having shared a nearly perfect life with Ken, I could understand that any threat to happiness—perceived or real—could arose intense emotions that were not always easily controlled.

So with much conscious effort, I allowed my breathing to slow and my mind to drift towards thoughts more pleasant than the day I had just spent learning things about myself that I hoped could be forgotten. I must have fallen asleep because I found myself back in my home in Boston with the only man I would ever love.

It was my first dinner party as Ken's wife. I had scrubbed, polished, moped and dusted our new home for an entire week wanting to make sure nothing was amiss. My new husband had been a prominent member of the community for years before I met him, and most of his friends were well-established professionals with sophisticated wives and several, well-behaved children. I was a country bumpkin who had been lucky enough to meet and fall in love with a wonderful man—who just happened to be my boss—but I had yet to prove my worth as a well-accepted and competent helpmate.

We had moved into our dream house immediately after the wedding. Ken had seen no reason to wait since he had the money available for a substantial downpayment. While the inside furnishings were still sparse, everything about the house, including its location and yard, were everything I had ever imagined having. We would make changes that reflected our personalities as we felt the need to do so.

Ken had thought I was silly for worrying so much about a party that was being held on the patio. But while I knew my fears were irrational, I couldn't dismiss them. He mowed the lawn, pruned the shrubs and made sure the grill was ready the day before our guests arrived. I swept the patio, washed the windows inside and out and hung colorful, paper lanterns everywhere. Then I made at least a dozen salads and desserts because we'd told everyone this celebration was on us.

We had decided not to have a wedding reception in Boston. His mother had been gone for a long time, and without any close family members to help plan one, he felt that having a party for his closest friends would be best. I was okay with that since we'd had a huge gala in Utah where we received all the linens and small appliances we would ever need. His father had given us a huge check that covered all the expenses when closing on the house as a post-nuptial gift.

I felt like a queen as I held his hand and made the acquaintance of people he had known for a decade or more. I could easily say it was one of the happiest evenings of my life because God had granted my every desire. Whenever I stole a look at my husband's handsome face, my heart literally soared it was filled with so much love and devotion.

The party was nothing fashionable, fancy or daring. It consisted of what I hoped was good food, interesting conversation, and a few games of volleyball and croquet. Ken believed that people either accept others the way they were, or it was okay to let go and move on. I had to concur because life really was too short for either pretenses or games.

After the last guest walked through the side gate, we wrapped our arms around each other and looked up into the dark, summer sky. I could feel tears of gratitude and joy form as I watched the stars dance above my head, but I wouldn't let them fall. I had never felt more safe, complete and joyously alive.

"Did you enjoy yourself tonight," Ken asked as his lips moved across the top of my head. It was a sensory experience that would never become old. "I know it was asking a lot to spring all my friends on you so soon after the wedding, but I was too exited to wait. I want everyone to know just how happy I am to finally have what they've been extolling for years. Creating a family was always a top priority but, regardless of the number of blind date my friends and their wives sent me on, nothing ever clicked until the moment I met you. You looked so young, impressionable and afraid, but I sensed an inner strength that would get you through anything—including my bad behavior. I still feel bad about knocking everything out of your arms, but I always assumed people would see me coming and automatically clear the way."

"And I ruined all those preconceived notions."

"Only in a good way," he responded with a mesmerizing smile. "Everyone appeared to have a good time tonight, and I have you to thank for being such a thoughtful, beautiful and perfect hostess."

"You give me too much credit. My only goal was to make it through the evening without causing some catastrophe with my clumsiness. You haven't forgotten about our wedding dance already, have you? I caught my heel on something in the grass and almost took both of us down. That would have wiped out the cake and at least half a dozen people watching from the sidelines. Besides, it was the least I could do after sabotaging your bachelor party by dragging you off to Utah to meet my extended family before the wedding."

"No one noticed what happened during the dance. I've got you now, Maya Holden—always and forever. And never apologize for having a closely-knit, big family. It's been just my dad and me ever since my mother died. He's told me more than once how much he appreciates being included in family activities he could never provide for me on his own. I can hardly wait to be a father. It will mean the continuation of what we decided to build together when you agreed to be my bride."

"That was the best decision of my life, and I hope I can tell you that we'll be adding to our family soon. I would love a dozen little Holden's running around our home. We truly have been blessed, haven't we?"

"I couldn't wish for anything more," he said, whirling me around in his arms and placing a kiss on my eager lips. "Now, why don't we leave the cleanup for tomorrow. There will be plenty of time, and I'll be home to help. Right now, I just want to lay in the hammock with you and enjoy whatever comes next."

My cheeks flushed scarlet and my heart began to race as he locked the gate and led me towards the row of tall trees beyond the flower garden.

"No," I cried out as a sudden noise in the kitchen shattered my perfect dream. It took a moment or two for me to remember that I wasn't back home in my own bed, and I still had some explaining to do.

I sat upright and waited for something else to happen. The digital clock on the nightstand said it was almost two in the morning. I should have booked a flight while I was waiting instead of allowing myself to fall back into a perfect memory. It made the present even more difficult to digest.

Someone coughed, and then I heard footsteps approaching my open door. I clutched the edge of the quilt to my mouth as I waited for a confrontation that would be anything but pleasant. For the first time since Ken's death, I was truly frightened about my ability to control my own future. I had allowed a woman I barely knew to manipulate me when it was abundantly clear that the suggested charade had every chance of spiraling out of control.

Lana had been very specific in her demands and what would happen if they were not met, and it had been hours since our clash in the kitchen. That meant she'd had plenty of time to state her case and make me look like an intruder who deserved to be reprimanded, if not suitably punished. My side of the story seemed less than plausible, even to me.

By the time a shadow was blocking the light coming from the kitchen, I had pushed the cover away and was sitting upright. It seemed like the most dignified thing to do, but I was no closer to defending my ill-advised actions than when I had unwittingly fallen asleep.

"Are you all right, Ms. Holden? I never meant to disturb you," Peter Richards said as he stood motionless with his hands hanging by his sides. "You should have gone to bed hours ago. There's no reason for everyone inside this house to go without sleep."

I rose to my feet but stayed hidden in the semi-dark. I could tell him what I need to without having him see my face. The less he remembered about me the better. "I was actually waiting for you, Mr. Richards. There's something I would like to explain."

"Lana said something about a disagreement the two of you had earlier, but I told her I didn't want to become involved in one of her petty tirades against my help. I'm not concerned with people's past. I prefer judging them on what I can see with my own eyes."

"That's a compassionate view since you've allowed a virtual stranger into your home. I would imagine there are a lot of women who would take advantage of a situation like this so they could get close to you."

He laughed but didn't move any further into the darkened room. "I'm used to people snapping my picture and wanting a scoop. That's why I try to keep both my personal and professional life as transparent as possible. I've found that most members of the press, whether legitimate or tabloid, will leave me alone if I give them no reason to come around. Besides, I doubt you're some serial killer. If there's something I have that you need or want, you're more than welcome to it."

"I can assure you that I have sufficient for my needs."

"Then why aren't you sleeping? If you're still worried about Lana, it's unnecessary. She wanted to stay over, but I told her I thought it would be good idea if she went home. I wasn't in the mood for any more drama, and we have an awards show to attend tomorrow night."

"That should be fun," I said, glancing towards the outline of his body and wishing I didn't feel so unsure of myself when it came to facing him in more than the dark. He had been nothing but kind to me. He had even helped clean up the mess I had made in his home.

"Fun isn't a word I would use to describe over four hours of sitting in the same place, trying to act interested in everyone's success and listening to almost identical acceptance speeches."

"Even when you're the one making them?" I asked. "I overheard Lana say that you're up for another award while I was serving dessert."

"Lana enjoys being in the spotlight more than I do since she's still trying to land her first big role. I've been in this business for over a decade. I got my break right out of high school and have been going to the same set every day since then. While it's nice to be recognized for the work I do, I'm afraid it has more to do with the storylines I've been given than my acting ability. Some of the men I'm up against have been doing this for more years than I've been alive."

"Still, it has to be an honor having your name next to theirs."

"Are you always so forthright?" he asked.

"I suppose I am."

"Then you won't mind telling me why I heard you cry out when I walked into the kitchen. I'm used to emotional women, but you sounded as if you were in genuine pain—the kind that doesn't come from a broken casserole dish or even Lana's sharp quips. While we don't know each other very well, I've been told I'm a good listener and sometimes strangers really do make the best friends. They can listen without judgment or unwelcome words of advice because they're not personally involved."

I clapped my hand over my mouth as I felt another giant sob rise to the top of my throat. Maybe I did need someone, other than family, to listen to my tale of lost hopes and dreams, but Peter Richards wasn't a man I could confide in. He was a celebrity, and I still needed to explain why I was in his home when I had no legitimate reason for being there.

"Listen, Ms. Holden," Peter continued when I didn't respond. "I'm sorry if I crossed some invisible line. I'm not in the habit of forcing my company on anyone. My main concern was knowing if you were okay. Mrs. Newbold only stays in that room when it's too late for her to go home after one of my parties. I shouldn't presume to know anything about you."

Quite suddenly, the night breeze coming in through the open window seemed to clear away what was left of the cobwebs in my head. I felt like a coward for still needing Ken so much, but our love was a once-in-a-lifetime miracle that would never be forgotten. Still, the best I could hope for right now was not an intervention but a reasonable reaction from the man I had tried to deceive. Then I could go home to my children and forget this horrid horrid trip ever happened.

"It's okay," I replied as I took a tentative step towards the doorway where his lean body was still standing. I had to admire his restraint. Most men in his position would have crossed that threshold without waiting for permission to do so. "I must have dozed off while I was waiting to speak with you. My outcry was simply a response to whatever dream I was having."

"I appreciate your candor, but I would like to see for myself that you're okay. Would it be asking too much for you to step into the light? You might not feel like sharing anything, but I could bring you a glass of brandy. Lana always says it calms her down and helps her sleep better."

A brief smile crossed my lips. Why was it that most everyone in the world thought alcohol could cure any condition? It was a depressant when used in excess, made people do uncharacteristic things and caused lapses in memory. Those were only a few of the reasons I had never indulged.

"That won't be necessary, Mr. Richards. Besides, I'm not exactly looking my best."

"A little smeared makeup and tousled hair doesn't bother me. I've seen women in almost every situation imaginable, but I will respect your wishes. We can talk in a few hours when we've both had a little rest. I just don't want you to feel like you've done anything wrong. We all have bad days, and Lana is prone to exaggerate when she feels threatened."

"Please tell her that she has nothing to worry about when it comes to me," I replied, wishing he would quit being so understanding. I certainly didn't deserve it. "I only came here to help."

"I'll make sure to do that," he said as he stepped away from the door.

The tone of his voice let me know I couldn't leave things as they were and get any rest, so I followed him.

"Please excuse my rudeness," I said my bare feet hit the tile floor in the kitchen. He was standing in front of the sink with his hands gripping the edge of the counter. "My tendency to speak without thinking is one of my least endearing traits. In no way did I mean to imply that you were not a desirable man. I simply meant that I'm not the kind of woman who would become involved with anyone who wasn't available."

He took a glass from the cupboard, filled it with water from the refrigerator and then handed it to me. There was a sadness in his eyes I felt responsible for putting there.

"Listen, Maya," he said. "Just because I'm a television star, it doesn't mean I think every woman I meet is going to fall in love with me, nor would I want that to happen. Lana and I have been together for nearly two years, and I care a great deal about her. But that doesn't mean I'm blind to her insecurities or her tendency to attack others when she's afraid of losing something she wants. In our world, few relationships last, and it's not because we don't want them to. We have to put on certain facades so we're marketable, and sometimes we get a little too caught up in them. I know you weren't trying to be rude, nor were you putting me down. I moved away from your door because it seemed like the right thing to do. You've been in a constant state of turmoil since I got home, and only a complete lowlife would take advantage of what could become a very delicate situation."

"You've been nothing but considerate. That's why I feel it's so important for us to talk."

"We can do that later. It's been a long day and even a longer night. So I'm going to bed, and I would suggest that you do the same."

He left me alone in the kitchen. But even if I tried to sleep, I doubted it would happen. There was too much noise turning summersaults in my head.

Chapter 7

Amazingly enough, I managed to sleep much better than anticipated. I awoke the next morning to the clanging and banging of pots and pans in the adjoining room, and the deep, base tones of a popular melody being sung. Daylight was streaming in through the lone window in the pleasant, but sterile-looking bedroom Mrs. Newbold used when she stayed later than normal. It took a moment to adjust to my surroundings. My head was throbbing from lack of restful sleep, and I was still wearing the light, summer dress I had put on the night before. I didn't bother checking the time as my feet hit the carpeted floor.

Recalling the events of the past twenty-four hours was more embarrassing than painful, but I still needed to set things straight. I would explain my unprecedented actions as soon as I changed my clothes and washed up. Then I would arrange for a flight and call a cab. Telling Aunt Lil what I had done could come later. It seemed a little callous to bother her with my problems before she'd taken care of her own. I just hoped she would be able to find Senator Hastings and convince him to come home. One of us deserved to be happy.

But when I got to the bathroom and saw my reflection in the mirror, I knew something that had always defined me as a person was gone. Deception, along with one moment of inquisitiveness, had distorted my reality and made me see things that weren't really there—like the strange glimmer in my eyes that had not been there before.

"I won't accept it," I said as I splashed cold water on my face to see if it would help. "I only said Peter Richards was a desirable man to cover up my blunder. In no way did I mean that I had even the slightest interest in him, regardless of how understanding, charming and attractive he might be. My heart will always belong to my husband. That's why I'm going back to my family where I can live in my lost dreams for the rest of this mortal existence if it's what I chose to do. They keep me grounded and sane. I don't want to be a woman who allows someone else to influence my behavior, nor do I care who thinks I'm crazy for wanting to live in the past. It's where I'm safe from influences that could make me forget."

I showered as quickly as I could, and while my hair was still wet, I put on a clean pair of jeans and a rose-colored sweater. I might as well get the inevitable over. Then I could put this unfortunate affair behind me and try to move on.

"Mr. Richards, I think it's time we had that conversation," I said as I pulled open the bedroom door. But when I saw him standing in front of the stove, his hands filled with breakfast foods, I felt shaken to the core. "What are you doing?"

"Fixing something to eat. I'm always an early riser and breakfast is my favorite meal, although with my schedule I seldom get to indulge. I thought we could enjoy it together. It seemed like the least I could so after the rough night you endured."

"But that's my job," I responded.

He was wearing a blue t-shirt and cargo shorts and looked as if nothing out of the ordinary had happened between us. But his open kindness was only delaying what had to be done.

"Nonsense. I know my way around my own kitchen, and my mother taught me all the basics when it comes to taking care of myself. I decided when I got out of bed that what you needed was a good breakfast and a little fun. And about this Mr. Richard's stuff. That's what people call my father. My name is Peter, and that's what I would like you to call me."

I glanced over at him with utter amazement. He didn't look as if he'd lost a moment's sleep, but what he was asking of me was impossible if I didn't want to dig myself a deeper grave.

"Is that what Mrs. Newbold calls you?"

"Let's not start with all the questions so early in the day. Mrs. Newbold is twice your age and has been with me since I first bought this house. She's more like my mother than anything else. I know you'll only be here for a few days, but I would like for us to be friends. You're easy to talk to, and I get the feeling that you're not as jaded as some of the other people I meet. That makes you a rather rare commodity around here."

He looked so contrite I felt there was no alternative besides agreeing to at least some of his simple requests. After all, I wasn't really a substitute housekeeper. I was simply doing a favor for one of Hildie's friends.

"You make it rather hard for a girl to refuse, Peter," I conceded, daring myself not to look away. "But only if we can have that talk before this day progresses any farther. Some of Lana's concerns are justified."

Before replying, he placed a package of bacon and a carton of eggs resolutely on the counter. "I prefer drawing my own conclusions when it comes to someone's character, but since it appears that you won't be able to relax until we do, why don't we go into the living room and sit down."

Without waiting for my response, he led me through the dining room, down two steps and into the pleasant room with overstuffed furniture, beautiful paintings and brightly-polished wood I had walked through the afternoon before. Nothing seemed to be out of place, except for six, dirty glasses and several empty liquor bottles that were sitting on the credenza next to the fireplace.

"Please sit down," Peter said, indicating the sofa with colorful throw pillows. He took a high-backed chair several feet away.

I suddenly wished we were still in the kitchen where I had at least done something useful. Maybe confessing everything wasn't necessary. Lana obviously hadn't given my identity away. That could only mean she wasn't sure she had anything that would turn him against me. All I needed to do was stay in the background, keep his house clean and then disappear at the end of the week. I had no intention of taking any money from him, and there was no way he could trace me back to Boston unless he found out something personal about me. It was clear he didn't recognize me from our brief meeting at Madame DuBois party.

"Look, Maya," he said after a few uncomfortable moments of silence. "I know something is bothering you. But you need to know that I could care less about your personal life, or your employment history, as long as you do your job. Mrs. Newbold wouldn't allow anyone disreputable to take her place. She's the most scrupulously thorough person I know."

"That's very kind of you to say considering all the trouble I've caused."

"What's one broken casserole? They're easily replaced."

"You seem to forget that I nearly ruined your dinner party."

"The food was great. And if you're still worried about anything Lana said, you don't have to be. I've already told her that how I choose to run my home is none of her business."

"But that's part of the problem. I know what it's like to be in love, and my very presence here makes her unhappy. That isn't fair."

"Not much in life is fair, Maya. Even the biggest breaks come at a cost. I thought I would be the happiest man alive when I signed my first contract, but I didn't understand what I would be giving up when my dream actually came true. I figured I would be in a position to make my own decisions and live life the way I wanted, but it's not like that. I have a manager, a publicist, a director, a producer, cast members, support staff, the paparazzi and every fan who supports my work to consider. I have to watch every word I say and every move I make or someone will call me on it. Believe me when I say that I understand what it's like to want to run away when things get tough."

"I'm sure it's been very hard," I replied, finding it almost impossible to concentrate on the details of the room where I sat so erect my back was beginning to ache. If everything he had just said was true, he knew how deep disappointment ran, but I couldn't tell him about Ken. Becoming personally involved with anyone else wasn't a risk I was willing to take.

The lines between his eyes deepened before he spoke again. "I seldom tell anyone how I feel. No one really cares as long as I'm doing what's required or expected, but there's an underlying sadness in you that's been tugging at my heart since the moment I saw you leaning over a spilled bucket of water in my kitchen. That unfortunate incident was as much my fault as it was yours. I should have apologized for hitting you with the door instead of demanding to know what was going on."

"You had every right to be upset. I had singlehandedly destroyed your kitchen."

"But I was more disturbed with the mess than your safety. I didn't even ask if you were okay. No wonder you want to leave. You must think I'm some kind of Neanderthal."

"It's not that I want to leave, Peter. It's just that I feel like I'm not doing you any favors by staying. Your home is immaculate, and Mrs. Newbold will be back in a few days. I'm sure you can survive quite nicely on your own until then, and I know it would make Lana happy."

"What about my happiness?" he asked. "I feel like a jerk for the way I acted last night, and I'd like to make it up to you—regardless of whether or not you decide to stay."

"Your apology is accepted, but there's no reason for you to feel like you have to make amends. Let's leave it at saying we've both made mistakes and go from there."

He rose to his feet, crossed the distance between us and sat down beside me. His nearness made me feel lightheaded, and it took every ounce of strength I possessed not to hurry away to my room until I had made arrangements to leave. I didn't want any man, other than the one I had married, getting close to me.

"I suppose we could debate the issues surrounding our meeting until sunset and nothing would be resolved, but everyone has the right to smile and be happy."

"Who says I'm not happy?" I asked. "I just get a little confused sometimes."

"Do I confuse you?"

"No!" I replied a little too abruptly. "You've been a perfect gentleman."

"Ouch," he said with a disappointed sigh. "Don't you know it's a fate worse than death to be called a gentleman in today's society? All the women I've ever met want a man who skirts the edges of the law doing seemingly heroic and noble things. They want someone who is exciting, unpredictable and even a little dangerous. Gone are days when a man gets noticed by an attractive woman for being chivalrous, honorable and dependable."

"Those qualities are important to me. But then most people consider me a little old-fashioned and slightly naive because I appreciate a man who respects women, obeys the law and lives what he believes. It's how I was raised."

He didn't say anything for the longest time. "If you really consider me a gentleman worth knowing, and without ulterior motives, will you let me do something for you?"

"Like what?" I hesitatingly asked.

"Nothing illegal or even compromising. I would simply like to take you away from whatever reality you've been living in for awhile. How long has it been since you've been sailing on the ocean?"

His proposition caught me off guard. "I've never even been swimming in the ocean. I'm not exactly from around here."

"Then before you go back to wherever you think you belong, that needs to be remedied." He reached for my hands and pulled me to my feet. "You've never experienced the ocean until you've been caught up in its waves and felt the tide carry you away."

"That sounds a little scary."

"It's not scary, but the ocean's majesty does tend to put a person in his or her place. It's breathtakingly beautiful when there's no land in sight."

"Even when a person can't swim?"

"There's always a life jacket, but everyone knows how to swim."

"Not me, and it wasn't from lack of trying. I grew up in the desert."

"And there weren't any swimming pools?"

"Of course there were. I just couldn't seem to stay on top of the water."

Peter's eyes were dancing. "Lead swimming suit."

"Along with being afraid to submerge my face. I almost drowned when I was two. My aunt yanked me out of the water in time to save my life, but I can still recall the sensation of floating away until everything turned black."

"So there was no blinding flash of light."

"Hardly! It happened quite fast. "

"That must have been terrifying for a child, but haven't you tried to learn as an adult? Everyone needs to know how to swim. There are large bodies of water all over the country."

"Believe me, I understand the liability that comes from not being able to help someone who might be in trouble. I even took swimming in college, but the teacher said he had never worked with a student who put up such fierce resistance."

"I bet I could get you to swim. All I would have to do is throw you off my boat in the middle of the Pacific Ocean."

"Wouldn't work," I said with a solemn shake of my head. "The sharks would get me if a heart attack didn't."

"Care to make a little wager on that?"

"What kind of a wager?" I asked.

The conversation we were engaged in had a familiar and painful ring. I still hadn't purchased a new rug for the den back home. I wanted to leave everything as it had been when Ken was alive.

"How about dinner at the restaurant of your choice if I can't get you to swim in one easy lesson?"

"And if you can?"

"Dinner anyway. I feel like having fun today. How about you?"

I was so caught up in his enthusiasm that I replied without thinking. "I suppose it wouldn't hurt, but I know there's a little work to be done around here after the party last night."

"That can wait until we get back. There's only one today, and it would be a sin to waste it. I like you, Maya Holden, and not in some perverted or impractical way. You're a refreshing change from the people I usually meet everyday."

"It could only be for a few hours since you have an award's show tonight. Lana would never forgive me if you were late."

"No need to worry about that. I'm not ready to give up on Hollywood yet and know what it takes not to be discarded. But I will take whatever time is available away from the rat-race. It gives me the lift I need to face another day amongst one of the most fickle societies on the face of the earth."

His honesty touched a chord in my heart. It couldn't be easy living the life he had chosen, but he seemed to know how to take advantage of opportunities when they arose. Besides, it wasn't a sin to try something new, and a day sailing the ocean might offer a diversion from worrying about what had brought me to his house in the first place. Perhaps I could even learn something that would help me adjust to the life I'd been dealt if I gave him a chance.

"Then I suppose I should try to find something appropriate to wear. Any suggestions?"

"Something lightweight and comfortable. You might also consider bringing a jacket. I haven't listened to the latest weather report but the spraying water can be a little unpleasant for someone who isn't used to it."

"Yes, sir," I replied with a smile. Maybe Peter Richards really was an okay guy. He was certainly getting to me in a very unpredictable way.

"You need to do that more often, Maya," he said. "You have a great smile. Now why don't you change while I pack a lunch."

"What about the bacon and eggs sitting on the counter? I thought you wanted to eat breakfast."

"We'll have them tomorrow. Some toast and juice will hold me until we find the perfect place to eat, unless you need more than that to survive for a few hours."

"Sounds perfect to me," I replied.

"Then it's settled. I want to show you how I live when no one else is calling the shots."

"What about Lana?" I asked as we returned to the kitchen to prepare for our outing. Regardless of the fact that she had nothing to fear from me, if I went with Peter today and someone found out, it wouldn't be good for anyone.

"Lana will sleep until noon. Then she'll get a massage and go to the salon to have her hair and nails done. That's just how things are done before any public appearance. She has no interest in my activities, as long as I'm not late picking her up. And if you're worried about someone seeing us, I know how to keep from being followed. I'll even tell Lana where we went when I see her tonight if it will make you feel any better. She does plenty of things with her male friends that don't include me. I just want a peaceful day on the ocean and would like to share it with you."

In less than thirty minutes, we were on our way to the garage. Peter was carrying a lunch basket and cooler. I didn't ask what they contained. I merely walked behind him with the blanket and towels he had waiting on the table when I emerged from my room. I wanted to chastise myself for being weak and unable to resist another temptation, but I hadn't felt so lighthearted in months. It was as if I had stepped into another person's life where all the pain, sorrow and weighty responsibility of the past few months no longer sat quite so heavily on my shoulders. All I felt was an acute awareness of being alive. It was a very heady experience.

"We'll take the truck," Peter said as the garage door lifted. "It's what I usually drive when I go to the beach. It gives me room to carry what I need, and few people recognize it. You can put your stuff up front while I make sure we don't lose our food and beverages on the way. While my truck doesn't have all the bells and whistles most people think are a necessity today, I overhauled it as a kid and haven't been able to trade it in for something newer."

"There's nothing wrong with that," I said, looking at the dark blue, Ford pickup with the rounded cab and single seat I had seen the day before. "I'm not a connoisseur of vintage anything, but it reminds me of the one my grandfather drove when I was a little girl. It took us to a lot of fun places."

"That's what I like to hear. This fine piece of machinery belonged to my maternal grandfather—may he rest in peace. He gave it to me when I was twelve and told me I would always have a job if I knew how to fix every part of it. He spent the next three years teaching me all he knew about rebuilding an engine and taking out dents. It was ready for a paint job before he died."

"What a wonderful memory," I said as I climbed inside and waited for him to join me. Just knowing that he valued the more simple things life had to offer made me feel better about joining him for the day.

He pointed out landmarks, so I could get a better feeling as to where we were, as we wound our way through the hills surrounding his home. I loved the early morning hours, and driving with the windows down because the truck didn't have air conditioning wasn't a burden so early in the day. He lived several miles closer to the water than Aunt Lil, and it didn't take long until we turned north on a freeway that ran parallel to the ocean. The parking lots were filled with vehicles and the beaches already crowded. I could see color everywhere from sunbathers relaxing on the sand to surfers riding the waves.

"Do you surf?" I asked, glancing at his profile instead of the passing scenery. I had a feeling that his level of discomfort matched my own now that we had decided to spend the day together. Nothing about our lives was compatible. He was outgoing, charismatic and adored by countless numbers of women around the globe, while only my closest neighbors and the people at church even knew my name.

"I've been on a board a time or two, but it takes years to master that sport. And quite frankly, I prefer to spent what limited leisure time I have away from the crowds. That's why my boat it docked at a little marina further up the coast where wanna-be journalists and photographers have little reason to go. Besides, all their efforts will be focused on being in the right place for tonight's festivities. That should give us plenty of time to make it back to the house before the lights on the cameras start flashing."

"What if we run into something unexpected?"

"Quit worrying about things that haven't happened. I always carry my cell, and my manager knows where I like to spend my Saturdays. He'll send out the calvary if I can't be reached when he needs me."

It was shortly after ten when we pulled into a private marina where Peter had to show a pass to get through the gate. For as far as my eyes could see, small sailing vessels of every size, shape and color were lined up along the sides of wooden docks. There was a clubhouse and several fueling stations. Owners were already scrubbing down decks and backing carefully out of their stations. At least one man in a uniform was patrolling the area.

Peter smiled as he opened his door, climbed out and stretched his arms towards a brilliant, blue sky. The smell of sea weed, salty air and marine life penetrated my nostrils as I joined him in the warm morning breeze than was coming in from the ocean.

"I can't think of any place I would rather be," he said, removing the strap that kept the containers in the truck's bed from bouncing around or blowing away. "The freedom that comes from being on the ocean is the drug of choice for me. I would live on my boat permanently if it wasn't so far away from the studio."

"But then it wouldn't be a place for retreat," I responded as I gathered the things I had brought into my arms.

"Smart woman," he replied. "I knew there was a reason I wanted to share this day with you. I hope you won't be disappointed when you see my lady. She isn't large and glamorous, but she's sturdy, fast and all mine. There's sleeping room for four inside the cabin and plenty of space for supplies. I could be away from shore for a month and not run out of essentials."

"It sounds like you're ready for anything."

"I like to keep my options open, but I'm on set five days a week. I leave home at four in the morning, and I'm lucky if I make it home by seven or eight at night. That doesn't leave much time for anything but dreams."

The vessel he led me to was painted red with white trim and had highly polished, dark wood on the deck. He put the lunch basket and cooler inside the cabin before helping me aboard.

"She's lovely." I said as I tried to steady myself against the slow rocking beneath my feet. I had never been aboard anything larger than a motorboat that pulled jet skis on Lake Powell and hoped I wouldn't get sick.

"You don't have to pretend that she's anything spectacular. I know her weaknesses, but she's perfect for me," he replied, taking the blanket and towels from me. "Would you like a tour before we weigh anchor? I think I even have some dramamine below. I forgot to ask if you get seasick easily."

"I'm not sure how I'll feel once we get underway," I responded as I followed him down some stairs and stepped into a room that was a combination kitchen and living area. Lights hung at intervals along the tops of the walls so it was easy to see everything as I swung around. "Like I said before, I've never been on the ocean and would hate to ruin the day."

He opened a cupboard, removed a small box and tossed it to me. "Then I want to make sure your first trip is as pleasant as possible. Why don't you take one of these just to be on the safe side. It shouldn't take long to kick in. There's a bedroom and bath at the other end, and the couch pulls out into a bed."

I followed him behind the stairwell to the rooms beyond. While it wasn't a large space, it was functional and every bit as inviting as any travel trailer I'd seen advertised. "This really is nice. I can see why you like to spend time here."

"It's my home away from home. Why don't you grab a bottle of water from the fridge and take a pill while I make sure everything is ready for our departure."

He left me standing in front of a full-sized bed. I heard him take the stairs two at time. He was giving me permission to look around. But after my invasion of his workroom the day before, I did nothing more than poke my head inside the bathroom before getting the water and swallowing one of the pills. Then I put what remained in the box back in the cupboard and joined him on deck. I watched as he pushed knobs and dials on the instrument panel.

"Did you always want to own a boat?" I asked.

"Not really. I was born in the midwest away from any large bodies of water. But when I decided to come here, I figured I owed it to myself to try most everything at least once. I went skydiving, rock climbing and even tried my hand at flying a small plane. But it was the ocean that captured my heart. I decided after the first year that if my career tanked I would sail the oceans and see everything this beautiful world had to offer."

"I bet Lana would be thrilled to go with you."

"Hardly!" he responded as I heard the boat's engine engage. "She's only been on board once. She said it was too confining, and she wasn't a fan of anything that ruined her makeup and messed up her hair. It was her way of not criticizing my investment in something that needed a whole lot of work."

I took another look at the freshly pained deck and polished chrome. "I think you boat is charming."

"It's changed a lot of the past few years, but when Lana saw it there wasn't a speck of paint anywhere. She even picked up a sliver walking across the deck in bare feet. I'm afraid she merely tolerates my obsession when there are so many other things we could be doing."

"That's sad, but it's hard to believe she hasn't come back to see how much work you've done."

"Lana's not a sun bunny like most of the other women around here. She comes from an affluent, New York City ancestral line where everything was diamond-studded and glamorous. She's only here because there are more opportunities to become famous for more than club-hopping and spending the family fortune."

"I went to New York City once," I said, not wanting to spend the entire day talking about my nemesis. "I didn't see all that much glamour, just a lot of people who made me nervous. I'm sure she'll be back now that you have it all fixed up. She loves you."

"So she says, and I do care about her, but you can't change another person's basic nature. I guess I wouldn't want to even if I could."

"I think that's wise, but I would like to ask you one question before we leave the shore, if it's okay."

"Fire away, as long as whatever you want to know doesn't crush my tender heart. I know men aren't supposed to be emotional, but most of the ones I know feel things rather deeply. They just don't want to admit it."

I looked up into his dark, brown eyes and smiled. No wonder Peter Richards made such a good actor. He was handsome, virile, passionate and attentive, but he was also in-tune with the part of his nature provided by his mother's DNA. That made him a rare find for any woman who might be looking.

"My question is generic. I only wanted to know how your boat got her name? *Shattered Lady* doesn't inspire much confidence."

"Spoken like a true land-lover," he said, nodding towards a bright, yellow lifejacket on the deck before the boat began inching backwards. I picked it up and then reached towards the nearest railing. "It came with the name, and after Lana's rejection it seemed to fit."

"It's certainly not one that could easily be forgotten, but from where I'm standing, she needs something more lighthearted and happy now that she's fully restored?"

"Like what?" he asked.

"I don't know. I'm not nautical."

"How about *Miss Maya*? That has a nice ring to it."

His eyes found mine again as he turned his head away from the rippling water behind us. I hadn't been fishing for a compliment, but that didn't stop my heart from feeling like some wire had been tripped. I knew what being shattered felt like, and I wouldn't wish the experience on anyone.

"Don't be silly," I replied, dropping my gaze and looking out to sea. The ocean was immense, and I felt as if I was about to be swallowed up in it. "Lana would only want to sink it if you did."

"That may be, but I doubt she'll ever see it again. Now, where would you like to go? I want to make this day unforgettable, and there are some incredible places to see."

"You're the captain, so I'll leave our destination in your capable hands. I'm only here because you made me an offer I couldn't refuse."

"In that case, what about Mexico? We could be back in a couple of days."

"I've never been there, but I don't have a passport with me."

"Neither do I, but that wouldn't be a problem as long as we don't go ashore. We could eat the provisions I have stored away, sleep under the stars and think about nothing but relaxing."

"While that sounds delightful, you have an award's show tonight, and I would hate to be the one responsible for disappointing your fans. They expect you to be there to receive your award."

"What makes you so sure I'll win? I'm up against some very talented actors."

He didn't give me a chance to respond. We were moving forward now, and I knew it wouldn't be long until we left the marina behind. I was ready to cast my problems aside for a few hours—to be free from the pain, the frustration, the responsibility and the loneliness of the past eighteen months. The problem was, I knew that whatever I experienced with Peter was nothing more than a momentary illusion of freedom from both our worldly cares. Once we returned, we would go about our normal routines as if this interlude had never occurred.

I watched the colorful boats that lined both sides of the docks as Peter maneuvered us closer to the open water. How Ken would love this. He was always open to new adventures. I was the one to drag my feet, except when it came to giving our children the experiences they needed to grow into confident, productive adults.

I had called them every morning, except for today. They were having a marvelous time with their grandparents and extended family members. Kenny was learning how to drive a tractor, feed cattle and change water. I kept cautioning my father about keeping a close eye on him. He was a city boy who had always lived a very structured life. As for Landi, my mother was keeping her busy with activities that would culminate in entries at the county fair. She was learning how to make jam, bake pies and sew a straight line on a sewing machine. She wouldn't tell me exactly what she was making, but I had a feeling it was an apron or a skirt with elastic at the waist. That's how my mother had started my sewing experience.

"Hey, Maya, what happened to your smile?" Peter asked as we watched the boat in front of us leave a trail of white, manmade waves. We would take off as soon as she was far enough away. "You aren't sorry for coming already, are you?"

"Not at all," I replied with a shake of my head. "I was just thinking."

"That's never a good sign, although I do spend a lot of my time out here contemplating what my life might have been like if I hadn't chosen acting as a career. Half of me wants the attention, the money and the honors, and the other half of me wants to leave it all behind and sail off into the sunset with a woman I love where anything imaginable can happen."

"I suppose it's hard for anyone to leave dreams behind."

"You sound as if your life isn't all you wished it could be either."

"It's not, but rare indeed is the truly happy person."

We were underway again, and I was glad because I didn't want to tell anyone what was really in my heart. I had known complete happiness with Ken, but that part of my life was over, and somewhere there had to be at least a modicum of peace.

But instead of revisiting my past as I so often did, I pushed my fears aside. They would come back soon enough, and I wanted to enjoy the sense of release that came from flying through the whitecaps with the damp wind blowing through my hair and the salty, ocean mist adding a glistening sheen to my upturned face. The heaven's were an unclouded blue above my head, and I felt a closeness to deity that had not been there since the moment I learned that my husband had been injured while trying to help someone else.

"You want to steer?" Peter shouted after we had been alone on the open sea for long enough for me to get my bearings.

"I'm not sure that would be advisable," I called back above the sound of the boat's motor and the crashing of the waves. "I'm perfectly content being a passenger and wouldn't want to wreck the *Shattered Lady* after all the work you've put into her."

"That's not going to happen with me showing you how it's done. You simply replace my hands with your own. It's not that much different from driving a car, unless the waves become rocky. I'll take over if they do."

Peter stepped back, and I found myself sliding underneath his arm and putting my hands on the black, smooth surface of the wheel.

"Just make sure there's nothing in the way before changing courses," he instructed as his hands came to rest on my shoulders.

His close presence was disconcerting, but I felt a moment of genuine panic when his warm breath brushed over my ear. I hadn't been that close to a man since becoming a widow, and I was glad the thickness of the lifejacket prevented any further physical contact. I just hoped my knees wouldn't give way. I could feel them shaking as I tried to remain upright.

"See that outcropping of rocks in the distance," Peter said, pointing in the direction of an old lighthouse a few miles away. "That's where we'll have lunch, and then I'll show you a few other coves I've discovered over the years. These waters used to be filled with treasures brought to the coast by explorers and settlers who had more money than sense. That's when pirates roamed the seas and took whatever they pleased."

"Have you ever found anything that was left behind?"

"I have a few Spanish coins but nothing that will make me rich. Anything of real value was found long ago. It's how many of the ancestors of the truly wealthy in Los Angeles became that way. I've always enjoyed history, and listening to the stories some of the old-timers in the marina tell only fuels my imagination. I often wonder what kind of person I would have been if I had lived during those years."

"You would have been a dashing, sword-carrying pirate who rescued damsels in distress and ran your hands through the contents of your treasure chests."

"That's what I think too, but most of them were far from being honorable men. Hollywood is responsible for creating the anti-hero —that man, or woman, who breaks the law and gets cheered on for doing it."

"We do seem to enjoy rewriting our past and distorting the present. The true heroes are people like Washington, Lincoln, Victor Frankl and Martin Luther King, but I think you need to take over. Those cliffs are getting closer, and there doesn't appear to be much of a beach."

"Why don't we do it together."

It was crazy, but a sudden flash of longing made me feel lightheaded. I wanted to be important to someone again. Not important as a mother, child, sister or friend, but important as a woman who was loved by a man. The thought was terrifying, and I forced it from my mind just in time to see a jagged mass of rocks a few feet in front of us.

"We're going too fast," I cried out.

Memories of the avalanche that could have left my children orphans were coming back with such clarity that my head flew backwards and landed on Peter's chest.

"Oh, ye of little faith," he responded, removing one hand from mine. "We're not going to crash. I've been here a hundred times and know exactly how deep the water is."

He pushed up on the lever that was supplying gas to the engine and inched the boat forward until we were just a few feet away from a shoreline that was nothing like the sandy beaches we had left behind. Driftwood was scattered everywhere—large and small pieces whose bark had been stripped clean by the pounding of briny water. Perhaps this was where he came to get the wood for his carvings. There was certainly plenty of unique remnants to pick from.

"Why don't you do the honor of letting down the anchor," he said as the engine quit running, and he stepped back so I could move away from him.

I scurried away. Ken had been the center of my life for almost fourteen years, and I would never stop loving him. But Peter was making me feel things I thought had been buried forever.

"Ready to go?" he asked after I managed to lower the heavy, silver piece of metal into the water so the boat wouldn't float away while we were ashore. He had the hamper carrying our lunch in one hand and the cooler in the other. The blanket I had brought from the house was thrown over one shoulder.

"Sure," I replied, removing the unbecoming life jacket and stowing it beneath a cushion in the seating that ran along both sides of the main part of the boat. "Why don't you let me carry something."

He extended the wicker basket in my direction. I watched the way the muscles in his upper body rippled beneath the light, damp shirt he was wearing as he made his way to the edge of the boat and then dropped to the ground without relinquishing either the cooler or the blanket. I handed the basket to him and then waited until he was ready to help me. Landing on the shore with my face in the sand wasn't any more appealing than twisting an ankle. But when his hands caught my waist, I almost wished I had been brave enough to jump the way he had.

I didn't like the emotions that were coming to the surface. They made me feel as if I was being unfaithful to Ken, but instead of letting Peter see my distress, I glanced up at the towering, cylindrical lighthouse that seemed to dominate the small island while he picked up what we had brought. Its surface was smooth and painted a brilliant blue, red and white so it would stand out from the grey rocks, green trees and low-growing shrubs that surrounded it. I wondered if we would climb the winding pathway so I could walk the circular stairs to the top, but Peter was the one with the schedule to keep.

"It's gigantic!" I exclaimed. "Is it deserted?"

"More or less," he replied. "The Coast Guard no longer uses it to spot smugglers and vessels that might be in trouble, but they still patrol the inlets and try to keep vandals away. It's a historic landmark, and I would hate to see it destroyed."

"So would I," was my response. "Too much of our past is being dismantled by people who have no conception of what others sacrificed to give us the freedoms we no longer seem to cherish. It must have stood on these rocks for decades warning sailors."

"There's no doubt about that. While I support people's right to disagree with how things are done, nothing is ever accomplished by violence or destruction."

"We sound like a couple of mature adults who have grown beyond the need to protest with every movement that comes along."

"I still let my views on some things be known, but I have no desire to be ruled by the masses who have nothing better to do than incite riots, bash others and destroy their communities. Maybe that comes from attending my share of parties as a kid where underage drinking, among other things, went on. But I can honestly say that I've never used illegal drugs, stole anything or sprayed obscenities on someone else's property. I have more self-respect than that."

"That's good to know. I stayed out of trouble because I knew what would happen if I didn't. My parents believed that a well-deserved spanking was good for a child. But I do remember some of the boys in my school accidentally burning down one of our neighbor's barns because they thought it would be the perfect place to set off fireworks and smoke a little weed."

"Did they get caught?" he asked, taking my elbow and leading me away from the cliffs and the water.

"Eventually, but they were kids, and the farmer didn't want them to end up with prison records so he didn't press charges."

"That was forgiving of him."

"It's the way things were done where I grew up, but the poor man was struggling financially anyway. People need what farmers and ranchers produce but have no idea the risks they take just to keep planting their crops or raising their animals. When his insurance wouldn't cover the cost to replace the barn, I think he just gave up. I don't know what happened to him or his family, but one day I just heard they were gone."

"Sometimes hope is the only thing people have. My great-grandmother refused to believe that her husband wouldn't be coming back from World War II, even though he was listed as missing in action after his first battle on German soil. She raised four children on a small government pension, supplemented by cleaning office buildings at night. She lived to be ninety-one, and no one ever heard her complain."

"Did she ever find our what happened to her husband?"

"No, but that didn't stop her from growing and living. She took strangers into her home and gave them everything she could. I had more adopted relatives than anyone in the county."

"She sounds like a wonderful woman."

"My Nanna was the best! I just wish there were more individuals like her today—ones who believe in hard work, integrity, and the importance of family life."

"There are still people like that," I said as my heart began to race. Peter had said nothing about religion, but if he wasn't a Christian, he certainly sounded like one.

"Not in Hollywood," he responded. "Most folks here want two things—fame and money—and they will go to almost any lengths to get it."

"If that's not what you want, then why do you stay?" I asked as he spread the blanket on a smooth stretch of sand in a cove that looked as if it would only see water when high tides came in.

"I'm not saying that I don't want those things. I'd be a fool if I didn't, but the older I get the less important they seem."

"Does that mean you're getting ready to settle down and raise a family."

Peter looked at me and smiled. "I've thought about it, but it can't be done alone."

"Lana seems more than willing to make a commitment."

"Only in front of others. We've talked about the possibility of marriage, but she wants to get her career off the ground first."

"What does she do?"

"She's a modern, interpretive dancer, among other things."

"I've heard of that, but aren't there more opportunities for dancers in New York City than there are here?"

"That's part of the problem. She thought she could make it big in films like Flashdance, Dirty Dancing and Grease, but musicals have lost their appeal. Action-adventure and fantasy have captured the interest of moviegoers worldwide, and they're much cheaper to produce."

"Why is that?" I asked.

"Because most of what is seen on the screen in today's blockbusters is computer-generated. That means fewer people are needed to build sets, supervise stunts, do hair, makeup and costumes or take non-speaking roles. Moviegoers just want to see alien or mythological creatures, human beings in danger and things being blown up or destroyed. They no longer seem care about mortal's real problems."

"That is a rather sad commentary on our society."

"But it is one most people have accepted without questioning where the philosophy came from. My biggest concern with Lana is not in her ability to achieve her dreams, but the fear that she'll compromise both her talent and her health if she doesn't quit drinking so much. She says it helps her relax and be more creative."

"I'm sorry," I said, sitting down on the blanket but waiting to open the basket or cooler until he told me it was time to do so. It wasn't exactly warm in the shade of the rocks but at least we would see the crabs and other forms of animal or sea life before they made it to where we were.

We didn't say much of importance after that. I think we were both a little afraid of getting into a discussion that would take away the simple beauty of the day. Peter had bread, cheese, some deli meat and green, stuffed olives for us to eat with fresh fruit and bite-sized frozen eclairs for dessert. He drank red wine while I had a bottle of water. He didn't ask why I refused to indulge.

I watched the gulls soar overhead and listened to the waves crashing against the shoreline while he told me about his latest storyline. Since I had no idea who his character even was, I merely tried to respond with what I hoped were appropriate comments. We looked for seashells after putting the things we had brought with us back on the boat, but our main finds were broken pieces of glass, an old, green bottle and a stranded, pink starfish that he threw into the water so it wouldn't dry up and die.

I tried not to trip over anything when he took me up a small incline so I could get a better look at what lay on the other side of the island, but there wasn't time for a tour of the lighthouse. He promised to bring me back another day when a pressing engagement wasn't keeping us from further exploring. I knew that would never happen, but it felt good just hearing the words. I was glad I had come on our spontaneous excursion until he asked my opinion about an interesting-looking piece of driftwood. That inquiry brought back my unintentional snooping from the day before, and I had to bite my lip to keep from admitting what I had seen in his workroom without asking permission.

People were milling about everywhere when we returned to the marina. Peter spoke to several of them while he secured his boat and made preparations for our drive back to the city, but he didn't introduce me to anyone. I kept my head down while we walked down the pier and through the parking lot to his truck. He had taken a risk by spending part of his day with me, and I hoped neither of us would live to regret it.

Chapter 8

The phone on the wall was jingling when we walked through the kitchen door later that afternoon. I was a little sunburned and confused, but my outing wasn't an experience I could share with anyone. My parents would think I had lost my mind, Landi would want to make a mountain out of less than an ant hill, and Aunt Lil would use it as ammunition while she tried to convince me that she had been right all along about my need for more than just family-related companionship.

"I'll get it," I said, crossing the threshold in front of him.

"Is Peter there?" A sultry voice demanded the moment I had the receiver to my ear.

"Yes, he is. He'll be with you in a moment," I replied.

My day in the sun had come to an end, and it was time to tell Peter the truth. No more hedging. No more excuses. I would explain what I had done as soon as his conversation with Lana ended.

But the dialogue they were having seemed to drone on forever. And from the changing looks on Peter's face, I knew it was anything but pleasant. I finished unpacking the picnic basket and wiped out the cooler as quickly as I could and tried not to listen. But that was impossible since we were both in kitchen, so I slipped away to my room and lay down on the bed to think.

Ken would not completely disapprove of what I had done by going with Peter, I decided as I put my arms over my forehead and closed my eyes. He wanted me to get on with my life, but following Aunt Lil's lead and taking risks in a foreign culture wasn't the way to anything productive or permanent. While today had provided a much-needed diversion from a world that had lost most of its joy, it had mostly reminded me that I wasn't ready to even think about meeting someone new. I wanted to be with my husband again, and no mortal man—regardless of how charming and accommodating he might be—had the ability to make me forget.

A knock on the door interrupted my reveries, and Peter asked if he could talk to me. So I rose to my feet and opened the door for him.

"You weren't resting, were you?" he inquired, looking at the rumpled bedcover with one eyebrow arched.

"No, I was just thinking."

"Pleasant thoughts, I hope."

I tried to stifle a fervent sigh. "What else would they be after such a pleasant day on the water? If I am prone to seasickness the Dramamine certainly took it away. Is there something I can help you with? I know there isn't a great deal of time before you have to leave."

"My tux is waiting in the closet, and it doesn't take long for me to shower. I just thought you might like to go to the awards show with Lana and me. You said this morning that you thought it might be entertaining."

"I didn't say that so you'd ask me to go with you."

"I know, but it might be a novel experience since you've never been to one before, and I'm sure I could rustle up another ticket. It might be in the back of the theater, but there are always last minute cancelations."

"Tonight is for you and Lana. Besides, I can't do everything in one day."

"She doesn't care if you come."

"Are you sure about that?" I asked as my hand seemed to clutch the door nob more tightly than was necessary. "You know as well as I do that she isn't overly fond of me."

"Come on, Maya," he almost pleaded. "I don't want our day to end, and I know you would enjoy watching the proceedings as part of the live audience. Everybody will be dressed to the hilt, especially the ladies. Most of them have been searching for the perfect evening gown for months. Men have it easier since styles with tuxes seldom seem to change. Only designers seem to know if a male celebrity is recycling."

"I thank you most appreciatively for your kind offer, but an awards show is no place for me. Besides, I have nothing to wear, and I don't want to be responsible for causing any more rifts in your relationship with Lana."

"You haven't caused any rifts. I thought you and I were becoming friends."

"We are, Peter, but I'm a realist. We live very different lives. I'll watch you on television while stuffing my face with popcorn."

"I think I would rather be doing that. It's going to be a long evening of pretense and adulation, and I do like popcorn."

My smile was immediate. "Then I'll save some, but right now, you need to get dressed before Lana shows up and figures out that you weren't alone on your boat all day. I'm supposed to be your housekeeper, not an honored guest who was treated to an adventure most women only dream about. Did you tell her about what we did?"

"Destroying her evening when she has a captive audience is not the action of a rational mind, and it would throw you into a spotlight I'm more than certain you would find unpleasant. The media can be ruthless when they get wind of what could turn into a provocative story."

"Then it really is best that I don't play into anyone's hands. What we did today was fun, but it can't happen again. In a few days Mrs. Newbold will be back, and then both our lives will return to normal. I hope you have a wonderful and profitable night. I'll be rooting for you."

"Just promise me that you won't sneak away while I'm gone? Despite how Lana might feel, I like having you here. You've made my house feel like a real home."

I swallowed back a sudden bout of remorse. Perpetuating lies and keeping secrets was not the way I'd committed to live. But I couldn't walk away without acknowledging what I had done, and

Peter already had enough on his mind for one night. My confession would have to wait until later.

"We'll talk when you get back," I said.

His look of concern immediately vanished. "In that case, I suppose I do need to hurry. Lana was going to meet me here. It would save over an hour of back and forth driving, but there was a malfunction with her dress and . . . "

"You don't have to explain. Just do what you must. I'll see that everything is straightened up around here."

I almost placed my hands on his chest to push him away but decided that additional physical contact would only cloud my judgment. I had stood within the circle of his arms and felt his heart beating. I didn't know about him, but that experience had profoundly affected my self of well-being.

It didn't take long until the kitchen was tidy, and I was moving on to the rest of the house. I straightened everything that was out of place and threw the empty liquor bottles away. Then I wished Peter a good night and told him to be safe when he emerged from his bedroom looking like the television star I had only imaged him to be. Without conscious thought, I watched him leave the house through the back door. But I wasn't prepared for the moment of regret that washed over me when I heard the garage door open and close. I could have gone with him, but I let propriety, fear and a certain amount of guilt stand in my way.

With nothing of importance left to do, I took shower and put on something comfortable before fixing myself a bag of microwave popcorn. Once it was in a bowl, I grabbed a soda from the fridge and made my way to the great room. It felt odd sitting on the sofa in front of Peter's 70 inch plasma screen, but I did it anyway. And then with the remote in my hand, I surfed through the channels until I came to the one that was covering the award's show.

There was a two-hour interval until the programmed aired. I hoped Peter and Lana would make it in time. I wanted him to be happy, and I wanted him to win. While I watched a portion of the news and a program about the mating rituals of African lions, I ran my fingers through my damp hair and contemplated what I had knowingly allowed to happen. Playing Peter's housekeeper was a mistake, but going with him on his boat was a recipe for a fiasco. If the media got wind of our outing, they would make a mockery out of an innocent, platonic friendship. And I never wanted to be labeled as Peter Richards' mystery woman or lover. It would be an insult to both of us.

The show was less than riveting since I didn't know any of the people involved, but I couldn't bring myself to watch anything else. I waited with what could only be described as an aching knot in the pit of my stomach to see his face. And then his name was flashing on the screen as a nominee for best actor in a daytime series and a few scenes from his show were shown.

A second camera cut to his face, and there was Lana, in a dress of silky amber, clinging to his arm and smiling as if there was nothing more important than being with him. She jumped to her feet when his name was changed from contender to winner and placed a long, searing kiss on his lips. His acceptance speech was brief. He thanked his parents, his colleagues, the producers, directors and writers for the honor but didn't mention anyone else. When the camera passed over them again, Lana had her head resting against his shoulder.

Peter didn't come home that night. I knew his whereabouts was none of my business. I had no claim on him, but it was the first time I had felt even a remote sense of betrayal. He had led me to believe that we would talk when he got back, and he'd left me dangling.

I awoke to tears of frustration but had no one to blame but myself. What I had initially done wasn't such a bad thing, but I needed to remove myself from further temptation before something that couldn't be explained away happened. I would leave Peter a note and get out of his house. I simply wasn't meant to be a member of society at large. I needed my family and something productive to do. Without that, I was a walking disaster and fair game to anyone's manipulation.

The jingling of the telephone on the wall in the kitchen startled me from my dismal musings, and I hurried to answer it. "Peter Richards' residence."

"Maya, darling," a familiar voice responded. "I was hoping to catch you."

"Aunt Lil!" I said as my brow knit in confusion. "I thought you were in Switzerland."

"That was my intention, but plans change. I need to talk to you in person. How soon can you be ready? I'll have Otto pick you up."

"I'm ready now. It will just take a minute to throw what I've been using into my suitcase. You don't know how glad I am to hear from you. Things have only gone from bad to worse since you left."

"Let's leave the rhetoric until we can speak privately. Nothing about what I've asked you to do has changed."

"Please don't say that. Lana knows who I am. I've just been waiting for Peter so I can explain my side of the story. He promised we would talk when he got back from the award's show."

"Don't hold your breath when it comes to that," she replied. "The post-award's show parties can go on for hours, if not days. I've been to plenty of them over the years. As for Lana, you don't have to worry about her. She won't tip her hand unless thoroughly provoked. Now, be a good, little niece and trust me just a little longer. You'll be back long before Peter gets home, and I really do have your best interest at heart."

"That's a laugh!" I declared as I nearly slammed the receiver back on the wall. Land lines were a thing of the past. Peter had kept his for a reason, but that didn't explain why Aunt Lil had used it instead of my cell. Maybe she was just trying to stir up more trouble while she still had the chance.

Otto picked me up a few minutes later. He didn't say anything as we drove the mostly-quiet, city streets. His jaw was set in a firm line, and I knew the eyes behind his dark glasses were hiding something I needed to know. But questioning him was taboo. He worked for my aunt, and he would never be disloyal to her. He escorted me into the house through a back way.

Aunt Lil was waiting for me in her living room, but she wasn't alone. Senator Hastings was sitting beside her on the red velvet sofa, his arm resting protectively around her shoulders. Neither of them rose to greet me, but my face must have registered nothing short of surprise when I saw them sitting so calmly together.

"Don't just stand there with your mouth gaping open, Maya, sit down," Aunt Lil instructed.

I dropped into the nearest chair. "I didn't expect to see you here, Senator Hastings."

"You're not the only one, my dear, but Lil has an uncanny knack for getting what she wants."

I was just about to agree with him when my illustrious aunt spoke again. "Now Tom, you know you wanted this just as much as I did. We may be old, but no one in their right mind would call us fools. We did the only thing we could"

"What are you talking about?" I demanded, totally at a loss as to why I had been summoned if it wasn't for release from what had turned into a perpetual nightmare.

"I thought you were more perceptive than that," she responded, holding her left hand up to the light so the monstrous diamond on her ring finger could wink at me.

"You didn't," I said, fighting back tears of both surprise and joy as I looked at her serious, yet beaming face.

"But we did! Not only engaged but married."

"How is that possible? It's only been two days."

"One day is all it takes if you know the right people," Senator Hastings replied.

"You make it sound so ordinary, Tom," Aunt Lil interjected. "Do you mind if I tell her the whole, romantic story? After all, she is partially responsible."

He looked adoringly at her. "You can tell her anything you wish, Lil. Just don't make me look too malleable. I still have a reputation to maintain."

"Quit worrying about how your past constituents will react to our news. They're only going to wonder what took us so long. I ran into Tom at the JFK airport. It seems he was in such a big hurry to get away from me that he didn't take into account the layover he had in New York City. My flight was more direct. I saw him sitting in a lounge having a drink when I walked down the concourse and decided that we might as well have it out before we got on another plane. Needless-to-say, one drink led to another. By the time our flight was called, we had decided to stay where we were and work things out together."

Senator Hasting squeezed her hand. "I saw what watching my wife die did to Lil, and I didn't want to put her through that again. I wanted her to remember me as a virile man who could take care of himself. But when I looked into her gorgeous, blue eyes and realized how much she was sacrificing for love, I decided it was time to forget my bruised ego. She had dismissed my first proposal because she wasn't ready to make such an all-consuming commitment. But when I asked if she would marry me for a second time, she told me she would."

"How could I refuse?" Aunt Lil told him. "I always wanted to be your wife, but I didn't want to come between you and your memories of Helen. I know how much you loved her."

"Helen was my first love. I'll never forget her, but my heart is big enough for more than one woman, especially when she's as courageous and selfless as you. I feel honored to have known two such remarkable women."

"That's a heartwarming and beautiful story, but why didn't you wait so I could be at your wedding?" I said as tears slipped silently down my cheeks. My aunt was a very spontaneous woman who obviously wasn't afraid to admit that she'd made a mistake. "You should have had someone standing by your side as you made your vows."

"A lavish wedding was never an option, even if we had married when Tom first asked me. Our public lives have always been fair game for both the legitimate press and the tabloids. But what goes on inside our own homes is private. We didn't want anyone questioning our motives or speculating on what may have gone on in the past. Tom was always faithful to Helen, and we wanted her memory to remain spotless."

"So what did you do?"

"Tom contacted a judge he'd known since his days in Washington, and we were married in a lovely ceremony at his home yesterday. We flew home last night."

"What your aunt isn't telling you, Maya, is that I was trying to do the noble thing for all the wrong reasons. I didn't want anyone to know I was dying, and I certainly didn't want emaciated pictures of me showing up anywhere. So I decided to go away before the medication could no longer control the pain and my body had deteriorated to the point where I could no longer get out of bed on my own. I'm dying from lung cancer, in case Lil hasn't already told you, and it's a beastly way to go."

"Isn't there anything the doctors can do? New treatments are being discovered all the time."

"I waited too long. I thought the nagging cough and shortness of breath would go away by itself if ignored. Besides, the doctors would have told me to quit smoking and a life-long habit is pretty hard to break, especially when the damage has already been done."

"How long have you known?" I asked.

"I think I knew before Lil left, but I didn't get an official diagnosis until a few weeks ago. The doctor wanted me to undergo chemotherapy, or at least radiation, but I told him I had no intention of spending what little time I had left hooked up to machines and in agonizing pain. If I had to die, it would be on my own terms, and not in some cold hospital room where people were only there because it was their job."

"But you're not alone any longer, Tom," Aunt Lil said. "We're going to do this together."

"That we are, but I'm tired and need to lie down. It's been a busy and emotional few days, but it was nice to see you again, Maya. I'm sorry my condition has ruined the remainder of your vacation, but I hope you will listen to Lil. We talked about you almost the entire way home on the plane. Her methods may seem a little unorthodox and extreme, but I've never known her not to get the desired results. She wants you to be happy and she's lived long enough to know that fear—in any of its various manifestations—will only stop you from accomplishing what you were meant to or could."

I drank lemonade on the deck while Aunt Lil got her new husband situated in bed. After the revelation I'd just received, I didn't have the heart to bring up my own petty concerns. I would deal with Peter Richards the next time I saw him, and I would leave my aunt to take care of the senator. I was glad she had finally given in to her secret desires, but my situation bore little resemblance to hers. I had already lost the man of my dreams.

No one came to talk to me until she returned. I wished there was something I could say that would bring comfort, but the journey through loss, grief and acceptance was an individual one.

"I know you're upset about the game I've asked you to play, Maya, but if you could just hold on for a few days longer. Hildie and I have our hands full with Tom right now, or I would send her over to Peter's."

"I would never ask you to do that. You need to keep the senator as comfortable and stress-free as possible. I really don't mind continuing with our charade, but Peter doesn't need a full time housekeeper. And I'm not entirely convinced that keeping anyone in the dark is the right thing to do."

"You're probably right, but I can't deal with anything else right now. Tom doesn't want his condition leaked to the media because reporters have a way of manipulating information to get the a story that will keep readers interested. He's a strong and proud man, and I can't take those things away from him now. As for Peter's housekeeper, she trusted us to protect her job. She needs the money, and she's too old to find anyone else willing to give her a chance. Peter has been kind enough to let her work for as long as she's up to it. She has no retirement, and no one can survive on Social Security these days."

"I guess there's a lot I don't understand," I said.

"Sometimes the truth is more detrimental and destructive than being a little underhanded. I didn't want to disclose everything I knew in front of Tom, but I had Hildie check into the severity of his condition while I was gone. I'm going to keep him active and involved with living for as long as I can, but his time is limited. The doctor says less than three months, but every moment of that time is going to count. After what August did to me, I closed off my heart because I was afraid of being hurt again."

"It's no crime to do that."

"Maybe not, but I went too far. I told myself I could only love one man, and since he betrayed me, I wasn't going to give anyone else a chance. That's really why I ran away from Tom. I was afraid I might lose myself again. Any all-consuming love has the power to do that."

Aunt Lil wasn't trying to be insensitive. She just wanted me to understand that she had finally been willing to take another risk with her heart.

"But you're happy now? That's all that really matters."

"Tom is a wonderful man, but we'll never have a typical marriage. My reluctance to accept his first proposal saw to that. I wish there were do-overs in life. I wouldn't worry about propriety or hurt feelings, and I certainly wouldn't chain myself to some desk because I was afraid of making a few mistakes."

"You didn't know it would turn out like this."

"Well, I should have. I've never admitted this to anyone before, but I'm sorry I walked away from the family. I thought that defying my humble beginnings made me better than people in the community who went to church every Sunday and were dishonest with their neighbors the rest of the week. I decided when I was still in loafers and short stockings that I would never marry a dirt farmer and spend the rest of my life raising babies and praying for rain. I thought that the world, and everything in it, was mine for the taking. So I ran away with August Farrow and never looked back. How could I have been so wrong?"

"You were young."

"Youth is no excuse for stupidity. I exiled myself from everything of value. Sure, I've made plenty of money over the years and have a lot of casual friends, but the past forty-eight hours have taught me that going after the superficial is mostly a waste of time. I envy you, Maya. You have two beautiful children, a husband who adored you and memories that can never be taken away. All I have is a mausoleum of a house, a few servants to mention in my will and enough money left over to keep several charities in the black for a decade or two."

"You have Tom, and he loves you very much."

"I feel the same way about him. He's my entire life, but he's going to die, and I'll be left alone again. How could a merciful God be so cruel?"

It was a question I had asked myself many time over the past eighteen months, but it always came back to faith. Did I trust that my maker had a plan for me, or would I blame him because things did not always go my way?

"Can I call you later?" I asked as she walked me to the front door. Otto would be waiting next to the limo to take me back to Peter's house the moment Aunt Lil gave him the directive to do so.

"You're welcome to call, but I might not be able to talk. Tom needs me more than I ever thought he could. I'll have Hildie prepare a light lunch for us once Mrs. Newbold gets back. That will give you time to sort things out with Peter, and I might know more about Tom's condition by then. I intend to ask very specific questions once an appointment with his doctor can be made."

I left it at that, and Otto took me back to my housekeeping duties. Aunt Lil had given me plenty of food for thought without realizing it. I pondered what she had said the remainder of the afternoon as I waited for Peter's return. But by five, my stomach was growling so loudly that I removed the leftover stew from the refrigerator and cut and buttered a thick slice of homemade bread. It had been over twenty-four hours since I'd heard from Peter. That might not seem like a reason for concern to anyone else, but I was a mother and worrying was just something I did.

After washing and drying the few dishes I'd used, I picked up a magazine from the rack beside the living room sofa and sat down to read. But I was too anxious inside to concentrate, so I called my parent's home. Landi answered the phone. She and Kenny had been busy all day with chores, church and a barbecue with their cousins. They were going to watch a movie before going to bed, so neither of them had time to talk. I told them that was okay, and I would call again tomorrow.

But when Landi asked if I wanted to speak to either grandma or grandpa before she hung up, I made a flimsy excuse about having something important of my own to do. I might be able to fool two children into believing I was having a glorious time, but my parents would see right through my deceit. Since I couldn't tell them about Aunt Lil and Senator Hastings without permission, and my fiasco at Peter Richards' home was something I hoped would remain a secret until the day I died, it was best to say nothing at all.

Chapter 9

I fell asleep sometime in the early morning hours and didn't open my eyes until the sun was streaming into the kitchen. I had left the door to my bedroom open so I would hear Peter if he came in the back way. But that hadn't happened, so I had no choice other than staying the course I had already set and hoping he was okay.

Aunt Lil needed to concentrate on the senator. Mrs. Newbold needed her job. Hildie needed to know I could be trusted, and no one in my family ever needed to know how I had spent the last week of my vacation in Hollywood. All I had to do was keep my mouth shut until Friday, and then I could disappear. Lana would never mention where she had seen me before, and Peter would soon forget that I had ever been in his home. It was obvious that our outing on Saturday had been nothing more than a simple deviation from his normal routine. He was back in his element, and I would soon be back in mine.

I had just finished running a dry mop over the floors and watering the plants when the phone rang.

"Good morning. Peter Richard's residence."

"And a good morning to you. How is my favorite housekeeper?" a cheerful voice responded.

"I'm fine, but I was getting worried," I said as a feeling of relief washed over me.

"Whatever for? I've been out on my boat. I told you I did that whenever I needed time alone to think."

"I hope everything is all right."

"We can talk about my personal life later. Right now, I need a favor."

"I'm at your disposal. Just tell me what you need."

"I guess it isn't so much a need as a request. How busy are you this afternoon?"

"Funny you should ask," I laughed. "I'll be busy trying to find things to keep me busy. Your house is spotless, and you're not even here for meals. I haven't done a moment of honest work since Friday night."

"I'll make it up to you. You can call the dry cleaners and ask what happened to my favorite shirt. They were going to fix a rip in the seam, and it didn't come back with the rest of my things."

"Gladly! Anything else?"

"Yes! You can join me for lunch at the studio."

"You don't have to invite me to lunch," I said, leaning into the counter for support. Peter Richards certainly knew how to deliver a surprise. "I can take a walk around the neighborhood if I get too bored."

"I wish you wouldn't," he said. "Our favorite journalists have been having a feeding frenzy since Saturday night. Occasions like that always bring new liaisons to the forefront and see the demise of others. Besides, it's not safe for any woman to be out walking alone, even in my neighborhood. I wouldn't want you to get hurt."

"You don't have to worry about me. I've been on my own for a very long time and can take care of myself."

"Maybe you can in the country, but this city is like no other on the planet. I've seen what can happen to unattended females. There are rapes, muggings and murders every day of the week, and they don't always happen in the dark."

I was tempted to tell him that I had lived in Boston for almost 14 years and had taken a self-defense class while Kenny took karate, but something stopped me. If I was going to make a clean break on Friday, it might not be wise to give him too much personal information.

"You don't have to caution me about the dangers of living in a city, Peter. This isn't the first time I've been in one."

"I didn't mean to sound patronizing, but I really would like to see you today. Would you reconsider my request if I asked it a different way?"

Quite suddenly, my reluctance seemed a little childish. There certainly couldn't be anything wrong with joining him for lunch at the studio. Friends must do it all the time. Besides, it was a once-in-a-lifetime opportunity and would help me get through another long day away from all that was familiar.

"Say I agree, isn't it a little unusual for an employer to take his housekeeper to lunch?"

"This is no ordinary working relationship, Maya, and what's wrong with doing something for someone else? I promised you we'd talk, but I don't know what time I'll be home. I have an hour for lunch and thought I could show you around the set after we eat. Don't you want to see where I spend most of my life?"

"Of course I do, but what about Lana?"

"She left for open auditions in San Francisco yesterday and won't be back until the weekend if all goes well."

I felt the muscles in my jaw tighten of their own volition. "I hope I'm not responsible. I know she isn't happy having me at your house."

"Her leaving has relatively little to do with you. She's been debating trying out for this production since it was first announced. It's a commitment that will last as long as the show runs with very little time off. Things haven't been right between us for a long time, and we're both hoping a little distance might help clear the air."

"I don't know what to say, except that I'm sorry."

"Me too, but life goes on and people adjust. Right now, I need both a distraction and a friend. I was hoping you could help me with that."

It only took a moment for me to make up my mind. "Say no more. Just tell me when and where."

"Really? he replied. "I thought you'd put up more of a fight, and I haven't given you my best reasons for coming yet."

"And what might those be?"

"Only that I'm the most charming, lovable and thoughtful man on the lot and loads of fun as a luncheon companion."

I chucked. "A regular Casanova."

"Hey, I have to be. It's part of the game."

I heard voices in the background.

"Listen, Maya, I've been called to the set. I'll see you at one in the commissary. Just call a cab and tell the driver where you're going. He'll make sure you get to the right gate. There's some cash in the strongbox in the bottom, lefthand drawer of my desk. The key is under the computer mat."

And with that, he hung up his end of the conversation.

I would never take money from him, but that didn't stop me from reminding myself that this wasn't a date as I changed into a light blue sweater and white denim jeans. Peter was trying to make amends for not contacting me sooner, but his comment about Lana concerned me. Women didn't run away from the men they loved without a good reason. Something had convinced her that now might be the time to make a life-altering decision.

By twelve forty-five, I was standing in front of the impressive-looking black, iron studio gates with canvas sandals on my feet and an oversized shoulder bag dangling down past my waist. I felt curiously like a native Californian.

But as I approached the guard stationed in his small, square booth some of my bravado began to wane. I was walking straight into another foreign environment, and this time I had no one to blame but myself if something less than desirable happened.

"Excuse me, sir," I said in my most commanding tone. "I'm supposed to meet Peter Richards in the commissary for lunch. Can you point me in the right direction?"

"I would be happy to once you show me your pass. It needs to be stamped before I let you onto the lot."

I lifted my shoulders in surprise. "Peter didn't say anything about needing a pass. I'm afraid I don't have one."

"Then you can't go in. Only authorized persons are allowed beyond this station." He put his hand on the holstered gun at his side and patted it almost affectionately. "If I let anyone else through these gates, I would lose my job. There are a lot of crazies running around out there."

"No kidding," I muttered to myself.

This was the second time today I had been warned about the unscrupulous people in Los Angeles, and both times by people who should know what they were talking about. But I wasn't going to let this unfortunate turn of events ruin my day. It had taken too much effort to get where I was.

"How do I go about getting a pass?" I asked. It would do no good to tell him I was a visitor to the city and would be gone in a few days when he already had his orders.

"You'll have to get in touch with Mr. Richards. He's the only one who can clear you, unless you know someone else who works here. I'm sorry about that, but I don't make rules. I only enforce them."

I bit my bottom lip and frowned. "It's not your fault. I'm sure it was just an oversight. Is there any way I can get a message to him? I would hate for him to think I didn't make the effort to come."

"I'm sorry, miss. I'm not authorized to give out private numbers. Why don't you use your cell and give him a call if you're such good friends."

My level of frustration was rapidly rising. I couldn't call Peter because I didn't have his number. He'd called the house on the land line because he didn't have my number either. But if I couldn't think of something soon, he might end up believing I had changed my mind without even trying to let him know.

"Please sir," I said. "I don't mean to be a problem, but I don't have his cell number with me. Could you make that call to the studio for me? I promised to meet him at one, and it's almost that time now."

"Oh, heck," he said, looking at me again. "You don't look like some crazy groupie to me. Give me your name, and I'll see if I can reach him for you."

I did as he asked, and he dialed a number on the phone in his booth.

"Connie," I heard him say. "I have a lady here at the gate who says she's supposed to meet Peter Richards for lunch. Do you know anything about it?"

There was a long silence, except for the guard tapping the end of his pencil on the bottom of the window casing.

I glanced at my watch. It was almost one o'clock. I might already be too late.

And then the guard was speaking to me again. "I'm sorry, miss, but no one at the studio knows anything about you."

"What about Peter? Did they try to reach him?"

"Connie tried, but he didn't answer his pager. I'm afraid there's nothing else I can do. Would you like me to call a cab?"

"Yes, please," I said as an aching loneliness filled my heart. Why had the promise of a pleasant afternoon disappeared like so many other things in life?

I waited while the man in uniform, sitting behind safety glass, made the call. There was no reason to be upset with him. Rules were in place for a reason, and no one inside the gates would get anything done if visitors were allowed to roam wherever they wanted. But I couldn't go back to an empty house where there was nothing for me to do. I would ask the driver to take me some place where I could buy gifts for my kids. Returning to Hurricane without them would be a mistake.

"Your cab will be here in a few minutes," the guard said before I had time to contemplate the real reason behind my disappointment. "You can wait on the bench in the shade if you like."

I didn't like, but it appeared that I had no other choice.

"Thanks for your help," I said, forcing an unfelt smile. "You've been very kind."

"I wish there was more I could do, but we can't be too careful. If we let everyone in, who claims to have a right to be here, there wouldn't be enough room left on the lot for the people who are here to work."

"Perfectly reasonable," I replied as he returned to whatever he had been doing before my arrival. "I suppose someone will tell him I was here."

When he didn't respond, I moved towards the metal bench that sat beneath the branches of towering palm tree. But there wasn't time to sit down before a bright, yellow cab turned the corner. I moved towards the curb so he wouldn't have to wait. I just hoped it wasn't the same driver who had dropped me off less than fifteen minutes earlier. That would be more than a little embarrassing.

"Where to, lady?" A different cabbie asked as I climbed into the back seat and closed the door.

I was about to tell him that I wanted to be taken to the closest mall when I heard someone call my name. I looked out the window to see Peter forcing his way through the ornately arched gate. The cabbie gave me a dark look when I told him to wait, but his angry words were for Peter who had opened my door and was helping me to my feet.

"Hey! What are you doing with my fare? She got into my cab. That means I need to be paid."

Peter thrust a wad of cash into his hand. "I'm taking her to lunch, and this should be enough to cover your expenses."

As soon as Peter was standing upright, we heard the scrunch of metal and the sound of squealing tires. The cabbie was on his way down the street, and I doubted that anything would enhance his foul mood.

"That was close!" Peter said, taking my arm and guiding me across the sidewalk to the guard who had been watching us with studied amusement. "I got all the way to the commissary before I realized I hadn't seen to your clearance. The scene we were taping took longer than expected, and I didn't even think about having someone else take care of it."

"I knew you hadn't done it on purpose."

"You're being more than understanding since you took the time to get ready and come. I'm just glad I got here before the cab left."

"Me too," I said, touched by his honesty. "I was looking forward to another delightful afternoon with you."

His smile told me everything I needed to know. Two friends spending time together wasn't anything to be ashamed of, and he would not have extended the invitation if he had something to hide. "Then let's get you through that gate. I have to be back on the sound stage in less than an hour, and I'm famished."

"Likewise," I admitted. "And I am excited about 'doing lunch' with a bunch of stars. Not many country bumpkins are given an opportunity like this."

Peter Laughed. It was such a pleasant sound to hear. "We're just ordinary people with rather unusual jobs, Maya. You should know that by now."

"I do," I said. "Some of you were even raised outside big city limits like me."

"Hey, Frank," he said as we stood in front of the guardhouse waiting for the gate to swing open. "What do you mean by turning my lady away? Couldn't you tell just by looking at her how special she is?"

The man I had spoken to before looked at us with surprise. "I don't make the rules, Mr. Richards. I just enforce them."

"I know," Peter relented. "I'm the one at fault here, but the next time this young lady shows up at your gate I want you to admit her. She's welcome on this lot any time."

"I'll be sure to do that, Mr. Richards, as long as she has a pass."

The lavish gate swung inward, and I followed Peter past tall, concrete buildings towards the main part of the lot. I had taken the time to see what I could find out about the studio before coming— having the internet at my fingertips was a marvelous thing—but it hadn't prepared me for the immensity of the world I had just entered. The entire compound covered several city blocks and had sound stages as large as apartment buildings that were filled with dressings rooms, costume and props department, makeup booths and spaces large enough for complete sets to be built. There were areas where outdoor scenes could be taped and plenty of room for offices, rehearsal and editing.

I had even reviewed the names of cast members and the roles they played. But now that I had entered a universe that had to be kept from the public, I no longer felt as sure of myself as I had when waiting to be admitted. I didn't want to embarrass Peter by making some slip that would let anyone know I hadn't seen so much as a single episode of the daily drama he starred in.

He stopped walking when we rounded the first corner. "I need a moment to look at you before we go any further."

"Why?" I asked. "Should I be wearing something else?"

"No," he replied. "You look amazing."

"Even better than standing in a room full of water?" I asked.

"I have to take the fifth on that," he teased. "I liked you even then. You looked like a naughty child who'd been caught with her hand in the cookie jar. It brought out the protector in me."

"Really," I said as my bottom lip began to quiver. "I still feel bad about destroying your kitchen and have every intention of replacing the casserole dish."

"That's ancient history," he responded, touching my arm almost apologetically as we moved forward again. "Mrs. Newbold can get another one when she gets back, if she fills the need to. It's not like I have dinner parties every day of the week. I'm just an ordinary guy who prefers most of my meals coming directly from the grill."

"They're probably healthier that way."

"Tell that to the character I play 250 days a year. Dr. Daniel Sutherland was born with the proverbial silver spoon in his mouth. He was supposed to take over his father's empire of crooked deals and unprovable espionage, but he chose to become a crusader in third world countries. Now he's back at the family mansion trying to keep his drunken, socialite mother, and the rest of his over-privileged family, from doing anything that can't be undone. That isn't easy because he spends most of his time solving highly unusual medical cases—some of which reveal that he isn't as squeaky clean as he pretends to be."

"Thank you for telling me a little about him. I feel bad that I've never watched *Secret Shadows* before."

"Never apologize for staying away from what most people consider trash. I would prefer a nighttime gig myself, but it's hard to break into a different genre when most everyone recognizes my face."

The genuine way he expressed himself brought an odd sort of comfort, but people couldn't become real friends in just three days. "I guess that means you've tried."

"You'll see my name in the credits for a few shows, but my schedule keeps me more busy than I would like. I'm glad I found you in my kitchen, Maya Holden. I love the way your eyes dance over the simplest things, and you're not afraid to talk about unpleasantries. You've even given me a compliment or two, and I get the feeling that isn't easy for you to do."

"I suppose I am a little out of practice when it comes to things like that," I said as the smile on my face faded.

"Then I feel doubly grateful that you can see more than just my outward appearance. In this society, no one seems to care what someone else values as long as their own needs and agendas are met."

We were walking past an outdoor set now—a sidewalk restaurant with a three-foot iron railing, a juice bar and several tables. The backdrop was a red, brick building that could be altered when the need arose. Even the concrete we were walking along was lined with glass, trees, flowers and enclosures that could be turned into a park or a private garden. I could see marks where camera tripods had been set up and worn spots in the grass where people had paced or stood for more than a few minutes at a time.

"Do you know where the term *soap opera* comes from?" I asked to keep my mind from drifting. There was so much to see, and it would be a shame to miss anything.

"We prefer the term *Daytime Drama*," he responded as the corners of his lips turned upwards again. "It sounds more professional. Why should it even matter?"

"I suppose it doesn't. I just find bits of trivia interesting."

"Then I would hate to be kept in the dark since it is my profession."

I wasn't sure if he was being serious, but talking about something that no longer mattered to anyone who wasn't interested in history was easier than being drawn into another personal conversation.

"It came from old radio shows of the 1930s. They were sponsored by soap companies like Ivory and Lava and had a captive audience of housewives who rarely left their homes. The programs were filled with dialogue, corny sound effects and less than realistic plots, but the women loved them. I suppose part of that had to do with the great depression and rarely being able to leave home. Of course, that was long before the woman's right movement of the 1960s that gave new meaning to the word liberation."

"You sound like a walking encyclopedia," Peter teased.

"I only remember things I have strong feelings about, and I took a class in radio and television production when I was in high school."

"That must have been interesting."

"I loved the history part, but I was never any good at editing packages on the computer for our daily news broadcasts. I was much better behind the camera and writing scripts."

"So you do know more about this business than you let on."

"Nothing I didn't learn from a book, but the class sparked a real interest in how completely the media can control what society thinks about and does. It's a frightening concept considering today's political climate."

"You're right, but there's little an individual can do to change anything when the wealthy, and those in positions of power are already in control. That's just another reason I love to get away on my boat. I need the clarity I can find no where else just so I can survive another day amongst all the chaos."

"I'm sorry," I said. "I didn't mean to turn the afternoon into some debate. I have no idea what your political, moral or religious beliefs are. I should have stuck with the weather. It's a much safer topic."

"Nonsense, Maya. I like to see the passion in your eyes, and you have yet to say anything I don't agree with. I want a wife and family some day. I've already said that, but it really doesn't matter to me who works and who takes care of the kids as long as our fundamental beliefs are the same. Still, it would be interesting to know what other things you feel passionate about. I sense some real fire underneath that calm exterior."

If he was trying to fill the void Lana's departure had left by flirting with me, it would never work. I was homespun through and through, and the only man I had been truly intimate with was my husband.

"Sometimes I think life causes us to forget about our passions and dreams. It takes all the energy I can muster just to survive."

"Well spoken, but I happen think you have a very passionate nature, and I mean that in only the most respectful way. Now why don't we grab something to eat? I need to be back on set by two, and no one likes to be kept waiting in this business."

He led me through a set of double doors into a big room where mouth-watering smells wafted through the air, and chefs in white hats stood behind counters filled with so many delicacies it would take an hour just to decide what I wanted to eat. But there wouldn't be time to sample much of anything. I would follow Peter's lead and eat what he did, whether it was a salad or a three course meal.

It seemed as if people from every department in the industry were there so it was doubtful anything but a little trivial conversation would take place. That was okay with me since I had already said enough about myself and starting the conversation we needed to have would only spoil what little time we had.

While we waited in line, I glanced around at the various diners. Some were sitting in small groups where much laughter and conversation could be heard, and others were sequestered in corners where they appeared to be studying scripts. In a way, it reminded me of a noisy college cafeteria, but these people were living their dreams, not merely preparing for them.

"Don't let the intensity around here bother you," Peter said as he handed me a tray. "We're really just regular folk who need a few minutes to unwind during the day."

"Thanks," I replied as I watched him take a shrimp salad from the cooler. "I had no idea it would be this busy."

"I wanted to take a later lunch, but the shooting schedule had already been set. I promise to make it up to you. Right now, we'll eat what we can, and I'll introduce you to a few of my colleagues. I hope you don't mind that I told them you were an old friend from back home. I didn't want anyone getting the wrong idea, or pestering you with questions. Just tell anyone who asks that we went to the same high school in Laslo, Indiana and have been friends ever since. You were in town for a few days and wanted to see where I worked."

"What if they want to know more?"

"I'm sure they'll think we were romantically involved the minute they see you, but you don't have to tell them anything more than we took a few classes together. Most of them are aware that I've been dating Lana for the past two years. I've never given anyone a reason to think I've been unfaithful to her, and I'm not about to start the rumor mill spinning now."

We ate lunch with some of Peter's co-workers. Small, happy talk continued until a stagehand poked his head inside the door to tell the cast that they were wanted on the set. Afternoon taping was about to begin.

"Are you coming with us," Jessica Luke, Peter's costar and love interest on the show asked as she rose from the table to leave.

She was a pretty girl from Pennsylvania with loads of wonderful auburn hair, green eyes, and perfect teeth that literally dazzled with whiteness every time she smiled. I wondered why Peter had not fallen in love with her. She was certainly more relaxed and personable than Lana.

"I'll be right there, Jess," he said. "I just need to talk to Maya for a moment."

"Take what time you need. I'll let everyone know you're on your way. It was good to meet you, Maya. It's been a long time since Peter brought one of his friends to the studio."

"She's seems nice," I told Peter as we rose to our feet once she was gone.

He gave me a cheerful smile. "Jess is great. And just in case you're wondering about the extent of our involvement, she has a loving husband and a two year-old daughter. That's one of the reasons I find her so charming. She's already figured out what is most important in life and isn't afraid to let everyone know it. She reminds me a great deal of you."

"How so?" I asked as my face flushed scarlet. "Does she have a clumsy side too?"

He took my tray and slid it onto a conveyer belt after his. "I would never breath of word of that mishaps in my kitchen to anyone without your permission. I hope you believe that, but I'm not sorry it happened. For the first time since moving into that house, I'm actually looking forward to spending more time there. You've made it seem like a real home."

"I'm glad you feel like I've made a difference, but this arrangement is only temporary. Mrs. Newbold will be home in a few days."

"I know, and I would never turn her away. She's been with me for over ten years, but I'm tired of the dating game. I want something permanent to build on, and I feel like this isn't the first time we've met. That may sound like some overused line, but it's how I feel and why I needed some time alone. What if destiny brought us together for a reason we have yet to discover?"

My breath caught in my throat, and I was tempted to tell him everything. But doing so in such a public place wasn't fair. Peter had been nothing but understanding and kind, and I really didn't want to be remembered as a charlatan who took advantage of anyone.

"That's a very sweet thing to say, and I do believe in fate, but you know nothing about me."

"I know everything that's important. You're a very real, sensitive woman who isn't afraid to stand out in a crowd because her beliefs don't quite mesh with those of the masses. Everything else can be learned as we spend more time together. I feel like we have a connection, but if it's one-sided all you have to do is tell me. I won't push for something that isn't there."

I stood for a moment outside the commissary as the hot rays of the sun seemed to beat mercilessly down on my shoulders. I was part of a conspiracy that would destroy what was left of my self-respect if I didn't change directions soon. But my feelings were not the only ones to consider. If I could just stay the course until Friday, I could leave and never look back. If I did anything to cause waves before then, I would only make everything worse.

"What about Lana?" I asked to keep from admitting the extent of my follies. "I thought you were committed to seeing if things could still work out between you."

"I'm not sure she'll even be back to stay. She wants her shot at fame more than she wants to be with me. But that's not what this is about. Maybe I'm just being selfish, but I don't want you to leave on Friday. I want you here where we can see what might happen between us."

Despite the fact that I was having trouble thinking, I pulled him into the shade of a tree and then glanced around to make sure we were alone. I would not become anyone's rebound romance, and he needed to know that.

"Listen, Peter, I'm not sure what I'm feeling right now. I can only tell you that I won't jump into anything just because time is running out. I would like to get to know you better, but we're both experienced enough to understand that a casual relationship isn't what either of us really want."

"Then let's take whatever time we need to make sure we're under no delusions. I just don't want you disappearing to a place where I won't be able to find you."

"We still have a few days before that happens. If you really believe in fate, there's plenty of time to decide if it's working for or against us."

"I suppose you're right," he conceded. "I know how fickle strong feelings can be. They often disappear once the urges have been satisfied."

"That's because there wasn't anything more to them than unadulterated lust. I prefer friendship to emotional euphoria, at least in the beginning."

"In that case, why not watch me tape this afternoon? It will give you a chance to see how I interact with others. I've already made arrangements, and once I'm finished for the day, we can grab something to eat before going home."

"I'd like that," I replied, not wanting to ruin what was left of the afternoon.

He escorted me across a network of sidewalks until we came to another large building that housed sound stages for the daily filming of *Secret Shadows*. It was bustling with activity. He introduced me to the director who was in charge of the scenes he would be filming before heading to his dressing room to change clothes and have his makeup redone. The fact that a man who was so obviously virile had to wear anything on his skin made me smile, but I knew it was a necessary. The cameras picked up every imperfection when they got close enough. Acting wasn't a profession I would ever choose, but people had the right to do what made them feel good, as long as it didn't interfere with the rights of anyone else.

I was told to sit in a tall, canvas chair just a little to the left of the main cameraman. It was hard not to be impressed by people who could work harmoniously in such tight quarters. I had no names for the individuals who called out orders and those who responded without verbal interaction. But it was nothing more than an unusual workplace environment until a wooden clapper came together and Peter stepped onto the sound stage.

His presence seemed to fill every corner of the setting. He was talking to the woman who played his onscreen mother. I had no reference point for knowing what had prompted her anger, but Peter was trying to get her to admit that she was responsible for the argument he'd just had with the character Jessica played.

They went through the scene three times before the director called it a take and they moved on to something else. I wasn't particularly interested in the exact dialogue, but I couldn't deny my mixed feelings of admiration and wonder as I watched Peter work. He was confident, self-assured and sensitive to the feelings of everyone around him. It appeared that he worked like he lived, putting every ounce of strength into just being alive.

I hadn't felt that way since the day Ken died, and a throb of pleasurable pain shot through my heart as I allowed my thoughts to drift from present to past again. Ken had been my life, and I had loved him with every fiber of my being, but he was gone now. And time, which had seemed so precious when we were together, now loomed ahead like some vast wasteland I didn't want to cross alone.

My children still needed me, but before too many years had come and gone, they would be off on adventures of their own. What would I do to occupy myself then? An existence taking care of other people's financial security would not stop the aching loneliness I felt inside.

I forced my mind back to the soundstage. Maybe there was something to be said for having a career that allowed escape into a fantasy world for a few hours each day. It was certainly preferable to living in a sort of limbo waiting for the next shoe to drop. I worried constantly about my children's welfare and what they might have to face as they grew older. They had already been through so much, and a parent was suppose to protect her offspring.

Peter was talking to Jessica now. She was tired of his mother's derisive comments just because she came from the wrong side of the tracks. If something didn't change soon, she was going to walk away for good. He was trying to comfort her when I realized that the dark-haired man at center stage had never questioned my motives or made any demands. In fact, he had treated me with nothing but respect, even when my blunders were more than obvious.

"You're a fool," I told myself as the scene in front of me continued to play out. "Peter isn't offering you a ring. He just wants you to let him in so he can decide if there might be something more than physical attraction. You know how he feels because there's been a stirring inside of you too. The only difference is that he's willing to take a chance while you refuse to step away from the past. It isn't being unfaithful to Ken to want to feel alive again. You've become nothing less than a machine, and if that isn't bad enough, you're being dishonest with everyone. You can't even tell your children what you've been doing."

I leaned back in the form-fitting, canvas chair and allowed my thoughts to flow where they would. Life was hard, and waiting on God's timing was often more than difficult. All I had ever wanted was to be happy, and I had been that way with Ken. No matter what anyone tried to tell me now, I couldn't dismiss my past simply because it was an inconvenience to others.

"Are you tired, or did we simply bore you to death?"

I looked up to see Peter Richards towering above me.

"Neither," I replied, stretching my back. "I was just thinking about your make-believe problems. They seem so real."

"We want the audience to identify. That's what keeps them wanting more. I just wish you felt like you could confide in me. No one should be so sad all the time."

"I'm not really sad, just a little preoccupied with certain things from my past."

"We all have pasts, Maya, but we also have futures. We just need to decide which one is more important."

"What if one feeds directly into the other? Sometimes a complete break isn't possible."

"I'm sorry if I'm pushing too hard. I often forget that what I do here isn't the way real life operates. And thank goodness for that. We'd all be too traumatized to move forward with anything under such constant turmoil. If you would rather not go out to eat tonight I'll understand."

But there was nothing for him to understand, except the fact that I had unwittingly decided to quit living because I couldn't endure another loss. Ken would hate the person I had become—sad, despondent, humorless, and even more alive in my dreams than when awake.

A cold chill suddenly penetrated my body. Maybe Peter was that legendary stranger—who makes the best friend—that could help me navigate through another hurdle towards fully embracing what life had yet to offer again.

"I don't want to go home," I said. "I want to go with you."

"Then give me a moment to change, and we'll be on our way."

I stayed where I was until he returned, and then merely took my hand and led me out of the building to where his convertible was parked and opened the passenger door for me.

"How about a hot dog and a walk along the beach? It's a date guaranteed to take the blues away."

I smiled as he slid in behind the wheel and started the engine. In no time at all, we were cruising along the freeway in heavy, afternoon traffic. I watched the tall buildings and lacy-leafed trees disappear in rapid succession as the wind whipped through my hair and tried not to squint into the sunlight that was heading rapidly towards the horizon. It was nearly seven in the evening. Peter's work days were long, and I felt a jab of remorse because he might not get the rest he needed before heading into a new one. But this side-trip was his choice, and I really didn't want to go back to being alone.

I was being given a chance to learn something new about myself. So I watched the passing scenery and glanced at his profile when I knew he wasn't looking at me. He was so different from Ken, except for being tall, but that didn't mean he wasn't worth getting to know. Maybe some of his composure and self-confidence would rub off on me if I gave him half a chance.

My reveries stopped when the car engine did. We were back at the ocean where sunbathers were loading their vehicles with surfboards, umbrellas, blankets, coolers and chairs.

"I hope you don't mind that I brought you here," he said, turning in his seat so he could get a better look at my face. "I was going to take you to my favorite Italian restaurant but wanted a place where we could talk without being interrupted."

"This is perfect," I replied as I spotted a hotdog vendor's wagon at the top of a wooden staircase that lead down to the beach. It must be incredibly hard for him to go anywhere without being recognized.

"I'm glad you feel that way because Tony makes the best dogs in the world—all smothered with chili, cheese and onions—and I haven't had one for ages. You're not a vegetarian, are you."

"Hardly," I replied as we both climbed from the car. "I grew up on a farm where we raised our own meat—cows, pigs, chickens and even an occasional turkey for Thanksgiving."

"I wish I'd been there to watch you take care of them. I like stories with humble beginnings. They remind me of where I came from and just how unimportant the world's view of success really is."

"In what way?" I asked. "You seem to have done very well for yourself."

"Lady Luck has smiled on me, but I've seen what happens when people stop viewing themselves as regular folk. No one needs more money than can spent in ten lifetimes, and it's impossible for anyone to have more than a few close friends. I never want to get to a point where I value what I have more than the people who helped me get it. That's why I try to stay out of the limelight or the tabloids. I don't want my actions to disappoint anyone who might look up to me."

He bought two chili, cheese dogs and placed one of them in my hands. We munched in silence as we descended the well-worn staircase. Dozens of gulls were hovering near—their wings flapping and their sharp beaks ready for any cast-off morsels of food. White-capped waves were whipping against the rocks as a gentle mist swept over us. I brushed a lock of damp hair away from my eyes.

How easy it was to feel God's presence in such a setting. The sun was beginning to set and a pinkish, orange glow had settled on what appeared to be the edge of the world. It brought back memories of the many moments of nature's beauty Ken and I had shared believing that there would never be another sunset or sunrise quite like the one we were experiencing together.

"You look deep in thought," Peter said as he finished his hot dog and threw the paper wrapping in an already overflowing trash can. "Have I lost you again?"

I smiled up at him, took my last bite and then followed his example. "No, I was just thinking about how incredible nature is. I'm glad you brought me here."

"This beach is pretty spectacular," Peter admitted. "Every element known to man can be found here—wind, rocks, sand, water, animals, minerals and sea life of more varieties than I can identify. Do you believe the theory that man originally evolved from the sea?"

"Not exactly," I replied, cocking an eyebrow. "I believe we have a Heavenly Father who created us in his image. I also believe he created this world and everything in it."

"Even all the murderers, terrorists, racists, rapists and junkies?" Peter asked.

"God didn't create man or woman to become any of those things, but he gave them the gift of agency. We choose to be as good or as bad as we want."

"That doesn't sit well with me when innocent people get hurt," he replied. "Why don't you let me help you with your shoes. The sand feels much better on bare feet."

I rested my hand on his shoulder and unlatched the strap on one sandal. Then I reversed the process and stuffed both shoes in the oversized, shoulder bag I had been carrying all afternoon.

"Do you want to put your shoes in with mine?" I asked.

Peter was looking around as if trying to find a place to stash his where they would still be there when we got back.

"If you don't mind. I would like to trust my fellowmen, but I'm afraid I've experienced the results of sticky fingers once too often. If there is a God, why would he allow all the ugliness to continue?"

I placed his shoes in my bag and stepped onto the sand before responding. I didn't want to come off sounding like some religious fanatic when it appeared he had doubts about the very existence of a higher power.

"Do you really want to know what I think, Peter?"

"I wouldn't ask if I didn't."

"Then I can only tell you that I believe God has a plan, and he won't force anyone to follow him. Coercion, and all the reprehensible things that come with it, are Satan's way of destroying eternal happiness."

"I'm more concerned with all the injustice of today. It makes me wonder if I'm being selfish just thinking about bringing a child into this world."

"It's never selfish to want a family for the right reasons," I said as my thoughts went immediately to my two beautiful children back in Utah with my parents. But I couldn't tell Peter about them if I wanted to make a clean break come Friday. "Do you come here often?"

"Whenever I can. I think this stretch of beach is one of the main reasons I stay here, other than my work and my boat."

While he spoke, my eyes were drinking in everything around me that was so masterfully etched between the sky and the sand. The rugged cliffs that lined the water's edge were majestic with their rock formations, hidden enclosures and spiny outcroppings. And the waves that pressed against the sand and then rolled away with a swooshing sound like nothing I had ever heard before let me know that I would miss the ocean when I was land-locked again.

"It does make one feel rather insignificant," I replied as the ambience of the ocean at dusk continued to seep into my soul.

"Maybe that's why I come here as often as possible. I spend my days so caught up in a make-believe life of an imaginary person that I need a place of sanctuary where I can remember who I really am."

"And who are you, Peter," I asked as I stubbed my toe on something I couldn't see. I almost cried out but didn't want to spoil the moment.

"Just an ordinary guy who already has more than he ever anticipated. The only thing missing is someone special to share my life with. But then we've already had this conversation before."

"That doesn't mean it isn't important to reaffirm our inner desires," I said while looking out towards the ocean and the dozen little lights that pointed the way to shore. "Finding that special someone is what preserves the human race."

"You sound like you've been there—in love, I mean."

I bit my lip to keep the tears from forming. "I have, but some things are just too good to last."

"I know exactly what you mean," he replied. "Lana isn't my first love. I was engaged when I came to Hollywood, but Bethany couldn't take big city living. So a year after we got here she returned home and married someone else. Last time I heard, she was expecting her third child."

"Do you wish you'd made a different decision?"

He stopped walking, and it was impossible not to notice how strong and magnificent he looked standing in the moonlight. "Bethany deserved to be happy, but that didn't stop me from dating too much and too casually until I met Lana. We've been together a long time, and I still love her, but sometimes I feel like I'm suffocating. Nothing is ever relaxed. It's like turning on a hot or a cold shower. She's either all over me, or she's off on some tangent because I hurt her feelings or disappointed her in some way."

"I'm sure that can be exhausting, but I know she loves you."

"Maybe love isn't enough. My mind tells me I should stick with her because of all the time we've invested in the relationship. But my heart tells me that I only want to get married once, and I might be making the biggest mistake of my life if I propose. Sometimes I feel like I'm still waiting for that special someone that was meant to be mine all along."

"Do you think you'll know when it happens?"

I had fallen hopelessly in love with Ken the moment we knelt together on the floor outside the elevator to collect my scattered belongings. My greatest joy in life had come from a rather bizarre encounter, and I fleetingly wondered if the same thing was destined to happen again.

"Hey, I don't know," Peter said as he nodded towards an outcropping of smooth, flat rocks that looked as if people had used them for climbing to the top of the cliff for generations. "I always thought true love would be something like an atomic explosion, but I'm not even sure about that anymore."

"I guess the time does come when tenderness and caring are more important than fireworks."

I crossed the sand in the direction he indicated. The hard surface I chose to sit on was large enough for me to bring my knees to my chin and wrap my arms around them. He followed but didn't try to sit beside me. He simply rested his shoulder against a bolder a short distance away.

"Just tell me that all the melancholy talk hasn't ruined your evening," he said. "I don't know why my love life has to play a part in every conversation we have. Sometimes I just want to forget it even exists."

"But it does, and you have to deal with it. If my presence helps you sort through some of the details I'm glad. Everyone deserves to be truly in love at least once."

"Do you feel like talking about the man who stole your heart? I would be more than willing to listen."

"Not right now, but that doesn't mean I'm not glad that you brought me here. I love sitting outside on a warm summer night, but I never expected it to be quite so near the ocean."

"We should have thrown some blankets in the trunk. Nothing is more beautiful than watching the sun set and rise over the Pacific Ocean."

"Isn't there some law about sleeping on the beach? I thought you wanted to remain as inconspicuous as possible when it comes to your private life?"

"People do it all the time, regardless of the restrictions. But you're right, I don't want my face plastered on the cover of some less-than-reputable magazine for spending the night with a beautiful lady in a place where I know I might get caught. I'm sure you must think I sound like a broken record when it comes to how the media can distort even the most innocent situation, but they're in it to make money, not preserve the sanctity of anyone's life."

"Then why take such a blatant risk tonight? I could have fixed something for us to eat like a normal housekeeper."

"That's just the problem, Maya. You aren't a normal housekeeper, and I can't seem to forget that you'll be gone in a few days. What if this is just a pleasant interlude, and fate has no intention of us being anything more than ships passing in the night?"

I wanted to reach up, take his hand and pull him down beside me. But nights like this could become dangerous, and someone had to make sure the situation didn't get out of hand.

"We can't make something happen just because we want it."

"Why not?" Peter asked. "I think we're responsible for making our own dreams come true."

"But what if it simply isn't meant to be? What if our dreams are dashed to pieces like those waves crashing against the rocks? How do we take those shattered fragments and form them into something new?"

Suddenly, he was sitting on the rock next to me and reaching for my hand. I felt powerless as his fingers closed over mine.

"You're asking the impossible, Maya. Some things can be broken beyond repair, and there is no alternative other than to relinquish them. Then it's going through the motions until something else comes along that brings a little hope for a brighter tomorrow."

"You sound like a philosopher spouting off some pet theory," I countered as I watched a star fall from the sky. I had never felt so needy, and what would it really matter if I allowed myself to be comforted? I wanted to feel truly connected to someone again. "No one chooses to go through experiences like that."

"Maybe not, but few people make it through life without some heartache. I don't think we were meant to have only one dream. I believe our visions for what will make us happy change as we grow and develop, or as circumstances change things for us."

"But how does one go about getting enough courage to make a new dream happen?" I asked, daring myself to look quickly his way. It would only take a slight movement on my part, and one of his arms would be around me.

"Courage is hard to define because everyone has different challenges. What do you think would happen if the series I'm in was canceled, or the producers found someone to take my place?"

"I don't know you well enough to answer that."

"I think you do, but I'll spell it out just so there will be no misunderstanding. I wouldn't give up and turn to booze, drugs, gambling, women or any other risky behavior some of my fellow actors have fallen victim to when their careers took a nosedive—or even when they skyrocketed. I may not believe that some heavenly being created us like you do, but I do believe that we were put on this earth for a reason. And it wasn't to feel sorry for ourselves because life didn't turn out like we planned. If my acting career turned to cinders, I would find something else to do with my life."

"Like what?"

"Maybe I would go back to Indiana and open a restaurant, a gym or an after-school program for kids. I might even try my hand at building something that would do nothing but bring others joy. This city is no place for the faint-hearted. Most people only want me around because I might be able to help boost their careers."

"It sounds a little lonely."

"Sometimes I wonder why I ever came here, but I decided to go for broke when I was a kid. For the most part, I've enjoyed what others only fantasize about. But that doesn't mean I haven't sacrificed to get where I am."

"We're talking about having someone special to share life with again, aren't we?"

"I can't seem to let it go. Maybe I'm just feeling my age, but I want someone around who cares about me as a person, not just a means to an end. And I want kids while I'm still young enough to be a real father, not just some name on a birth certificate."

I knew what he was hinting at, but I couldn't reciprocate the way he might want. He was on the rebound because he wasn't sure about Lana, and my memories of Ken were still poignant and fresh.

"Why don't we table this conversation until later," I said, turning so I could see his face. "You've helped me see a few things much differently, but I'm afraid of what might happen if we stay where we are."

"Are you sure?" he asked.

I was on my feet in an instant and pulling him up with me. The night had lost some of its innocence, but nothing irreparable had happened yet.

"Absolutely! I want to take a walk along the beach. It would be real shame to waste all that glorious sand."

Chapter 10

The alarm on my phone went off at a quarter to four the next morning. I tried to sit up, but my head was spinning and my eyes refused to open any wider than slits. It was dark and silent outside the bedroom window, and the warm cocoon I had made for myself the night before was too comfortable to leave. But I had promised myself that I would make sure Peter had something to eat before his workday began, and he would be leaving the house soon.

It was impossible for me to understand how anyone could function at such an early hour. I wasn't a morning person and the thought of getting up before dawn was repugnant. I hadn't done it since college, unless someone in my family was sick or needed help.

"Easy does it, old girl," I cautioned myself as leaned against the edge of the bathroom sink while the blood returned to my head.

I knew Peter didn't expect me to see him off. In fact, he'd told me to sleep as long as I liked. But that hardly seemed fair since I'd left him alone to memorize lines after we returned from the beach around eleven. I even apologized for keeping him out so late, but he told me he wouldn't have missed one moment of the time we spent getting to know each other better. And if he needed some extra sleep, he would catch a short catnap between takes. That would never be enough for me.

But instead of returning to bed—where I most wanted to be—I filled my hands with cold water from the tap and splashed it lavishly over my face. It didn't feel nearly as refreshing as I had been led to believe, and I shivered before wiping it away with a soft, fresh towel. Then I took a moment to study the refection that was staring back like I had done the morning after I arrived at his home.

The continual change in my countenance was nothing short of miraculous. I looked almost happy for the first time in months. But why was the transformation happening now? I didn't want to forget a single moment of my past with Ken, and I certainly didn't want another man complicating my already messy life. Nonetheless, it didn't take a genius to recognize that something about Peter's words of encouragement the night before had kindled a spark of remembrance. I had never been a quitter who took to my bed when life got hard. My grief was real, but it was time to move into the next stage of healing—that of acceptance.

My husband was gone, but I would see him again. And when that glorious occasion came, I wanted to face him as a strong, independent woman who had not given in to sorrow or fear. That meant coming to terms with where I was at right now and moving into an uncertain future with the courage Ken had so much admired. God had not forgotten me. He had simply given me an unwanted test. It was up to me if I passed or failed. Before I left Peter's home, I would find a special way of thanking him for helping me see life more clearly and becoming a friend I would never forget.

So I ran a brush quickly through my hair and pulled my robe tightly around my shoulders before heading to the kitchen. I might not have time to fix bacon and eggs, but I could manage a couple of slices of toast and pour a glass of juice.

A loaf of the bread I had baked on Friday was sitting on the counter, and I was just pulling my hand from a drawer when an unexpected noise startled me. The knife between my fingers dropped to the floor, and I looked up to see Peter standing in the doorway. He was dressed in jeans and a light, grey sweater and had a look of utter surprise on his face.

"I'm so sorry," I said. 'I seem to be nothing but clumsy around you. I should be wearing a sign that says *disaster area* ahead, but I thought you might like something to eat before leaving."

"My stomach would revolt if I did," he replied, taking a step towards me. "I told you to stay in bed. No one should have to get up at this hour without a reason."

"What about you?" I asked.

"I'm used to it, but you look like you could use a strong jolt of caffeine before you topple over. There are several flavors of coffee in the cupboard next to the stove. Feel free to fix whichever you like most."

I wriggled my bottom lip until I had it between my teeth. "I don't drink coffee. I don't even know how to make it. I assumed you didn't either because there wasn't a coffee maker on the counter when I got here."

"That's because Mrs. Newbold clears everything away the moment she's through with it." He moved in my direction and retrieved the knife from the floor before I could reach down for it. "I usually grab a mug to go at the commissary before heading to my dressing room. You could practice brewing some if you run out of other things to do. Although it might be a challenge if you don't drink it. I generally take mine unadulterated, black and hot, but Lana likes something a little more exotic. The coffee maker in the lower cabinet next to the sink."

"Why are you always so forgiving when it comes to my shortcomings?" I asked, trying not to wilt under his steady and accepting gaze. "You could have yelled at me any number of times these past few days with complete justification, but you've treated me more like a guest than a housekeeper."

"Maybe that's because I view all people as being equal, regardless of what they do for a living. Besides, yelling never gets a person anywhere, and there's always an explanation for why mishaps occur. Do you think trying to be understanding makes me look weak? I know men are supposed to take charge and act like they know everything."

"Not at all," I replied, once again surprised at his depth of patience and understanding. "I appreciate people who look for the good in others. Not everyone is capable of doing that."

"Only because they refuse to take responsibility for their actions. But now isn't the time for a discussion about all the unrest and bigotry in the world and what can be done to stop it. I appreciate the effort you made in seeing that my day started right. I haven't had anyone offer to make me breakfast in years, and that includes Lana. She's never at her best until early afternoon."

I wanted to tell him that would change if she got the role she was auditioning for, but it seemed a little cruel since he had no idea if she was even coming back so they could decide what they were going to do about their rather tumultuous relationship. The Lana I had met would avoid any unpleasant confrontation, unless she was the one to start it.

"What time will you be home?" I asked as he made his way towards the back door with the folder containing the script he had gone to his office the night before to memorize in his left hand. "I would like to have at least one meal ready on time before I leave."

"I'm shooting for seven, but why are you talking about leaving? The week isn't up yet." He turned to face me again, and I caught a glimpse of sadness in his usually sparkling eyes. "I thought we weren't going to talk about that until we'd both had time to do a little additional soul-searching."

I looked up at him and smiled. "You're absolutely right, but I really would like to show you that I can take care of a house and fix a few edible meals."

"As I see it, you've done far more than anyone could have anticipated," he replied, using his free hand to reach for one of mine. I tried to move away, but there wasn't time. "You've brought life into this house and made it feel like a real home. Mrs. Newbold is great, but she makes me feel like I'm still living with my mother. She picks up things before I even drop them and nothing is ever out of place. She's more like a robot who acts on command, and we've never had so much as one truly personal conversation."

"But isn't the role of a housekeeper to keep her own problems to herself and make sure everything is done so her employer has no complaints?"

"I suppose, but having you around is more fun. Why don't we check out that little Italian restaurant I told you about last night when I get home. It isn't too far away, and we could both be in bed by ten."

The warmth of his fingers around mine almost made me reconsider. But we were not two ordinary people—at least he wasn't. There were people everywhere watching and waiting for him to do something out of the ordinary they could write about and exploit. And there was no telling what Lana might do if she learned we had spent any more time together.

"I'm not sure that's a good idea if we truly want to get to know each other better. We've been lucky so far that no one with a camera has seen us together away from the studio. I don't want anyone making assumptions, or writing untruths, before we've figured things out for ourselves."

"Both beautiful and practical," he replied. "But I understand where you're coming from. People in this town can be ruthless, and I really don't want to ruin anything either."

"Then let me fix dinner for you tonight. I promise not to poison you or destroy your kitchen again, and I really would like to make amends for a few of my blunders."

"I like your blunders. They're a refreshing change from the regimented life I live. Nothing out of the ordinary ever happened around here until you came."

"I'm sure it didn't, but won't you be late if you don't leave soon?"

He dropped my hand and moved towards the door again. "You should be a diplomat. You know just how to keep a man in line without causing a national incident. We'll talk more about whether you leave or stay when I get home. Mrs. Newbold plans to retire at the end of the summer so I will be interviewing for a new housekeeper anyway. I hope you will keep that in mind as you go about whatever needs to be done today. I know she left a complete list of responsibilities for you. If you need to go anywhere, the keys to my truck are on my dresser. Feel free to use it for anything."

I watched from the kitchen window until his car disappeared. It was four-fifteen in the morning, but I was too wired to sleep. Thoughts were zooming around in my head, and I really didn't want to stop them. I liked feeling excited about something. Not that fixing dinner was such a unique experience. I had done it thousands of times in the past, but being around Peter made me feel less alone and more like a woman who still had a purpose for living.

I loved Landi and Kenny with all my heart. They were constant reminders of how beautiful life would be when we were with their father again. But I had to make it through a lot of years without becoming a bitter, resentful and sullen woman first. That would only happen if I broke away from the safe and familiar and accepted new offers of friendship. Peter was extending that to me, and I would be gone before anything really life-altering happened.

So instead of climbing back underneath the covers where I would only mull over every decision I had ever made, I got the dust mop out of a corner cabinet and started to go over every hardwood floor from the dining room to Peter's office. Mrs. Newbold had been very specific about daily chores and which rooms in the house needed extra attention on Tuesday. That was the time specified for bathrooms and laundering the bed linens and towels. I had the sheets in Peter's room changed before I heard the first bird singing.

It was barely six in Utah when I decided to call my parents. I hadn't talked to them for a few days, and I didn't have to worry about waking them up. No one in my family slept past dawn when there was work on the farm to be done. Besides, a camping trip was being planned, and in an odd sort of way I felt bad because I was going to miss it. I hated sleeping in a tent, being bitten by bugs with pinchers or stingers strong enough to inflict pain and not being able to shower. But that was also the time for smores, Dutch oven meals and sitting around the campfire at night while my father told stories about our ancestors.

I liked being able to say that I was a descendant of sturdy, heroic and impassioned   pioneers who blazed trails and faced both hardships and death so they could settle in a part of the country few white men had ever seen. Many of them had crossed the mighty Atlantic Ocean in overcrowded ships where they slept on wooden planks and nearly starved to death just to find freedom from religious and political oppression. They had given away their fortunes, been separated from their homelands and family and taken unimaginable risks just to live in a place where sagebrush, scorpions and rattlesnakes had to be eradicated before they could even think of long-term survival.

As I waited for someone to answer, I realized that in many ways, I was like them. Not that I had ever known any of their hardships, but I was certainly blazing my own uncharted trail now that Ken was gone. I still missed him so much I felt as if I could barely breath most of the time, but I couldn't deny the legacy he'd left for me to watch over and cherish.

When I saw my children again, I would no longer conduct myself in the selfish, over-protective and fearful way I had done since Ken's death. I would be their moral strength and support as they continued to grow into the fine adults they were destined to be. And I would be a true friend—one just as accepting, patient and comforting as Peter had been to me.

I was surprised when Landi answered the phone before I could leave a message. She sounded as if she had been running.

"Mom, is that you?" she panted. "I tried to get to the phone sooner, but why are you calling so early in the morning? You've never done that before."

"Maybe I was just missing you. Are you ready for your big camping trip with grandma and grandpa? I know you'll have a wonderful time with all the hiking, fishing and looking for Indian artifacts."

"Is that what you did when you were my age?"

"It sure is. Haven't I shown you all my treasures?"

"You mean that box of stuff in the top of your closet where all the shiny, black rocks and pieces of broken stuff are?"

"Those aren't rocks. They're flint arrowheads made by the Indians who once roamed all over this part of the country. The men hunted for food and fought off members of other tribes while their wives baked clay pots in the hot sun, looked for water and made clothing out of animal hides."

"What did the kids do?" she asked.

I took a deep breath before answering. Now really wasn't the time for another history lesson, but sometimes I just couldn't help myself. So much of our country's past was being changed or left out of books completely. I never wanted Landi and Kenny to forget the sacrifices others had made so Americans could enjoy the freedoms most of them took for granted.

"Much of the same things you and Kenny do. They helped out where they could, but they also played games and learned about life and nature from the elders in their tribe. But I don't want to keep you from something important. I remember how much work had to be done before we left for even one night."

"We already came back," she replied.

"But I thought you weren't leaving until today."

"We decided to go yesterday, but it didn't turn out to be much fun. We didn't even get to sleep in the tent we put up."

My anxiety level was rising fast, and it was hard not to let my concern show in my voice. "Why not?"

"Kenny wanted to explore every creek bed, clump of trees or cave and almost got eaten by a big, ugly snake. It was coming back to check on its babies."

"Is everyone okay?" I asked, sinking down on the edge of my bed. I was shaking almost uncontrollably. Deserting my children to see Aunt Lil had been a horrid mistake. I should have known that taking care of my son would be too much for my parents. They were getting old, and he was a very active little boy who had no fear. "I can catch a plane home today."

"Please don't," she pleaded. "I want to stay longer. This place is lots more fun than Boston. And grandpa said we'd all learned a valuable lesson, and nothing like that was going to happen again."

"I should hope not," I said. "But if I stay until the end of the week what will you and Kenny be doing?"

"We'll stay out of trouble, I promise. Grandpa lets us give the baby animals their bottles, and we can play with them if we're careful. He's even taken us out to the orchard to see the beehives, but we can't get close to them unless he's with us because they'll attack if they get mad. He made candy from some of the honey and let us stretch it when it was cool enough. We never get to do cool stuff like that when we're home."

"What about grandma?" I asked.

"Besides having us check the garden twice a day to see what vegetables are big enough to pick, we go out every morning to pull weeds and make sure everything has enough water."

"Do you also put puzzles together, paint rocks and go for long walks?"

"Of course, but we're mostly busy getting ready for the fair."

"I suppose you're in good hands then," I said. I would not mention the snake again until I talked to my father. While I wished my son was less fearless, I never wanted him to be afraid. "Those are exactly the things I did as a kid."

"Then why did you ever leave to go to the city? I could stay here forever."

I swallowed back a heavy lump of nostalgia before answering. My children would never completely forget their father, but being with my family was helping their pain to heal. "I wouldn't have met your dad if I'd stayed in Hurricane, and you'd still be waiting in heaven to get here. Don't you miss Papa H., your friends and your home?"

"Sure, but we could visit them. I like it here. It's quiet, and there's always something to do."

"I'm not sure you'd feel that way if you had to work on the farm until you were out of high school. I never got to have sleepovers, take dance lessons or go to the zoo or an amusement park on the weekends. There was always too much work, but I am glad that you're having fun."

"What about you?" she asked. "Are you having any fun?"

Her question was much too insightful for me, but I had to give her something or she would just keep hounding me. "I suppose, but it's different with adults. Aunt Lil has taken me to see a number of incredible things, but she has a every demanding life. I'm actually doing a little favor for her right now."

"What did that crazy, old busybody do now?" a male voice broke into the conversation. My father was listening in on the extension.

"Dad, where did you come from?" I asked.

"The barn, and I'm mighty glad I did. You shouldn't be doing favors for Lillian Farrow when she was the one who asked you to come."

"It's complicated, and I'm not sure now is the best time to try to explain."

"Then put Lil on the phone, and she can tell me herself."

I swallowed back another bout of personal remorse. I had been concealing the truth for days, but I couldn't lie to my father. He had raised me better than that. "I'm afraid that isn't possible, dad."

"Why the hell not?" he demanded.

That's when I knew he was mad. Swearing was not something he did unless truly provoked.

"Because I'm not at her house right now."

"You're not in any trouble, are you? If that woman has involved you in one of her hair-brained plots, I'll wring her withered, old neck."

"Dad, remember your blood pressure," I said, envisioning both the straight and curved blue vessels sticking out all over his forehead. "You don't want to have a stroke."

"That will only happen if I don't get some answers. What possible favor could you be doing for her when you don't know anyone else in the city?"

I wasn't ready for an inquisition, but I could lessen the damage done by giving him some of the least incriminating information before we talked in person. "Did you know Aunt Lil got married."

"No! I thought she still had an aversion to men. When did that happen?"

"Two days ago. She got married in New York."

"You mean that old biddy left you all alone in a city like Los Angeles to go off to New York and get married. Why didn't you just come home?"

"It has to do with that favor I was telling you about."

"Quit hedging, Maya. You've never been any good at lying. You're not going to be punished. You're an adult now. But if you don't tell me what's going on, I'll be forced to fly to L.A. to find out for myself. And you know how critical it is for me to be home right now. Fall is a very busy time of the year."

Fall was no busier than any other time of the year for framers who raised animals and most of the food they consumed. But I didn't want my dad checking up on me. I had things under control and would be leaving all my supposed troubles behind in less than three days.

"You don't have to come here, dad. I'm sort of playing housekeeper to a television star."

"Wow!" Landi was back in the conversation. "Is it someone I know?"

"Probably not! He isn't a teenager. His name is Peter Richards, and he's a very nice man."

"I know who he is," Landi almost cooed. "I've seen pictures of him in magazine's at Walmart. Some of my friend's moms watch *Secret Shadows* and think he's the dreamiest guy on television. When do I get to meet him?"

"Probably never, and once this week is over I won't be seeing him again either. He has a beautiful girlfriend who is madly in love with him."

"You're beautiful too, mom. Maybe he'll fall in love with you. Wouldn't that make all my friends at school jealous?"

I laughed at my daughter's naivety. "I was under the impression that you didn't want me to get married again?"

"I don't, but it would sure improve my popularity if Peter Richard's was my stepfather."

"You're popular enough, and there will be no second marriage for me. I'm still very much in love with your father."

"Enough small talk," my dad interrupted. "Now hang up the phone, Landi. I need to speak to your mother alone."

"Okay, grandpa," my daughter meekly relented. "But I need to ask mom if she can get his autograph for me. No one will believe me when I tell them if I don't have proof. Have him write something nice and personal."

"I'll see what I can do, Landi, but I can't make any promises. He's a very busy man. Now give Kenny a kiss for me, and remember that I love both of you very much and will be back at the farm in a few days."

"I love you too," Landi said. "And I'll make sure Kenny behaves."

"Now, dad," I said as soon as I heard the click that let me know my daughter had done as her grandfather asked. "What is it you have to say that you don't want my daughter to hear?"

"Only that I don't approve of what you're doing. You shouldn't be working for some stranger, regardless of how nice or famous he is. Lillian Farrow has done some strange things in her life, but I never expected her to go this far. I should have put my foot down when she first suggested this trip, but she made it sound as if she had nothing but your well-being in mind."

"Aunt Lil has been wonderful, but she can't control fate any more than we can. The man she married is dying. It really is a long story, and one that I would like to tell you about in great detail, but most of it isn't mine to share."

"I'm sorry Lil will be facing such a loss, but that doesn't explain why you're impersonating a housekeeper. You should have come home when she left."

"That was my intention, but she'd already given her word to Hildie."

"Who's Hildie?"

"The cook and main housekeeper Aunt Lil depends on for most everything. There's also a maid, a gardener, a butler and a driver. Hildie was going to cover for a friend who was called to her grandson's bedside quite suddenly, but Aunt Lil needed her help."

"And you volunteered?"

"Not exactly, but it hasn't been an entirely unpleasant experience. I've learned a lot about myself and actually feel less sad than I have in a long time. Peter Richards is a good man. I think even you would like him. He grew up in the country."

"Maybe I would, but that isn't the issue here," he replied. "You're a beautiful woman like Landi said, but you're also incredibly vulnerable being on your own for the first time in years. I don't like the idea of you being in a situation you might not be equipped to handle. Most men only have one thing on their minds."

"I know about men's needs, dad. You taught me about the birds and the bees when I was younger than Landi. Peter leaves for work at four in the morning and gets home barely in time for a late meal."

"You know I trust your judgment, Maya. If I didn't, I never would have allowed you to go all the way to Boston, without me, when you were barely twenty."

"And see how beautifully that turned out! I met the most wonderful man, and together we gave you two incredible grandchildren. I think I can handle playing this role for a few days.

After all, I've spent the last thirteen years doing exactly what I'm doing now—taking care of a house. I may not have a resume, but I am qualified."

It was a heartfelt speech that was more for me than my father, but he never needed to know exactly what had gone on since my arrival in California. I had allowed Aunt Lil to use me, but denying that anything good had come from her meddling wasn't fair.

"All right, Maya, I know how useless it is to argue with you when you've alreayd made up your mind. Just remember that your mother and I are here if you need us. You'll always be our little girl."

I left it at that and hung up my end of the conversation without even mentioning the snake. There would be time to discuss that later.

The sun was up by the time I was dressed, and the day loomed ahead like some vast open sea with nothing to break the monotony of the gently rising and falling waves now that I had nothing left on my list to do. Since it was still cool outdoors, I left the confines of the house and walked across the flagstone patio towards the back yard, making sure to stay away from the room in the garage where Peter created his masterpieces. I had fallen victim to curiosity once and would not let it happen again.

The yard behind the house was lovely with tall, swaying trees and freshly mowed grass set against a tall, brick fence. There was a fountain in one corner surrounded by lose, white pebbles and an oval-shaped pool in the center. I couldn't help but wonder how often Peter was able to use it, but as I took two full turns around the exterior, I realized something seemed to be missing—something homelike and comforting.

"There aren't any flowers!" I exclaimed as I stood next to a gate leading into the alley. There was a gardening shed to my right and a large pile of compost and dirt—behind a wooden partition where two garbage cans stood—to my left. "Every yard should have flowers. They make the world a more beautiful place."

Suddenly my mind was reeling with visions of what Peter's back yard could look like under the gentle hands of a woman. It never occurred to me that he might prefer his surroundings exactly the way they were. I was an avid gardener, and my back and arms were strong from having worked with soil nearly my entire life. People came from blocks around my home in Boston just to see what new varieties of flowers were in bloom. Besides, I needed something constructive to do. Creating a flowerbed for him would be my parting gift—an expression of gratitude for all he had done for me.

I found a shovel, bucket, garden hose and wheelbarrow stored inside the shed along with everything else I might need. That included redwood planks, unusual rocks, decorative bricks and several large pieces of driftwood. It was a gardener's paradise. Once I moved the wooden partition back a few feet—around the biggest portion of the dirt and leaving plenty of room for the trash cans and a smaller compost pile—I knew I could put a tiered, flower bed in front of it with very little effort. The ground underneath the loose soil appeared to be barren, and there wouldn't be a lot of heavy digging. Within ten minutes, I could see the beginning of the project I envisioned.

It would be a reasonably large mound, and I would include varieties of flowers I was familiar with like daisies, iris, mums, bluebells, lupins, peonies, feverfew, carnations, delphiniums, coneflowers and China pinks. I would consult with someone at a local greenhouse about which varieties would grow best and set each clump off in a way it could be appreciated. Peter needed something a little old-fashioned that would remind him of home and the simple values he had learned while growing up in the country. Just thinking about the touch of antiquity I was creating caused a shiver of delight. If a few annuals were added each season, he would have a delightful showing of color year round, and it would be minimal work for his gardener.

After moving ing the last load of dirt, I began hauling decorative items from the shed where I used them to fashion borders and backdrops within the mound. I used some of everything I found, including one piece of driftwood that would act as the focal point of the entire garden. By the time I stood back to get a better view of what I had done, I realized that my simple project had taken on a life of its own. It would take over thirty plants to fill all the spaces I'd made.

Leaving everything where it was, I hurried into the house and took a quick shower before heading to a nursery. I was almost certain we had passed one on our way to the beach on Saturday. But I didn't have to rely on memory to find a place where I could get what I needed. That's what smart phones were for. If all went as I hoped it would, the flowerbed would be finished and dinner on the table by the time Peter got home from work.

It was almost ten-thirty when I pulled on a pair of jeans and a top, tied a ribbon around my dripping hair, and grabbed Peter's pickup keys from off the top of his dresser. The side roads were quiet, and I would have no trouble following the directions on my phone. I had been using it for years to make my way through the labyrinth of freeways that encircled my neighborhood back home. The only thing I worried about was getting into an accident. Peter loved his truck, and wrecking it would be a justifiable ending to all my mishaps of the past few days.

But I pushed back my fears, and in what seemed like no time at all, I was signaling to pull off the freeway. I found a parking space in the morning shade at an outdoor complex that housed a small shopping mall, grocery store and the nursery I needed. I would look for something for my children first. I had the usual assortment of nicknacks from the places Aunt Lil had taken me, but I wanted them to have something special that really came from my heart.

Landi loved new clothes, but picking just the right outfit for a budding teenager was no easy task. She had her own ideas as to what looked cool and what didn't. There were shorts and tops, jeans and boots, and shirts and sweaters. Everything seemed rather ordinary until I spotted a lacy Sunday dress that was fashionably cut and would make my daughter look like the princess she was to me. I purchased it without reservations and moved on to find something for Kenny.

He was at another awkward stage—too old for little boy toys and too young to appreciate anything practical. Thinking about my precocious, yet innocent, son made me smile. He was trying so hard to be a man now that his father was gone, but I wanted him enjoy what was left of his childhood. I had been thinking about getting him a watch for his birthday, but perhaps now was even a more appropriate time.

I found one I thought he might like in a department store near the front of the mall, but before leaving with my purchase, my eyes riveted on a small, crystal sculpture in a display case. It was a swan —wings gracefully spread, head erect—and reminded me of the ones that nested each year on the lake near my parent's farm in Hurricane. It was a rather extravagant purchase for something so small, but I knew my mother would love it and my father would appreciate what it represented. I also picked out a driftwood paperweight for Ken's father.

My gifts secure in the locked pickup, I headed to the nursery. I told the first salesperson available as much as I could about my project and how many plants I would need to complete it. She led me to the area where perennials in every variety and color imaginable sat in rows along metal shelves where they could be easily watered and cared for. I had to take one of nearly everything so there would be no gaping holes.

After paying a three-hundred and forty-five dollar bill, she gave me a written guarantee. If any of the plants did not make it through the first growing season, they could be replaced without additional cost. Then she helped me load my purchases into the bed of the truck where I hoped they wouldn't go into shock on the drive back to Peter's house.

But before pulling out of my parking space, I ran into the market and selected two top-sirloin steaks and two Idaho baking potatoes. I added to that a pre-made pie crust, a few ears of fresh corn, some large strawberries, a bag of fresh, bakery rolls and a bouquet of colorful, cut flowers. I wanted everything for our evening meal to be perfect. It never crossed my mind that what I was doing might be considered excessive or give Peter the wrong idea. I simply wanted to do something that would make him happy and help atone for all my deception and blunders in the process.

I left the pickup in the alley when I got back to Peter's house and went straight to the house to fix a fresh strawberry pie, wrap the potatoes in foil and marinate the steaks. When that was done I returned to what I hoped would not soon be labeled as nothing short of *Maya's Foley*.

But before putting the first plant into the soil where I thought it would look the best, I uncovered the barbecue grill and made sure the propane tank was full. Then I placed the flowers I had purchased in a vase and put them on the patio table. I would shower again and set the table once the garden was finished.

It was nearly four by the time all the flower pots were sitting in the shade of a tree, the bed of Peter's truck had been swept clean, and it was back in the garage where it belonged. I was exhausted, but I couldn't afford to quit now. Even if what I had done was a mistake, it would take more time to put things back the way they were than finish what I had started. So I tapped the first plant out of its pot and set it in a hole at the top of the mound before adding a generous amount of water and replacing the needed soil.

Time was slipping by so rapidly now that I found myself working as if some demon were driving me. It was warm, almost to the point of being hot, and the moisture was streaming down my cheeks. But I couldn't afford to take time away from my work, even to get a drink of much-needed water if I wanted to be finished by the time Peter got home.

But each time I stood upright to stretch my back, I looked over at what I had accomplished and felt a jolt of satisfaction. The flowerbed would be both unique and beautiful, and the sprinkling system would give the plants enough water to thrive once the roots had taken hold. The only thing that remained was Peter's acceptance.

Still, it was more than luck that nothing had gone wrong in the execution of my plans, and I marveled at how rapidly everything had fallen into place. I could smell the potatoes baking when I got out of the shower for a second time and put on something to wear that Peter had not seen before. The sour cream had already been mixed with herbs, the corn husked and ready to place in hot water, and the grill hot enough for the steaks by seven.

I was putting silverware, cups and plates on the patio table when I heard the garage door open. Peter was home, and I felt as if my heart literally leaped to my throat when he called my name.

"I'm outside," I called back to him, clasping my hands behind my back.

Suddenly I was scared—more scared than I had ever been—excluding times of illness and death. My impetuousness might become the basis for a lawsuit, and only this morning I had told my father that I could take care of myself and stay out of trouble. Well, it hadn't seemed so wrong when the idea of building Peter a flower garden first popped into my head. It was simply a living gift to a man who had helped me see that I was capable of moving away from some of my grief.

Peter walked through the kitchen door onto the patio and gave me a warm smile before whistling. "You look lovely."

"Thank you," I said as my jaw beginning to quiver. Perhaps if I escorted him directly back into the house he would never see what I had done to his yard until after I had gone.

"Something smells delicious, but I wish you hadn't gone to all the trouble," he said, glancing around with a perplexed look on his face. "It would have been a pleasure to take you out and show you off."

My own brow furrowed. "We both know why that wouldn't be such a good idea. Despite a few issues that need to be resolved, you and Lana are still a couple, and my time here is almost over."

"It doesn't have to be, Maya. I already told you that Mrs. Newbold is going to retire, and I haven't heard from Lana since she left."

"That doesn't mean her feelings about you have changed. Nor does it mean that I can stay here as your housekeeper on a permanent basis. I just wanted to plan a quiet and relaxing evening. It's the least I can do after all the havoc I've caused."

"Stop with the apologizing!" he exclaimed, and I knew I was pushing too hard. "I'm tired of talking about a water-covered floor and a broken casserole dish. If there's something you feel the need to tell me, just do it. If not, let's have the quiet evening you've planned and leave all the heavy discussions until later. Even if you don't want to believe it, having you here has been a real pleasure."

If I said anything about my subterfuge now, the rest of our time together would be strained and decidedly uncomfortable. I had to stick with my plan of silence until Friday so there would be no more discord and hurt feelings.

"You're right," I said. "I'm overthinking everything because I've never been in a situation like this before, and I'm not sure how I'm supposed to feel or act. I came here to take care of your home while Mrs. Newbold was away and ended up making a new friend."

"Does that make you uncomfortable?" he asked. "I would never force myself on anyone. I actually take pride in never having been part of a scandal. I've watched what happens to reputations and careers when accusations are made. The press has a field-day and lives are destroyed. I've worked incredibly hard to make sure that doesn't happen to me."

Without thinking, I reached out and touched his arm. "I know I have nothing to fear from you, Peter. But you have to admit that our relationship has been a little unusual."

"That's only because it wasn't the traditional meeting at some party or club. Would you feel better about spending time with me if we'd been introduced by a mutual friend?"

He was getting so close to what I was trying to hide that it made the hairs on my arms stand erect. I would only have to mention Madame DuBois or my aunt and he would know we had met before, and I wasn't at all who I pretended to be.

"I guess it doesn't really matter how, when or where we met. It only matters that we like and respect each other."

He uttered a sigh of relief as I removed my hand from his arm. "That's certainly how I see it, and I really do appreciate the fact that you're not like other girls I've met in this city."

"It's probably because I'm not a native Californian," I replied, taking a step towards the back door of the house. I needed to start the water boiling for the corn and get the steaks on the grill before it got any later.

"Maybe," he said, following me. "California girls, and the ones who come here to make a name for themselves, tend to lose some of the gentleness I see in you."

"I don't know about that, but you've made me feel like I belong, and I can never thank you enough for that."

"In that case, why don't you sit down in one of the lawn chairs and let me cook the steaks? I don't get to do it nearly often enough."

"Are you sure? I wanted to fix this entire meal for you."

"From where I'm standing, you've already done all the real work. Grilling steaks is fun for me, unless you're afraid I don't know how to do it."

"That thought never crossed my mind," I replied. "If you're sure, the least I can do is get them for you. I marinated them in a sauce I hope you'll like. I didn't even think about asking if you preferred them plain."

"There's little anyone can do to ruin a good steak, except for overcooking it. I'm sure I'll like whatever you put them in."

He moved towards the grill while I hurried inside. Once the stove was on, I returned to the patio with the steaks on a plate. But Peter wasn't where I had left him. He was standing in front of the flower garden, and from the back, he didn't look pleased. I almost did a one-eighty. If I was quick enough, I could make my escape before he figured out who had made an unsanctioned addition to his yard and call the police.

But as I stood there with a plate in one hand and a grilling fork in the other, I knew I hadn't done anything horribly wrong. His yard looked lovely with flowers in it, and the worst he could do was yell at me and demand that I restore it to the way it had been that morning. The only things lost would be a great deal of beauty and more money than I had intended to spend. My sore, aching body would take care of itself.

"Maya," Peter called out as I set what I was holding on the arm of the grill. "Would you mind joining me for a minute."

I squared my shoulders before stepping onto the grass, but my hands were locked behind my back by the time I got to where he was.

"Where did this flowerbed come from?" he asked.

My reply was simple. "Don't you like it?"

"It's absolutely incredible! But it wasn't here this morning. I would have noticed. You were here today. Who put it in?"

"Does it really matter as long as you like it?"

"It matters a great deal. Someone has gone to a lot of work, not to mention expense, and I would like to thank whomever it was properly."

"Would it suffice you to say that it was done by a special friend as a way of saying thank you?"

"Let's not play games, Maya. I don't have friends like that. Not here, anyway. Besides, it would take a grown man several days to do a job like this. Did someone instruct you not to tell me?"

"No, but it could done in a relatively short amount of time if the person knew what he or she was doing and had all the right materials."

"So you do know who did it?" Suddenly he stopped talking and looked at me in a way that made my heart almost ache. "Are you trying to tell me that you're responsible?"

I bit down on my bottom lip. He had given me a way out, but I was tired of lying about everything. Besides, it wouldn't take long for him to recognize that everything, but the flowers, had come from his shed. "I guess I am."

"But how and why? I've done nothing to deserve it."

"The how is simple. I've loved gardening my entire life and when I saw that stack of dirt I couldn't seem to leave it alone. All I had to do was move the partition a few feet and there was still be plenty of room behind it for trash cans and a compost heap. I really didn't make a final decision until I looked inside the shed and saw the bricks and stuff. I'm sorry for using things you may have been storing for something else."

"Nothing in that shed was earmarked for a specific project, and I can't imagine anyone doing a better job. But I'll never understand the sacrifice you made in giving me slice of heaven in my own back yard. I recognize a lot of those flowers from my childhood. Like you, my grandmother was a master gardener who knew just how to breath life into something ordinary."

"So you really like it?"

"I love it, Maya."

"And it will give you color most of the year—at least that's what the saleswoman at the nursery said. I used perennials, but you can fill in with annuals if I've planted anything too far apart."

Peter took a few steps forward so he could get a better look at the individual flowers. "I'll weed it myself. I don't want anyone else messing with it."

His show of appreciation made tears well in my eyes. "You don't have to do that, but I tried to make sure the sprinklers wouldn't wash any of the dirt away. I have a guarantee in the house saying that if a plant doesn't survive the first year it will be replaced at no cost to you."

"You've thought of everything, haven't you?" he replied. "But I still don't understand why you did it. All I've done is treat you to one picnic on the beach and a hotdog."

"You forgot lunch at the studio."

"A minor oversight, and not exactly something that would rival this."

I let the air slowly out of my lungs. "I wanted to leave you with something beautiful. It was the only way I could think of to show you how much your friendship means. It came at a time when I truly needed it."

"But all this?" He waved his hand through the air above the garden. "A simple thank-you would have been sufficient."

"I'm not good at expressing how I feel in words."

"I'll value it forever, but I'm the one who should be thanking you," he replied, taking my hands in his.

But the physical pain made me pull them away. I hadn't taken the time to find a pair of gloves, and my palms were red, swollen and blistered.

"What's wrong?" he asked as I hid them behind my back again.

"Nothing, but the steaks won't cook by themselves," I responded.

"They can wait. I want to see your hands."

When I didn't relinquish them willingly, he pulled my arms from behind my back and forced my hands open. A look of shock or pity, I wasn't sure which, suddenly appeared on his face. "I don't know what to say. Your gift has truly humbled me."

I stood as if rooted to the spot, unable to look away from him, as he lifted my hands to his lips."I only did it because I wanted to, Peter. It was no big deal."

"No big deal! Just look at your hands." He held them up in front of my face. "You won't be able to use them for a month."

"They're not as bad as they look. This isn't the first time I've given myself blisters, and it certainly won't be the last. Now quit fussing, and let's eat. I'm starving. Can't you hear my stomach growling?"

He let go of my hands almost unwillingly. "What you just said about wanting to leave me with something special has me worried. Have you decided to disappear from my life completely? I thought we agreed to make that decision after we'd both had time to think about how we really felt."

"The arrangement was for a week, and that's nearly over. We can't postpone the inevitable forever."

"Nothing is inevitable if we don't want it to be that way."

"Are you sure about that?"

"As sure as I can be about anything. If you need more money, that won't be a problem."

"It's not a matter of money, or even employment. We've each committed to a certain life, and mine isn't here."

"Then where is it?" he asked.

"About as far away from here as anyone can get. I would tell you all about it if I thought it would make the slightest difference, but it won't."

"Why don't you let me be the judge of that? Can't you see what's happening here? I'm falling in love with you."

The earnest look on his face let me know that he believed what he was saying, but love couldn't happen that fast. Even Ken had waited until we'd been dating for over a month before declaring how he felt. And I wasn't at a place where I could even think about letting another man into my life, especially one who had a girlfriend who had already told me what she would do if I got in her way.

But even knowing what I did, I didn't move away from him as I should have done. I simply stood where I was looking up into his intense, brown eyes until his arms encircled my waist and his lips came to rest on mine. And when they did, I seemed to welcome his touch as a thirsty woman welcomes water. I justified what I was doing by calling it a kiss of friendship, but it was much more than that, and I knew it. I was awakening to the life Ken had wanted for me, only I was still too afraid to admit it.

When the kiss finally ended, Peter held me close and whispered in my ear.

"I probably shouldn't have done that since nothing has been settled between us yet. I know you're fighting ghosts, but whatever it is in your past that you're finding so hard to forget, I know we can face it together."

Not unaware of what I was doing, I ran the back of one hand gently down the side of his face. "You are an incredibly, wonderful man, Peter Richards, but I can't get involved with you as long as Lana is part of your life. It wouldn't be fair. Besides, you know very little about me."

"I know everything I need to. You've opened up a part of my heart I never even knew existed. Can you honestly say that you feel nothing for me?"

"You know I can't, but we're not sitting in a place where a commitment of any kind can be made."

"I'm not asking for a commitment. I know we've only known each other a few days. I just need you to tell me that you won't disappear until we can figure out what's really going on between us."

I forced a smile, but my heart was heavy. I had become a participant in a deception that never should have happened, and I would pay an unfathomable price for not telling Peter the truth before reciprocated feelings became involved.

"You don't have to worry about that. I'm here until Mrs. Newbold gets back. That should give us plenty of time to think about what just happened. A relationship built on regret or rebound is worse than no relationship at all. Now, why don't you cook those steaks. There's fresh strawberry pie for dessert, and I know the corn is boiling by now."

Peter didn't say anything more. He simply led me back to the patio where we ate a delicious meal. We kept the conversation from focusing on us. It was better that way because I was in over my head and had no idea what I was going to do. I didn't want to run away, but I wasn't sure I could fulfill my arrangement with Aunt Lil any longer. No one was supposed to get hurt, but it was doubtful that anyone would walk away from this fiasco unscathed now.

Chapter 11

Peter went to his office around ten to study his lines for the coming day. I washed the few dishes we had used and straightened the kitchen before closing the door to my room and laying down on the bed to think about everything that had happened during the past few hours.

I couldn't fault Aunt Lil for pressuring me into coming I couldn't even blame Peter for making a return move after the garden I had created for him. I was the one who had given mixed signals.

Tears soaked into my pillow as I recalled each moment of our short relationship and tried to determine when I had given him any encouragement that could be construed as something other than friendship. Perhaps my evasiveness was the problem. Most men enjoyed the chase almost as much as the conquest, and I had been so determined not to let him know how I had been duped into coming to his home that I had made everything about my life seem mysterious.

What did that say about me as a woman who had promised to cherish her husband forever? I felt as if my love for Ken had been desecrated because I had not pulled away from Peter's kiss. I could still feel his lips on mine and knew I wanted more.

By midnight, my thoughts were in complete turmoil. Aunt Lil had certainly proven her point about me needing someone else in my life to love, and I almost hated her for it. How could I allow myself to have feelings for a daytime television star when I had been married to a man like Ken? Peter could never give me the security, peace of mind and family life my husband had. He was part of a world where indiscriminate sex, illegal drugs, drinking to excess, pursuing fortunes and power and doing whatever felt good at the moment—regardless of the personal or societal consequences—was perfectly acceptable.

It hardly mattered that he was kind, patient and handsome enough to turn any girl's head. His lifestyle was a million light years away from mine, and I couldn't let a single emotional encounter destroy all the years of happiness I had enjoyed with Ken.

"I've got to get out of here!" I exclaimed before jumping to my feet and stuffing clothes and toiletries into my suitcase. "I don't care who gets hurt or upset. I need to be around people who believe and think as I do, and who are satisfied with living an orderly and uncomplicated life. I'll go back to school and get that advanced degree so I can help Ken's father with the business until my kids are old enough to decide what they want to do with their lives. Maybe I'll even take a more active part in the community. Boston is where my safety lies, and I'm not going to leave it again."

When everything was ready, I called Otto on my cell. It was twelve-thirty in the morning. I knew he would be in bed, but I was counting on him to make good on his promise of being there if I needed him. I wouldn't give him any details about what I was planning to do because I didn't want him tell Aunt Lil. She would only try to dissuade me from leaving, and I wasn't about to take her advice again.

I would call her from Hurricane and give her whatever excuses I had come up with by then. It would be easier than facing her in person. As for Peter, I would leave him a note. He might hate me for leaving so abruptly, but at least he would not be able to figure out where I had gone. And in a few weeks, he would forget that I even existed. Lana, or some other available woman, would see to that. It seemed the most logical—not just the most cowardly—thing to do.

I dug around in my purse for a piece of paper and then scribbled a brief message asking for his forgiveness. The rest of the note explained the basics. How I had come to his house under the guise of being a replacement for his housekeeper—a plot devised to get the two of us together. I didn't mention my aunt's name or why I had allowed myself to be drawn into such an underhanded scheme. I didn't even give an explanation as to why I hadn't come clean when we first met. It just seemed less complicated to let him believe I was an unprincipled fake who had finally developed a conscience. If what Lana had told me about him hating deception was true, he was going to despise me anyway.

When I finished, I quietly opened the bedroom door and slipped into the kitchen. Feeling around in the dark, I placed the note on the counter, along with the house key. Peter would surely see them when he got up for work. Seconds later, I was closing the back door behind me.

I almost ran to the end of the driveway hoping Otto would be waiting for me, but not a single car was in sight. Every now and then, while chewing on my bottom lip, I would steal a glance at Peter's house to see if any lights had come on. I really didn't want anyone to see me standing in the dark with a suitcase and call the police. Telling an almost unbelievable story to strangers wasn't how I wanted this unfortunate charade to end.

My parents would try to be understanding when I called to tell them that I was sitting in the Salt Lake City International Airport and needed a ride to their house. Even my children would welcome me home. But I wasn't sure I would ever get over the fact that I had allowed myself to become a pawn in someone else's lunacy. I had always been such a level-headed, calm and slightly retiring person.

A car was coming down the street. I felt my heart begin to race and stepped backwards into a shadow until it had passed by the house or came to a stop.

"Is this a letter of resignation?" An angry voice boomed from just inches away. I hadn't heard anyone approach I was so intent on keeping from being seen until Otto arrived. "I'm not in the habit of losing my domestic staff of one without two weeks notice. What have you got to say for yourself?"

I swallowed back all my pride, my fear and my self-respect. I should have known that God would not let me disappear into the night like some lowlife who had committed a crime. If I ever wanted absolution, I would have to admit what I had done. So I swung around to face the man my actions had harmed the most.

"This isn't exactly what it looks like, Peter," I said. "I am not your domestic staff of one. It's all been a huge mistake. I explained what I could in the note."

"I would rather hear it from you."

Peter was wearing lightweight shorts and a sleeveless t-shirt and looked as if he had not been to bed yet. Without saying anything more, he raised his arms and tore the note into tiny pieces. I watched them flutter away in the cool, night breeze.

"You shouldn't have done that," I retorted, suddenly too afraid of what might happen to recognize that a serious confrontation could be avoided by simply telling the truth.

"And why not? Have you been stealing my silverware?"

"Never! I already told you there's been a mistake. The sooner it's over, the better it will be for all of us."

He folded his arms across his chest and continued to stare at me with a mixture of confusion and pain. "Why don't you let me be the judge of that? I know what I said about falling in love with you a few hours ago was sudden, and maybe even a little out of line, but I never dreamed it would offend you to the point where you felt the need to run away. I thought we were friends, and friends just don't just disappear without an explanation."

"I have my reasons."

"Then share them with me. I think you owe me that much."

"I did that in the letter."

"Well, the letter's gone, and you're here. So start talking."

Tears of remorse and frustration were tickling the end of my nose, but the last thing I would allow myself to do was cry. "I can't. And even if I could, there isn't time. I have a car coming."

"So you really were going to run away after you told me you wouldn't."

"Yes," I replied without flinching.

In the half-light coming from a street lamp, he looked as if he'd been gut-kicked. I deserved his wrath, but I hadn't been around him long enough to know if there was a streak of violence underneath the composed veneer he allowed others to see. We were alone on a dark, deserted street, and he had already told me it wasn't safe to roam anywhere in L.A. at night. I watched as his face moved through a series of contortions before he spoke again.

"Disappearing without a trace and leaving me to wonder why you had gone and if I would ever see you again isn't fair."

"I wasn't thinking about being fair. I was doing what I thought was right for both of us."

"And what gives you the right to decide anything for me—other than what I might like to have for dinner? I'm a grown man who has been managing my own life for over a decade. I've thought a lot of things about you, Maya Holden, but I never once considered you a coward."

My eyes began to flame with sudden indignation. I might be doing a cowardly act right now, but I had waged the greatest battle of my life the past eighteen months. I had fought to make myself get up in the morning, and I had fought to make a life for my children. I was anything but a coward, except when it came to letting someone new gain access to a place in my heart.

"If it's an explanation you want, Peter, then you'll get it," I said as my lips quivered. "I'm not a housekeeper. It was all a game of pretense that started out innocently enough, and turned into the biggest debacle of my life. No one was supposed to get hurt, or even know it was happening. But I overstepped the role I was assigned to play, and you got caught in the middle without even knowing it."

Peter's chest was heaving with anger. "What the hell are you talking about?"

I spread my arms wide. "This whole charade. I came here because Hildie couldn't and my meddlesome Aunt Lil thought it would be a great idea if the two of us got to know each other."

"Pardon my bluntness, but who the hell is Aunt Lil?"

Quite suddenly, I didn't care whom I involved. Hate was a powerful motivator, especially when turned inward, and I had never felt such self-contempt. I had allowed myself to be used by someone I barely knew and a consequence would have to be paid.

"Lillian Farrow, queen of the corporate world and women's rights, and the biggest busybody imaginable."

"I must be losing my mind," Peter said as his look of anger turned to bewilderment. "I thought you were sent here by an agency."

"That's exactly what you were supposed to think. It was all part of a carefully executed plan so you wouldn't know what had hit you until it was too late."

"Are you trying to tell me that you were part of this scheme to deceive?"

"Only indirectly! I could have refused when I found out that Mrs. Newbold was expecting Hildie to cover for her. I guess they've done it in the past."

"They have, but why volunteer for something you aren't trained to do? Mrs. Newbold isn't a slave here, and it's not like I can't manage on my own for a few days. I've just become accustomed to having people wait on me."

"I could claim a moment of insanity, but the truth is that everything had been decided before I was let in on the plan. I haven't known my aunt for long, and she makes it rather hard to say no."

"From what I've heard, she can be a formidable opponent. That's why she's been so successful, but I still don't understand why you agreed to come if it isn't your line of work."

"I suppose one could say it was an ambush! I came here for a short visit, but Aunt Lil had to leave town on personal business. She needed Hildie's help and figured I would have plenty of time to work through some issues of my own while taking care of your home. It didn't seem like such a horrible idea until I got here and found out how serious your relationship with Lana really was."

"You could have told me what was going on right after you got here. I would have understood then, but . . . . "

"Not now," I finished for him. "I don't blame you for being angry. No one likes to be duped. But if you remember, I kept telling you that I had something important to say, and you kept putting me off. I'm not trying to justify what I've done, or lay any of the blame at someone else's feet. I accept full responsibility for my actions. I only wish I hadn't allowed Lana's warning to cloud my better judgment."

"Lana knew about this?"

"Not everything, only that Lillian Farrow was my aunt. She didn't know I wasn't a real housekeeper. She just thought I was out after her man."

Peter took a step away from me, and I knew by the set of his shoulders that I had done more than wreck havoc with his home. I had destroyed a major part of his life.

"It seems this little trick has backfired on all of us. I just got off the phone with Lana, and she's been offered the part."

"Is she taking it?" I asked.

"Most likely. I told her she deserved the chance to have the career she's always dreamed about."

"I thought she wanted to be an actress."

"Lana wants to be in front of an audience that's devoted to her, and she's tired of waiting around for me to make up my mind. I never wanted the jet-set life like she did. Now, I no longer have a girlfriend, and the woman I thought I was beginning to care about has turned out to be a phony. How surprising life is."

I felt the sting of his words, and they cut me deeply. "I can't change what's happened, Peter."

"So why not leave things as they were until the end of the week? Your charade would never have been detected."

"Maybe not, but I would still have to live with the guilt. And after what happened a few hours ago, I knew I couldn't play the game any longer."

"And what was it about our encounter in my back yard that so reformed you?"

"You already know the answer to that."

"How could I when I'm the fool who thought I was falling in love with you?"

"You're not a fool, Peter. You sparked something inside of me that I thought was dead, and it terrified me."

He looked at me with blank confusion, but I knew our promise of friendship was over. There was nothing left for me to do except plead for his forgiveness before Otto arrived.

"That makes no sense, Maya. We discover we like each other. That should bring us closer together, not drive us apart."

"I don't expect you to understand. I'm not running away from you, or even from the unethical things I've done the past few days. I'm running away from myself."

"Running never solves anything. What about your bogus commitment? You owe me two more days."

"You don't need me, Peter. You never have. Why would you even want me around after what I've just told you?"

"Under normal circumstances I probably wouldn't, but I don't feel like our relationship is strictly professional any longer."

I sighed and sank down on my suitcase before burying my face in my hands. "You don't know where I come from, why I'm here, or what I'll be doing when I leave."

"None of that seems important right now."

"But it is! I have a family and a home of my own to think about."

Blurting out the truth was the last thing I intended to do, and I looked up in time to see Peter's face turn as white as the shirt he was wearing.

"So everything has been a lie, especially pretending that you cared about me. I've met conniving people through the years, but you top the list. You had me convinced that you actually believed in family values and abstinence from sex, alcohol and rushing into anything. I didn't even care that you were a housekeeper. It's an honorable profession, but it never once entered my mind that you had a husband somewhere. I'll get my checkbook and see that you're properly paid for services rendered, and that includes the flowerbed."

My heart plummeted. "I don't want your money, Peter, especially for the flowerbed. That's the only honest thing to come out of this entire mess."

"Well, you're going to get it. I refuse to take anything from you."

He left me sitting on the suitcase, but I couldn't stay where I was. I rose to my feet and ran blindly from the driveway into the front yard. I wanted to scream—to let all the pent-up emotion of the past year and a half come to the surface in one agonizing breakdown that would evaporate with the rising sun and finally leave me at peace.

But only time could mend a broken heart, so I fought back the cascading tears as I threw my injured hands against the gnarled bark of an ancient maple tree and pleaded for deliverance. I should have stayed in Boston with Landi and Kenny where my world was stable if not complete. A good man telling me that he cared wasn't sufficient reason to send me over the edge, but I was in no condition to challenge what might be left of my sanity.

I'm not sure how long I stood there as my fragile world continued to crumble, but it seemed as if my entire past moved in front of my eyes like some silent movie on a large, outdoor screen. I saw myself as a child running through the canyons around my home in southern Utah, as a student with dreams too big to contain, as a young wife and new mother, and as a woman who lost everything when her husband died.

"Please forgive my unchivalrous behavior," Peter said as his hand came to rest on my shoulder. The unexpected physical contact made every vision fade. "I should have given you a chance to explain before cutting you off. I only said what I did about the flower garden to hurt you. I know it was given in friendship."

I turned my head just far enough to see his face before brushing some of the tears from my eyes. I had every right to grieve and even feel sorry for myself. I had been denied the chance to grow old with the man I loved, but the man standing just inches away—whose breath was caressing my neck—deserved to know what was really behind my impulsive behaviors.

"It was given in friendship, Peter, and nothing about this has been your fault. I got in over my head without realizing it."

"We all do things we wish we hadn't," he said as his hand dropped to his side. "And you can't assume all the blame. I was the one making advances. You were always a perfect lady, representing everything I have ever looked for in a woman. Maybe that's why I started to fall in love with you. I apologize for throwing your husband in your face. I only did it to cover feelings of rejection. How could anyone not want to be with the man or woman who was truly loved."

"That's just it, Peter, I do want to be with him."

"Then go home and enjoy what you have, but tell him that he'd better treat you right. If he doesn't, he'll have to deal with me."

Peter's sincerity should have made me smile, but it only brought more tears. "I would do that if I could, but I'll never get to be with him again, at least not in this life. My husband was killed trying to help others the winter before last."

Peter's arms reached out as if to hold me, but something stopped them from making contact. "I'm so sorry. I had no idea you were fighting such a burdensome monster. Do you feel like talking about it?"

"I'm not sure I can. I took this trip hoping it would bring added perspective, but all it's shown me is that I need a keeper so I don't get into trouble. At least I can say that I've seen a new side of life. It isn't mine, but it's opened my eyes to things I haven't been willing or ready to face."

He looked at me with my head pressed against the tree and the tears still flowing from my eyes, and I saw the tenderness in his countenance return. After everything I had done, he still felt compassion for me.

"You're not the only one who's felt overwhelmed when life takes an undesirable turn, Maya. There have been times when I didn't want to come back after a short trip home, but I needed to prove to myself that I wasn't afraid of failure or anything else. I'm sorry I put so much pressure on you. You seemed to be doing okay until I stepped out of line."

"Please don't apologize. I'm only leaving because I didn't know what else could be done to right a very serious wrong. I was more than fortunate in finding a true and lasting love. That doesn't happen very often, or so I've been told."

"Your husband was the lucky one. Not many women feel that kind of love, or loyalty, to their husbands even when they're alive."

"Ken made it easy for me to give everything I had to him. He became my heart and soul after we were married. We had a lovely home and two beautiful children. He was happy with his career and made sure I wanted for nothing while I raised Landi and Kenny."

"Sounds ideal."

I wrapped my arms tightly around the tree as if to gather the strength necessary to continue. "People used to tell me that young love was the ultimate experience of living, but they were wrong! Our love just got better and grew deeper as the years went by. We thought we would grow old together, but then Ken was killed and all I have left are memories."

"How did he die?" Peter asked. "You made it sound like an accident."

My eyes looked up at the swaying branches above my head while my mind searched that dimension called memory again.

"We were on a skiing trip—a celebration of twelve years of pure bliss. We spent the first night laying on the floor in front of a raging fire and planning our future. We slept late and had a lovely brunch at the lodge. Then we headed to the top of the longest run. I was still a novice skier but determined to prove to the man I loved that I was worthy of all his admiration and love. We even made a silly, little bet. He promised to buy a new rug for the den if I made it to the bottom without capsizing.

"I was halfway down the mountain when there was a rumbling under my feet and freezing ice particles began swirling around my head. It was an avalanche, whose origins   seismologists had somehow missed, and we were caught in the middle of it. I was completely buried underneath the snow. Ken clawed with his bare hands to free me, and then breathed life back into my body. My left leg was crushed and my right ankle sprained. I thought we had paid a big enough price for our outing by the time we made it back to the lodge, but I was wrong.

"A lot of people were missing, many of them presumed dead. The local search and rescue department kept asking for volunteers. Aftershocks were shaking the mountain, and they wanted to find any remaining survivors before it was too late. Ken stayed in the hospital with me until I was out of surgery, and then he went with them."

"And you didn't try to stop him?"

"I couldn't pressure him into doing something he would only regret. Ken wasn't the kind of man who could sit back and do nothing when others were in trouble and his own family was safe."

"He sounds like a saint."

"He wasn't a saint in the true sense of the word, but he was probably the closest to it of any man I've ever known. He loved life and wanted everyone to enjoy the same kind of blessings he had."

"That included you and your children."

I smiled. "Among other things. When we were married, it was a forever commitment. That knowledge is the only thing that's kept me going the past few months. I know we'll be together again when I die."

"How can you be so sure? Even those who come back after near-death experiences are a little vague about what we can expect after we die. Maybe we'll stay in our graves forever."

"We won't! I know that as surely as I know that the sun will rise from the east in the morning and set in the west at night. We weren't created just for this life. We have always existed and always will. Mortality is just part of a vast eternity, albeit the most important part."

"If you really believe that, why are you always so sad? That's the first thing I noticed when I saw your eyes. I remember now. We didn't meet in my kitchen. We met on Madame DuBois yacht. I was talking to you when Lana came up and made such an unpleasant scene. She recognized you from before. That's why she came down on me so hard after the dinner party at my house ended."

"What did she say?" I asked as I turned around to face him again. I didn't know how long we had been talking, but it couldn't take Otto much longer to get there.

"Only that you couldn't be trusted, and I needed to get rid of you before I lived to regret it."

"So why didn't you do as she asked?"

"The only people who make decisions for me are my manager and my director. I figured Lana was just upset because you didn't look anything like Mrs. Newbold. As beautiful as my former girlfriend is, she never allowed herself to trust any woman I found attractive or interesting. But I don't want to spend any more time talking about Lana. I want you to finish your story. You haven't told me how your husband died."

It would have been less painful to refuse his request, but he deserved to know the rest.

"Ken was supposed to be back some time the next day. I was beside myself with worry, but I couldn't even move. My left leg hung suspended from a pulley, and I had several cracked ribs. He was brought in over thirty hours later. The team he was with must have encountered a ground storm or got caught in another tremor. No one could ever tell me what really happened, but he wasn't the only one who went over a cliff. Ken knew that mountain like the back of his hand. He'd been skiing there all his life. The doctors did what they could, but there were too many internal injuries. He was in a coma for six weeks and then he was gone."

"Your children must have been a great comfort after such a horrendous ordeal."

"I would never have survived without them. They've spent the last two weeks with my parents. It's funny, but my daughter is the real reason I came to L.A. Imagine an eleven-year-old being perceptive enough to know that her mother needed time to regroup."

"She sounds like an amazing kid."

"Landi is bright, beautiful, kind and gentle. Of course, there are those inevitable times when she throws a tantrum or teases her brother."

"That's just being a kid."

"So the experts say. But knowing how fragile life is, I wouldn't trade even the bad times. My children are the best part of my life now that Ken is gone."

"I'm sure they are, but children can't fill all the hours of the day. What's going to happen when they don't need you as much as they do now?"

"That's the question I've found most perplexing lately. Sometimes I think I would give almost everything I have just to feel alive again."

"If I had the answers you were looking for, I would give them to you for free."

He was standing so near that I found myself reaching for his hand. Peter Richards deserved to find the kind of woman he was looking for—one without a past that would stop her from loving him with her whole heart.

"I know you would, but your kindness and understanding are only part of the reason you mean so much to me."

"Are you trying to shatter that macho image I've been trying so hard to maintain?" he asked as his fingers closed more tightly over mine.

"Not at all. I believe a man can be macho and sensitive too."

"That's what my mother keeps telling me. She still can't understand why I prefer tinsel town to stacking hay."

"I can," I replied as the electricity in the night seemed to make my heart a little beat faster. "Nobody in my hometown could understand why I wanted to move to Boston. I was supposed to marry the boy on the adjoining farm and live happily ever after."

"Why didn't you?"

"Probably for the same reason you moved away from Laslo. I wanted to experience more than I had growing up. Besides, I had this crazy belief that I would find the man of my dreams in Boston."

"And that's where you met Ken. Maybe we both outgrew our hometowns."

"I'm not so sure about that. We all need roots, and Ken and I often talked about moving back to Hurricane when we retired. There's something peaceful about living in the country."

"That's why I have my boat, the beach and a few other hobbies that help keep me grounded since it would be career suicide to leave this city right now."

"Like your carvings?"

He released my hand so abruptly that it slammed into my side. "How did you know about them? They are the one thing I do not discuss."

It was too late to retract what I had said, but explaining why I had invaded his privacy by snooping was a conversation I had hoped we would never have. "I was trying to get a feel for your home and went too far. I'm sorry for violating more of your trust, but I'm not sorry I saw them. They're magnificent. Those faces look like they could actually breath and talk. I found myself wondering what stories they had to tell."

His sigh was heavy, but it let me know that he wasn't going to censure me any further. "In that case, I'm glad you got to see them. In fact, I would like you to have one."

"I couldn't accept it," I said. "They're very personal and should be saved for the people who mean the most to you."

"And you're not sure you qualify?"

"How could I after everything I've done? I have no right to expect even friendship."

"Is that because you're the only one who has ever made a mistake? My friendship is never given lightly. And if you look deep within your heart, I'm sure you will see that what we have is the beginning of much more than that. I really wish you felt you could give it a chance."

His words made the blood pound in my temples. If I stayed, I would get caught up in something I couldn't control. Whether it was the right thing for me wasn't even an issue. I simply wasn't ready to let another man into my life. To stop the disabling dizziness, I leaned my head against the tree and closed my eyes. When I opened them again, Peter was gone and I could see Aunt Lil's limo in the driveway. I hurried towards it.

"I'm sorry it took so long, Mrs. Holden?" Otto said as he put my suitcase in the trunk and then opened the back door for me. "The car had a flat."

"Maybe things worked out better this way," I responded, sliding onto the leather seat and dropping my purse to the floor. "There were a few things that needed to be taken care of before I left."

He adjusted his seatbelt before looking at me through the rearview mirror. "Do you want me to take you back to the house?"

"I don't think so. I need to go home. Tell Aunt Lil I'll call her when I get there."

"She'll be very disappointed. I know she likes having you here, especially now that things aren't going so well."

"Is the senator worse?"

"No worse, but no better. That's the way it is with cancer."

"I wish things were different, Otto. I want to be there for her, but it just isn't possible right now. You'll give her my love, won't you?'

"It would be better if she heard it from you. She's a very special woman, Mrs. Holden. Only she's been hurt in the past and tries to hide it by pretending she doesn't care."

My eyes suddenly darkened. I knew what Otto was trying to say. Life without the right kind of love was hardly worth living. I was glad Aunt Lil had Senator Hastings, regardless of how much time they had to spend together. As for me, I had to relinquish the past before it consumed me.

I came out of my musings to hear a thumping on the roof of the car.

"Open the door, Maya," Peter was saying. "I have something for you."

I hesitated, knowing that if he touched me again I might never leave. I needed a man in my life just as much as Aunt Lil had told me I did, and Peter was one of the most handsome, forgiving, kind, sensitive and considerate men I had ever met.

"I didn't know where you'd gone," I said, pushing the button that made the window go down.

He handed me an object wrapped in white tissue paper. "I went to get this. I figured you should have a part of me to take with you. That way, you'll never forget what we've shared the past few days."

"I couldn't, even if I tried."

"Then stay and see what might happen between us. I meant it when I said I was falling in love with you."

"But what about the things I just told you—my marriage, my children and the things I can't seem to get over?"

"We all have pasts, and while I was surprised to find out that you had been married and were a mother, it hasn't stopped how I feel about you."

"But it has presented some rather unique complications?"

"Nothing in life is insurmountable when two people are heading in the same direction. I've always wanted a family."

"But not an instant one," I said.

"It's not how I thought it would happen, but they're a part of you. How could I not want to care for and cherish them?"

My eyes filled with tears, and I smiled tenderly up at him. "You're a wonderful man, and I know you mean what you say. But everything has happened so fast I can't even think straight right now."

"I'll help you."

"What about your own life? Taking on a wife and a new family could seriously hamper your friendships and your career. I have a home in Boston, church and civil responsibilities. And that doesn't include my father-in-law and the promise I made to help keep the firm in the family until my children were old enough to make an informed decision about a career. I just can't walk away from my past and everything I've worked for and believe in as if they never existed."

"I would never ask you to do that. But if the people in my professional life, along with my personal friends, can't adjust to a change that gives me everything I've ever wanted, they aren't worth having. I just want to be a part of your life, and I'm afraid that if you leave now I'll never see you again. Can you really walk away and never look back?"

"No! But I have to try to put the pieces of my past where they belong or there will never be a future for me."

"What about us? You can't expect me to forget these past few days. They've been some of the happiest of my life."

"Mine too."

"Then stay!"

My eyes clouded with tears.   Now that I had made the commitment to leave, I could admit to myself that I was just a little in love with Peter Richards. "I can't. Maybe someday."

"That may be too late, Maya. All we can be certain of is now."

He turned and walked away. I didn't try to stop him, but I held the package he had given me all the way to the airport without opening it. I knew it contained one of his carvings, and the thought made me sad. I had already taken so much from him—his strength, his courage, and even his love. All I had given to him in return was a flowerbed.

There was a two-hour wait at the airport after I secured a ticket. As I sat there watching people walk along the concourse, I thought about my first encounter with Aunt Lil—the smart fur stole, the red spiked heels and the attitude of compete composure and control. It was all an act designed to keep people at arm's length so they would never get to know the misunderstood girl who had sacrificed everything of real value to get what she thought she wanted.

But she had allowed me into her carefully guarded world. Perhaps she had sensed a kindred spirit who needed the kind of guidance only she could give. Or maybe she simply didn't relish the idea of dying alone. Regardless of the reason, deserting her when she needed me wasn't fair. So I took out my cell phone and tapped the icon that represented her land line number. I wasn't leaving Los Angeles because I wanted to. I was leaving because everything I believed about myself and what I treasured was being challenged.

"Good morning, Hildie," I said when a sleepy voice answered. I knew she never slept late because Aunt Lil didn't. "This is Mrs. Holden. Would it be possible to speak to my aunt?"

"Mrs. Farrow been pacing the floor since Otto got back but was afraid to call you herself. She's a proud soul and couldn't understand why you would leave without saying good-bye."

"That was wrong of me, but then I've been doing a lot of ill-advised things lately."

"And I'm partially to blame for that. Mrs. Farrow just needs to know that you're going to be okay. She's in the conservatory. I'll have her take the call from there."

"Thank you," I replied.

My aunt was being far more understanding than I deserved, but what did she expect after all the demands and unexpected news? I wasn't one of her servants who got paid for carrying out her wishes. I was a member of the family she had discarded so she could live life exactly the way she wanted.

"Maya," she said a few moments later. "I hope I haven't caused you too much distress. That was never my intention. I merely wanted you to have an experience that might bring some added perspective. What I was offering on my own didn't seem to be helping."

"My anguish is my own doing, Aunt Lil. Everything would have been fine if I had just stuck to the original plan and stayed out of Peter's way."

"Has he done something to hurt you?"

"No, he's been more than considerate when it comes to my inadequacies and poor decision-making skills."

"Then why are you leaving?"

"Among many other less-palatable things, Peter told me last night that he thought he was falling in love with me."

"But that's wonderful, Maya! It couldn't have happened to two finer people. I never dared hope things would turn out so well."

I wanted to laugh but couldn't seem to get past the pain. "Love isn't a panacea for everything. I think you're seeing life through those rose-colored glasses alluded to in *The Wizard of Oz* because you finally have your wonderful senator."

"Yes, but for how long? Life really is fragile, and you must grab opportunities when they come. That includes finding and keeping love."

"I'm glad your opportunity for experiencing real love has finally arrived, but it can't happen like that for Peter and me."

"Why not? You're both young and single."

"But we're not unattached."

"If you're talking about Lana, that was only a passing fancy. Peter is too smart to marry a woman who can't see beyond her own desires. He fell in love with you because it was destined to happen."

"My destiny was fulfilled when I married Ken. He gave me a home and a family. I can't see it happening again."

"I am aware of your nearly perfect past and supposed liabilities of today. But it isn't right to spend the rest of your life alone when there is a wonderful man who has already told you what most women would give nearly all they possess to hear. Despite my rather fallacious example, I do believe in committed love."

"There's more to building a successful relationship than that. Peter may be an extraordinary man who would treat me with great love and respect, but what about my deeply held beliefs? He isn't sure God even exists, and I've relied on him from the time I was old enough to kneel down and pray."

"Then convince him otherwise."

"I can't do that."

"Why not? If you have something you truly feel will make another person's life better isn't it your responsibility to share it? Maybe Peter is drawn to you because he sees something he likes but can't explain."

"What about his personal values? He does things I've avoided my entire life."

"So he drinks a little and has made love to more than one woman. Few people believe in complete abstinence from any of life's pleasures, and you're not exactly a virgin."

"That's different. Ken and I were married before we let our relationship progress that far."

"I'm not going to fault you for having somewhat antiquated beliefs, but you have to understand that you're in the minority. I don't condone illegal drug use, gambling away money that is needed elsewhere, drinking alcohol in excess or sleeping with anyone who's available. But sometimes people need a little motivation. How long has it been since you read the Bible? Christ loved the sinners. He never put himself above them. He got right down on their level and taught them correct principles so they could change their own lives."

"That's not fair, Aunt Lil. I'm more than willing to share my beliefs with someone who really wants to learn about them."

"But not if your heart is involved. You wouldn't be running away from Peter if it wasn't. You're afraid of what might happen if you stay."

"I'm trying to survive."

"No, you're making excuses because there is a risk involved. Don't you think Peter is worth it?"

"Of course he is, but how could I explain my involvement to Landi and Kenny and Ken's dad, not to mention my own parents? We've only known each other a few days."

"Fast doesn't mean wrong or impossible. Some of us need an unexpected kick in the derrière so we'll pay attention to what is really going on. Do you think it was easy for me to go after Tom? I had already rejected him once and had no reason to believe he would even talk to me. But he gave me a chance to explain and forgave me for squandering time we could have spent together. You've already lost one good man. Do you really want to take the chance of losing another one?"

"You make it sound like love conquers all, but it doesn't. Peter deserves to have a relationship that can last forever. I already have one."

"If I were you, I would leave details like that up to someone who is much wiser than we are. You can't tell me there isn't going to be a lot of sorting out when we get to the next life. At least that's what I'm counting on. I may have wasted a large portion of my mortal existence, but I still want to be with the people I love as much as you do."

Chapter 12

As I thought about what Aunt Lil had said while waiting for my flight, I knew she was right. I was afraid of everything I couldn't control and didn't understand. That wasn't the definition of a bad person—just a confused and vulnerable one who was scared to take another chance. If I left L.A. now, I might be walking away from exactly what God had in mind for me. But instead of returning to Peter's house as my heart told me to do, I boarded the plane and was soon back in red rock country with my family.

Landi and Kenny were delighted to see me. They loved their gifts and were so excited to tell me about their adventures that the subject of my vacation, or why I had cut it short, didn't even come up my first day back. In fact, no one mentioned my trip at all until I was sitting at the kitchen table with my parents the night before we flew home to Boston.

"Thanks for keeping the kids. I really appreciated it," I told them as my mother served fresh peach pie with ice cream on top. It had been a struggle getting my children to bed since they knew we wouldn't be back for at least a year, but I didn't want them overly tired on our early-morning flight. They'd had their dessert early.

"We loved having them," mom replied. "I just wish you didn't have to leave so soon. We haven't even talked about what happened while you were in California. Both dad and I are more than curious after what you told him, but we decided not to push for answers or explanations until you were ready."

I didn't want to cry, but tears tickled my nose as I set my fork down on the table. Telling my parents what I'd been through would bring much-needed relief, but I couldn't burden them with all my troubles. They had enough of their own to worry about. Still, I would never forget my time in L.A. Aunt Lil, Senator Hastings, Otto, Hildie and Peter had all become a very important part of my life, and it seemed unfathomable that I might never see any of them again.

"Oh, Ken," I thought as I sat there staring at my plate. "What am I supposed to do now?"

And then through a very penetrating darkness, I heard my father's voice and felt his hand on my arm. "I do believe my little girl is falling in love again. Only this time it isn't quite the Cinderella story it was with Ken."

I looked up at him through blurry vision. "Why would you even say something like that? Have you talked to Aunt Lil?"

"No! I've simply learned how to read between the lines over the years. You're much too practical to be swayed by one of your great-aunt's schemes unless something in your heart prompted it. It's not a crime to care about someone else, Maya. Ken doesn't want you to be alone."

"But I don't want anyone else!"

"I know that's how you feel right now, but the journey through the rest of your life has just begun. Living in a vacuum called the past isn't healthy. Landi and Kenny need the mother they had before their father died so they will feel more secure about their own futures."

"Did they say that?" I asked.

"More than once. They're lost and sad too, but they're ready to put some of the pain aside. They need you to be a vital and involved part of their voyages of discovery as they figure out who they're destined to be."

"Having some man in my life—regardless of how kind and accepting he might be—isn't a panacea to all our problems. It would just confuse the issues we have yet to work through."

"Perhaps, but it could also be the means for solving some of them. I'm not going to tell you what to do, but if you ever need someone to confide in your mother and I are always available."

"I know that," I said as my eyes searched the scarred surface of the wooden table that had been in our family for generations. "What concerns me are the consequences some of my actions have produced. I've never intentionally hurt anyone before."

"And you're sure you've done that?"

"Unfortunately, yes! I don't seem to know what's right for me anymore. When I met Ken everything fell into place. I truly believed he was the only man for me, and now I discover that there might be room in my heart for someone else. I don't want to be unfaithful to Ken."

Mom handed me a hankie—one of the dozens she had embroidered with colorful birds, flowers, geometric shapes and intertwining hearts. "You gave Ken everything while he was here and made him one of the happiest men alive, but I think you're doing a disservice to his memory by burying your heart. He's the one who taught you how to love without restraint, and finding out that you can care about someone else doesn't mean he will ever be any less important to you. It only means that you were meant to learn and grow in a slightly different way."

"How?" I skeptically asked.

"By showing him that he made marriage and loving someone so special that you would rather take a few risks and try it again than put an end to that very important and fulfilling part of living."

"It would be more than just a few risks, mom. Landi and Kenny don't want another father, and I have no desire for another husband. I still love Ken with every fiber of my being, but there's this aching loneliness inside because I want to be important to someone again. That said, Peter Richards can't possibly be the man Ken would approve of to help raise his children. He isn't even sure God exists."

"That is a dilemma," she said.

I fell into silent thinking as I sat in the homey, well-used kitchen where I had spent a joyous childhood and had first learned about loving other people. I had been attracted to Peter at the party aboard Madame DuBois' yaught—as women would always be attracted to him—but it would never have gone any farther if Aunt Lil had not interfered.

Nonetheless, I couldn't keep blaming her for my confusion or my actions. I had gone to Peter's house of my own free will. But instead of finding a man who was self-centered and knew how to manipulate women, I had found someone who was accepting, understanding and had a real passion for living. He had helped me smile again and had put aside his own feelings and possible desires to protect and defend me. But without common religious and moral beliefs, the ability to get along might not be enough to build on.

"It's more than a dilemma, mom. It has failure written all over it. My marriage to Ken was perfect. I won't settle for anything less."

"Even if it means spending the rest of your life alone? Marriages are never perfect. Heaven knows your dad and I have had our differences of opinion, but that doesn't mean we don't love each other. It only means that we're two different people who made a commitment to each other and to Heavenly Father. Growing together as one in love and purpose is the way it was meant to be, but don't make the mistake of idolizing Ken just because he's dead. He was a man—a very good man—but he wasn't perfect."

"Is that what you think I'm doing, putting Ken on a pedestal that no other mortal can reach?"

"Only you can answer that," she replied. "I haven't been where you are, and I won't tell you how to live your life any more than your father will. Agency is man's greatest gift, but living with the outcomes of our decisions is part of the process. I can only tell you to put your trust in God and follow your heart. Any other advice would be less than fair."

"I love you both so much," I said, rising to my feet and pulling them into my arms. I had never appreciated being part of a family more, but it was true that the decisions I made over the next few weeks had to be my own. "Maybe I am idolizing my marriage to Ken, but I can't remember any bad times until the very end."

"That's the way it should be, Maya," dad said. "I only want to add one thing to what has already been said. Opportunities generally only come along once."

I wanted to protest, but his look silenced me.

"I'm not telling you to run off and marry some guy just because he's there. I'm only suggesting that you look at things from every perspective before making a decision that can't be undone. I've discovered that many things in life are not simply black and white, right or wrong. There are degrees. And sometimes situations that seem completely hopeless can be turned into something wonderful."

"Peter did give me something before I left, but I haven't had the courage to open it," I admitted.

"Why not?" dad asked. "I've never known you not to be curious."

"I'm curious enough, but I already know what it is."

"And that displeases you?"

"Not in the least. It just makes me feel guilty because I invaded his privacy when I first got to his house."

"You went there to be his housekeeper. It only stands to reason that you would want to become familiar with your new surroundings."

"That's not the point, dad. I was snooping in his garage, found a key, and without considering the consequences opened the door to his workroom. I've never done anything remotely like that before. I even handled some of his wood carvings. They were magnificent. It was almost like looking into his soul."

"We all have lapses in judgement," mom said. "Was he upset with you about it?"

"No, he just looked at me with surprise when I let the nature of my transgression slip."

"Then no real harm was done, other than to your pride."

"Maybe not, but I always thought I was a much better person than that."

"You are a good person, Maya, but humans make mistakes. If he's given you one of his carvings as a reminder of the time you spent together, he can't be all that upset with you."

"I'm not sure Peter has an unkind bone in his body. I'm just not comfortable being around someone who is always in the spotlight and has women from around the world fawning over him."

"So it isn't the man himself you have issues with?"

"Hardly! He was a true gentleman."

"Then remember that when making a final decision. Not everyone we meet is spouse material, but we can never have enough friends."

"Thanks for the pep-talk," I said before kissing my parents good night and climbing the staircase to my old bedroom. "I'm going home where I belong. I need a highly-structured routine. When left to my own devices, all I do is get into trouble and confuse myself."

At the top of the stairs, I tiptoed quietly into the my old bedroom so I wouldn't awaken my daughter. But when I turned on the lamp by the edge of the bed so I could find the package Peter had wrapped, she opened her eyes.

"Is it morning already?" she asked.

I moved to her side before responding. "Not yet. It's just a little after eleven. I didn't mean to wake you. I just came in to get something."

"Your present?"

"What present is that?" I inquired.

"The one in the top dresser drawer. I thought it might be for me, but you already gave me so many things, including that beautiful dress."

"So you really like it? I wasn't sure girls who were almost twelve still wore fancy dresses, except to church on Sunday. All I ever see you in is jeans."

"They're not just jeans, mom, they're brand names."

She sounded exasperated, but I couldn't blame her for that. I had been raised in a family where my mother made most of clothes I wore until I was old enough to work and buy them for myself. The only brand name I had ever known when it came to jeans was *Levi*.

"Sorry, Landi," I said. "I really am trying to modernize."

"I know, and the dress is awesome, but you forgot the most important thing."

"What was that?"

"An autograph! How am I ever going to convince my friends that you met someone famous without it? You didn't even take a picture of him."

"It must have slipped my mind. Everything happened so fast."

"Like what, mom? You were in his house for days."

"Just grown-up stuff like work, trying to fit in without getting into trouble and some very heavy conversations."

"Yuck!" she scowled.

"It wasn't all yuck, Landi. Peter is a good man who made allowances for my many blunders. Remind me to tell you about the broken casserole and flooding his kitchen."

"You can tell me about it now," she yawned.

"I think you need to be fully awake for a story like that. Now go back to sleep. I will be getting you up in a few hours."

"Why can't you just call and ask him for an autograph? I know you have his number."

"I don't have it on speed dial, but I'll see what I can do." There was no reason to upset her because I had made so many mistakes. She was a child who just wanted something exciting to share with her friends. "What happened to you not wanting me to be interested in another man?"

"Peter Richard's isn't a man. He's a television star."

Her naivety made me smile. Men were men no matter what they did for a living. "And that makes a difference?"

"It sure does. He gave you that present, didn't he? Can I see what it is?"

I walked over to the dresser, opened the top drawer and removed the crumbled package. A surge of emotion almost overcame me just holding it in my hands again. "Why don't you do the honors, Landi?"

She eagerly tore at the paper as if it was Christmas morning. I gasp when I saw what she had unwrapped.

"How did he know that was the one?" I whispered as I gazed in wonder at the carving of the fisherman—the gnarled face, the rough hands, and the eyes that held the wisdom of the ages.

"This is cool," Landi said. "Where do you think he got it?"

"He carved it," I replied, gently taking it from her. "He had an entire workroom filled with them, but this was my favorite."

I was studying each minute detail when Landi's next words caught my attention. "He sent a note. Do you want me to read it to you?"

"Sure," I said without thinking.

"It's kinda strange, mom."

"In what way,?" I asked as my heart began to pound.

"Because it doesn't make any sense. What does *When you can finally see, please come back to me* mean."

"I'm not sure," I responded, grateful I was sitting down. "That whole adventure with him seems rather unreal."

But something about the note and my attitude towards it bothered her. "You aren't planning to leave us again, are you?"

"No, Landi," I said, gathering her into my arms and resting my cheek against her satiny hair. "I'm not going anywhere except back to Boston with you and Kenny—the only three pieces of the puzzle we'll ever need."

Chapter 13

Back in Boston, both Landi and Kenny settled into their former routines much more quickly than I did. School was about to begin, and they were anxious to resume accustomed activities and be with their friends. Their summer had been a refreshing change from the one before where we all sat around the house in a state of numb agony and disbelief because Ken was no longer with us.

They had action-packed tales of adventures of farm living that could be embellished if they so desired. No one they knew had ever been to the sun-baked land of southern Utah where the rocks were red, the weather hot and the flora and fauna decidedly different than most anything that could be found in the city.

Landi hounded me about Peter's autograph for several days. His home number was firmly fixed in my mind, but opening Pandora's box again was something I simply couldn't do. Whenever I thought about our last few hours together the confusion became so intense that I felt as if I might become physically ill. Not only did I have the kiss to feel guilty about, but I also had the note he'd included with the carving to ponder. What did he expect me to see, and why would I even consider returning to the place where I had become a woman I no longer knew? If he truly believed he was falling in love with me, he could contact Aunt Lil. She would set him straight about the advisability of reaching out to me.

I had Ken's father over for dinner the night after we got home. His expression of relief when his grandchildren threw themselves into his arms was all the proof I needed that I had done the right thing by coming back. We were all he had left, and changing the course of my existence simply because an attractive man had expressed an interest wasn't something a rational, mature woman would do. He thanked me for the paperweight, and listening attentively throughout the entire meal as Landi and Kenny told him about life on the farm with my parents.

It was a pleasant evening, and I was ready to tell him I had come to a firm decision about going back to school so I could be a functioning member of the firm. I ached with a loneliness that was even greater than when I lost Ken, and empty hours with nothing more productive to do than take care of the house and my children would give me too much time to think. I was already having trouble remaining focused on simple tasks like doing laundry, pulling a few weeds or opening the mail.

My love for Ken was as strong as it had always been, but I couldn't seem to forget about Peter. I would hear his voice and his laughter in my head at the most inopportune moments. And when I closed my eyes at night, it was often his face I saw and not Ken's.

But my decision had been made, and since I wasn't about to change my mind, I did the only thing I could. I pushed my feelings aside and plunged headlong into my new commitments.

Ken's father was delighted with my resolve and invited me to join him at the office for on-the-job training while I was taking classes via the internet. I could set my own hours and be available when my children needed me. It was an ideal situation, and one that gave me a reason to get up in the morning. Landi and Kenny didn't seem to mind when I told them our routine might be somewhat different than it had been in the past. They were used to helping out, and I wasn't going to require anything that would take away from their childhoods.

I was given Ken's old office. At first, I thought there would be too many memories to work there and be happy. But just the opposite proved to be true. I loved sitting in his chair and running my hands across his desk's smooth surface. I loved looking at the pictures we had chosen together and put on his walls. And I loved finding those special memos he had written by hand. The room was alive with his presence, and my labors were like a voyage of discovery with my husband at the helm, rather than a room filled with nothing but sorrow.

Todd Foster, the associate that had been brought in when Winston Turner decided he was definitely going to retire at the end of the year, wasn't exactly happy to see me. He wanted to become a full partner. But I outranked him just stepping in the door, and I had very little practical experience and no degree in the field. That made him suspicious of everything I said or did, but he couldn't openly go against me because I owned a third of the stock in the company and had the right to take an active part. So he treated me with what could only be descried as reserved indifference as I tried to make myself useful.

On the other hand, Ken's cousin, Jeff Talbot, and I became immediate friends. He had accepted the offer to merge his small, independent firm with Turner, Holden and Holden. The paperwork was complete. All that remained was adding his name to the plaque outside the building and to the letterhead inside the office. He was in the process of closing the doors to his old office and contacting all of his clients about the change. He would take up permanent residence as soon as Winston Turner walked out the door. That would happen the first of December since Fiona wanted to spend the holidays abroad.

Jeff was single and more than grateful for my frequent invitations to dinner. Ken's father always joined us. After the children had said their nightly prayers and were tucked safely in bed, we would pour over files and consult with each other about tax laws and what was happening in the stock market. We planned mergers and decided when it was time to pull out of one commodity and buy into something else.

I knew Jeff didn't need the mentoring since he had run his own company for several years, but he was entering the big leagues now and recognized the value in learning everything he could from a master. And H. Holden held nothing back. He explained tactics, semantics and personal values as many times as was necessary until we understood exactly what his position was and why. His company had been built on the integrity of the people who worked there, and knowledge meant nothing if it wasn't used appropriately.

I had a lot to learn, but my mind was open, and I definitely had the incentive to succeed. I wanted to lead my children by example so they would never be afraid to take on a seemingly impossible challenge.

That made three students in our home—one of whom had been out of the classroom for almost a decade and a half. I thought my decision to become a student again might create undo havoc, but I soon learned that blessings often come in disguises. I was so busy studying at night—when I wasn't going through things with Ken's father and cousin—that Landi and Kenny soon decided it was more fun doing homework at the kitchen table with me than it was watching television or playing computer games. This renewed interest in their own educations soon brought dramatic results. Instead of the C's they had been receiving since Ken's death, they we back to A's and B's.

I was proud of them for that. They were putting the past where it belonged and getting on with their lives. That set a powerful return example for me. Feeling sorry for myself when there were so many rewarding things left to experience was unproductive and selfish. God had never told anyone that life would be easy, only that it would be worth it when the bigger picture was seen.

We still missed Ken dreadfully and talked about him everyday. But instead of continual sorrow raging in our hearts, we found we were beginning to make plans for a more pronounced future. Both Landi and Kenny were determined to go into the family business. I didn't discourage them, although I knew they would likely change their minds any number of times before a final course was set. But for now, those dreams provided a sense of security and gave us a chance to build something that included Ken without having him with us.

Leaving my home, and the hundred and one little things I did everyday that made it such an intrinsic part of who I was, proved a real challenge. But after a few weeks of leaving everything behind and many things undone, I began to adjust. Not that it was easy. I was a tidy, organized person by nature, and having dishes in the sink and laundry waiting in baskets to be done kept me awake at night. But sacrifices had to be made if we wanted to see different results.

Then one day, I realized I was starting to feel like a different person simply because I was no longer the little housewife who lived and breathed under the watchful and tender care of a loving husband. I was a wife put on hold, a widow, and that meant that I needed to grow up and discover the strong parts of my personality that would allow me to become an independent person who could be happy and useful despite her loss. That was certainly a new insight, but it took a powerful amount of courage to follow through.

"Don't you think you're pushing it just a little too hard?" Ken's father asked me during one of our late night study sessions in early October when Jeff wasn't with us. He had a date with a cute redhead he'd met at the gym. Her name was Angela, and she taught first grade in a local, private academy.

"It's what I need, dad," I replied. "You don't think I'm neglecting my children and my other community and church responsibilities, do you?"

"Of course not. You've always been able to multi-task, and you're going to be a wonderful business partner someday, but you never take any time for yourself."

"I don't need to. I enjoy what I'm doing. Besides, there's so much to learn, and with my children, my home and everything else I really don't have the time."

"But you're young. You should be going out occasionally so you can meet new people or reconnect with ones you already know."

"I could say the same thing about you. Come to think of it, I haven't seen you with Violet James lately."

"We still see each other occasionally."

"But not like you used to."

"I suppose not. We decided we liked being friends too much to ruin what we have by getting married. She wants to be free to lavish her time and money on her grandchildren, and so do I. But what about you, Maya? You've said next to nothing about your trip to the coast. I was afraid you might meet someone and never come back."

"I did meet an interesting man, but I wasn't in a place where it could turn into anything serious."

He swallowed hard, and I could tell that he was fighting to keep the tears from forming. As much as he lectured me about getting out and developing a social life, he was afraid that if I actually found one it would take me and my children away from him.

"You don't say," he finally responded. "Why is it that you never mentioned him before?"

"Because he's a television star, a daytime television star."

"No kidding! I thought all they cared about was ratings, fame and money. How did you meet?"

I wasn't going to explain what Aunt Lil had talked me into doing. Even my parents only knew half of that story. My only thought in mentioning Peter was giving my father-in-law a reason to quit suggesting that I put myself out there so I could meet someone new. I had already tried that with almost disastrous results.

"Let's just say that it was a comedy of errors that is best left in the past. Aunt Lil knew him and thought I should too."

"Have you watched his show since you've been back?"

"No, dad. He's on a soap opera."

"Ken's mom watched a few of them when she was sick. I think she felt a connection to some of the characters, and the storylines helped her forget what she knew was coming."

"I'm sorry for all the losses you've had to endure, dad."

"So am I, but I can't dwell on the past any more than you can if I want to be a contributing member of society. I need you to know that I'm here if you ever need someone to listen. And I'm not just talking about business. You're my daughter, and I want you to be happy. If that means finding someone new, I want to know about that too."

"If that ever happens, you'll be one of the first people I tell."

He let out a sigh of relief. "I hope so. I know how strong your loyalty is to my son, but if you did find someone else, I wouldn't be upset about it. You should get married again."

"That's not a possibility I'm even considering right now. I have a very full life just the way it is. I couldn't add anything more and survive."

"You say that now because you're still grieving."

"I'm not sure that's ever going to change. Ken was the love of my life, and that only happens once."

"I felt the same way about Beatrice. We were married for forty years, fifteen of them before Ken was even born. You only had twelve, and you're too young to spend the rest of your life alone. Ken would want you to feel loved and cherished again."

"Maybe if the right man came along, and all the other circumstances fell into place, I would consider it. But that isn't likely to happen, so I'm not going to worry about it."

"Then I won't say anything more since I'm not sure living with a soap opera star would be all that good for my grandchildren. They see enough of the seedy side of life right here. Still, it isn't healthy to spend all your time working and studying. You need to have a little fun."

"I'll think about it," I said.

That seemed to satisfy him. I was glad because Aunt Lil and I were still trying to make peace after what had happened during my trip to the coast. I talked to her every few days. Sometimes she was happy. Sometimes she was worried, and sometimes she was scared about the inevitable. But she was never bitter about the fact that Senator Tom Hastings was dying. She seemed to accept that as part of her destiny—something I was still trying to do with Ken.

"I've never known what it's like to lose someone I really love," she said to me one evening when I answered her call to get away from the lesson I was trying to decipher on the computer. "I'm afraid I was a little rough on you when I first called you last summer. I thought it should be easy to just let the past go and get on with the task at hand because that's what I've always done. But during these past few weeks, I've begun to realize that I let August Farrow destroy the most important part of my being a woman. I forgot how to feel until I met you and learned of your special relationship with Ken. I understand now that my life will lose much of its meaning when

Tom dies. I love him so much. Do you have any idea what we've been doing lately?"

"No," I replied.

"I've been going back to church, and I've been taking Tom with me when he feels up to it. He's on oxygen all the time now and barely has enough strength to get out of bed, but he does what he can because he knows it pleases me."

"I'm sorry his condition is deteriorating so rapidly, but you haven't been inside of a church since you left home as a teenager. What prompted that change?"

"Once again, you did," she responded. "I know I'm going to lose the man I love, but I also know it won't be forever if I can get my act together. We've even been reading the Bible and praying together. At first he resisted since he's a confirmed agnostic, but I think he's finally at a point where believing there is something beyond the grave doesn't seem like such a bad thing. Won't your folks, and all the people back in Hurricane who remember me, get a laugh over that one? Old Lillian Farrow, straight-shooter and women's libber, finally deciding that marriage and family are important. Do you think there's any hope for an old reprobate like me?"

"Of course there is, Aunt Lil," I said. "It's never too late to accept the Savior's atonement."

"But I've wasted most of my life. When I think of all the good I could have done . . . Well, it makes me more than sick inside."

"God knows what's in your heart."

"I'm beginning to understand that principle now," she said. "I only hope I have time to make amends for some of the things I've done in both my professional and personal life. In some ways, I'm jealous of Tom. He never thought about religion until recently, and I've spent my entire life running away from everything I was taught as a child because I didn't want to be encumbered by what I thought were archaic and stifling beliefs."

"I've often wondered if people who found God later in life were better off than those of us who have always been believers, but I hate to think where I may have ended up if I'd been left to my own devices. I've always needed someone to lean on, and I can't deny that my blessings far outweigh the struggles."

"Blessings I missed out on trying to prove that Lillian Farrow could make money with no one around to help her."

"Money's important."

"But not at the expense of everything else."

"You've supported a lot of charities."

"That's true, but I've never had to dig deep for what I've given. It was usually just the excess from some investment, and it could be claimed as a tax deduction so it was never a real loss. I've been totally selfish with my liquid assets."

"But you've changed, and there will always be people who need help."

"Quite true, and I intend to do more of my share. But what I really want is to leave most of my estate to you."

"That's totally unnecessary, Aunt Lil," I replied as what she was suggesting started to sink in. "Ken left me well provided for, and I'm starting to earn a little on my own."

"I'm glad you've found something productive to do since running away from here, but you're a mother first and should be home taking care of your children."

"Landi and Kenny are having fun studying with me, and I'm only away from home when they are. I want to keep Ken's business alive for them."

"Ken was everything August wasn't, but I don't need the money either. Besides my own, Tom is leaving everything he has to me, and that's a considerable amount as well."

"Then you should decide what you want to do with it together."

"We've already done that, but neither of us feel right about giving everything to strangers when there's someone in the family who could put it to better use. What you don't know about financial management, you'll soon learn. That puts you in a perfect position to manage the bulk of our estates. You can use what you want and invest everything else. Not every charity can be trusted, especially when the ones running it

change. You might as well give it some thought because I won't change my mind. The
adjustments to my will are already being made."

I could have brought up my parents, my uncles and aunts or even my brother as
possible alternatives to share her fortune, but she hadn't seen any of them since leaving
home. If I did as she asked, it would be huge for our company and make me a bonafide
investor. But if the economy tanked, I could lose everything.

"I'm still learning the ropes, Aunt Lil. Don't you want someone with more
experience?"

"I trust you, Maya. I know your character and values. When I'm gone, it's not going to matter to me what happens to my money. I just need to know I'll be leaving what I have in the best possible hands. And I am sorry about forcing Peter on you the way I did. Naturally, I didn't think about complications like your children or your religious or moral beliefs."

"You did what you thought was right, and you weren't so far off the mark when it came to thinking I needed a friend. Peter taught me a great deal about myself. Have you heard anything about him recently?"

I hoped I sounded only casually interested, but when she hesitated, I felt my heart sink. Thoughts of what our life together may have been like if all the complications were stripped away had been invading my waking hours as well as my fantasies.

"Nothing concrete, only that he's more or less taken himself out of circulation. I don't know what that means, but I could check on him if you like."

"That won't be necessary," I replied. "I was just curious. He's a good man and deserves to be happy."

"I suppose he's doing as well as the rest of us. I only know that he hasn't been seen at any of his regular haunts recently. It's caused quite a stir. A man like Peter Richards doesn't come along everyday, and the women in Hollywood know it."

"Don't Aunt Lil," I said.

"I wasn't going to rub your face in it, but have you even tried to contact him since you went home? It's been over two months."

"Time isn't going to change what went wrong between us. Deception is never the basis for a lasting relationship, and I wouldn't know what to say to him if I did."

"I'm sure you could think of an ice-breaker."

"Not after the way I botched things up. He deserved to be treated so much better."

"I'm sure he did, Maya, but I think Peter is more understanding than you give him credit for. All you need to do is be honest with him. I wish I had learned the value of truthful feelings years ago. It would have prevented a lot of heartache, but I am glad I put my pride on hold for Tom. Our relationship means everything to me."

"This isn't a matter of pride. I have a family and a great many other responsibilities. Besides, I'm sure he's found someone else if Lana hasn't come back. I know he's interested in marriage and family."

"Fancy that!" Aunt Lil said. "Well, I've got to run. Tom and I have a date with the doctor in the morning, and I want to spend some time with him before he drifts off to dreamland. Pray that we'll get some good news. We could really use it right now. I'll call you when I know more."

"Okay," I responded. "Give him my love."

She ended the call, and I went back to studying. I had a huge test the following day and didn't stop until midnight. My head was pounding and I hoped I would sleep, but that wasn't what fate had in mind. Just as I was just turning back the bedcovers my cell rang again.

"What's up?" I asked when I saw who was calling. I had spoken to Aunt Lil less than three hours earlier. "Is everything all right?"

"No, it's not," she replied. "I was reading to Tom from one of his favorite books and thought he'd fallen asleep. But when I brushed a lock of hair away from his forehead, I knew he was no longer breathing."

"Did you call for an ambulance?"

"He was already gone, and I needed some time alone with him before all the questions and decision-making began. I'm sitting in our bedroom holding his hand. He looks so peaceful now that I've disconnected the oxygen and morphine drip. I wish I could go on looking at him forever."

She sounded so young and tender that the tears came quickly to my eyes. "Do you want me to come?"

"If only you would. I thought I could get through this by myself, but I've discovered during the past two and a half months that I never want to be alone again. I'm just a foolish, old woman who never let anyone in until it was too late for more than a few weeks of happiness. I even messed up meeting you."

"That's not true, Aunt Lil. You helped me out of the downward spiral I was in."

"And now I'm in one myself. Do you know what I really want to do? I want to be around children. I want to hold them in my arms, tell them stories and pretend they're the grandchildren I never thought were that important before."

"You could do that with Landi and Kenny," I suggested. "Why don't you come and stay with us once everything is settled in California?"

"Maybe I will, but I don't want anyone feeling sorry for me."

"I'd never do that, Aunt Lil. I love you."

"Did you know you're the only person who's told me that nearly my entire adult life, with the exception of Tom?"

"He's a wonderful man."

"The best, but I'm not going to mourn for him. I'm going to get right on with the plans we've made and hope I'll see both him and Helen again some day."

"I'm sure you will. Our relationships don't have to end just because we die."

"That's what I'm counting on. But I need to spend a little more time with Tom right now. Once word gets out, I won't be able to do that."

"Take all the time you need. That's what I did with Ken."

"Oh, Maya," she cried out, suddenly unable to suppress her feelings of agony any longer. "I'm not sure I'll make it through this. Tom was all I ever wanted, and we had so little time together. It just isn't fair."

"That's the way it is when we lose someone we love. I never expected to be a widow before I was thirty-three. But the real tragedy would be never having shared that kind of love at all. You'll make it through this, and I'll be there to help you any way I can."

"Then I'll see you soon."

"As soon as arrangements can be made."

When I sat down at my computer to look at available flights a short time later, I questioned the propriety of taking children to the funeral of someone they had never met. Senator Hastings had been a popular, public figure for many years, and Aunt Lil would be occupied with plans for a memorial service and listening to expressions of condolence.

But the more I thought about it, the more certain I became that taking Landi and Kenny with me was the right thing to do. Aunt Lil was reaching out to her family for the first time in over 50 years. She needed our acceptance, understanding and love. We needed her spontaneity, wisdom and self-assurance.

Besides, I had a selfish reason for not wanting to leave my children behind. I didn't want to go alone, and there was so much I still needed to teach them before they ventured out on their own.

Ken would be delighted with how far they had come. I was the one who was still learning that trying to shield them from life's hard knocks and tragedies would not help them become happy, productive adults. That's why I was making plans to take them out of school for a week, and I wasn't worried about lessons any of us would miss. They could be made up later. I wasn't even concerned about whether or not Aunt Lil would send Otto to the airport to meet us. I was simply living for the moment and doing what had to be done.

I called my mother early the next morning to let her know what had happened and what I intended to do. She said they would accompany us, but I told her it wasn't necessary. Under the circumstances, a simple card or a phone call would be enough. She was surprised by my attitude.

"You've turned into a wise and responsible woman, Maya. Not that you haven't been an adult for a long time, but few months ago you were afraid to even come home with the children."

"I'm definitely a different person now," I replied. "I've finally accepted the fact that Ken isn't coming back, and if I want a life that is filled with more than sorrow I have to make some adjustments."

"Like going back to work while you're attending school. It seems a bit much to me."

"I need to stay busy, and the kids are flourishing in their own studies again. It helps to finally understand that Ken's death is just one challenge in a whole slew of difficulties I'll have to face if I want to go where he is when I die."

"You'll get there," she replied. "I like to remember that our Heavenly Father will never ask us to take on the seemingly impossible alone. Even if we can't be with the one we love most, there will be others to help us along the way."

"I know," I responded as memories of an unforgettable night on the beach with white caps crashing against the rocks and salty air brushing across my cheeks came floating back. "All it takes is the courage to let go of the past and try something new. A dear friend once told me that."

Early the next morning, I pulled three suitcases from the front closet before sending an email to Landi and Kenny's principal telling her that there had been a death in the family, and we would be out of town until the following Wednesday. Then I called Ken's dad. If he was concerned by my impulsive behavior, he didn't say anything. He merely told me to be careful, and he would see to everything that needed to be done while I was gone. He offered to take us to the airport, but I told him we had decided to take a cab. Our flight was leaving at one, and that was the middle of his work day. I was just putting my cell phone on the counter when Landi came bounding down the stairs.

"Mom, it's nearly eight. You forgot to wake us up."

I stepped from the kitchen in time to see the look of fear on her face when she saw the suitcases. Despite my resolves, our world was still very fragile.

"You're not going away, are you?" she asked.

"Not without you and Kenny," I clarified.

"But, mom, it's Tuesday. You never let us miss school unless we're running a fever or throwing up."

I smiled at my beautiful daughter. "This is an exception. We're going on a trip."

She looked at me as if I had lost my mind. And Kenny, who by now was standing at the top of the staircase, hollered, "Are we going back to the farm?"

I motioned for him to join us. He did—two steps at a time all the way to the bottom. "No, we're going to Los Angeles to see Aunt Lil."

Landi frowned and reached up to place her hand on my forehead. "You must be sick. You said California was no place for us."

I brushed her hand away. "Things change and so do people. I've been holding all of us back because I was sacred. I realize now that it's important to take a chance once in awhile. That's how we grow, and it's what your father would want. He made each day count because he wasn't afraid to show others how much love he had in his heart. That's what we must learn to do. It's part of our legacy to him."

"But why California?" Landi asked.

I took them into the family room where I could explain our reason for going. Landi sat down in a chair, but Kenny snuggled next to me on the sofa.

"Aunt Lil called late last night. Her husband died, and she wants me to come and help with the funeral."

The color drained from my daughter's face. "I don't want to go to another funeral. Why can't we just go back to grandma and grandpa's house?"

"I suppose that could still be arranged, but I would really like you to go with me. It was a spur-of-the-moment decision. I haven't even told Aunt Lil that we're all coming. But I think she needs us."

"Why? She doesn't even know Kenny and me."

"Because we understand what she's going through and might be able to help. No one expects you attend another service, but I think you might enjoy swimming in her pool, having your meals fixed by someone who does it for a living, and maybe even taking a side trip or two if there's time. The beach is wonderful, and there are plenty of other sights to see."

"Like Disneyland?" Kenny asked.

"I can't make any promises, only that it will be another adventure you can tell your friends about when we get back."

Landi and Kenny were packed before I was. It was amazing how fast they could move when an activity that held so much promise was involved. But my anxiety level only rose as I made sure nothing had been left behind. And by the time the taxi arrived, I knew I had been somewhat hasty in making such a momentous decision. But backing down after the discourse I had given them would only undo any progress we had made towards accepting life as it was now.

The flight was uneventful, and Otto was waiting for us at the end of the concourse when we walked into the Los Angeles International Airport a few hours later.

"It's good to see you again, Mrs. Holden," he said, inclining his head. "These must be your children."

"Yes, they are," I replied, wondering if he had even been told they might be coming with me. "Landi and Kenny, I would like you to meet Aunt Lil's chauffeur, Mr. Otto . . . "

"Just Otto," he finished for me. "If you'll come with me, we'll get your luggage and be on our way.   Mrs. Hastings is anxiously awaiting your arrival."

I wanted to ask him how she was holding up, but he seemed as remote as he had been the first time we met. However, he did let Kenny sit up front with him in the limo, and my son chattered happily the entire way to Aunt Lil's villa high in the Hollywood hills. He was definitely his father's son. Ken had never met anyone he didn't consider an instant friend.

Landi sat beside me in the back seat, her eyes staring out the tinted window next to her right shoulder. She appeared to be oblivious to most everything I tried to point out, other than the fact that she was in Los Angeles where anything could happen and usually did. I spent most of my time wondering what I would say to my aunt when I saw her. Telling her how sorry I was for how I had acted again hardly seemed enough.

It wasn't long until we pulled up to the iron gates that separated Aunt Lil's house from the rest of the world. They opened automatically, and we were immediately greeted by the same overpowering fragrance of roses I had noticed three months earlier.

"Wow!" Landi said, looking around, her eyes as big as saucers. "That house looks like a hotel."

"I know," I replied. The grandeur of my aunt's home had impressed me on first sight too. Even now, I had trouble believing that one person could amass such a fortune, but a price had been paid for her wealth. There were no cars in the driveway, and I questioned Otto about it. People had been at our home continually after Ken's death.

"The word isn't out yet," he said, removing our suitcases from the trunk. "Hildie and I would have helped her like we've always done, but she wanted you here before a notice was put in the paper. She said she needed her family."

I now understood his reticent and somber attitude. Until my arrival, he and Hildie had been Aunt Li's family. Resenting me for upsetting that dynamic was a very human reaction. I would do what I could to make sure my presence now didn't cause any further upsets.

Otto opened the ornately carved, wooden door to the house for us before carrying our suitcases inside. "Mrs. Hastings is in the drawing room. You know the way. I'll see about getting rooms ready for the children."

He nodded and left. Landi and Kenny gripped my hands as we started down a wide hallway with freshly polished floors towards the back of the house. I knew exactly how they felt. Everything around us suggested an audience with a queen. Aunt Lil came rushing towards us when we got close enough for our footsteps to be heard.

"Maya, darling, how good of you to come so . . . " Her words stopped in mid-air when she saw Landi and Kenny.

I was momentarily afraid I had done the wrong thing by bringing them, but Aunt Lil simply dropped to her knees and held out her arms to them. I gave them a gentle push in her direction.

"My little angels," she said, pulling them close before looking up at me. My children looked almost frightened, but there were tears in my aunt's eyes. "I was hoping you would bring them. I wanted it so much. They're like a breath of spring air after a hard, bleak winter."

"I love your house," Landi said to hide whatever she was feeling.

"So do I, my precious one," Aunt Lil replied. "I'll have Hildie show you around while I talk to your mother. I hope you brought your swimming suits. I have a big pool out back just waiting for you."

"Do you have any toys we can play with while we swim?" Kenny asked, not wanting to be outdone by his older sister.

Aunt Lil ruffled his hair as I so often did. "I'm sure something can be found, but until then, could I interest you in a snack? Hildie has been baking all morning."

The reason for our coming wasn't mentioned until my children had been escorted away. I knew they would be okay with anyone on my aunt's staff, but not having them next to me brought a moment of unease. I couldn't bear it if something happened to them.

"How did you know I needed your children?" Aunt Lil asked as I sat down on the sofa while she chose a stately, high-backed chair.

I bit my bottom lip before replying. "I didn't, and bringing them wasn't an easy decision to make. A funeral is no place for children, especially ones who have so recently lost their father. But I've finally come to terms with the fact that my husband is gone, and I can't shield Landi and Kenny from all of life's disappointments and sorrows forever. I had hoped you would meet them under better circumstances."

"I'm meeting them now, and that's all that really matters. They can stay at the house with Hildie during the service. I know she wouldn't mind. Didn't I tell you they would see California soil before the snow flies in your neck of the woods? How long can you stay? It really is so good to see you again."

Her sentences were clipped and a little disjointed. That's how she maintained control, and I had learned not to push. She would let me know when she was ready to take the conversation to a more emotional level.

"Until Tuesday, unless more time is needed. I'm afraid I encouraged my children's truancy from school."

"They will get more education here in five days than they would in five weeks at school," Aunt Lil retorted. "We'll show them everything we can."

I eyed her curiously. Was she trying to deal with Senator Hasting's death by pretending it had never happened?

"Don't look at me like that, Maya. I haven't forgotten why you're here. They took Tom away early this morning to perform an autopsy. I don't understand why. His doctor can verify the cause of his death, but I suppose there will always be speculations of foul play when a person has been in the public eye as long as he has. And our recent marriage hasn't helped. Some unprofessional journalist will try to fabricate a story about me marrying Tom for his money and not because I loved him."

"That seems a little cold."

"It's the price one pays for being part of a world where nothing is sacred. You probably made the right decision by walking away from Peter. He could only protect you from so much."

I took in more air than was necessary. I couldn't afford to think about Peter Richards now that I was back in L.A.

"Let's not talk about him, Aunt Lil. I came here to be with you. What can I do to help?"

"Tom had everything worked out when he first learned he was sick. He was going to have a big, elaborate, Catholic funeral and wake, and then be cremated and have his ashes thrown out to sea."

"I thought he was going to Switzerland so no one would know when it happened?"

"That was a knee-jerk reaction because he thought I couldn't handle it."

"So what are the plans now?"

"I guess that will be up to us. He deserves to have a grand sendoff, but I'm not sure I feel comfortable going through some rituals I'm not familiar with. I've never even been inside a Catholic church."

"You said he'd gone to church with you. Is a simple Christian funeral out of the question?"

"We didn't discuss it. We thought we had more time."

Her eyes filled with tears, and she lowered her head into her hands. That was my signal to move close and offer what comfort I could. So I knelt on the floor in front of her chair and put one hand on her shoulder. It took a few moments until she was able to look at me again.

"I'm sorry, Maya. I didn't mean to fall apart."

"Never apologize for loving someone, Aunt Lil. Tom will approve of whatever you decide."

"Are you sure?" she asked. "Helen had a big, Catholic service, but then she was always more into religion than Tom. I only know that regardless of his original plans, cremation isn't an option. He wants to be buried next to her, and he wants me to be buried next to both of them."

"Then you have at least part of your answer already. You'll say goodbye to him in your own way, but the people who knew him over the years need a chance to pay their respects. I doubt it really matters where, as long as you feel good about whatever is decided."

"See why I needed you," she said. "You are my voice of reason right now. I've never planned a funeral before, not even for August. I just let the woman he was living with take care of it. I didn't even attend the service. Does that make me an awful person?"

"It makes you human. Do you know when the body will be released?"

"The coroner said he could have it to the mortuary by Friday. Since all the initial decisions have been made, we just have to meet with them to go over any final details. He would have loved seeing your children, Maya. They're everything you said they were. When I think of all . . . "

"We can't change the past, Aunt Lil," I responded.

"I know, but I can't help thinking how cynical fate can be. Life should bring us together, not death."

"Sometimes that's the only way it can happen. I was so busy taking care of my family when Ken was alive that there was little room for anything else."

"And I spent over fifty years amassing an empire the government will only seize the moment I die if you don't agree to what I've asked."

"We don't have to talk about that right now. There's plenty of time to get everything in order."

"That's what I thought until last night. I'm not bitter over the way my life turned out. I'm only sorry I let my confusion and pride take away the years I could have spent with Tom. These past few months have been the happiest of my life because he loved and needed me. I didn't mind leaving all the superfluous activities behind to feed him, change him or cleanup after him when he was sick. And I couldn't bring myself to be out of whatever room he was in for more than a few minutes at a time, even when he was screaming out in pain and pleading for the end to come. I lived in my head, not my heart after August did such a number on me. Now I understand why you fought me so hard for meddling in your life when it came to Peter. Once you've shared even a few weeks with the perfect man, no one else will ever compare."

I was grateful for Aunt Lil's candor. She understood now because she was living through what I had experienced not that long ago. And I could help her with Senator Hastings' funeral arrangements, without feelings of overwhelming agony, because I could now see the blessings of both life and death more objectively.

At Aunt Lil's request, I contacted the mortuary and made an appointment for the following day. The woman I spoke with promised that everything we needed would be taken care of without delay. After that was done, I placed a call to someone from the church she had been attending. Two men arrived at her home that evening. We'd barely had time to feed the children and get them ready for bed.

When the first man shook her hand, I was afraid she might break into tears, but she simply looked deep into his eyes. "Thank you for coming. I know what I'm asking is a little unorthodox. Tom wasn't a member of your congregation, and I've chosen not to be affiliated with religion most of my life. I don't believe in deathbed repentance or someone mortal being able to absolve sins. I think we're responsible for all the mistakes we've made and need to seek proper forgiveness through complete and total repentance. However, that is not what we are here to discuss. I want Tom's funeral to be held in a church where his life can be celebrated for the good man he was. Can you help me with that?"

The poor man she was speaking to looked as if the wind had been knocked out of him, and I waiting anxiously for his reply. Aunt Lil wasn't trying to be difficult or dismissive of personal beliefs. She simply knew what she wanted and didn't feel like wasting anyone's time.

"Dear Sister Hastings," he said after a short pause. "Christ's mission was one of kindness, acceptance and charity. He didn't care about a person's past. He simply stood ready to help where he could while explaining the Plan of Salvation to anyone who was willing to listen. I never knew Senator Hastings personally, but I admired his convictions. He was an honest and a dependable man who spent his life helping others. It would be my pleasure to help you give him the kind of service you want."

"Thank you," Aunt Lil replied. "It won't be anything fancy—just a few songs, a eulogy, and any remarks people in the audience might like to give. My husband was known for his forcefulness in protecting the rights of the people in this state, but he led a simple life away from the public."

In less than an hour, the arrangements for a funeral service had been made. It would be held at noon on Saturday. Members of the congregation would take care of the flowers and direct traffic. Aunt Lil didn't want a special luncheon. Hildie would prepare what we needed at home.

She asked me to read Senator Hastings' life sketch. They had written it together during the weeks he had mostly been confined to bed. He wanted his passing to be a time of joy, not one of sorrow for those who had been left behind. The words committed to paper gave a vivid account of a life filled with extraordinary opportunities, passionate feelings and the love of two very special women.

I wasn't convinced that I should be the one reading it since I had only met him on two occasions. He had a sister-in-law and two nephews living in the area. I expressed my concerns to Aunt Lil.

"You have to understand that I'm going against everything Tom's family has ever believed in by not having a priest give him last rites. According to Alice, his brother's widow, I'm sending Tom straight to hell. And if I insist on continuing with this lunacy, as she calls it, no one in the family will attend the service. It's a matter of that old adage: *you do this and you'll no longer be a part of us.*"

"Maybe you should reconsider," I said. "A person's family is very important. They should be there."

"What they do is none of my concern. They didn't have time for him while he was alive and just want to make sure they get some of his money. That's not going to happen. They can contest his will, but it's ironclad."

I knew better than to argue with her once she had made up her mind. Aunt Lil knew how to stand her ground.

On Thursday, we selected a casket, made arrangements for flowers and accepted the condolences of persons who got close enough to be heard. Aunt Lil never cried when anyone told her how brave she was. Her tears would come later and in private.

Landi and Kenny were little angels of mercy bringing a spark of joy and life into an otherwise sorrowful situation. They splashed around quietly in the pool, helped Hildie polish silver and fix meals that went mostly uneaten, and slipped their arms around Aunt Lil's neck whenever they found her alone. I was so proud of them for being able to give and receive love from a woman they barely knew.

As the time for the funeral approached, Aunt Lil began questioning her decisions and her resolves. She had never shied away from difficult situations, but she had never been truly in love before. Knowing how some people viewed her sudden marriage to Senator Hastings put her in an awkward position. She wanted his service to be one of dignity and respect, not fodder for unprincipled journalists. That's why she refused to have a viewing the night before the service. She only wanted people who really cared to come, along with limiting the amount of media coverage.

"It's too late to worry about it now, Aunt Lil," I told her early on Saturday morning as we were making preparations to leave the house for the church. The casket would be open for two hours before the memorial service. She had gone to the mortuary alone the night before to say her final goodbye.

"But what if nobody comes?" she lamented. "What if my desire to stop a potential scandal backfires, and people simply decide to stay away?"

"That's not going to happen," I assured her. "You made decisions out of love. No one can fault you for that."

But inside I was a little worried too. An obituary notice had been placed in all the local newspapers, and his death had been mentioned on both the radio and television news. Nonetheless, people liked social conventions, and a Father Christopher had contacted her about giving him a proper funeral at St. Mary's Cathedral. We both knew who was behind that.

At the last moment, Landi and Kenny decided to go with us. Since I would be giving the eulogy, Aunt Lil would be sitting alone. I scurried around like the proverbial chicken with its head cut off to get them ready, but we still managed to arrive at the church in the limousine with Otto at the wheel by nine. Senator Hasting's casket was already nestled amongst a glorious array of flowers.

I made sure my children were sitting on a sofa in the corner of the room, with something to keep them occupied, before joining Aunt Lil. I didn't like having to introduce myself to strangers, but she needed my support. So I shook hands and smiled for over an hour until I felt a disturbing presence. I looked over the heads of countless numbers of people to see Peter Richards standing in the doorway.

Our eyes met, and I wondered if he could detect the sudden, rapid beating of my heart or see the flush that rushed to my face. I managed a tentative smile. He looked so strong and dependable as he broke protocol and approached me.

"Excuse me for a moment, Aunt Lil," I said. "There's something important I need to do."

I doubted she even heard what I said. She was busy talking to an old friend, and the line would keep moving past Senator Hastings' casket even if I wasn't there. So I hurried to greet Peter, wishing I could just throw my arms around his neck.

But we were in a very public place, and at least one reporter had already made it past the security team that had been put in place to make sure the service proceeded as planned. Senator Hastings had given up his political career when his first wife got sick, but not everyone had agreed with the propositions he'd supported over the years.

"How are you?" I asked, holding my hand out to him while the air around us seemed to crackle with tension.

He fingers closed over mine and their warmth caused a tingling in my veins that could not be stopped. "Never better. How about you?"

"Good," I replied, wishing I had something a little more memorable to say after all I the time we had spent apart. "It was nice of you to come. Aunt Lil will appreciate it."

"It's the least I could do. I was hoping you would be here."

I bit my lip to keep it from trembling. "I had to come. My aunt needed me."

"So did I," he replied, still holding my hand. "Why didn't you come back? I thought all you required was time."

"It was a little more complicated than that. Ken's father needed help in the family business."

"And he couldn't find anyone else?"

"No one with the same same incentive I have to keep it alive for my children once he retires. I'm not excusing what I've done, I'm merely trying to explain why I had to stay in Boston. Besides working with him at the firm, I'm going back to school to get my degree in financial planning. I still have so much to learn, but at least I'm becoming more independent."

"You were always independent, Maya. You just didn't have to be that way because you had Ken."

"Maybe you're right," I said. He seemed to know me so well, but I couldn't say the same thing about him. I had kept him at arms length because I didn't want to become involved. Now, I almost wish I hadn't. Seeing him again, even in such a bizarre situation, had reawakened feelings I believed had been put to rest. "That talk you gave me on the beach about courage helped me put my life back in order, but . . . "

He looked at me tenderly, almost pleadingly. "But there's no room in it for me. Is that what you're trying to say?"

There wasn't time for me to respond. Both of my children had come running up to us.

"Wow," Landi said, looking up at him with complete adoration. "You're Peter Richards, aren't you?"

"In the flesh," he replied. Turning away from me, he took her hand and kissed it. "You must be the delightful Landi. You look a great deal like your mother. You're both very beautiful."

Landi blushed, and so did I. Fortunately, nobody seemed to notice.

"I'm Kenny," my son boldly announced. "I look like my dad, but he's dead."

"He must be very proud of you, wherever he is," Peter responded as my son stepped deliberately in front of him. Landi had already moved to my side.

"He's in heaven building a new home for us. We get to be with him again someday."

"You don't say," was Peter's reply.

"It's the truth! We needed him here, but Heavenly Father needed him more so he died. It's really neat up there. He gets to be with Grandma Holden and everyone else. Even Aunt Lil's husband is there now."

"You're pretty young to know so much," Peter told him.

"Oh, I know lots of things like what really happened to the dinosaurs. Do you know why all of them died?"

"Haven't a clue!"

"Kenny," I said, grabbing his hand. "Mr. Richards is here to pay his respect to Aunt Lil and the senator. You shouldn't be bombarding him with questions and other trivial things."

Peter's arm came to rest around my shoulders. It was a very heady experience. "Let him talk, Maya. I happen to be very fond of kids. In fact, after the service is over, I would like to take yours sailing. If it's all right with you. I know you will be needed for other things."

Kenny looked up at me pleadingly. "Can we go, mom? I promise to be really good."

I glanced down at my children—both starry-eyed and beaming—before looking at Peter again. His eyes seemed to be pleading with me too. "I don't know if it's the right time for an outing like that. I'm sure Mr. Richards has more important things to do on a Saturday afternoon."

What I really wanted to do was tell my offspring how dangerous sailing could be, but that might undo all the progress I had made in letting them experience the new and impromptu parts of living like most other children were allowed to do.

Peter seemed to sense the reason for my hesitation. "I'll guard them with my life, Maya. I know what they mean to you."

Hundreds of people arrived for the funeral, so many that the doors to the building had to be closed before all of them were inside. Landi and Kenny sat with Aunt Lil—one on each side of her. It made my heart swell with pride to see the way they took care of her. Every now and then she would reach for their hands, and I knew the strength and comfort that gesture could bring.

The congregation was nothing more than a blur of faces when I took my place behind the podium. I was terrified, but I took a deep breath. And when my vision cleared, I saw Peter sitting a few rows behind Aunt Lil and my children. There was an intensity about him that flowed into me like a tide into an empty lagoon giving me the strength to do as I had been asked. I tried not to stare at him and do justice to the task at hand, but my mind was not in the present. It was thinking of all the sadness that lay behind me, and all the emptiness that lay ahead, unless I was willing to take another risk.

While the final song, *How Great Thou Art*, was being sung, my thoughts continued in the same unrealistic direction. Peter was all about caring, about living life to the fullest and loving with an open and gentle heart. How many men, let alone a rather famous television star, would offer to take the children of his pretend housekeeper sailing? Especially when she had withheld the truth multiple times, snooped around his home without permission and run away when all he asked for was a chance to see where things might lead.

Once the song ended, a prayer was said, and then we were on our way to the cemetery. I watched Aunt Lil's eyes fill with tears as Senator Hastings' casket sat above the hole in the ground where he would be laid to rest. It was a clear, bright fall day and the lawns and trees were still wearing their summer finery since the temperature in L.A. was almost always pleasant. Birds were singing above my head, and my memory automatically turned to the last days I had spent with Ken.

We had shared a wonderful life, but today was bringing personal revelation for me. Standing silently with people I loved, I suddenly realized that I no longer harbored any regrets, anger or bitter feelings over what had happened to Ken and me. We had followed our convictions and loved each other completely. Our hearts and souls were bound together forever, but it was time for me to pick up the pieces of my fractured life and go on.

As I looked over the crowd again, I saw a familiar, dark head. Peter had come to the cemetery too. Could it be that he still had deep feelings for me?

Chapter 14

Over the next few months, Lillian Farrow was a frequent visitor at our home. Landi and Kenny adored her, and it wasn't just because she assumed the role of a Fairy Godmother—bringing lavish and thoughtful gifts whenever she came. They cherished our time together for the same reason I did. Aunt Lil saw life as it was and yet found a reason to love everything about it. The fact that hers was no longer what she wished it could be was rarely mentioned.

She seemed to be just as comfortable playing board games with my children around the dining room table as I imagined she had been directing her empire. Over time, she transferred the bulk of her holdings to Turner, Holden and Holden. My father-in-law was ecstatic over having such a wealthy client. They got along well on a personal level too, but I knew their relationship would not develop into anything more. They were happy just being part of the same family. If my parents were upset by the place Aunt Lil was assuming in our lives, they never let it be known. They even flew out to join us for Christmas.

It was during that short holiday visit when I pulled my mother aside and asked how she really felt about all the changes in my life.

"We're all part of the same family, Maya, and it's about time we started acting like it. While I will admit that I was afraid your illustrious great aunt might try to replace us, she hasn't. She's been a lonely woman all her life and deserves a little compassion and happiness now. I wouldn't be following Christ's example if I denied her that. Besides, I know my grandchildren love me, even if I'm not rich. I think I can afford to be generous."

It was just another wake-up call for me. Loyalty could be bought, but true affection was earned through sharing multiple experiences together over an extended period of time. That's why I didn't become too upset when my aunt informed me that her will had been altered again, and she was leaving her home in Los Angeles to me.

By the first of the year, Ken's cousin, Jeff Talbot, had moved into Winston Turner's old office. He and Fiona were off to see as much of world as they possibly could—with the stipulation that they would return as often as feasible to spend time with their children and grandchildren. Todd Foster, the more-than-promising associate, soon decided he wasn't happy being low man at the firm and went off to find a greener pasture.

And so I come to the end of my story. The past two years have been hard, but I've learned a thing or two. A lost member of our family has been found. Turner, Holden and Holden is flourishing. Landi and Kenny are happy and doing well in school. I'll soon finish my bachelor's degree so I can become a bonafide member of the firm, and I've finally adjusted to being alone.

"But what about Peter?" you may ask.

Well, one Saturday afternoon in the early spring I was digging around in my flowerbeds, clearing off dead leaves, and checking for first signs of budding. That's when Landi threw open the screen door and hollered at me. "There's someone here to see you."

When I turned my head, there stood Peter Richards, dressed as I most liked to remember him in a t-shirt and jeans.

"Is it really you," I cried out while struggling to stand. "What in the world are you doing here?"

"What does it look like?" he asked, the expression on his face as serious as the tone of his voice. He then showed me what he was holding. "I've turned into quite a gardener thanks to the flowerbed you left behind, and I'm here to help you."

My mouth sagged open as I looked at him. What a man of contradictions he was—a daytime heartthrob with a gardening spade in his hand.

"But why?" I nearly stumbled over the words.

"Because you're not the only one who needed time to make a few difficult decisions, and I was afraid to come empty-handed."

"You could have called."

"What I have to say cannot be said over the phone."

"You make it sound ominous," I responded, advancing a few steps towards him while wiping a light sprinkling of moisture from my brow. "Do you want to come into the house?"

"I think it would be easier to do this out here."

He sat down cross-legged in the shade of a tree and then motioned for me to sit beside him. I felt my teeth catch the inside of my bottom lip as I tried to keep my eyes from mirroring all the love I had kept so carefully hidden for such an extended period of time.

"Come on," he said, patting the grass beside him. "I promise not to bite. And if what I came to say makes no difference, I promise to leave without causing any further complications in your well-ordered life. You seem content, almost happy."

I sat down beside him and clasp my hands together in my lap. "How did you even find me?"

"Your Aunt Lil and I have become friends."

"She didn't tell me."

"That's because I swore her to secrecy. I knew how determined you were never to see me again, but I couldn't understand why. Friends aren't supposed to desert each other."

"We were becoming more than mere friends."

"Maybe that's why I haven't been able to forget about you, and believe me when I say that I've tried. I dated every woman who seemed the least bit interesting. But every time I closed my eyes, all I could see was you kneeling in a puddle of water in my kitchen."

"That must have been a perpetual nightmare. I looked like an idiot," I replied, removing my gardening gloves so I wouldn't have to look at him.

"You looked adorable, just the way you do now." He brushed the backs of his fingers against the side of my cheek, and I quivered. "See, you're still not entirely indifferent to me."

"I already told you I wasn't."

"That was a long time ago."

His open, honest look made me flinch, and I looked up to see where my children were. But Landi had taken her brother inside. No doubt Peter had given her some incentive. While I was deciding how I could best respond, he continued.

"I've missed you, Maya. I've missed you like crazy."

"Don't, Peter," I said. "Nothing has changed."

"I beg to differ. Why else would I have come to Boston? I can get enough rejection in L.A."

"Your series hasn't been cancelled, has it?"

He laughed. "I guess that answers one of my questions. You obviously haven't been watching my show. It's number one in all the daytime dramas. But that doesn't matter anymore either because I've taken a short leave of absence."

"But why? You love what you're doing."

"I guess I love something else more."

His words made me frown, but that didn't stop what he had left to say. "I know you loved your husband. And I'll admit that I didn't understand the depth of that devotion until I sat down with Lil, and we had a very enlightening conversation."

I felt my world sway, but Peter's arm held me upright.

"You were holding out on me. If I had known even half of what I do now when we met . . . But we can't live in the past forever, now can we?"

By this time, I had recovered part of my senses, but I still wasn't entirely sure what he was getting at. I only knew that my aunt had a lot of explaining to do.

"We have a future together, Maya. You can throw any objection my way, but I'll only accept one—that you don't love me. You see, I'm a verified, church-going Christian now, just like you. I know all about Christ's time on earth and how he felt about the vices and behaviors most of us so readily accept. I want to give everything I possess, including my eternal love, to one woman, and I'm ready for an instant family. I know Ken's memory will always be part of our lives, but that doesn't stop how I feel."

"But I would have to talk about him sometimes, and there is no way of knowing what will happen once we leave this life. That's just the way it is."

"Accepting that isn't a problem, as long as I can have a place in your heart too."

"You already do," I said.

With that, he pulled me into his arms, and I felt the remaining darkness disappear when his lips found mine. My journey was far from over, but as our kiss reached inward to the depth of my soul, I knew I had found another beginning.

"Does that mean you love me, Maya Holden?" he asked when our search for more completeness ended.

"I guess it does. I'm sorry for being so scared and confused."

"Then you'll understand that I've felt the same way. I've been afraid my love was all one-sided."

"Never," I replied. "I've loved you for a very long time."

"Then why didn't you tell me?"

"Because I couldn't see us as a couple who had any chance of making it. We had so little in common, and there's still a lot stacked against us."

"That may be true, but I happen to believe we can overcome anything if we do it together. You see, Maya, I'm not afraid of ghosts. What we have is special, and I have no desire to take anyone's place. I just want to be part of your family, and I would like for us to add to that family someday. Don't you see the wonderful gift we've been given? We may not have all the answers, but we do know what's important."

"Being together," I replied.

"Forever and ever, if that's what God intends."

*****

We're all going out to dinner together tonight. Landi and Kenry are excited. They like Peter, and he's not going to push them for anything until they're ready. I don't know what's going to happen, but I've made a commitment to follow my heart. That's what I did with Ken, and I've never regretted it. The same thing could happen again.

The End

Other Titles From Jan Hill Books:

Final Allegiance - Reagan Sinclair, FBI - Book 1: by JS Ririe

Reagan Sinclair defies her family's wishes to join the Federal Bureau of Investigation believing she can make a difference by helping the downtrodden and defenseless. Her motives are pure, but her first undercover assignment proves that true bravery comes from the heart. Loaned out to the Drug Enforcement Agency to infiltrate a compound in the Colombian jungle, she is forced to face her own mortality when the mission is compromised and she attempts a daring escape without the necessary backup.

Resilience - Reagan Sinclair, FBI - Book 2: by JS Ririe

Life is beginning to return to a semblance of normalcy when Reagan is approached about another undercover assignment with the DEA. Seeing her former partner again is intriguing, but she will never forget Agent Fielding's cold arrogance and ruthless behavior in the Colombian jungle. How will she ever pull off the role of his make-believe wife?

Safe Haven - Reagan Sinclair, FBI - Book 3: by JS Ririe

After trying to come to terms with more than just the fallout of a very heart wrenching assignment in Mexico, Reagan returns to FBI headquarters with a new price on her head. Eloise Seville has vowed to destroy her life, and with a mole somewhere within the ranks of the DEA, she knows that discovering her true identity won't be hard.

Unsheltered - Reagan Sinclair, FBI - Book 4: by JS Ririe

Stunned, hurt, and afraid after the tragedy at the safe house and a brutal demand, Reagan is forced on the run with baby Sam knowing they might never see their family again. A strange and unnerving encounter gives her the ammunition she needs to start a return battle against the evil monsters that have stolen so much of her life.

Welcome Redemption - Reagan Sinclair, FBI - Book 5: by JS Ririe

Not wanting to spend time in a Mexican prison, Reagan agrees to testify at Eloise Seville's trial. But her uncanny ability to see things others often overlook tells her that the subpoena was merely another ruse. Treachery, broken hearts and a return to the country where her journey began test Reagan's commitment to all she believes as she and Agent Fielding go up against their ruthless and formidable enemies in a calculated showdown where only one side will be victorious.

Indecision's Flame - Book 1: by JS Ririe

Brylee Hawkins was prepared to enjoy a bright, hopeful future until her fiancé convinced her to return to the Australian Outback to confront her father. On her own in a harsh and unforgiving land, she is forced to face an unsavory past and an even more disturbing and dangerous present filled with unrelenting lies, secrets and cover-ups.

Lost - Indecision's Flame - Book 2: by JS Ririe

Torn between her family and the obligations of a promise made to her father, Brylee longs to return to the United States and to her fiancé, but fate has other plans. Jake, the brother of her father's wife, decides to take her under his wing and teach her the ropes of running the ranch—mostly in an attempt to get rid of her before she learns of her father's legacy and the part she is to play if she wants to help keep it alive.

Exposed - Indecision's Flame - Book 3: by JS Ririe

With LeAnn gone from the ranch and the aftermath of the flood to deal with, Brylee is forced to assume more responsibility than she is prepared for in raising her little brother, Trevor, and trying to keep the family heritage intact. Her troubles deepen when a secret she was keeping from her fiancé is revealed through an unexpected source.

Betrayal - Indecision's Flame - Book 4: by JS Ririe

Despite a fractured heart, Brylee must forge onward in support of her cousin, Molly, who has suddenly decided to get married. Tension and violence quickly ignite in the outback when a nugget of gold is found on a neighboring homestead and a man is killed for not revealing its source. Brylee and Jake are forced to put aside their differences as they are pulled deeper into a web of misunderstandings, cover-ups and danger.

Reawakening - Indecision's Flame - Book 5: by JS Ririe

Jake's cryptic note forces Brylee to reconsider remaining in the outback where personal heartbreak and unrelenting responsibility are reducing her to a shell of the woman she has once been. And the arrival of an old aborigine from her past, who sincerely believes in the mythical Rainbow Serpent, and whose revelations about her childhood and omens for the future make leaving impossible.

Unraveling - Indecision's Flame - Book 6: by JS Ririe

Brylee's avoidance when it comes to revealing parts of her curious past, along with her refusal to accept the bewildering and callous powers of the aborigine's Rainbow Serpent lead her back to the cave of drawings. While Trevor's disappearance fuels LeAnn's involvement with their neighbor, Raymond Tucker, whose only goal has been to acquire every ranch in their part of the outback by whatever means is necessary.

Destiny - Indecision's Flame - Book 7: by JS Ririe

Beth effectively ruins Christmas with an unexpected visit and Raymond steps in to help save the day, further ingratiating himself into the family. LeAnn's accepting behavior towards their unwanted benefactor causes additional rifts as Brylee and Jake race to figure out what he's up to before the secrets of the mountain become common knowledge and bring the unsavory element that nearly cost Jake his life back to their part of the outback.

About the Author

JS Ririe is the pen name for Jan Hill who spent her youth in the country where she learned to appreciate solitude, making her own fun, and reading romance novels from some of the masters like the Bronte sisters, Louisa May Alcott, Victoria Holt and Phyl.is Whitney. She penned her first novel as a teenager but never pursued what is now her greatest passion until becoming the lead witness in a federal case brought against the school district where she taught broadcasting and journalism. Reagan's story is her second series after writing Indecision's Flame and its sequels as she waited two years to testify. She lives in Utah and has two children and two living grandchildren who bring meaning and joy to her life.

A Note From Jan

Thank you so much for reading this novel. I'd love to stay in touch with you. Please consider joining my MAILING LIST so I can send you periodic newsletters about upcoming book releases, special offers and more. The link to sign up is: http://eepurl.com/dCPYVf . I promise not to spam you or sell your email information to anyone. It will be treated with care.

One last favor: Your rating/review of this book helps promote my work and encourages me to keep writing. A short, but honest review would mean a lot. It shouldn't take more than a minute or two. You can reach the page directly at http://bit.ly/IFReview

Thank you again.
JS Ririe

www.JanHillBooks.com
For contacting the author: JSRirie@JanHillBooks.com